HELLO, REST OF MY LIFE

RICK LENZ

Chromodroid Press

Hello, Rest of My Life

Copyright © 2021 Rick Lenz. All Rights Reserved.

Chromodroid Press
ISBN: 978-0-9848442-6-5 (Trade Paperback)
ISBN: 978-0-9848442-8-9 (eBook)

Maps by Linda Lenz

Publisher's Cataloging-In-Publication Data
(Prepared by The Donohue Group, Inc.)

Names: Lenz, Rick, author.
Title: Hello, rest of my life / Rick Lenz.
Description: [Van Nuys, California] : Chromodroid Press, [2021]
Identifiers: ISBN 9780984844265 (trade paperback) | ISBN 9780984844289 (ebook)
Subjects: LCSH: Actors--California--Beverly Hills--Fiction. | Husbands--California--Beverly Hills--Fiction. | Time travel--Fiction. | Motion picture industry--California--Beverly Hills--Fiction. | Dogs--Fiction.
Classification: LCC PS3612.E557 H45 2021 (print) | LCC PS3612.E557 (ebook) | DDC 813/.6--dc23

For Linda

Also by Rick Lenz

North of Hollywood
The Alexandrite
Impersonators Anonymous

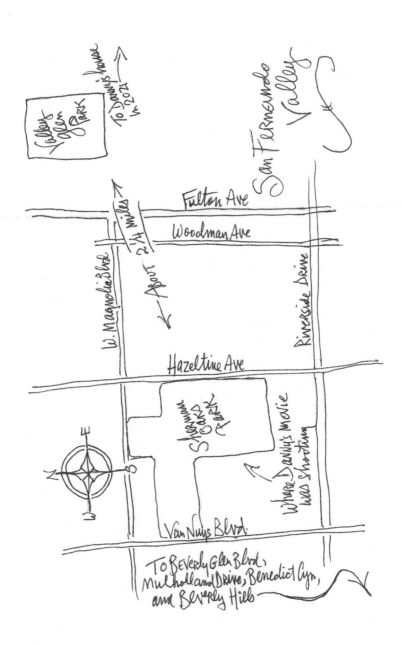

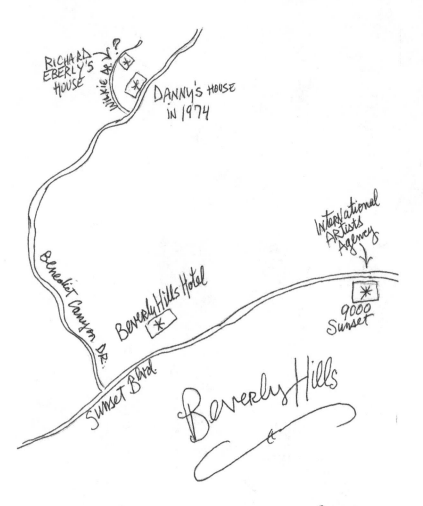

RICHARD EBERLY'S HOUSE

Wilkie Dr.?

DANNY'S HOUSE IN 1974

INTERNATIONAL ARTISTS Agency

9000 Sunset

Benedict Canyon Dr.

Beverly Hills Hotel

Sunset Blvd

Beverly Hills

• Benedict Canyon Becomes Canon Dr when it crosses Sunset Blvd.

• Its about 4½ miles from Benedict and Sunset to the Casa del Sol apartments

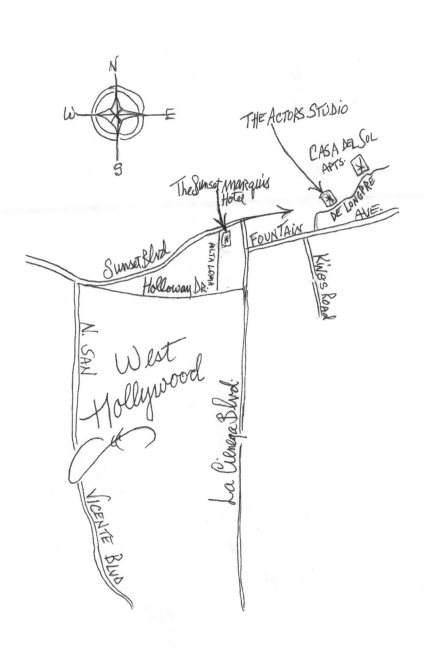

San Jacinto Valley / Riverside County

About 86 miles from Los Angeles to Hemet

San Jacinto Peak

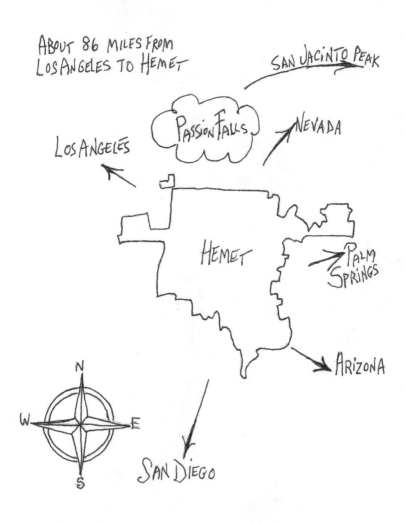

Passion Falls

Nevada

Los Angeles

Hemet

Palm Springs

Arizona

N
W E
S

San Diego

"The minute I heard my first love story, I started looking for you, not knowing how blind that was. Lovers don't finally meet somewhere. They're in each other all along."

— Rumi

"Time is
Too slow for those who Wait,
Too swift for those who Fear,
Too long for those who Grieve,
Too short for those who Rejoice,
But for those who love,
Time is not."

— Henry Van Dyke

1

(2021) SAMANTHA

I live with my wife Samantha in Valley Glen in the San Fernando Valley in Los Angeles.

I never thought I'd have it this good.

It feels, in some part of me, that I loved Sam even before I stood outside her apartment, anxious from blind date nerves.

She answered the doorbell, looked puzzled, then relieved, and said, "Not bad."

I didn't know what to say to that, so I grinned and said, "Hi. I'm Danny Maytree."

She took my hand, smiled warmly at me, and said, "It's nice to know you."

You just don't get good blind dates. At least I never did. You get: *"I've had this flu that keeps hanging on, but it's getting better ... I think. Are you divorced?"*

"Yes, a few years now," I say.

"You're an amateur," says this date that won't work out for either of us. *"I'm a three-time loser, but my shrink says that's all behind me, and he should know, I guess."*

Which she doesn't explain.

But *Samantha*, who says "*Not bad*," has no problems, or doesn't tell me about them on our first date, a blind one—which is odd.

Her eyes, I could fall into those eyes.

She speaks of this and that, and so do I; it doesn't matter because I just fell in love with her, in her doorway. Or maybe I loved her even before that.

So I came in and stayed.

One night, early in our years together, Samantha seemed to have drifted off to sleep, lying on her stomach. As I was about to turn the lights off, she said quietly, "Pet me."

I didn't move for a few moments, trying to decide exactly what that meant. No one had ever said anything like that to me. Something about the confidence of that sort of command amazed me. It combined self-dominion with trust, as if in her life, when seemingly insignificant requests had been made, they had been automatically granted. And I was going to grant this one, and it felt good.

I rolled over on one elbow and gently, beginning over one eyebrow, stroked Sam's forehead, moving my hand softly over her light brown hair to behind her ear.

At first it felt sort of odd to me, petting her, but pretty soon I fell into a tender and natural rhythm. I lightly smoothed back her hair, concentrating on doing it so that even if she were still awake, she might be almost unaware she was being petted. And I got lost in a ritual kind of affection I didn't even know I was capable of.

I slid my right hand down to her neck and left shoulder, and as far down her back as I could comfortably reach without disturbing her rest. Eventually, I stroked up and down her left arm until I reached her hand. It was smooth, but it was also the hand of a peasant girl, made to work, to do labor. At the same time, there was a graceful vulnerability to her hand.

I studied her in the lamplight, her face relaxed and at peace. I was pretty sure she would be sleeping serenely even if I weren't lying next to her. It was nice being a part of that peace; it made me feel calm, and I began to get sleepy.

It could have been five or fifteen minutes later when I rolled over, turned off my bedside lamp, and dropped off to sleep.

I had a bad day yesterday.

I'm working on a new novel, a time travel story that was coming along beautifully, I thought, but now it's making no sense at all. I've painted myself into a corner and I don't see any way out of it. I had stupid notion on top of stupid notion, and for the rest of the day I couldn't let go of the careening thoughts and sensations that reminded me of my loose cannon younger days when, as often as not, I employed the whole nest of my malevolent emotional demons to steer my life. It feels as if I'm trying to bludgeon the story in my novel with identical finesse.

Before dawn today—it was still dark out—I woke up and started rehashing my problems, a real effective technique for beginning a happy day.

A little while later, Sam woke up and asked me what the trouble was. I told her and she suggested I try to get some more sleep. I heaved a big sigh and lay down beside her.

The next thing I knew, she was running her fingers over my head, caressing my neck, shoulders, and upper back … petting me.

When I woke up, I felt better.

Over forty years after we met, Sam and I are having our magic hour before dinner. The light is a cinematographer's dream, the day's toil is done, and our dog Tali is at our feet. At the moment his chin is resting on my left foot, which is getting all pins and needles because I don't want to disturb his peaceful sleep. Anyway, as far as the three of us are concerned, all is well with the world. At the moment we're reminiscing—an activity, I confess, usually initiated by me.

"After we'd been together a few weeks you called and said you wanted to come over and talk about something," says Samantha. "I thought, he's either going to ask me to marry him or he's going to break up with me." A whisper of sadness mixed with surprise. "And you broke up with me."

"I was going off to do a job. I didn't want to …"

"Leave me hanging?"

"Well, exactly. I was trying to … I don't know, do the right thing."

She sips her wine and says, "You probably thought I was a snob because I didn't like that tacky restaurant you took me to where they had mashed potatoes and gravy."

"Well, you *were* kinda snarky about it," I say. "You know how you can get snarky? Well, you got snarky. Up until that night, I'd only taken you to nice places."

"I was bummed out that night. I thought, oh God, I really … liked him but he's … *ordinary*. He likes this depressing place. Maybe it hit me that way because I'd been raised in Carbon Falls—you can't find a more depressing little patch of Pennsylvania—until I was ten and we moved out here. … And it was visceral; that little restaurant felt like scrimping and saving and S&H Green Stamps. Anyway, if you'd taken me to the Cupid's Hot Dogs stand on the corner that night, I would have been fine. I would have been delighted. And then you would have asked me to marry you. I still would have said it's too soon, but

..." She looks down into her wine. "And then you broke up with me."

"But none of that was the reason. You were too ... *nice*. I remember when I got back from location in Portland and I called you. Do you remember what went through your mind?"

"Well, I was glad that you were still interested in me. 'Cause in the meantime, you'd been gone for ... how long?"

"I'm not sure," I say. "As you know, once in a while my mind and the conventional notion of time drift a little out of synch. I guess I was gone about a month." I smile. "If you don't count the forever before the month."

Sam smiles back. "Yeah, well, in the meantime, I went to Palm Springs with Mike. I was sad."

Mike was her previous boyfriend. She'd dated him off and on for ten years. He married someone else after Sam and I got together the next and forever time.

"You were still sad about me," I say, "a month after we said goodbye?"

"Sure I was. I'd started to care about you. You broke up with me. And of course you were important to me in another way, but ..." She gazes into my eyes. "Then you went off to do that ... whatever job in Portland. But I thought, well, okay, he doesn't want this relationship. I'll go to Palm Springs and spend some time with Mike, and with my mother and Grace." I smile at the mention of Grace's name. Sam goes on, "I'll ... just try to get on with it. So when you called and said ... Do you remember what you said?"

"I think I said I miss you. I want to see you."

She frowns. "Yeah. So why did I come to *you*?"

"I don't know, but you got in the car and drove over to my apartment."

"Did you think it was weird that I came to you, not the other way around?"

"No," I say. "I didn't think it was weird. Actually, I was kind of flattered."

"If I'd been one of those girls who was savvy about guys, the ones who know how to play all the games … I didn't know how to do that."

"I did," I say. "I'm afraid sometimes I was sort of trying to be a 'player' until you came along. But a smart friend of mine said, 'Why don't you join a church group or something, meet a girl that way.' I thought he was crazy and tossed that idea out, but the drift of his advice floated around in my mind until I understood what he meant. He thought, as I looked for someone to be with … for *life*, that I should do it not only on the basis of physical attraction, but also that it might be a good idea if she was—what a concept—*a nice person*."

Sam says, "Well anyway, I got in the car and came to you. It shocked me that I did that. I'd always been so cautious. Having divorced parents makes you that way." She shrugs. "It didn't seem to matter though; I came to you. Also, I had to think of … other people. I *had* to give you one more chance."

I nod. "I buzzed the front door and came out of my apartment and met you coming up the stairs and I felt like …"

Sam smiles. I've told her this before. "Hello, rest of my life?"

"Yeah, hello, rest of my life. Yes. That was what it felt like. It was the closest thing I'd ever felt to total … is there a word that combines relief and joy?"

Her impossibly blue eyes twinkle. "Euphoria?"

She's joking, but I'm not. "Yes, that's it. Euphoria."

2

(2021) TALI

I'm lying on the floor under a skylight in the dining room of our little cottage in the San Fernando Valley.

Life is precious—maybe especially so because we survived 2020 and, so far, the COVID-19 pandemic. Above me, clearly visible in winter between the branches of an old silver maple, is the only harvest moon there will be this year. I am healthy, in the middle of writing a novel, the subject of which has run away with my imagination, and am married to a woman I wouldn't be lucky enough to find again in a hundred lifetimes.

Tali curls up next to me, the most mystifying, inscrutable so-called dog in the world. He's what some people refer to as a "rescue," although I can't imagine anything he wouldn't do to rescue us. He seems to think that practically anything either of us decides to do is great. If you've ever had a pet you love almost as much as your child, you know what I mean. Tali wasn't always that nonjudgmental. He became ours seven years ago, soon after we'd gone to the Animal Rescue Center one day, thinking we might bring a dog home with us.

When we first spotted Tali in the back of his cage, he was curled up, not quite ignoring us. It felt to Sam and me as if he was the one doing the choosing. He regarded us motionlessly for about two minutes, then slowly got up, walked to the front of the cage, and watched us for a while longer. One at a time, he looked us straight in the eye, then swung his gaze appraisingly back to the other. I'd be wrong to say that his look was human, but it was awfully close. He didn't blink, just deliberately—it seemed—shifted his gaze back and forth between us. He wasn't pleading; no, it felt as if he were saying, "Where have you been? What took you so long?"

His dark chocolate brown eyes reminded me of King Kong's when he says, in effect, "How could you do this to me, cage me up like this?" Tali made one last appraisal before his tail wagged. "Okay, we'll let bygones be bygones." He was smiling now, unquestionably smiling. "We're family," he said. "Let's go home and be together the way we're meant to be."

But he wasn't available until the morning after next.

Two days later, when the waiting period was over and Tali became officially eligible for adoption, we got to the Animal Rescue Center at 6:15 in the morning in order to be the first in line at the seven o'clock opening. We both knew he was the perfect dog for us and we didn't want someone else to get him.

We were more than disappointed when we saw that someone had arrived sooner. A well-put-together Beverly Hills type of lady. Sam couldn't stop herself from asking her what kind of pet she hoped to adopt. The lady described Tali exactly, a light tan poodle-something else mix, maybe some kind of retriever—no one ever knows for sure—with a large irregular brown patch on his right side. Sam and I were brokenhearted. First come, first served. There was no bending the rules. Beverly

Hills Lady was going to adopt our dog; there was no reason for us to stay.

We got back in our car and started our dejected drive home.

Halfway there, the Animal Rescue Center called. Tali had nipped Beverly Hills Lady, who then changed her mind. She didn't want a dog that bit. The man at the rescue center didn't have to ask if we were still interested. I was already turning the car around as Sam said, "We're on our way. We want him."

Tali has been ours for over seven years now. He's never nipped either of us. He's never bit anybody since that moment he was specific about whose dog he wanted to be.

Actually, we don't consider him a dog. He's the son we never had—a most uncommon son.

How he came to be called Tali is a mystery.

The simple explanation is that it's the name he came with. The Animal Rescue Center produced a collar he'd been wearing when they picked him up. It had a faded silver tag attached to it. Part of whatever had been inscribed on that tag had worn off. Tali seemed to be the first part of his name; there were more letters, much fainter, after that. No one could make out what those letters had been.

The details of the story are more baffling. On that same tag was what looked like an antiquated telephone number, barely visible. It seemed to be one of those numbers that goes back to the sixties, early seventies at the latest, when they used numbers that began with a word. We were able to make out what seemed to be a CR prefix, followed by -627. We couldn't read anything beyond that. It didn't make sense. We think he was about three years old when we got him, so why he wore a tag with a phone number dating back fifty years or more, no one could figure out.

In any case, Samantha and I liked the name Tali, and that's why our dog held on to the name. As for the CR prefix, I guess we'll never know. There used to be a prefix in Beverly Hills called Crestview. For two seconds we considered calling him that, but it felt too much like crestfallen, and Tali is anything but that.

I know nothing of his backstory, but whatever it is, it's got to be fascinating. The strangest, most singular thing about him, among many strange things about Tali, is that as much as he loves Sam and me, our home, and our life together, now and then he disappears. No matter what we devise to prevent him from escaping, he manages to figure a way to outwit us. We've erected various kinds of fencing around the backyard, even a wall to keep him from escaping. None of it works. There is nothing Tali cannot dig under, and we can't keep him inside all the time.

He always comes back and he's never gone for long—at least as I perceive time—but even as I say that, I realize that sometimes it *seems* as if it's a long while. I know that doesn't make sense. Samantha has a similar sensation.

Perhaps more bizarre than the lengths of his absences is the nature of them. They're hard to describe. It's as if he has not run off to anywhere in our neighborhood, or even the San Fernando Valley. Sometimes he returns with his fur covered in vegetative substances that don't grow anywhere near where we live. One warm spring day, he came home with bright pink wild prairie roses twined in his fur. Wild prairie roses don't grow within three hundred miles of the San Fernando Valley. Once he came home to us covered with what I was pretty sure was beach sand. Three small shells, called bean clams or Gould's Wedges colloquially, and found all along the Pacific Coast of California, were snarled in Tali's matted fur. We live twenty miles from the nearest beach.

Sometimes, when he gets back, he doesn't even look like the same dog. But he *is* the same. He loves us the same. He acts the same, and it's not long before the eerie feeling of his ... strangeness lifts. Then he's back to being the Tali we know and love.

The oddest single experience we had was the time he came back to us covered with mud. We have a friend who works in the geology department at USC. We asked him to analyze it. He called several days later, puzzled. We had told him that a great deal of the mud had been found caked in our dog's fur.

"Have you been out of the country with him?" our friend asked.

Sam had picked up the extension. "No," she said, "as far as I know he's never been out of the state."

There was a pause on the other end as our friend seemed to ponder. Then he said, measuredly, "Well, your dog—some kind of a poodle mix, I take it—seems to have come home to you matted with mud from the Dead Sea."

All three of us were silent. Finally I said, "It has to be some kind of prank."

"I have a tube of facial mud mask purportedly from the Dead Sea," offered Sam.

Our friend chuckled. "You brought me a good bit of that substance. It seems to me that would be a pretty extravagant joke to play. And it's unlike any prank I ever heard of."

We never solved that mystery. Of course, we know that it has to have been a gag of some kind, but we don't know who was behind it or why they did it. At this point, I'm thinking we probably never will.

Now, as I lie on the floor beneath the skylight, Tali nuzzles into my side and stomach, once again offering his tender affection. My father once told me only human beings have souls, not animals. With Tali, it feels as if there is a depth of perception in his heart I can no more than aspire to.

I'm wearing my robe. Sam is sleeping in the bedroom, twenty paces from where Tali and I lie. I have her robe over my knees, which are bare because I wear a nightshirt for sleeping. I can see what look like faint gray islands on the moon, which is pure white at the moment. As I barely swivel my head, it changes shape slightly, transformed by the domed glass of the skylight. The moon seems to send out shafts of soft frosted light like satiny spokes from a round, luminous axle.

I don't know why, gazing up at the moon in the middle of the night—maybe it's the fullness, the newness of this moon—but for a moment I remember what intoxicating fun it was being a young actor in Los Angeles. And a little predictably, I'm afraid, my mind skips to the one role I really wanted but didn't get: *Barry Lyndon*. Then I shake myself out of those thoughts and tell myself that by the final days of it, I didn't mind that my career had gone south.

On the other hand, I know I will *always* feel a little regretful about how close I came to playing the title role in a film by Stanley Kubrick. It's silly, I understand, but that little tinge of regret never entirely evaporated. According to my agents, Kubrick saw every piece of film I was ever in, but Warner Bros. insisted on a big-name, bankable star. Kubrick's first choice, Robert Redford, turned the role down. He finally settled on Ryan O'Neal, whose star had ascended with *Love Story*, *Paper Moon*, and *What's Up, Doc?* I was an adolescent in a man's body, susceptible to the most transparent flattery, so coming that close to—and then not getting—that role practically unhinged me.

Soon afterward a couple of people told me Kubrick regretted going with Ryan O'Neal. He began to think Ryan was too pretty, so the gossip said. I was good-looking enough I guess, but no one would ever have called me pretty. Anyway, I got over it and my career did all right for several more years. And then, right around the time I was beginning to lose most of the "heat" I'd ever had in Hollywood, I met Samantha. After that I didn't obsess about my career anymore. I didn't have to. I had Sam.

I glance over at Tali and see that he's watching me intently, as if he's having thoughts about my thoughts. It feels as if he knows something about me, but he can't—or won't—tell me what it is. Maybe he's telling me it's time to go to bed.

How did I get this lucky? Tali and I will get up from the carpet in a couple of minutes, go into the bedroom, and lie down next to my wife, Tali on a posh dog bed Sam has put together for him and placed on the floor next to her side of the bed. Sam sleeps between us as beautifully as she lives her conscious life. I will sleep through the night with her. When I get up, Sam will have coffee ready and Tali will smile at me, get up, and come over for his morning scritching.

Usually between Sam and me there's a touch, a pat, a kiss, it doesn't matter; it's a genuflection of gratitude. I'll eat oatmeal with a drizzle of maple syrup as we take turns reading from whichever spiritual book we're in the middle of. I guess this wouldn't have sounded so sweet to me … X years ago; it probably would have felt saccharine. But now it's lovely. I recall that when I broke up with Sam during that moment of my extended insanity, she called me shortly after I'd gotten back to my apartment and said, "This hurts." Then she added, with the same combination of sweetness and self-possession she had when she asked me to pet her the first time: "You don't know what you're missing."

Since a month after that call, when I buzzed her into my apartment and she came up the stairs, I've always known exactly what I would have missed.

I look up at the moon of our ancestors, the pulsing harvest moon I've been watching for several minutes from the floor of our dining room, and draw no conclusions.

What's the point?

3

(2021) BE OH-SO-CAREFUL WHAT YOU ASK FOR

'm trying to write, but I don't seem to be able to focus today. My damned dog is watching me with what seems to be a disapproving look. He doesn't do it often, but every once in a while he looks at me as if he's judging me. I hate it when he does that. It makes me think of my father.

I can't let any of this bother me. I have to allow my mind to go where it will. It doesn't matter where I let my thoughts wander right now; I have to relax and give them free reign.

When I was still studying and working as an actor in New York, I got my first job in a film. It was called *I'll Live Till I Die*. As you may have guessed from the title, it wasn't a great movie—not as bad as it sounds. … Okay, almost. It's hardly ever played on television and most people have never heard of it. To the extent anyone has, it's because it starred an actor named Henry Devane (not a relative of William) a few years older than I am.

Henry died about a month ago, and although he was most well known and respected for his work on stage, both in New York and London, he also did a handful of movies, which are now receiving memorial attention. Sam and I attended a screening of *I'll Live Till I Die* last week. It's kind of an adventure thriller that takes place in Los Angeles, where it was shot. I was a little uncomfortable as we watched it. Some actors have the knack of film acting the first time they step in front of a camera. I was not one of those. I looked self-conscious and awkward in every one of the few scenes I was in. I was embarrassed to have Sam see me at my worst, although afterward she said, "You were wonderful. You looked like a kid, but you were wonderful." Sam thinks I'm terrific even when I'm pretty sure I'm not. But then, Sam loves me (and it doesn't hurt a thing to keep reminding myself of that).

There are a couple of aerial shots in *I'll Live Till I Die* of two of the canyons in the Santa Monica Mountains between the Los Angeles basin and the San Fernando Valley. One of the reasons I wanted to see the film again was to rewatch those shots, one in particular. That one is over Benedict Canyon where I later lived with my first wife, Fleury, when we moved to Los Angeles from New York. The shot I'm talking about clearly shows the white adobe California Spanish house Fleury and I bought a couple of years after relocating.

It was a gorgeous place. We were lucky to be able to buy it. For a short while, at the beginning of my career, I was able to afford some luxuries, among them that beautiful hacienda. I wish I'd been able to live in that house with Samantha. She would have loved it.

As we watched the unmemorable movie that first brought me to California, I whispered to her that the shot I'd told her about was coming up.

And then it did—the complete aerial shot.

My house at 1809 Benedict Canyon Drive was not in it.

The scene was intact, but the house was missing.

I wanted to stand up and shout to the projectionist that he should run the film back because somehow we had missed seeing the house I'd lived in with Fleury.

I went back the next day and sat through the film almost twice. My house, which was built in 1933 and is still there to this day—sometimes I pass it when I drive over Benedict Canyon—was not in the movie.

Sure, someone could have replaced a mile of familiar terrain via the magic of computer-generated imagery (CGI)—but at a cost of about twice as much as it took to finance the entire B-movie in the first place. Maybe it would be possible, but almost anyone who knows film—and the terrain being photographed—would be able to see the difference.

I'll Live Till I Die was made a long time ago. I don't know anyone still living who was connected with it. And even if I did, no one, not even the savviest film technician, could explain to me why my house disappeared.

The disappearance (on film) of the house I lived in for four years will never stop haunting me.

As I think about it right this minute, it seems to be troubling me more than ever. That house hasn't disappeared in real life. I know I'm repeating myself, but I pass it fairly often on the way to or back from Beverly Hills.

In fact, even though I know it's crazy, it felt as if I was *in* that house … yesterday? I suppose I could blame it on my uneasy relationship with time, but that doesn't make sense; I haven't actually been in that house for over four decades.

But I do wish I could be in it again, one time—just to take a look.

And still Tali is watching me as if he knows some cardinal rule of being that I don't, and he thinks I'm violating it. I want to tell him I believe in the science behind what most of us call reality, but like most people, I assume, I sometimes wonder what's behind the science. Another reality? If so, what's behind that?

"Go find Mommy," I say.

But he doesn't move and that look is leveled at me.

I've had four back operations. Two of them probably weren't necessary. I can't replay that, but my attitude is better now and the pain is mostly history. Except at night, when the day's aches set in. Before bed, I take a couple of opiate pills, which help me sleep. The next morning, after I start to move around, I'm fine for the day.

One night though, after Sam and I have had our wine and after I've taken my pain pills (a little earlier than usual), I have an atypical urge to do a little nighttime writing, hoping the slight buzz I have will give me a new slant on my novel and the cul-de-sac my protagonist finds himself in. The genre called "time-slip" can be fun to write. But, for me anyway, it's also easy to get stuck, especially if you don't write chronologically—which I haven't been doing so far in this one. After a couple of no prog-ress days, I find myself getting that claustrophobic feeling that comes with writer's block.

In my latest time-slip tale, a love story, I have not drawn on the most commonly used time travel approaches. I've never been able to write authoritatively about time machines; I'm not mechanical. In a similar vein, slingshotting my protagonist around the sun or sticking him into a black hole doesn't work for me. I've played around with wormholes, but not with much success. Speed of light manipulation isn't my cup of lunacy. I like soul or life essence transferal; that's fun, but it's never the whole answer for me. I also like drugs and comas, to various degrees and in varying combinations. Encountering old artifacts is nice but works best with children's fantasy.

My preference is to ask for help from the cosmos. Understanding I probably won't appeal to hard-line, set in stone atheists, I still like leaning on God, or the Universal Creative Force, or whatever you like to call ... the Deity—knowing that *The Author of Everything sees time in a way that passes our understanding.*

Having said that, I don't recall any holy books telling us that God will zip someone backward or forward to a point in time they would whimsically like to visit ... or revisit. On the other hand, philosopher Ernest Holmes says, "Miracles are natural." Over the past few years I've come to believe that's true. I don't *know* anything about God's miracles. I'm not personally acquainted with anyone who does, but I do like to leave that door open.

I had begun my first draft of this story with some material about dimensions: length, breadth, width, and duration (time). I began with: *"H. G. Wells anticipated Einstein when he said it was theoretically possible for someone to go backward in time and shake hands with himself."* But I threw that approach out because after writing this kind of thing for a while, I've found that my favorite shortcuts to heaving my hero backward or forward in time involve *not* having to make the reader buy into something that, practically speaking, is silly.

With this new book, I had begun with what physicist David Bohm, in his discussion of the order of the cosmos, called "*the plenum*" *of space*, which turns the ideas of matter and space upside down. It's something based in real or at least theoretical physics—and what it means, if I'm understanding it correctly, is that *all* rules are turned upside down. What you'd heretofore thought was impossible in time and space becomes its fundamental reality.

One magic hour I talked about this to Sam. She blinked, looked off into the sanctuary of her private thoughts, then crossed her eyes and made a silly face. Her honest, open countenance is a joy to live with, but not so useful if she thinks I'm trying to get away with storytelling perjury.

Back to the drawing board (at least as to how I approach my narrative): my hero is an actor (surprise, surprise). I want him to go back to the time in his career when, primarily because of emotional immaturity, he made stupid decisions. Until then he'd had bright potential. Sadly though, he almost single-handedly drove the nails into the coffin of his career.

I think about my age. If I'm not fooling myself, I am blessed to have more mental acuity than I had at any previous time in my life. Also, as I've indicated, I have some experience with what I'm attempting; I've written time travel books before, done my research, and have a little theoretical understanding of the form.

But again, most of all—and I don't know this for sure—I think the wild card for anyone who wants to be creative is to realize that the source of knowledge human beings are able to draw from is as infinite as we conceive the universe to be. Since I can't account for all the variables in Creation, *but I AM one of the variables in Creation*, I'm limited only by my own imagination, which I try to convince myself is—like the universe—forever expanding.

Theoretically then, my mushrooming imagination being the key, I am allowed to begin my story at a moment when, in real life, my "hero" gets a call from his acting agency.

The phone is ringing. I answer it.

It's a voice I don't recognize. She's one of my old acting agent's assistants, a spooky-sounding woman who says her name is Velma, like the scary femme fatale in *Farewell, My Lovely*. She has a low, velvety voice. Someone—an old friend I ran into at one of the rare Hollywood-type parties we still go to—has asked to see me for a movie role. This old friend, has told my agent, through his casting director, that he can't imagine anyone better than me for a small but nice role in a movie he's co-producing. It will just be a meeting with the director and star; I won't need to audition. I don't bother to ask who the director and star are. I'd be unlikely to know who they are these days.

I say, "Thanks, Velma."

"You're welcome, darling," she replies in surprisingly familiar, mellow tones.

"What's the name of the project?"

"I don't have the script in front of me, but I'll be dropping it off at your house later. I live in The Valley too. Are you still at the address in Valley Glen?"

"Still here," I say. "Why would you be dropping a script off? I thought you said this was just a meeting."

"I guess they want you to know what you're in for in case it works out. I may not be getting out of here until late." Her voice sounds like a low, distant fog horn. "I'll just leave the script on your front step. Have a pleasant evening, darling." She hangs up.

She'll leave it on my front step. A sign of the times. In the old days she would have rung our doorbell and handed me the script. Now most people are (still) reluctant to get close to each other. "Darling?"

I'm excited, probably too excited, and take a tranquilizer, forgetting for a moment that I already took the pain pills. I don't know if those these things mix. I also had the wine. I know this isn't smart, but I think it's okay; I won't be expected to read for this job, only go in and meet the director/writer and the star.

Thinking about this, I realize I'm getting a headache and that it's not going away. I have some old, pretty powerful pain capsules in the back of our first-aid drawer. They're amber-colored. Call them Ambers. They usually work for headaches whereas the opiates don't. So now I've been drinking, I've had my opiates, two tranquilizers, and two Ambers. I add a third Amber because the first two didn't kill the headache, and what can one more really hurt, anyway? Outside of the fairly mild opiates, none of these things are actually *that* strong.

I sit in my office, listening to Pink Floyd's *The Dark Side of the Moon* (original title—*Dark Side of the Moon: A Piece for Assorted Lunatics*). Not a huge surprise when some little leak erupts in my visual cortex and rainbows of phosphorescence gyre and gimble through my ventral occipital lobe, and a psychedelic paint stain flows across the floor and up the walls around me as New York and the Tinseltown of my youth wash over me. I hear my old psychotherapist—a lot of people had one back then for a couple—sometimes more—spins around the sun. She says, "You seem nonchalant about the drinking and drugs."

And it's true; I smoked a little pot—for a couple of years. I was stressed. My therapist was cool ("hip" in those days), so I told her, "Okay, I also took a few Quaaludes when the pressure got to be more than I … et cetera, et cetera."

"And the other thing?" she says.

"Two times," I say, morally indignant, "I took cactus tabs." I translate for her the way hippies and post-hippies were so charitably inclined to do with their treasured cultural secrets. "Mescaline.

It made me feel goosey and wired; I didn't like it, so I never took it again." And even though it's possible that's true, she is smiling at me with the look of a loving but worried mother, who has decided a lecture at this moment isn't going to help.

Still in my office, not having moved from the chair I first sat down in, I'm driving through the southern, flat part of Beverly Hills. I notice Cañon Drive to the left as I turn right for the umptieth time, just past the sort of quivering and slowly spinning Beverly Hills Hotel, onto Benedict Canyon Drive. I'm aware that I'm becoming … I'm becoming … a … uh … Well … And to the south of Sunset, the street is called Cañon. The Spanish pronunciation of cañon is canyon, but most Americans—and I suppose Brits as well, including Pink Floyd—pronounce it cannon, without the tilde. Cañon isn't in a canyon, but Benedict Canyon, to the north, *is* a canyon, and is appropriately called Benedict Canyon as it winds upward out of the canyon and over the Santa Monica Mountains to the San Fernando Valley on the other side—where they don't have any canyons.

It feels as if I'm becoming … um … I blink my eyes a few times and it occurs to me that the combination of meds I took a while ago just … *may* not have been well thought out.

This reminds me of my father, but I can't think about him now.

Tali, who has been sleeping at my feet, sits up and looks me straight in the eye.

I don't admit this to anyone, even Sam—I don't think she'd understand. Sometimes, especially during moments that fall under the heading of the kind of experience I'm having now, Tali consents to talk to me. This may sound as if he's snooty, but that's not it. I mean that during the occasional daft moments when Tali and I converse, it seems to be on his terms, never mine.

Right now he says, in soothing, gentle tones, like an unusually sure of himself twelve-year-old boy, "You know there is no time, no place, no space. There is only your unconscious, your bewildered conscious, and eternity. You know that, don't you?"

As always, at moments like this, I am confused. "What's that mean?" I say.

"It means you need to take your mind off the trivia once in a while."

"Again, what's that mean?"

"I don't know," says Tali. "I just make this shit up. No, no, wait. It means that in some disturbed part of your brain, you think you're about to go somewhere you've always wanted to go."

"Where?"

"I'm not sure," he says. "I'm not God."

"You're God backwards."

Tali makes a weary face. He doesn't always find me amusing. "That's an old line. You'll have to do better than that when you get there."

"I don't know that I've got better in me."

It seems now as if Tali is pulsating; his fur shimmers in shifting, swirling vortexes. Dazzling rainbows of color whirl feverishly as "Brain Damage" throbs around and through us. "Take my word for it," he says. "You have better in you. It's not always apparent, but it's there."

I'm having trouble concentrating on his words. It crosses my mind that whatever crazy thing is going on with him, he is, after all, a dog. He licks his balls, sniffs other dogs' butts, all the usual stuff. When I confronted him about this once, he said, "You're right; I am a dog. What do you expect?"

"How is it that you think you know so much?" I ask him. "I'm the advanced species."

"Who told you that?"

"Some very smart people."

"All of them trapped in their tunnel vision, wearing their little individual sets of blinders."

"No. I'm talking about the huge mass of scientific wisdom that goes back to long before Aristotle."

"Anyway," says Tali, "what do *you* know about this? You're an actor. Actors are not known for the depth of their wisdom."

"I'm not an actor anymore."

"No, but you'd like to be."

"Yeah, I guess."

"Don't guess. You've been living in that regret since I came to you."

"Maybe."

"No *maybe*. And I should take this opportunity to tell you that to reminisce is one thing, to live in the past is another. For example: Sam. You always want to go back in time with her, always initiating conversations about the old days the two of you had together. And it's not coincidental that during those times, you were still hanging on by your fingernails to your vision of yourself as a big shot."

Tali is morphing in and out of being himself and some creature born of the music of Pink Floyd, his fur a cascade of oscillating, undulating colors, billowing, surging, then contracting into a fairyland hurricane eye, Tinkerbelle on cocaine, touching down, then scattering *Koyaanisqatsi*-like—a million iridescent marbles, flung by some cosmic pointillist, around the warp and woof of what I used to think of as my dog. I remember reading that when Roger Waters, of Pink Floyd, exhausted in every way, took a reel-to-reel copy of *The Dark Side of the Moon* home and played it for his wife, he sat next to her, not watching her as she listened to the entire album. When it was over, he got up, switched off the tape machine, turned back to her, and saw that her face was drenched in tears—as mine is now, watching Tali in his kaleidoscopic, parti-colored vestments giving me the best advice he has.

Maybe, because I've been here before, none of this, including my drama queen tendencies, seems all that surprising to either me or my dog.

"Back to my acting," I say, drying my tears with a sleeve. "I do sometimes wonder how can I ever know what could have been … unless I know? And of course, I understand there's no way to *really* know. But imagine this: if I could go back and relive some pivotal moments, for one thing I'd be better for Sam. When I met her, I would no longer have any bitterness, any regret."

"Sometimes you're stupid enough to make me want to jump up on your bed, if it wasn't Sam's bed too, and poop on your pillow. How do you know that the second time you would ever even meet her? By the time you got to her, she might have already been scooped up by someone of great taste. You might not ever lay eyes on her again. What about that?"

"Yes, but we're talking hypothetically."

"Are we? Please, oh master of mine, tell me what *hypothetical* means."

"It means imagining something else in place of what is."

"You can do that?"

"Sure."

"I am *not* so sure," says Tali. "If you could see the effect of doing what the desperado in the outback of your brain is contemplating, I don't think you'd take the chance you're about to take."

4

(2021) GOODBYE, OLD GIRL

When I wake up in our bedroom, it feels as if I am still under the influence of the drugs I took last night. I don't remember going to bed. I'm not sure what I'm supposed to do today. I know I have to go to Beverly Hills, but I have no idea whether it's for a job interview or if I'm going to see a doctor. I think I remember my agent's assistant, someone with a velvety voice, saying something about leaving a script on my front step. I go out, open the front door, but there's no script there. Maybe that whole thing was a dream.

I'm not only confused, I feel like an addict without his drug, as if someone has been hacking at my spinal column with a carrot peeler. I know my appointment in Beverly Hills isn't until one p.m. Since it's still early, I get back into bed and manage to escape my body's revenge for a while as I catch a few more winks.

My next awareness is of being in Beverly Hills.

But that's not possible. I don't remember driving here.

I do not know how this happened. The carrot peeler has been replaced by a furry tangle of anxieties and an almost physical sensation of solitude.

After gobbling down a little oatmeal with sliced banana and honey, I got ready for my interview. I remember that.

Since then, something has gone badly askew. I feel like I'm underwater, at the helm of a submarine, except I don't know how to drive a submarine, and my claustrophobic nature isn't helping. My best intuitive powers, which I desperately need, have leaked out into the inky ocean around me, and I'm left dependent on the part of my brain that can't unfold a folding chair without written instructions. There is something deeply disturbing about the aftermath of the meds I took last night. But I don't think it was the meds themselves, just the combination.

My God, I can rationalize anything.

Sam said, "Are you okay?" I remember that.

I shrugged it off. "I'm fine," I told her. "Promise." But I sensed an edge to my voice as I said "Promise." I hate being impatient with Sam. Not liking myself around Sam scares me in a way I may never figure out.

"Really?" She looked worried.

"Really." I kissed her. She was frowning. I got the keys to my sky blue 1971 Pontiac Firebird out of my pocket, but it was already unlocked.

Sam grimaced; she knows how sensitive I am about that car. "I'm sorry," she said. "I had it last. I guess I forgot to lock it."

I smiled "forgivingly" in a way that didn't feel forgiving, and headed off to Beverly Hills.

But I don't know how I got here. And I'm not positive what I've described is exactly the way it happened. Maybe it's no more than a disturbed circadian rhythm. In any case, I don't think I've looked through a glass this darkly for a long time.

I pass Cedars-Sinai Medical Center. I don't think that's where I've been. I thought I had a meeting for a movie, but if I did I can't remember who was there or what was said.

For some reason, I've almost completely lost my bearings.

This "living in the now" business, and all that goes along with it, is a lot trickier than the people who write about it lead you to believe. They tell us that if you stay in the moment, as the moment is happening, then you have the opportunity to get all the juice out of life, and along with it, you end up being the kind of person who makes the world a better place.

This sounds swell to me. The problem is that living in the moment is easy to talk about—otherwise there wouldn't be the hundreds of books available on Amazon that tell you how to do it. But if living in the now is the straightforward, transparent answer to how to have a happy life, why is it such a murky, impenetrable riddle to learn how to actually live such a life? Why did so many people have to write books about it? I've read some of them, both religious and metaphysical. I've even done survey reading on quantum physics. I recently bought a book called *String Theory For Dummies.* I guess I'm a lot dumber than the average dummy, because I don't even understand the foreword, where they explain to me how easy it's going to be for me to understand how easy it's going to be.

Back to "the now" and the brainteaser that goes along with it: does such a thing as now, and for that matter time itself, even exist? Sometimes, in the morning, I get up and I know I'm awake, but I've had an erratic mix of dreams. It feels as if I'm in two realities at once. What time is it? I don't mean what time of

day; I mean what time is it in the whole wash of time? Still strad-
dling the "real world" and the dream world, I am lost in time and
space and in every other way, and I couldn't with confidence
swear who I am. If the race mind (the group consciousness of
humanity) is not seriously out of whack, then my brain is.

No matter how you slice it, it appears I'm ... kind of lost. I
wonder what it would be like to be *really* lost in time. Imagine
that. No Samantha. We came into this world alone; the spiritual
books Sam and I read every morning tell me we'll go out alone.
I'll have the Universal Life Force with me, the gurus say, but I
worry they're implying I won't have Sam. I watch her sometimes and pray in my cramped fashion that I learn to make other
human beings anywhere close to as dear to me as Sam is.

One of the last roles I played on stage was the older version of
Joe in a revival of *Damn Yankees*. I'm humming "Goodbye, Old
Girl," the song I sang in that show. A smooth-talking hustler
named Mr. Applegate (the devil in disguise) gives Joe the chance
to be young again and play baseball for his favorite (but peren-
nially pathetic) team, the Washington Senators. But before he
leaves, the older version of him—my role—sings "Goodbye, Old
Girl" to his sleeping wife. I love that song, but at this moment,
I can only hum it. I can't think of the lyrics. If I had a meeting
for a movie and they cast me, could I even remember the lines?

"Goodbye, old girl ... and then what?"

Not being able to remember the lyrics to the song is distressing. It shouldn't bother me. I haven't sung it for a long time. I'm
old enough to play that role now without makeup, but maybe
that wouldn't be possible because I can't remember a single word.

And again, I'm not sure where I am—maybe the lower, flat
part of Benedict Canyon, still Beverly Hills, on my way to The

Valley on the north side of the Santa Monica Mountains (which, if I haven't mentioned it before, separate the San Fernando Valley from the Los Angeles Basin—Hollywood, Beverly Hills, etc.).

I reach for my cell phone to call Sam and realize I must have forgotten it. It's not in any of my pockets or on the passenger seat or in the glove compartment.

This doesn't happen. I never forget my phone.

I try to trace back in my mind to where I've been. I think *maybe* I had a meeting for an acting job, but I couldn't swear to it. The only time I've come over to this side of the Santa Monicas lately is to see my doctor near Cedars-Sinai—normal checkup stuff.

But I don't think that's what I've been doing.

There it is. It exists. It is real. I remember seeing *I'll Live Till I Die* last week or so and feel now as if someone is siphoning ice water up my spinal column as I glance over my shoulder and see my old house, 1809 Benedict Canyon Drive. I think about Fleury and wonder what she would've felt if she'd seen the screening of my first movie, realizing 1809 Benedict had disappeared from it.

At around Easton Drive, I pull my Firebird over to the shoulder of the road, open the door a crack, wait for three cars to whiz by, get out and open the trunk. Lifting the spare up from its well, I find a partial pack of crushed Marlboro Lights, drop the tire back where it goes, slam the trunk, get into the car again, and push in the lighter.

I'm still confused. I try not to think about it. I know it could have to do with the unnecessary cocktail of pharmaceuticals I took last night, but I can't see how that would affect me to the unnerving degree I'm feeling ... whatever this is.

As I wait for the lighter to heat up, I notice there's lots of junk in the car, papers, candy wrappers, an old movie script, magazines. That's not like me. I always keep my Firebird neat. For some reason I've become almost anal about it, unlike my old (younger) self. The lighter does its little popping thing; I pull it out and light one. It doesn't matter that this scrunched cigarette is at least five years old. It tastes wonderful. I inhale deeply, enjoying an expanded lungful of rich, stale, R. J. Reynolds fine tobacco.

Now, for reasons I can't begin to understand, I start backing down Benedict. You have to be careful, doing a thing like that—there's a lot of traffic on both sides of this street.

Smoking and concentrating on backing up, it occurs to me that this is a truly crazy thing to be doing. Apparently I'm planning to back all the way down to 1809 Benedict and … what will I do when I get there? Stare at it?

I reach it and turn off the engine.

It's the white two-story California Spanish hacienda I remember. It has two balconies on the second floor with decorative wrought iron guardrails. There was never much of a view from those balconies, but they looked good, and Fleury and I used to sit outside our bedroom suite to have morning coffee and croissants (we had a little kitchenette with a small fridge and coffee maker in the office that connected to our bedroom). There were nice parts about being successful for the short time I was—during a halcyon period in LA that Neil Diamond in his song "I Am … I Said" called "lay-back." He also mentioned that the cost of living was low. Not anymore.

In the end, Fleury and I didn't work out. My fault. We've been divorced for well over forty years. Samantha and I have been married now for thirty-eight (we lived together for a while first).

There's a whitewashed, six-inch-thick stucco wall in front; and on the south side, facing onto a small street called Wilkie that winds up into the hills behind my old house, a wooden gate—wide enough, when it's open, to drive a car through. That gate looks like it belongs on a ranch. Fleury and I liked it and left it alone. The first house on Wilkie, a little smaller and only one-story high, overlooked ours, but because of trees and a back wall, we were hardly ever aware of it.

The long wooden gate and the house behind us are still here.

There is a driveway to a rear garage on the north side of the house and a short pull-in parking place off the main driveway in front. In that pull-in is a midnight blue Audi Fox that looks astonishingly like the one I leased when I lived here.

I get out of my car, shut the door, stamp out the cigarette, wait until traffic has briefly cleared, and cross the street to where the Audi sits empty. I look inside and feel a rush of déjà-vu. It's an exact replica, including the tan interior, of the Audi Fox I drove during the years I lived here. It's a much deeper blue than the Firebird, which I look back at and notice it needs a wax job. That's odd. I'm finicky about keeping it clean and shiny. I look at the Audi again, shocked, as this moment registers in the pit of my stomach; the power of long-term sense-memory is spine-chilling.

Maybe this is why I stopped and backed up. I must have peripherally seen the Audi in the driveway and it stuck in my unconscious in a way that finally made me decide to pull over and back down to the house I lived in, what, forty-six, forty-seven years ago?

I stare at it, trying to decide what to do next.

I move to the wrought iron gate, experiencing a dread I can't identify. It's like feeling a deep loss, but you're not sure what you've lost. I lift the latch and enter the front courtyard of this house I used to live in—which now, of course, belongs either to the people I sold it to or, I guess, the people they sold it to.

Outside the arched front door is a raised semi-circular entry-way; three stone steps lead up to it. I move up to the door, ring the bell, wait, knock, then repeat both actions.

I reach into my pants pocket and produce my keys.

I find an unfamiliar house key.

Feeling queasy, I insert it into the lock and turn it.

The door opens. I step in.

What is happening to me?

5

(2021) BEVERLY HILLS & VALLEY GLEN

'm standing in the entryway. High above me is a circular balcony with a wrought iron guardrail from which, if I were standing on that balcony now, I could look down and see me, two and a half stories below. In some unlikely manner I couldn't begin to explain, I can, in fact, see myself that way.

In front of me, toward the left, is a red–carpeted circular stairway that leads to the second floor. I used to climb these stairs, treading on this carpet. It must be great carpeting; it still looks fine, almost new, decades later. It also covers the foyer I'm standing in.

Is this a dream? No, it's too consistent to be a dream. I reach a hand out and touch the white, texturized plaster wall. I can feel the detail of this place. I can see it, smell it. Everything around me is … complete, vivid.

To my right, down two steps, is a large living room with a polished, dark-stained oak floor and a beamed ceiling. I can make out the faint stenciled nouveau floral designs still on the timbers and see the gleaming white fireplace at the far end of the long living room. There are two steps down to the fireplace. I used to sit on the top one, looking into the fire, sometimes drinking brandy, wondering what lay ahead in my "glamorous" movie actor life.

Voice lifted, but soft so as not to alarm anyone in the back of the house or upstairs, I say, "Hello?"

A little louder: "Hello … anybody?"

No response. My blood is not exactly running cold. Frozen is closer.

I'm not sure what to do. I can't turn around and leave. I don't know what's happening. Maybe whoever lives in this beautiful home I used to live in can tell me where I *really* am. I know I'm in the house at 1809 Benedict Canyon in Beverly Hills, but more along the lines of where am I in the whole vast spectrum of life, *my* life, *any* life, I don't care. I'll accept any answer right now.

Like why in hell a key on my key ring fits the front door of a house I moved out of a lifetime ago.

Ten minutes later, I'm in my Firebird again on my way to my home in the San Fernando Valley. When I realized no one was in the house I used to live in, I looked around the ground floor for a while. Everything was as I remembered it being in the seventies. In my mind I heard, "Shut your mouth." Since I was a kid, I've had the habit of letting my jaw drop open when a moment in life takes me totally in, like watching the shower scene in *Psycho* for the first time or finding myself in some situation that baffles me, like walking around a house I lived in over forty years ago and finding it exactly the same as I remember it.

I went into the library, turned on the television and saw that I was watching *American Graffiti*, the movie that gave the first big breaks to Richard Dreyfuss, Harrison Ford, and a few other good actors. I was seeing it on the Z Channel on Theta Cable.

Theta Cable went out of business in 1989. The Z Channel, devoted to showing uncut, commercial free movies, no longer exists; hasn't for over thirty years.

Four or five minutes ago, I was watching it.

I ran out of the house, slammed the front door behind me, almost got hit by a huge red Chevrolet as I crossed Benedict, and wrenched open the door of my Firebird.

I feel as if I'm driving through a sister version of the world I thought I lived in. I more or less recognize everything around me—not, to be honest, that I've ever much noticed the homes, gardens, and canyon sides to the left and right of me as I drive up Benedict. I never even walked up Wilkie Street behind my house when I lived there. But looking at Benedict Canyon now, it doesn't seem at all different from the last time I was here, either on my way over to Beverly Hills today or whenever I was last on this road. I know I didn't step through some window in time. Sane people know that's science fiction. Ask anyone but the fringiest physicists.

Could I have developed a brain tumor or some other physical anomaly? It doesn't seem likely that such a thing could have happened this suddenly. Has my whole mental landscape mysteriously shifted—a sea change in how my brain functions out in the real world, away from Sam and the cocoon I more or less spend my life in? I sit at home, writing, almost every day. Maybe, without feeling it, I've undergone a subtle but comprehensive alteration in the way my mind functions. Maybe the *me within* me, who watches my thoughts and emotions and everything physical in my life, has become so prominent in the balance of my psyche, that this ... *watcher* within me has become something other than what I supposed it was, something more alien than I could imagine.

Maybe I'm not the man I was, but never noticed it until something about this particular occurrence of passing the house I used to live in drew me back to it.

That doesn't make any sense.

Maybe, by some means I can't understand, I've reached a way station in my life, a sort of commuter stop on my journey through this ... whatever journey I'm on.

As I'm about to reach Mulholland Drive, I see the San Fernando Valley open up before and below me. The panorama of the west Valley is at nine o'clock and the east at three, as I look from six o'clock north toward midnight on the geographical timekeeper I'm traversing. I choose to aim for midnight instead of noon because I'm a night person, and although I love new days and dewy mornings, it's nighttime that holds the magic for me.

Where did that thought come from? It's as if some *Twilight Zone* giant, an immense little girl, has picked me up like a tiny doll she was furious with and shaken me violently, tumbling the lobes of my brain around like a bingo ball scrambler. This reminds me that even though I'm not young anymore, I still live in the pleasant delusion of my immortality. It's a kind of stubbornness athwart what the world calls reality.

I turn west on Mulholland, toward nine o'clock, and after about a third of a mile slide right onto Beverly Glen, headed north and down the mountain toward the San Fernando Valley.

As I descend Beverly Glen, quickly losing sight of the panorama of The Valley, my mind flips to its usual default setting: Samantha. The night of our blind date, I took her to a wonderful restaurant called the Red Lantern Inn, five miles north of

Universal Studios (not yet a full-blown theme park, although they had been running their pink and white striped "Glamor-Tram" tour around the studio backlot since 1964).

Sam and I sat down, ordered drinks, and were starting our second one when we both reached out at almost the same moment and touched hands.

"You must have thought I was brazen," she said later.

Well, maybe. I don't know. I do know I'd been waiting for her. She smelled right. She smelled of lilacs and lavender and lemon blossoms, "L" things. She was ... nice and interesting and interested, not to mention sexy. I believe *something* was telling me most of the way through my fourth decade on this earth: "*You're sitting next to the love of your life.*"

We'd both been in this city for years and never encountered each other, and now there she was next to me. I leaned in and, trying to be a *little* subtle, breathed in the sweet, feminine smell of her.

Not long after that we both said, "You're it." When you find that—at least when we found it—things started to fall into place, the world started to be okay at last—not only okay, but warm, *containing no fear*—and that's where I wanted to be. Ambition, show business, almost none of it mattered. I'd found my pearl of great price and I couldn't imagine being in any other "better place."

Years passed, and I don't know how many times she's asked, "Do you know how much I love you?" I say, "Yes, but tell me again. I can never hear it enough." Sometimes, when I think of her, I think of what is lately my favorite line in any song:

In this life, I was loved by you.

It's not news, I suppose, if I confess I'm a man who loves chick flicks.

In The Valley now, I take a left on Coldwater and drive north toward Valley College and our enchanted cottage a couple of blocks north of Grant High School. I turn into the driveway.

Sam's car is not there.

Where she is? Probably the store. She's one of the few people I know who likes to grocery shop. She loves Trader Joe's and Ralphs and Vallarta and the Armenian neighborhood market and even Costco. She talks to people. I don't mean it's her habit to open up to strangers. She's just unguarded and approachable, friendly. I'd like to be that way.

I get out of the car and walk toward the front door.

It's not there.

That's not true. It is there, but it's a different door. The house looks almost—no, *exactly*—as it did when Sam and I bought it thirty years ago.

I feel as if I've been deoxygenated or all the blood has drained out of my brain. Sam and I redesigned this house. We put a stained glass window in the front of the kitchen, which is at the southeast corner of the house. We built what is called an outlook onto the roof; it's several double beams that extend out over the walkway up to the house. Now, everything we did has been undone.

It's no longer the door to my house, not the door I opened and the doorway I passed through when I left the house this morning.

I find myself backing away from it like I've encountered Godzilla, and I don't like the idea of being picked up and eaten.

I go across the street and knock at our neighbor's door.

An old man, I suppose about my age, answers. "Yes?"

I don't know this man. I blink. "I'm sorry to … uh, bother you. Could I talk to Angel, please?"

"Who?"

"Angel."

"Who's Angel?"

"She lives here."

His eyes narrow. "No, she doesn't. I've lived here for thirty years."

We stare at each other for a few seconds before he says, "You have the wrong house."

"But ... you see, I live across the street." I point.

He frowns at me. "No, you don't. That's where Gary lives. He's my best friend. I ought to know." He sees something in my expression. "Maybe you're on the wrong street. These streets can look a lot alike. ... I don't know anyone named Angel."

"But I live ..." I again point to my house.

He frowns. "Sorry, you're mistaken. Good luck." He frowns again, puts one hand up, making sure I've received his message, and closes the door.

Sweat is streaming down my back. I don't know where I am.

I look around the neighborhood. It is not the same one I left to go over the hill this morning. *Was that this morning?* I feel as if I'm about to black out.

I don't know where I went this morning. If it was an audition, I don't know what it was an audition for. Maybe it was only a meeting. Yes. It was a meeting for a possible acting job.

I think.

I look around me. This is not the neighborhood I live in—at least not *now*.

I walk back to the sidewalk in front of Angel's house, only I just found out this is *not* Angel's house. I look across at mine, at what *used to be* my house. I can see the substructure of the place

I've lived in for thirty-plus years, but it's not the same house as the one I left this morning.

But I don't remember driving over the hill.

I look in every direction. I get in my car and drive down to the end of the block, the way I came. I turn to the right and see Erwin Park across the street where it's always been. I make a three-point turn, pull to the side of the street and turn off the engine, keeping my eye on the park. It's almost time for the dogs and their walkers to arrive, about four in the afternoon. I'm guessing. I don't have my watch on. I don't remember what my watch looks like or what kind it is. Something inexpensive. I've always worn cheap watches. They keep time as well as expensive ones. Besides, I keep losing them.

I sit in my car for … it must be close to an hour, staring at the park. It's been renovated in the past three or four years. They put in new trees and plants, some boulders, a playground for kids, and a walking path around the perimeter.

All those things are now … *not there*; the park is back to being what it was when we first moved to this neighborhood. A few people show up, some of them with dogs, but not one familiar person, not one familiar dog. I'd give anything right now to look out there and to see Tali galloping toward me, with Sam in tow.

I try to account for this inner collapse I'm going through, this unaccountable lunacy. But that doesn't help. As I mentioned, I take mild opiates at night to cope with the pain I still have after those back operations, but I don't take them during the day. I don't take any other drugs, nothing "recreational."

Anyway, it's not as if I'm stoned. I don't *feel* stoned. All I drink anymore is a glass or two of wine in the evenings, or a martini. Well, maybe last night was a little different. But how does that create this parody of reality?

Recently, I've tried to meditate more often. I've been hoping to learn to lift myself above the world's relentless chaos, the cybernated culture's inescapable pinging sonar din. But I don't know if it's helped. Sometimes it feels as if I've slipped into an oblivious state of existence in which I've accomplished no more productive thinking than you'd get from a cauliflower. Sometimes, seeing it from the everyday way of looking at things, I'm just *here,* serving no purpose, solving no problems. A lot of times, I can't even call it meditating or praying or anything that's in any way useful, which I guess in a way makes me another piece of the world's detritus, a lump of … nothing that matters.

I drive up to the mall, five short blocks to the north. It looks about the same. Parking in front of Vallarta Market, I think about ordering *Quantum Physics For Dummies,* which makes me giggle because I have no home, and therefore no computer, no access to Amazon, no way to order all the stuff I'm always ordering—most of which I don't need anyway. And the bookstores have mostly disappeared.

Why am I laughing?

Maybe I'm in two places at once. I wish I were where the other me is. I wonder what he's up to. Is he at home with Sam, wishing the next couple of hours would fly by a little faster so he could have magic hour with her? I'd give anything to know where his house is—actually, where either of our houses is. Maybe I live in an apartment. Maybe I don't live in LA. Maybe I'm a version of me that never moved out here from New York. Perhaps I never moved from the various Los Angeles Basin locales I was raised in to New York in the first place.

I see a guy getting into a Dodge truck. I don't know why, but I shout "Hi" out my window at him. He glances behind him to see who I'm speaking to, then looks back in my direction.

Finally, he manages a leery "Hey" and, frowning, gets into his truck and pulls out of his parking place. He doesn't look back as he drives away.

I get out and walk around the parking lot. I look to the west, out over a wash that was once, so I'm told, part of the Los Angeles River. Am I meant to be trying to reason this out? What do people do in real life when they find themselves confronted with madness?

Am I simply mad? What does that mean?

Okay, begin at the beginning. I am born. No, that's *David Copperfield*. Okay, I am hatched and stuck down on a slab of cracked asphalt next to a converted piece of desert, next to a bone-dry concrete ditch that people call a river, I guess because when it floods around here in wintertime, the water rushes down this "river" and goes … nowhere in particular; eventually out to the Pacific, I suppose, although I don't know. I've lived in this converted desert for a long time, and now I'm reduced to exploring the nonsensical. Nothing reasonable seems … *reasonable*. I don't remember ingesting anything unusual this morning. But for that matter, I don't remember eating breakfast. I thought I did, but now I'm thinking it's possible I'm remembering some other morning.

I remember yesterday. I had cocktails with Sam. I have nothing I could call a coherent memory after that. I don't remember going to bed.

There's a Sanskrit word from yogic teaching, *samskara*. It means "impression." It's a mark left on the *chakra*, one of the centers of spiritual power in the human body. I think it's the result of an emotional disturbance. Without meaning to, you latch onto some bad moment in your life and it leaves a *samskara*, a scar. Something upsets you and you're unable to let it go.

After a number of months or years or a lifetime, you have a part of your deep inner self that carries these scars, and whenever anything conjures up the "bad" moments that caused them, you're reminded of whatever it is and it re-involves you in it. And after you have enough of those scars in you, you can end up with triggers in your emotional makeup that cause you constant and deep distress. They can bring about depression and cause you to barely be able to function. All you can do is spin your wheels and go nowhere.

Have I gone through some major *something* that I don't remember, but that is nevertheless triggering a unique kind of depression? Maybe it's the culmination of my isolated life of recent years, almost exclusively defined by my marriage to Sam. Is it possible that something in my limbic system, which is particularly relevant to my brain's ability to process memory, has gone awry?

But I know I'm conscious. Maybe I've had a little blackout, but otherwise my memory is fine.

Oh, Jesus!

I've looked down at my hands resting on the steering wheel. *They're not mine!*

That's not true. I'm seeing a young man's hands on the steering wheel. They look like my hands used to when I was young. As I stare at them, I lift the loose-fitting shirt I'm wearing. I'm looking at a young man's stomach, not over-muscled but flat. Wow. Flat.

I look in the rearview mirror. I stare for I don't know how long at my years ago, just-moved-out-here-from-New York face.

I confess that, along with a kind of terror, I'm aware of a burst of adrenalin that feels something like the thrill of knowing that ... *something* has happened to you and it's something *abso-fucking-lutely* wonderful.

But what do I do now?

I look around me. That's not Vallarta. That's a Lucky's market. It was here when Sam and I moved to this neighborhood. Bally's Total Fitness to the left of it isn't there. Nothing's there. They haven't built up that side of the mall yet.

I start the car again, pull out of the mall and head east. I see an old bar I don't remember, and a place that advertises SWIM CLUB, MONTHLY MEMBERSHIPS; I don't remember that. There's a "new" delicatessen two doors east of the swim club.

I turn right on Coldwater, passing a bank that was a Starbucks a few days ago, and head south. Where is Sam? I'd like a glass of lemonade. I'd like to ask Sam what's going on with me. Not that she'd know. I feel like I'm in an old sci-fi movie, *Plan Nine from Outer Space,* or one of those things where some sad sack is held captive in a saucer and has no idea where or even who he is. And then Zsa Zsa Gabor shows up.

But I'm a young man. Again.

But where is Samantha? Is she young too? She can't be. If she is, I haven't met her yet.

I can't think about that. I don't own a conceptual apparatus capable of processing any of this.

As I proceed south on Coldwater, everything looks the same as I remember it. But that doesn't surprise me. During my acting training I was taught to be constantly aware of the people and places around me. I guess I'm out of practice at that—and a lot of other things.

Mostly, I stay home; Sam goes out and gets everything we need to stay alive: groceries, stuff for the house, and so on. The only time I go out anymore, unless it's to go over to the other side of the Santa Monica Mountains, is for dinner or a movie. For exercise, we've got an elliptical machine on the porch, and—not as often as I should—I lift light weights in the backyard and do some halfhearted stretches. I go to a nearby gym sometimes, but not as often as I used to, and lately not at all.

I take a sudden right on Magnolia, drive a mile and a half to Hazeltine, take a left there and then a hard right into one of the parking lots for the Van Nuys/Sherman Oaks Recreation Center. I have no idea what I'm doing. I get out of my car and slam the door, not bothering to lock it, and run past the baseball diamonds, heading west.

I notice a crew shooting a film at the south end of the park. It doesn't occur to me to go over and see what it is. I always feel a little, I guess, jealous when I pass a film being shot on location because it reminds me that I'm not working, or that most jobs I used to be able to do, I can't do anymore because I've aged out of them. There are four age categories in Hollywood jargon: juvenile or ingenue, leading man or woman, character man or woman, and old-to-dead. It's depressing.

I realize I'm gazing at one man. He looks a little like I did when I was young. They're setting lights on him. This is no doubt the actor they're about to film in the next shot. Or maybe it's his double, his stand-in. There's no way to know without going over and asking and I don't feel like doing that.

Now, it hits me why I'm here: to run. I can *run*.

I'm running as fast as I can. I was never a sprinter, I wasn't track team material, but I'm running as fast as my legs can carry me; I'm moving like a half-miler toward Van Nuys Boulevard, coincidentally a half mile away.

When I reach it, I drop down to the grass, gasping for air. I'm winded.

But my lungs are evidently fresh and pink because within a few minutes, I'm ready to go again. I get up and run back the way I came, to Hazeltine.

Yesterday, I was what the world calls an old man; today I have a kid's genius for running, for flying across the grass and gravel, heart pumping hard and steady, my blood surging as if I were bolting away from a fire. The sensation of wind on my face is exhilarating.

I haven't had this feeling for years and years and God, it feels wonderful, staggering. It might be a person's most fantastical dream come true.

Except for one thing.

How do I get back to Sam?

6

[197?] BEVERLY HILLS AGAIN

Now, *whenever now is*, driving east on Ventura, doing my best to assess from my *present* point of view—this new, terrifying/beguiling *young man's* reality (if there is *anything* real about it)—it strikes me that I have no idea how I got to be as lucky as I got to be in my *old man's* life with Sam.

Once in a rare while, I (the old me) was reminded of my age—a little arthritis in my hands, or I'd get my ID checked at a pharmacy; they wanted to make sure I was who I claimed I was. And sometimes somebody, seeing my age, treated me a little as if I didn't exist, but they didn't know any better, and it didn't bother me.

But now, it looks like there was another side or another configuration of my good luck. Did I lose perspective? Did I allow my life to become too precious? I wish I'd *known* one time that God was listening. I would have spoken to Him or Her in a way that mattered. I'd have said to Whoever it was, "I am more grateful for this beautiful life I've aged into than I could ever express. Thank you, God. I really, really adore You."

This is definitely a different *Valley*. A different Ventura Boulevard.

Look at that. An Orange Julius. That hasn't been there for at least thirty years. I think it's a Fatburger in 2021. Do they still have Orange Juliuses? I don't know. I stopped paying attention to stuff like that a long time ago. When did I start sleeping through my life? I could probably make a long list of things I've let drift into my bin of unawareness. I wish Sam were here. She could explain this to me.

Well, maybe not. She probably has no more insight on a cosmic level than I do.

But she *has* magic. From living for so many years in the peace and the light that go along with that, I imagine for a moment that I've become at least a tiny beacon of *light* in the cosmic tapestry, a pocket flashlight.

So why isn't some cosmic … *something* paying attention to me right now? If there's any reality to what appears to be going on at this moment, then *as far as I'm concerned* … there *is no Samantha Maytree. For the time being, Samantha doesn't exist.*

Then do I?

Although the driver's side window is open, the city around me seems unusually quiet, almost as quiet as it seemed for much of 2020, the last year the old man in me lived through (not counting the grim babble of politics—that was not quiet). A late afternoon third quarter moon hangs tantalizingly low in the sky, south of Mount Baldy to the east. It feels as if I could drive there by sunset. Maybe get a cosmic answer or two from the old-to-dead man in the moon.

I turn right on Coldwater and as evening approaches, head up the Santa Monica Mountains for (I *think*) the second time today.

Maybe I've become a night creature and when the sun goes down my life will return to my normal vampire existence. Maybe I've slipped out of the seat of my normal consciousness. I know I've read something about that. I believe it happens. But isn't that some sort of a spiritual thing? I don't think it translates into the material life of some guy living in the San Fernando Valley. And anyway, this is without question *not* the *Valley* I left when I went to the doctor this morning at Cedars Sinai in Beverly Hills.

Doctor? Did I see a doctor? I thought I had an acting interview. But I don't remember that either. And if I saw a doctor, I don't know which one, or why. And if I saw a doctor, it doesn't look as if he did me much good—unless you count the fact that SOMETHING has caused me to become more than forty years younger.

I'm in Beverly Hills again. Even though I no longer know this side of the hill as well as I used to many years ago, everything looks the same, or about the same, as far as I can tell.

"About" and "as far as I can tell": words that describe my *sweeping incomprehension* of the world I am living in—a big no-no for actors, for anyone. Ralph Waldo Emerson said: "Let us take our bloated nothingness out of the way of the divine circuits." And: "Let us unlearn our wisdom of the world." I've taken that way too far. I've unlearned everything I ever knew or thought I knew, and so far no luck with the divine circuits.

But this *does* look like the Beverly Hills I remember. If I have lived through some kind of nightmarish hallucination, maybe it's ending. It will always be something I can't explain. Years from now (I'd better make that not too many), I'll tell this story to our friends.

I ask myself where I'm going. I know almost no one, and certainly no one very well on this side of the Santa Monicas—at least that's the case for the Danny Maytree who left his home this morning and drove south over the mountains to Beverly Hills. In the fading sunlight now, I'm gliding, as I always seem to when I'm in Beverly Hills, under Mexican fan palms and sugar pines. I'm on Rexford. As I reach Sunset, I turn right and head west. I don't know why.

I take the second turn north after the Beverly Hills Hotel. If I'd gone south instead, I would have turned onto Cañon Drive. The Spanish pronunciation of cañon is canyon, but most Americans pronounce it …

Wait a minute. This is the second time today I've been here. In fact it feels in some part of me as if I'm perpetually making this turn, that I never come out of it.

Or I'm on a string, a yo–yo.

I saw a documentary about Yo-Yo Ma and several other international musicians in 2016 or so. I'm no longer sure 2016 has happened yet. I can't tell by the years of the cars the way I could when I was young. They all look the same, including my own '71 Pontiac Firebird, which looks again like I guess it used to when I was young and didn't take good care of it.

Approaching the California Spanish house I used to live in with my first wife, Fleury, I slow down. It's still rush hour. Lots of cars are streaming north on Benedict; I'm no doubt irritating the people driving immediately behind me. When I see the Audi Fox, I pull over to the right shoulder, stop the engine, get out of the car, and cross the street to the pull-in where, once again, the Audi sits empty.

It is definitely the car I leased … forty-five, forty-seven years ago is a good guess.

This time, I look at it more carefully. It's got an 8-track tape player and the control panel is exactly as I remember it, dark wood and a rich, elegant feel. I'm trying to remember if the tan interior is leather. I think it is. I guess at the time it *was* a luxury car. I'd just come out from New York with Fleury, having done the movie version of a play I did in New York, *Holiday in the Park*. The play had been a hit on Broadway. The film was one of the year's highest-grossing, although it was the rag end of frothy Broadway comedies being turned into frothy Hollywood movies.

And now I had a movie contract. I have a rush of all the feelings I had when I realized I'd ended up a success. "Ended up" is an incorrect expression. You don't "end up" until ... it's *all* over. I remember thinking at the time: *"This is it. I am a big success. Period."*

What I forgot, or hadn't learned yet, was that there are no periods in life, no *endings*—happy or otherwise—just commas; lots of commas, with the occasional semi-colon. You only get one *period* in life and most of us don't look forward to it, let alone think of it as a cause for celebration.

I open the side gate, walk toward the front door, climb the steps, and for the second time today, ring the bell.

There is no answer. I try the door. It's not locked. Why would it be? I didn't lock it when I ran out.

Was that ... experience ... real?

In any case, the people who live here *now* aren't home. If they were, they'd answer the doorbell. The doorbell works; I can hear it. I knock to be sure.

Still, no one answers. This place belongs to me again. I can feel it. Fleury and I owned it until I was about the age I appear to be at this moment. (I ended up with the house. She ended up with everything else, including her divorce lawyer.) I look at my young man's hand in front of me for maybe the twentieth time since I first noticed it in the parking lot of what used to be Vallarta Market.

I go inside and close the door behind me.

I'm standing in the turreted entryway again. High above me is the circular balcony with the wrought iron guardrail. There's not as much light coming in now. It's evening. The canyon loses sunlight, more so on this, the west side of the street, long before actual sunset.

And there it is again, toward the left: the red-carpeted circular stairway to the second floor. Glancing to the right at the living room with the beamed ceiling, this time I head up the stairs, noticing a spring in my step and feeling a rush of exuberance with it.

At the top I look down the hall toward the end guest room. To the sides are the three-bedroom suites. I walk past the first one and through the doorway into the one on my left. It's exactly as I remember it. More polished oak flooring, thick, pure white walls, opaque windows that would look out over the stairway if you could see through them. To one side of the windows are several pictures of me in various plays I acted in. There's the group picture from *Look Homeward, Angel.* After the read-through, before the first rehearsal, the wonderful woman, Mirabelle, who directed it said, "*Intuition is not enough, Danny.*" She was saying it was good that I had the passion I did, but that I needed craft too. She was telling me I needed something other than my right brain to be a good actor; that it was good to make intuitive choices that were emotionally "valid" (a word that later—I'm not sure when or why—became almost holy to me), but they also needed to be logically valid. I could use a little valid left-brained thinking right now as I stand here in what used to be my office.

On my desk, which, spookier than I can express, is exactly as I remember it, I find my wallet. I remember a friend doing an exercise in an acting class. He was told that he was suddenly thrust into a foreign situation, lost and alone. I could see that as my friend started to act this premise, he became physically panicked. The first thing he did was to pat his left hip pocket where many men carry their wallet. That was his first reaction to finding himself in alien circumstances.

I do that now. There is no wallet in my left hip pocket. All I have in the faded tan corduroys I'm wearing is a small pocket notebook, with a few notes, scene outlines, and so on in it. I carry it mostly to jot down ideas for later writing purposes. In my left front pants pocket, I find a fancy new recorder pen, called a Spy-Guy, I recently bought online. SpyGuy is the brand name of the device, which is a voice-activated pen-shaped recorder, good for sixteen hours of whatever audio material you want to document.

I've got plenty to make notes about and document now.

I look inside the wallet I've found on my desk. Thirty-four dollars and my New York driver's license, nothing else. I guess I'm not using credit cards yet. I look at the black-and-white picture of me in the wallet, then at the mirror. Yup, about the same age as the guy in the driver's license photo. Is he as bewildered by all this as I am? He sure doesn't look like a picture of confidence.

I walk from the outer room into the bedroom. Those are the same gauze curtains over the windows. There are eggshell white shades we used at night, but they're not pulled down at the moment.

And that's our bed. Well, my bed. I can tell by the absence of Fleury's personal items on the dresser that this is after she left me.

In the beginning it was my fault. In the end, it turned out she'd contributed her own part. Still, if I have to think in terms of who was most to blame, I have to pick myself. We had a bit of an if-you-do-it-to-me-I'll-do-it-to-you relationship developing. It was one of those marriages that happened at first because each one needed the other one, not out of love, but in order to heal some longstanding wound. We both found out too late that doesn't work. We'd gotten married too young and for the wrong reasons. It happens all the time. I don't excuse myself, but now, an old man's lifetime later, I think—make that hope—I forgive myself.

I forgave Fleury a long time ago. It's easier to forgive others than yourself. Well, some others. I think of my childhood. I didn't have a mother for most of it. She died when I was very young. For most of the years before I met Sam, I dated lots of women. My therapist later suggested that maybe I was looking for mama. No shit. When I met Sam, she volunteered to be a surrogate—to be devoted, to show me a definition of love I'd never known possible. It didn't kill all my self-doubt, but it did make me faithful to Sam.

I'm hungry. The little refrigerator is still under my desk in the other room. I open it and find three cans of Budweiser and most of a loaf of bread. I open a beer and drink half of it. The bread smells all right. There's no butter, but I'm ravenous. I eat two pieces, but stop in the middle of the third. Maybe there's something a little more satisfying in the kitchen. I finish my beer and head down there.

As I circle down the stairs in the turret that I've descended a few hundred times before, I think about the quicksilver quality of time, recollecting, reconfiguring, and arbitrarily replaying the moment of my unending turn from Sunset onto Benedict. I imagine a merry-go-round spinning in the wrong direction—not clockwise wrong or counterclockwise wrong, but because the horses are facing the wrong direction wrong.

I'm talking to myself, but I'm not sure who is talking to whom. I'm probably crazy. If not, I'm at least badly lost—but not in a way that would justify filing a missing person report; they'd hang up on me if I told them the particulars of my case. The only one I can imagine reporting myself missing to is Sam.

When I tell this story to Sam, I must remember to say that if she's looking for a chronological line of unfolding events, she's going to be unhappy with me. It's not that I'd be unwilling to tell this tale in a linear way, it's that I wouldn't know how to do that. The gyroscopic equipment many people were born with was not in the goody bag handed to me as I exited the birth canal. And now with today's turn of events, I'll have to beg whomever I tell this to, to please accept my apologies for my non-chronological soul.

There's a half-can of Dinty Moore beef stew in the fridge. I take it out, smell it, and, standing at the kitchen sink, eat it cold. It's delicious.

I walk into the library where I watched the Z Channel broadcast of *American Graffiti* on television earlier … today? I think so. It's an Admiral TV. It seems fairly new, 24-inch screen. Earlier, I'd thought it was small, but by seventies standards that's not true. I look at the books on the shelves. When Fleury and I lived here, I subscribed to a *Masterpieces of English Literature* series. For twenty-five dollars a crack, they sent me a new book every month.

I take one of those books off the shelf.

It's *The Secret Garden* by British-American novelist Frances Hodgson Burnett, Sam's favorite book from her childhood. This morning, *this same copy* of it was on my bedside table in the home I live in with Sam in the San Fernando Valley.

By the feel of the air, it's spring. Working back in my mind to when Fleury left me, I know it *has* to be 1974, forty-seven years ago.

"Jesus!"

There was a yellow wall phone in the hallway between the breakfast room and the library. Beneath it was a pad with important phone numbers on it. On the back of that pad I'd written my agent's home phone number. I step out of the library into that hallway.

The rotary phone is there today. On the dial is a little white circular decal with the same number I still remember from when Fleury and I lived here. I take the pad off the hook it's hanging on and turn it over. In my handwriting is written *John Yort*. The writing doesn't look forty-seven years old. I dial his home number.

After three rings, a woman's voice says, "John Yort."

"Hi," I say. "Is this ... Jenny?"

"Yes, it is."

"It's Danny Maytree."

"Oh, hi, honey. I thought that was you. You sounded so unsure."

"Would you let me ring through? It's kind of important. Do you know if he's home?"

"I think so. He picked up his messages. Go ahead and ring back. It better be important," she adds, "or I'll get in trouble."

"It is. Thanks, love."

I hang up and dial again. After six rings, John answers. John is one of the killer agents. He's not the worst of them and I do like him, partly I suppose, because he seems to like me. But I wouldn't want to have to negotiate with him. There are still a few of the old courtly lady and gentleman agents, but they've been mostly driven out by 1974, which I guess was always their fate, as the sharks steadily amputated them out of the sea.

"John, can I talk to you for a minute?"

"Maytree. What's up?"

"Oh, John, oh my God, John, if I could only answer that question."

"Pardon?"

I'm stuck already. I can't think where to begin. "Did we talk earlier?"

"You mean today?" he says, surprised.

"Uh … no, I meant earlier in the week."

"It was Monday. We talked on Monday. Why haven't you gotten back to me? Did you read the script?"

"Uh …"

"You were supposed to get back to me yesterday," he says. "What do you think?"

"About what?"

"About the script. About *Sunset Island*."

I actually remember that script, most of a half century later. That's how bad it was. I usually took whatever job John told me to. But I turned that one down. "It's horrible, John. I can't do that. No one will ever hire me again."

There's a pause. Now he sounds like a little boy. "You think so?"

"Yes. It's embarrassing."

"Don't lose your temper, Danny."

"Why would I lose my temper?"

"Because the same thing that makes good actors also makes working with them like living next to a volcano. Look, the money's good. And it's Stanley Blanchard. He's Altman's protégé. Everybody says fabulous things about him."

"He wrote it too, didn't he," I say without a question mark.

"*Yes*, he wrote it. His name is on the cover of the script."

"I can't help it. It's still horrible."

There's a short pause. "You pretty sure?"

"I'm positive." God, it must have been bad, to feel this strongly about *Sunset Island* forty-seven years later.

"Okay," says John, seeming to give in, which is surprising; he never surrendered that easily. "I gotta go eat something," he says. "We'll talk tomorrow. Oh, and Danny, please remember the people you meet on the way up are the same ones you'll meet on the way down."

I recognize this pearl of wisdom. "John, why do you keep saying that to me? I *get* the message."

"It's the most important message in the business for some-body like you."

"I've got it."

"You don't have to just get it, Danny. You've got to chew on it and digest it."

The last time I remember him telling me this, he may as well have been speaking to me in Swahili. Now, I get it. I say all right, then: "If I'm here again ... I mean I *am* here ... *now* and I know I've got to do it right this time."

"Pardon?"

"I've been thinking; some actors are making their own *breaks*. You know what I mean?" He doesn't respond. I think he knows where I'm going with this; I've probably mentioned it before. "If I can raise twenty-five or thirty thousand dollars, I can probably get a little more and shoot my own script. You know, a shoestring production thing. It's happening all over the place. I mean, I'm not exactly sizzling, but I'm hot enough that I can raise a little cash toward something worthwhile. By the way, what was the last job I did?" I can't believe I've asked him that.

"Are you smoking something?"

"Yeah. ... No. I was just ... I've had a few drinks. I mean I'm not working now, right?" Silence. "I'm only kidding. ... But I'm going a little crazy from not working for a while."

"Danny, you just finished that Paramount thing, what, three weeks ago?"

"Oh yeah, right right right. Actually I was asking about the last play I did."

"I don't know what you're on, Dan, but you are not going to go do a play now. You can't afford it."

"You're right," I tell him. "But I'm not going to do most of the same crap I did last time."

"Say again?"

"I've got to take some chances. If Altman himself offers me a job, or Coppola or Lumet, or ... one of those, I'll take it if it's any kind of a part at all, but other than that, I'm going to come up with something for myself."

Again, no response, then finally: "Do you know what kind of a gamble you'd be taking if you did that?"

"The film business is changing, John. The film business has *changed*."

"But this is now," he says. "You ain't gonna be hot next year, honey. And they aren't real big with second chances out here like they are in New York."

"Listen, John ..."

"I'm hungry," he says. "I'm going to go eat. I'll talk to you tomorrow. You're in Hollywood now. Get with the flow."

"John ...?"

"Try to talk some sense into yourself."

"I'll try. Hey John, do I have a … hot temper?"

"Well, you do go over the edge every once in a while. Don't worry about it; I'm used to it. It's who you are. Bye, Maytree." He hangs up.

Jesus. I sit in a woven rattan chair in the breakfast room, looking past the cabinet with Fleury's and my second-best set of dishes in it, still chipped, but still there. Why wouldn't they be? John Yort is still my agent. I *did* notice a little edge to my voice.

My agent. I get the giggles. I'm lost in the cosmos, out of my time, or in the wrong one of my times, and the first thing I do is call my agent. If that's any indication of my accrued wisdom, I've gone a whole lifetime and not learned a thing.

What would happen if, this time, I could make decisions that are even slightly rational? It hits me in a new way that I've been given a second chance to get a few things right, to make some half-smart decisions in an acting career that has, at this moment anyway, some potential. This time, I can let a career blossom that I pinched off in its infancy before. People don't get the chance to do things right after doing them wrong the first time, to not make the same mistakes; I know what mistakes not to make now. I have another chance.

Another chance. Is that how I got here? I wanted another chance?

Wait. It was around the time of *Sunset Island* that I turned down the lead in the pilot for the Mike Brookes series. (Mike is a classy TV producer of the time) I didn't want to do a series then; I remember saying that and John went along with me. He told me it was a firm offer, but he didn't know what it was going to turn out to be any more than I did. That series ran for seven seasons with a good actor in my role. I don't think they've cast it yet. Should I call John back and tell him I'll take it?

A second chance to do something good. This was one of the rare series during that period that had some intelligence, that wasn't just sluggish diversion. It was a sitcom, but it had some wit; you didn't feel like a zombie, watching it—as if someone has shot your brain full of novocaine and now you're a deadened lump of target audience, gawking at the telly as your life drifts by.

I could call John back. They haven't shot the pilot yet. I recall it took a while to find the actor who did the role. As I remember, that actor went on to do nice things later, although I can't think of his name. God, I'd hate to mess up his chance.

Maybe I shouldn't be making decisions now.

The first page of Chapter One in *String Theory For Dummies* begins: "*In Chapter One you gain a basic understanding of string theory.*"

It didn't happen.

In chapter one of my life, I was apparently asleep. Maybe this is just Chapter Two in my life, but this time I'm awake.

Or am I?

7

(1974) CACTUS AND A BATHTUB

'm getting the shakes. Once in a while, before an audition, I used to loosen up with a little pot, or a Quaalude, although I used them mainly to help me get a decent night's sleep before the day of an interview.

Once I had the job, self-consciousness became a private matter between the camera and me. Sometimes, it's possible to turn the camera into a friend and then everything's not just okay, it's exhilarating—the same stimulation that caused you to become a stage actor in the first place; if feels like you're a child being paid loving attention.

At this moment, having been tossed forty-seven years back in time, I feel the way I felt before an important audition: scared, anxious, lost—not to mention, in this case, a dark dread of the next piece of the past that lies ahead.

I kept my drugs in the top cupboard of a hutch in the laundry room behind the kitchen. I climb up on a stepstool now, reach into a cubbyhole in the back of that cupboard, and pull out the film canister I kept my Quaaludes in. If I ever needed a little escape from alleged reality, it's now.

There are four small white pills about half the size of a dime in the gray canister. I don't remember exactly what Quaaludes look like—there were lots of pills of various sizes and shapes in those days—but that's what these have to be. It'll be the perfect relaxant for the occasion. To be on the safe side, I swallow only one.

I do *not* know why I do what I do now.

I run upstairs and ransack my bedroom and office, looking for the script for *Sunset Island*. I must want to remind myself of what I've turned down. I find three movie scripts, none of them *Sunset Island*.

The keys to the Audi are on a key ring I keep on a hook next to the back door. I grab them, go out to the Audi, unlock it and look for a movie script. I look in the pockets on the doors, under the seats, and in the trunk. I don't find a screenplay.

I sit in the passenger seat for a while, aware I'm starting to feel a little funny.

Upstairs in the bathroom, I undress and turn on the faucets, catching sight of myself in the mirror. Not bad. Not exactly lean and chiseled; this is not the handiwork of a bodybuilder, but respectable enough. I look down at the water running into the bathtub. I'm going to fill the bathtub as near to the top as I can, allowing for the water I'll displace when I get in. I'm feeling very aware of my surroundings.

There was a lot of junk in my Firebird when I drove here today. I remember noticing a script on the passenger seat floor-board. When I got out of the Audi … a few minutes ago, I think—just before I came up here to take this bath—I walked over to the Firebird, opened the passenger side door, and even in the shadowy light from the street lamp I could see that my memory was serving me correctly; I reached down and picked up a movie script. I couldn't make out the title and I didn't have a flashlight with me. I went into the house through the rear entrance and looked at the script in my hand by the back hall light. The title was on the front of it in gold letters.

I had found the script for a movie the young me ... the *first* me had said no to, *Sunset Island*. I opened it up. Scrawled across the title page, in my handwriting, were the words: "No way! This is shit!"

I guess I really didn't like it.

But that screenplay was from 1974. I found it in the car I drove from Valley Glen to Beverly Hills today in ... But now it's 1974 ... again.

That script should have been in the Audi, not the Firebird. Who put it there? And how could it already have my comment written (by me) on it?

Oh! Lightbulb, man!

That was not a Quaalude I took.

I watch the spigot spurt down its tube of water into the bathtub. It looks like a hose without its clothes on. As I step in, I notice I'm not displacing *any* water. It's as if my body has no mass. Another thing I realize, now that I think about it, is that the walls are breathing like an animal, in and out. They're yellow, these walls. All the surfaces in the bathroom, including the floor and the ceiling, are composed of yellow, pulsing, breathing surfaces. Except the bathtub, which is made of porcelain white surfaces, also breathing.

My body mass returns and now, after several moments of feeling my bones are about to burst through my skin, I remember what Quaaludes look like. They're opaque, darkish capsules. The pill I took I suppose could be an aspirin, but why would I put four smallish aspirin in a film canister and hide it?

I swallowed a tab of mescaline.

Should I stick my finger down my throat?

Nope. Too late. The pink elephants are here.

I settle down into the bathtub, deciding it's as good as anyplace to begin the next few hours' journey, which reminds me I'm a piece of dust, spinning around on one of billions of planets in dark, empty space. I tell myself I'm still fine. This is the kind of thing I think about before I took any little white pills.

Of course, I am lost, but lots of people go through that.

Sunset Island. Is he kidding me? They think I'm going to act in a movie so cheesy that for the rest of my life I'd be the scarlet letter poster boy for cinematic salmagundi? I hear James Coburn's voice from the Cary Grant/Audrey Hepburn movie *Charade*: "My mama didn't raise no stupid chirrun."

Fleury's mama served me salmagundi one time and perhaps gave me an idea of what she thought of me. Salmagundi is a dish made from cubed stuff, fish maybe—catfish, I believe. And then you add chopped meat. It doesn't matter what meat you use because then you put in lots and lots of anchovies—at least that's what Fleury's mother did—and finally eggs and onions and some other things I don't think I should think about right now.

I'm starting to relax and nod off, my bones now snug as a bug in a rug in their corresponding sleeves, leg bones in my legs, arm bones in my arms, ears alert for the word of the Lord. I'm safe; my knees and head are well above the waterline. I am in no danger of drowning. Also, my keen-eyed attention has been drawn by a high-pitched mechanical noise, a buzzing, whirring sound.

On the water, between my knees, a trifle north of my privates, a spacecraft lands, a scaled-down, miniature flying saucer out of one of those fifties sci-fi movies. It's shaped like an aerodynamic-looking shuffleboard puck, but about the size of a compressed can of tuna. It appears to be made of something like buffed aluminum.

A tiny green rowboat is lowered into the water. On the stern, stenciled in tiny white letters I can barely make out, is printed: FOR ALIENS ONLY.

They came to the right bathtub.

In the boat are two teeny-weeny humanoids—evidently a man and a woman. The man turns the craft around and rows it toward my face; the woman sits in the bow, making pinging noises.

Now, the man stands up in the rowboat. In his right hand is a megaphone, about half the size of a piece of candy corn.

Clearly, the little white tab I took didn't have an expiration date.

Into his megaphone, the man says in a surprisingly forceful voice, "Don't move. If you speak, whisper." I notice he's got a Midwest accent—hard Rs.

"Yes, we *are* small. You will be too, in a moment, but only temporarily." He's reading my thoughts. Fascinating, Captain. He clears his throat. "You're wondering why we don't just beam you aboard. Well, we don't know how to do that. Give me your hand."

Next thing I know, I'm mysteriously—although it doesn't seem to surprise me—their size and am being helped into the rowboat.

The man is wearing Bermuda shorts and a Twisted Sister T-shirt. He's about forty, with a slight potbelly, and looks like an overage camp counselor. He extends his hand and introduces himself: "Jim Ball, Columbus, Ohio." He smiles warmly; his handshake is firm and friendly. "This is Mindy." He indicates the woman in the bow. She wears shorts and a halter top, has black hair cut in a pageboy, and thick, muscular calves. "She's from the Big Apple," says Jim Ball. "The Bronx actually—well, not really. You're a smart guy; you've already figured out we use those places for cover. Actually, we're both from Fregghx [which is what it sounds like to me] in a faraway galaxy." He chuckles.

I stare at the still-pinging Mindy, then ask Jim Ball what I think is exactly the right question: "What's happening?" I don't wait for an answer. "Where's Sam? Can you tell me where my wife is?"

"We're here to take you on a little vacation," says Jim Ball.

Mindy stops pinging. "Jeez, it's ugly," she says. "I don't know why we couldn't have grabbed a zebra. Now that's a good-looking earthling. And why is it doing *that*?" I'm crossing my legs and covering myself.

"He's protecting his dignity," says Jim Ball.

"Is he fuh *real*?"

"He's very sincere, stoned as a blizzard of butterflies, but we're not here to judge him." Out of the ether, he produces Bermuda shorts like his, plus a T-shirt and sandals, hands them to me, then returns to his rowing. My T-shirt says "Cadillac Ranch." With my back turned to Mindy, I slip on the shirt and find it hangs past my knees. I pass on the pants and sandals.

When we get to the spacecraft, we're lifted by an unknown mechanism up into the craft and plunked down into a ranch-style suburban living room complete with picture window, through which I see nothing but worn, white porcelain that, as I study it more intently, looks like cliffs of rust-stained limestone.

"Make yourself to home, Danny," says Jim Ball. "Like some rocks with your Gordon's?"

They know what brand of gin I drink. "I'll go without the alcohol for now," I say. "How'd you make me so small?"

"Size is a matter of attitude," says Jim Ball. "It's simple. Although it did take us a few of your millennia to work it out. We still haven't been able to pull off the goldang beaming thing. Folks are pretty ticked off about that. Lord knows we've been pickin' up your *Star Trek* and whatnot signals long enough. That's actually one of the things that brought us here. We thought you might be able to help us."

"Help you what? I'm not even able to stand up in this ..." I look down and remember my bathtub is currently a spaceship, although to be honest, it still looks like the bottom of a bathtub. "Can you tell me where—"

Mindy interrupts: "Only to find you can't even help yourselves." She looks at Jim Ball. "Jeez, he's not going to do us any good at all. Let's vaporize him."

Jim Ball looks balefully at his petite faux Bronxian companion. "You're a new soul, Mindy. We can't do that. He's part of the whole. If we vaporize him, we do it to them all—including the zebras. He's inseparable from the rest. Of course, most humans, in many ways the most backward of species, barely understand that."

Out the window, I see the coast of California and the Baja peninsula.

Mindy alights on the sill of the picture window and looks down at Northern California and Oregon coming into view on the right, along with an attenuated stretch of the Pacific Ocean.

"You humans have spent your existence assuming that everything you see and touch, everything you consider as having substance, is a *physical* construct, when it is in fact occurring in the mind of each of us. A donkey knows that. Yes?"

I start to speak, but he cuts me off. "I know you're going to tell me that if everything in the universe split off from the consciousness of each of us, that we would be dealing with a tangled infinity of parallel worlds, which brings me to your second delusion."

"What's that?" I say, as a convergence of pulsating donkeys leap out of the picture window.

"Delusion number two is your entertaining assumption that you, we, are separate from each other—that, for example, the core of your consciousness is separate from Sam's, from *anyone's*, even from those donkeys that just hurtled off into the cosmic abyss. We are all interconnected. If your Jesus Christ were sitting here with us, he'd tell you the same thing. So would every great sage in your mad little planet's history."

Some kind of preacher shows up now, looking all beatific and ineffable. He's costumed—not well—as Jesus. He smiles, makes the sign of the cross, frowns, cringes, says "Ouch," and floats out after the donkeys.

"But where does that bring me?" I say. "I'm marooned, adrift far from Sam, lying here in a T-shirt in a bathtub, even though I'm seeing what looks like the coast of Siberia out the window."

"What you should understand now is that without having set out to, you have put yourself on a laterally extending path."

"How do I leap back to the path I was on yesterday, with Sam? How do I get back to her?"

Mindy makes a lightning-fast orbit around the room—or space capsule; I'm not entirely sure—passes through Jim Ball on the way, and ends up where she began. "Can't we please, puh-leeeze vaporize this guy, fuh chrissakes?"

"Sam's important to Danny," says Jim Ball. "You need to understand that, to Danny, she doesn't feel intrinsically unified with him—a part of him. He's forgotten that she's with him right now."

"I don't know it unless I can see her and touch her," I tell him. "I'm not interested in parallel universes except if they're keeping me away from Sam."

Mindy is about to explode. She arches her eyebrows and points two accusing fingers at me, but Jim Ball says, "Mindy!" and stares her down. "Do you want me to put you in your sleep capsule?"

Mindy shrinks and looks contrite. In a conciliatory but rote-sounding voice she says, "Consciousness gives rise to everything, including the brain. The mind is everywhere. If you look inside yourself, you will encounter God, which is at the epicenter of who you are. You may think you're only a blip on a tiny planet, but you can also save that planet. All you have to do is practice love, kindness, and joy. Everything else will come along in its wake. Mind and matter are not separate entities, but different aspects of one whole, unbroken movement. The truth is, if you *understand* the word 'love,' that will do it. That's all you need."

Jim Ball shakes his head in disgust. "That's just an act," he says. "She's learned a lot of stuff out of your Bible, the Bhagavad Gita, the Quran, David Bohm's *Wholeness and the Implicate Order,* among others, but she doesn't know what any of it means, not really, not yet. She's young and extremely immature. I think on your planet you'd call her a very bad girl."

I try to formulate something fresh to say. "*Io vorei una camera doppia con doce, per favore,*" I tell him. "*Molto Buon Giorono, mi moglie,* Samantha."

Jim Ball smiles. "You would like a double room with a shower? And you wish Samantha a much good morning. Is that right?"

I burst into tears. "No, that is not what I meant to say. I don't need a double room. And I'm already in a bathtub. Or I was." I interrupt myself. "Wait wait wait, we're off the subject," I say. "Can we get back to Sam. I *realllly* want to find a way to retrace my steps to my wife. Where is she?"

"She works at her father's jewelry store on Ventura Boulevard," says Jim Ball.

"How old is she?"

"Still two years younger than you."

"How old am I?"

"How old were you when Fleury left your sorry ass?" inquires Mindy, all innocent smiles now and still smaller than before.

I have to think about that. "I guess I'm about twenty-seven," I say.

"Then Sam is twenty-five," says Jim Ball.

"Well, bring me back down from here," I say. "I gotta go find her."

"What will you say to her?" says Jim Ball. "She hasn't met you yet."

As I think about that, realizing I have no idea what I might say to her, he bows his head for I don't know how long. Finally, showing me a gentle smile, he says, "You're having extraordinary trouble with what you call time, aren't you? It's common knowledge—or should be—that time perception is in no way related to the physical senses, but is a contrivance of humankind. So there is no law in nature that governs it. Time, as you employ it, is a learned and arbitrarily imposed neural activity pattern. No two brains form the same synaptic connections, and therefore no two brains register what you call time in the same manner."

Most of his words are bouncing around in my head like pin-balls. He must note my confusion, because he says, "All right. I'll put it in broader terms. Newtonian gravity is mathematically …" He seems to search for the right words. "I know he was a blue-ribbon dude, very useful when he was useful." He makes an apologetic face. "But Newton was just … I'm sorry, wrong. First of all, his theory is incompatible with relativity—not to mention it's contradicted by observation. For example, the Global Positioning System, which is not yet in place in 1974, but will be when you, and a couple of other outliers you're going to run into, look back at it from the next century. You will learn—or have learned—that the internal clocks of the GPS satellites need to be adjusted periodically to stay in sync with the clocks on earth. This means, not only is the law of gravity as you learned it … incorrect, but as Mindy and I know, and you have intuited, time is out the window."

A large, dour-looking grandfather clock with long, skinny legs turns to face us, and, with a countenance made of all melo-dramatic woe, throws a hand across his clock face, and leaps out into eternity (whatever that is).

"What … outliers am I going to run into?" I say, sounding quite desperate, I know.

"Well, *I* can't name *your* outliers. I'm not equipped to do that. But I can explain what I'm trying to say. Think of a bell curve." He holds his hands together over his head, then spreads them to the sides, bringing them down and out in opposite directions to the outer lip of the imaginary "bell" he's illustrat-ing. "You, for example, seem to be on this outer lip." He nods at his two hands, denoting the bottom of his bell. "Again, we all have different synaptic clocks. You are, right now, at a singular point at *ONE* of the furthest points on a bell curve. The little ball that you are, in your probability model, has fallen into the outermost slot, and you appear to be the only one there—but that's only in *YOUR* little arc of the curve." He nods at the bottom of the bell again. "From your perspective, you are alone in the outer slot. But always remember: a 'probability model' in real life is not the same as the two-dimensional one against a flat wall at the Boston Museum of Science, or as *any* two-dimensional bell curve. The world you have spent your life in has depth, as well as height and width." He now uses his hands to trace a large circle. "So we are talking now about a *GREAT BIG, LIGHT YEARS, THREE-DIMENSIONAL BELL.* In real life, you are assuredly not the only one—unlike with a two-dimensional model—who has fallen into an outermost slot. Do you understand?"

"No."

Jim Ball nods, suggesting this is the response he expected of me. "Yeah, well, you will," he says. "The point is, you are not the only outlier."

"But what other outliers am I going to run into?"

He smiles broadly. "I'm only one creature, one alien. How would I know?"

"Okay," I say, having no choice but to accept his reticence— and or stubbornness. "One more thing I would like to know. What about the second law of thermodynamics? If cream is poured into a cup of coffee, mixing the cream and the coffee, you can't unmix it—which *has* to mean I *can't* have gone backward in time because *nothing* can do that. I came from 2021; I can't have traveled back to 1974."

Jim Ball smiles at me, glances at Mindy, then looks back my way more benignly than ever and says, "Oh, honey, nobody's arguing with you."

Although I couldn't swear to it, it may be that I slip into yet another state of reality for a while. I look around me and see that I'm now up on a ladder. Jim Ball, who was, now that I remember it, my camp counselor when I was about ten years old, is on another ladder. I'm in my young twenties in this one. He's the same as before. We're hanging stage lights, an array of kliegs and Fresnels. I think I'm doing the sets and the lights for whatever this production is. I'm the designer; my former camp counselor is my technician.

Hanging lamps is satisfying work. Being up on a ladder above the stage is an adventure, a rush of its own. Putting the gels—only one letter from gems—into the lamps is a treat. Each color is enchanting; the names of the gels say it: magical magenta, indigo and Tokyo blue, spring yellow, millennium gold. Chrysalis pink is actually deep lavender with a dash of rose blusher. Velvet green is a perfect nighttime hue—for off the main set, off beyond the windows. And play a comedy scene in any one, or a combination, of the three bastard ambers and the laughs will be bigger and better than the playwright ever dreamed. When you're working up in the air with flame, special rose pink, electric lilac, and virgin blue, you don't ever want to come down.

After the ground plan and the rear and front elevations have been drawn, the set pieces have been constructed, painted, locked into position, and the play has been lovingly rehearsed, you call the lighting designer—me, I guess. I've watched all of the parts of the show come together. Now, I get to do what I do.

"What do I do, Jim Ball?"

"Well, you've got your scheme and a valid concept. You know what the mood needs to be," he says. "You have the right gels in the right lamps. Go ahead and hang 'em."

"What are you doing up on a ladder too?" I say.

"I don't know. I saw you up on yours. It looked like fun. Go ahead and put the gels in the instruments—make you feel better."

"Call the doctor, wake him up?"

"No, put the gels in the instruments."

"I said, 'Doctor.'"

"Wipe that smile off your face," says Jim Ball, "and pay attention."

"You sound like my father."

He ignores that. "You want the perfect texture, tone, and mood, right? It's going to be opening night before you know it. Fantasy, adventure, romance, comedy; whatever the mood turns out to be. It all depends on you, pally."

"Please don't call me pally, Jim Ball. It makes you sound like Frank Sinatra."

"I could do worse. This is fun, huh?"

"Yes, it is," I say. "It is, but we need to be a little careful of all this electricity around water. By the way, Jim Ball, I forgot what this show's about."

"It's about the Spirit of Life, pally, not only your timeline. You think you're on a ladder or maybe a roller coaster. But you're not. You're astride a giant helix. You're doing okay on your space coordinates, but you've lost track of the fourth dimension."

"Time?" I venture.

"It is a triviality," says Jim Ball, "only one puny and arbitrary element, but it still has to be dealt with. Believe in yourself and you can get everything back." And now he raps:

"Put the gel in the instrument
Make you feel better
Put the cream in the coffee
If you *really* want to get her."

"One more thing, he adds. "A guy like you is going to have to go through the blues if you want to come out the other side."

"What am I supposed to make of that?"

If he gives me any answer at all, I don't hear it. I think I've drifted off to sleep. I would like to have known whatever he was going to impart to me next, but I guess I'm going to have to learn the rest all on my own.

I didn't take Mindy's threat to vaporize me too seriously because entertaining aliens and old camp counselors or not, I don't think much about them after Jim Ball implies that I might be able to find Sam. I know that, together, Sam and I will get the right gels in the right lamps, and we'll hang them.

And then we'll flick the master control and set the stage ablaze with indigo and gold, spring yellow and velvet green, and finally lilac and lavender with a dash of chrysalis pink.

And now, for one long-drawn-out moment, I do feel better.

"Do you mind if I stay here?" says Sam from somewhere behind me.

"Do I mind? You told me you'd never leave me. What do you mean, do I mind? Where are you?"

"I'm home."

"No, you're not. I came back after the doctor or … I'm not sure where in Beverly Hills, and you weren't there. Our house wasn't there, or at least not in any form I recognize anymore. And I don't mean to sound as if I'm blaming you, but I came home to you the way I always have and you were gone, and that's just not like you."

I think I'm crying again. A lot. I'm soaked clear through with my own tears.

"Take some zinc and cold pills," says Sam. "I think you're coming down with something."

"At least my back doesn't hurt," I say, sniffling. "I don't need to take pain pills anymore."

"I'm going to read our book," she says. "Do you mind?"

"No, I don't mind. I don't mind *anything* you do." I watch her mouth move as she reads to me from *The Secret Garden*. It's the part where Mary, formerly sickly and ill-tempered herself, has been transformed by the secret garden, and is telling the bedridden Colin his illness is psychological, and he will be well if he only makes up his mind to be. I can see the gleam of saliva on Sam's upper teeth. I never would have found something like that captivating in the old days. I see how nubbly the bottom joint on her thumb is. Her arthritis hurts her and it crosses her awareness from time to time, although she rarely mentions it, never complaining. I hate it that she *ever* feels pain. I'd do anything to stop it.

I reach out to pet her forehead, but I'm only a puppet, tangled in the strings of time, and she vanishes.

I get out of the bathtub, shivering, and grab a towel, noticing that my healthy young body is all pruned up.

I dry off, realizing as I do that the second chance I was thinking of, at least as far as getting my career right this time, seductive as it sounds …

I do not want it.

I want Samantha. How can I get back to her? She is the only career I want. I feel like a petulant kid, but I don't care.

8

STUCK IN LODI

I drive three miles south into commercial Beverly Hills and pull over to the curb across the street from Nate and Al's Deli. It's nearing lunchtime. The same people as always are standing around out front. Their clothes aren't so "designer" as they will be in forty-seven years, but they're all aiming in that direction. Everybody is as they were when I was a young man. They're all trying their best to impress everybody else, pretending to be what in most cases they're not. And even if they were, who cares? I was one of them, behaved the same way. It's not disgraceful or anything, it's just the fact of the delusion they live in. There's nothing exactly wrong with it; it's just … pointless.

Funny to realize that even though I was among them—not knowing I was—here I am again, in the same place. The main difference is that if you asked any of those people who they are, they would probably give you a sincere answer. With most of them it would be nonsense, but it would be an answer. If you asked me right now who I am, I'd have to say, "I dunno." I couldn't say I'm a lost old man trapped in his younger self's body, trying to find his way back to his wife. I mean, I could, but that would be no more than another kind of dumb. And now, again in front of Nate and Al's, here are all those folks pretending to be people they would unlikely be happy to be, steadfast in their belief that there's no other road to survival.

To the south of where I'm pulled over is the exotic old Beverly Theatre, on the other side of the street. They're showing a twenty-fifth anniversary revival of *Adam's Rib,* the sixth and perhaps best of the Tracy/Hepburn films. I wouldn't have thought it would be popular enough to warrant a revival this many years later, but maybe the movie they originally booked had tanked and they had to find a quick replacement. I can imagine it might have seemed a reasonable idea to revive *Adam's Rib.* It's a good movie, very successful in its original run.

As I look at the marquee, something seems wrong. ADAM'S RIB is in large block letters. I can also make out from where I am that Tracy and Hepburn are billed over the title. Maybe it's just the notion of learning there's a revival of a movie that was first released twenty-five years ago—before the forty-seven I've already lost—that's muddling my already defective gyrocompass.

Maybe some twisted something in the back of my brain allowed me to be misled yesterday, or for whatever crazy reason, I drove not to my home, but to an area that only looked like my neighborhood. Maybe I was on the wrong side of Coldwater Boulevard.

Today, doing my best to ignore the world it *seems* I'm now living in, I carefully follow my fully conscious mind's directions to my address two blocks north of Valley College in Valley Glen.

I don't know why I'm so surprised that I got confused yesterday. I often feel that way. It's not an age thing. Life is by nature confusing. I wish I could learn not to expect nature not to behave like nature. Actually, I might be happy if nature would explain herself to me, give me a program, some notion as to whether the next number is going to be a waltz or a polka, or since life is a tap dance anyway, maybe a time step.

And now I'm sitting in front of my house.

It's the same as yesterday.

It looks the way it did when we bought it. When houses like Sam's and mine were first built on this street, they called them "beach cottages" because they thought they might be more appealing to potential buyers, despite the fact that this part of Valley Glen is a long way from the Pacific Ocean. I think of some of the names they give motels in Las Vegas, almost three hundred miles from the Pacific Ocean: The Beachfront Inn, Malibu Park, Oceanside Lodge.

Sam and I rebuilt our house structurally inside and out. Such changes have not yet been made. And now that I *know* I'm some-how living well back into the seventies, it hits me that this whole area is a seventies neighborhood. They don't even call it Valley Glen. The subsection of Los Angeles called Valley Glen hasn't been named that yet. Now, it's back to being Van Nuys, almost as near as you can get to the bottom of the LA status ladder.

Sam is alive.

She's working at her father's jewelry store. A few times, in our future life together, she's taken me by her father's former jewelry store on Ventura Boulevard. Today, in this reality, she's twenty-five-years old and still working at The Jewel Box.

I get in the beautiful blue Audi and drive there. It's a sunny day as usual, but also surprisingly clear. There's a coffee shop across the street called Silvia's Sweets & Sips. No wonder Silvia went out of business.

I don't want to be obvious and ignorantly blunder into The Jewel Box, so I've decided to spy from a distance. I manage to get a window seat. It's eleven in the morning. I eat a croissant with butter and have a cup of coffee. I refuse to "sip" it.

I watch the front entrance for almost an hour before I become aware that the emaciated little man who served me is throwing more than occasional glances in my direction. Also, the lunch crowd is starting to filter in. Reluctantly I get up, pay at the cash register, never letting my attention wander from the front door of The Jewel Box, and head for the door. Despite a familiar voice in the back of my mind that says "*Bad idea,*" I decide to cross the street and pretend to window shop.

As I walk out of Silvia's, Samantha comes out of her father's store and heads west.

She's thirty yards away. I'm dizzy. I can't focus or see her clearly.

That's not true. Maybe I'm confused because her beauty defies even my credulity. She's wearing a cream-colored silk blouse, a pencil skirt, red. Her flowing honey-blonde hair is shoulder length. Perhaps because I know her face at many ages, I can see *exactly* how lovely she is, how graceful and unspoiled. Her looks don't cry out movie star gorgeous, but if you can see into the future as I can for the first time in my life, it's easy to believe she will be turning heads forty-seven years from now.

I have to be careful. If we met now, I don't think she'd pay much attention to me. Or maybe we'd have a couple of dates before she realized how self-involved I am.

I have to take a closer look at her.

Negotiating the Ventura traffic, my legs rubbery, I cross the street, slipping on the seventies-style oversize sunglasses I brought with me. I'm nearing her from the direction toward which she's walking. She's got a huge brown and black German shepherd on a leash. When I first met Sam, she had a photo album she'd put together. On the front, she'd printed BUNDY'S VACATION. I never met Bundy, but I've leafed through BUNDY'S VACATION at least a couple of times. It's full of pictures of Sam and Bundy at Pine Mountain, a community and recreation area in the mountains about a hundred miles north of Los Angeles.

As we approach each other I smile and say, "Hi, Bundy." Sam has always told me Bundy was a friendly dog and therefore an odd choice to be a guard dog at a jewelry store. Holding my hand down, my head lowered to make eye contact with Bundy, I scritch him behind the ears, which he obviously likes. "What a good doggie." I'm assuming Sam will think I've been in the store in the past, either when she wasn't there or was waiting on another customer.

My heart is pounding.

Now, I stand up and meet her gaze from behind my shades. Her eyes are as I remember them, deep as the ocean. I have a defiant impulse to look straight into them, not through these damned glasses. I take them off.

In this crystalline daylight, for one moment, the time it takes for a lump to form in my throat, I am looking into the depths of those fathomless waterfall blue eyes.

She gives me a friendly smile, frowns slightly and looks down at Bundy.

I realize how stupid this is. I put my glasses back on, give her a little wave, as if perhaps I *am* a customer she can't quite recall, and move off.

A thickset, redheaded man with a beard comes up behind her. "Hey, Sam, your dad changed his mind. He'll have a liver-wurst on rye. And cream soda for both of us."

As Sam raises a hand in acknowledgment and says "Okay," I've moved away from them, heading back toward Laurel Canyon.

I think Samantha half glances at me as I leave, but that's all. That's it. That's as close as I can get to the love of my life right now. If I'd stayed there any longer, she'd think I was a creep. I cross Ventura at Laurel, head to the parking lot behind the stores on the north side of Ventura, west of Laurel, and drive off in which direction I am, for I don't know how long, unable to determine.

I saw Sam. I saw her young. Age doesn't make any difference. Isn't that a nice thing about getting older? Your beloved stays as beautiful to you as she always was. I wasn't anymore attracted to the youthful Sam I just saw than the one I've spent my life with—each day, every night. There is no difference between the two Samanthas. None. So is it not a physical attraction? Has it become some kind of spiritual thing?

No, that's not right. Time, space, biology, all of life comes together in Sam into something there is no way I could imagine improving. When I look at her—for example, the last time I looked at her before today, in Valley Glen—I never see what a kid would call an old lady. I see everything about her, and it is nothing less than perfect. Beyond time.

"Guys who think they're big shots take big-shot risks. That's what you just did. You do understand that, don't you?"

I look in my rearview mirror and see him, growing larger, closer, realer. He's trotting toward me as I slow down, pull over to the side of the road and stop. I'm still on Laurel, about a hundred feet south of Mulholland Drive.

Tongue hanging, lips curled up as if in a smile, it can't be, but it is. My four-legged friend from another time just showed up.

"Right. And sometime when you're least expecting it, I'll do it again."

"Okay. Okay," I say. I've maneuvered my right leg over the gearshift console and am leaning over as near as I can get to the passenger side window. He's standing on the ground three feet from the car, looking at me from almost my eye level. "So meanwhile," I ask him, "what are you doing here? What do you want from me?"

He shakes himself all over as if he's materialized from out of a lake. *"Let's try to cast you in a positive light for a moment. You've gotten yourself caught up in something that seems to have turned out to be a mistake. Not knowing it was your suggestable mind that enabled it, you have attempted something unique. MAYBE it was a mistake. ..."* He looks me straight in the eye in that way he has. *"But it couldn't hurt,"* he continues, *"for you to remember Mr. Einstein's words: 'Anyone who has never made a mistake has never tried anything new.' What do you think?"*

"But how do I know my mistake is correctable?"

"You don't."

"Then what good are you doing me?"

"Do you remember telling me I was God backward? That it would even enter your mind to say that is one of the many swinging doors to your problem. You thought when you found me at the Animal Rescue Center that you were rescuing me. But if you will remember, it was I who chose you. I showed up in your life to rescue you, not the other way around. I'm aware that you recognize the God in me, but understand that I have always seen the emerging Dog in you, and to answer your earlier question as best I can for the moment, that's what I'm doing here."

9

MY MOCKINGBIRD

I wander around the house Fleury and I lived in for four years. About a year after she fell in love with her divorce lawyer and moved to Michigan with him, I began to fully see what a hash I'd made of my life. A friend of mine—the same one who, a few years later, fixed me up with Sam—gave me the number of the Southern California Psychology Association, and they referred me to Patricia, who became my therapist for five years. At the beginning, I felt silly, seeing a shrink; it seemed like a Hollywood cliché, but God knows I had reason to seek help. My exterior looked perfectly presentable, but inside I was a motley snarl of melted gummy bears.

Not only had Fleury and I come to the impasse I've described, but a little later, I spent two years on a limited TV series (not the Mike Brookes series) playing a police detective I disliked. I took the job because I wanted to show the industry I could play more than "light comedy." A couple of people I should have listened to told me it was going to have a different effect. They were right.

People started to identify me with my character; they saw me as the neurotic, humorless man I was playing.

It's fun to play a villain once in a while, but not all the time. If you aren't too sure who you are in the first place, you don't want to live month after month in the darkest part of yourself. I don't think when Dr. Jekyll felt Mr. Hyde coming on he ever said, "Oh, goody, look who's here!"

But I haven't taken that detective role yet. And when and if it's offered to me again, I'll say no, and if I'm going to take the kind of part in a movie or on television I might be identified with, I'll make it a character I'd *like* to be identified with. And I won't need a damned therapist.

Am I talking about *staying* here?

I saw Sam outside The Jewel Box, what, yesterday? The day before?

I remember a friend, a good actor. His name was Nicholas. It was the early eighties. After I'd introduced Samantha to him, we spent several evenings with Nick and his wife at that time. I remember he told me that his marriage was in trouble. He said, "I'd give anything to find someone like Sam."

"I thought your marriage was good," I said.

"Nah, she's as crazy as I am. You're the one who's hit the jackpot. I never met anyone as centered as Samantha. Ya lucky bastard."

Nick doesn't realize just *how* lucky a bastard I am. John Yort told me you don't get second chances in Hollywood, but he was wrong. I was offered a second chance with the Mike Brookes series. John doesn't know that I've lived through its whole seven-year run.

But if I had taken that second chance and the series had been as successful as it turned out to be, I would not have met

Samantha. And it was only through Sam that I discovered a life
that mattered. And what matters—to me, anyway—is that while
I live, I *live*. And I hope I've learned by now that living and loving are interchangeable, or should be. Looking for a meaningful
life as a television star is up there with trying to milk the bull. I
don't exist to make a lasting impression on the world. I exist to
do my best and spend as little time as possible as the oversexed
flea I first heard about around the age of thirteen, that floats
down the river on his back, yelling, "Raise the drawbridge!"

If I loved Sam, I can be loving. Isn't that what I'm here for,
to learn the meaning of love?

So, I don't call John Yort about that series.

I will do anything, try anything, to get back to Samantha.

How? I'm talking about time, over which I have no control.

I am persuaded that time *can* collapse in on itself, become
contorted and buckle back into the so-called past, like a heel
bursting through a worn-out sock. But wouldn't that work in
either direction? I cannot disappear from my life without a trace.

I go behind the bar I had put in at the end of the library and
get out a bottle of White Horse. The label informs me that it's
"Fine Old Scotch Whiskey." Am I to take it that this particular
bottle is forty-seven years older-than-old?

It tastes like White Horse. It's got that trademark earthy
moss bite.

As I look at the mariner's clock on the bar in front of me, I
imagine that as I watch the flow of time, it must be passing for
Sam too. A while ago I was in my bed trying to sleep. I couldn't
do it. I didn't usually have trouble sleeping when I was twenty-
seven years old the first time. I know why the new twenty-
seven-year-old me can't sleep. I once went back to New York

to do a job. By the time Sam was able to join me three weeks later, I had circles under my eyes. It was the absence of Samantha that killed my sleep. It's happening again, except this time Sam is not in another time zone, she's in another time—or to be more accurate: I do not know where in creation she is.

I look at this clock, a meaningless activity, watching another minute pass by. I remember staring at other clocks, wishing the time was later, wanting chunks of it to get out of my way. But it was my life. I discarded it by wishing it gone. Before I knew it, my wish had come true and I had urged huge chunks of my life into history.

God save me from my dreams come true (well, most of them). Somehow, lurking out there in the backwaters of time and space is that fourth or fifth … or whatever dimension, sitting at the end of the bench waiting to get into the game. You have to be careful what you wish for because, no shit, *you will get it.*

I don't think I'm as stupid as I used to be, and if the prayer that's in your heart most hours of your day is the one that gets answered, then maybe I'll be okay. This means I don't have any choice for now but to move from this barstool to the next moment and the next, and try to make whatever "time" I have here somehow fruitful, without letting go of my determination to discover a pathway back to Sam.

I'm going to need help.

Patricia, my therapist. I liked her. I was able to talk to her about things from a fresh way of thinking about them. You feel better and understand what's going on with your own psyche and your own life if you look at it through the eyes of someone who has no other purpose in being with you than to help you find ways to make life better. I suppose it's like having the best kind of smart, loving mother—something I know nothing about.

I haven't heard from my agent since I told him I wasn't going to do *Sunset Island*.

I've just come back from the bank and the grocery store. I don't have a lot of money in my account, but enough to feed myself and make the next couple of house payments. Fleury and her new husband, the divorce attorney, let me keep the house and my modest bank account, and I did pretty well on the little thing I did for Paramount. It's not much of a picture, but it paid nicely, so I'm okay for at least a while.

Standing at the sink again, I eat a can of Campbell's Chicken Noodle Soup, undiluted, and a peanut butter and grape jelly sandwich.

Through two large European white birch trees, I see the house behind me, on Wilkie Street, which winds, climbing maybe a half mile (I'm guessing) up into the hills behind us. The house is California Spanish like mine, smaller, but even though it's essentially on one floor (split-level) it's situated up the hill. Looking up from Benedict Canyon or through the trees, out my back window, it looms above my two-story house.

I see a teenage girl skateboarding down the hill from I'm not sure how far above my house—on the corner of Benedict and Wilkie. I can tell the girl is a good skateboarder. She enters from the right side of my field of vision. She must have started from quite a ways up Wilkie because she sweeps by me like a shooting star, and it's easy to see she's going way too fast—that when she reaches the bottom, she won't be able to safely stop.

She jumps off the board just before she reaches Benedict and rolls into a thick bed of ivy. The skateboard, meanwhile, sails across Benedict Canyon Drive and comes to rest on a dirt pathway across from my house on the other side of Benedict.

The girl does not rise out of the ivy, so I get up from the table and hurry out the back door and through the rear gate in the adobe wall that surrounds my house. As I reach my side of Wilkie, she sits up in the ivy and smiles at me. She's wearing jeans and a Blue Oyster Cult T-shirt.

"Hello," she says.

I don't remember this girl from the first time through. "You're going to hurt yourself one of these days," I tell her.

"Yeah, maybe." She looks around her. "But it's pretty cushiony, this ivy. How I'd really hurt myself is if I kept on doing this, and one day I stayed on the board when I reached the bottom. There's a lot of traffic here." She nods toward Benedict Canyon Drive. Seeing the concerned look on my face, she adds, "But I'm probably not going to do that—skateboard right onto Benedict."

"Probably?"

"Well, you never know." She grins and springs up, scampers across Benedict, picks up her board and, checking for traffic, ambles back to the corner of Benedict and Wilkie, where I'm standing.

"This is where you live, huh?" she says.

"Well, for the moment."

She frowns but doesn't question my unwillingness to commit to this place of residence. "What's your name?"

"Daniel Maytree. Yours?"

"Rue Lefanty. What do you do?"

"That's a funny question. We just met." I clear my throat. "I'm a ... an actor."

"You don't seem very sure about it."

I laugh self-consciously. "Well, I'm not really ... *lately*—an actor. I ... have worked a lot. I mean, I guess I still do. I did a little job three weeks ago. I have been an actor, for ..." *Why is this so hard?* " ... quite a while."

"But not lately?"

"Well, not for the last three weeks. ... Things will pick up again soon. That's the way acting careers go."

"I see."

Out of habit, I follow my show business instinct to discreetly aggrandize myself. "I've done some pretty decent movies. Light comedies mostly, but, you know, pretty good roles. One of them was something I did on Broadway. I was pretty lucky." I point to my house. "It got me this place."

"You said 'I *was* lucky.'"

I hold up my hands, self-effacing. It doesn't matter whom I glorify myself in front of, I always want to go back and un-say it, but you can't do that. And this is a teenage girl. I wish I'd never brought up this subject. No wonder my career crashed. Nobody likes people who tell you they're a VIP.

"Why did your parents call you Rue?"

"I don't know. Why does anybody call anybody anything?"

I can't think of a response to that.

She grins, shrugs, and heads back up the hill.

As I walk back into my house, I whisper to Sam, "You would have loved living in this place."

I hear a crow above me, look up and see that it's not a crow. It's a mockingbird sitting near the top of a fifteen-foot pear tree I don't remember being here *the last time*, which doesn't mean much; I'm pretty sure I was unaware of lots of things last time. I guess this mockingbird is "pretending" (do mockingbirds pretend?) to be a crow.

One summer when I was a kid, I learned to do that loud whistle thing that some people can do. My version is the one you do by pressing your lips hard against your teeth and blowing between the tip of your tongue and your upper teeth and hard palate. It was useful in New York for hailing cabs.

I do it now.

The mockingbird stops his crow impression, seems to think about it for a moment, then makes a sound not unlike the whistle I made. He pauses a moment longer, then does a call that sounds something like the sharp *yeep, yeep, yeep* of a robin.

I imitate his robin call. It's not too bad, if I do say so. I used to spend lots of time practicing this kind of whistling.

Now, the mockingbird produces the cry of some other bird; I don't know what species.

I imitate it. Again, I get pretty close to the sound he made.

He flies away from his perch, showing me the underside of his wings, which have a beautiful black-and-white Navajo-like design. He returns to his perch immediately and makes another birdcall.

Again, I do my best impression of the call he made. We repeat this several times.

He is silent for a moment, then makes a high trilling sound.

I can't do that and tell him so as a huge monarch butterfly, a living, breathing example of metamorphosis, flutters by.

Not that day, but a couple of days later, the mockingbird says what sounds very much like a foreshortened version of "I can't do that," then shows me his Navajo underwings and flies away.

In the next few days, I will talk to him several times. Does he have any concept of time? How could he, when I (who, I'm told, far outrank him on the evolutionary ladder) can't do something as simple as spin the hands of a clock that's mistakenly gone counterclockwise back the other direction—clockwise, to where they came from?

I've got to call Patricia.

First I go upstairs to my office, take the cover off the typewriter I've had for … I don't know how long, and start to work on the screenplay that's been percolating in my head, ever since I brought up to John Yort the idea of making my own movie. I don't have a title yet. Maybe I should call it *Working My Way Back to Sam*. Or perhaps *A Monomaniac's Parallel Universe*. No. I'll use the line that popped into my head when she came up my apartment stairs and back permanently into my heart: *Hello, Rest of My Life*.

In my mind, my mockingbird says, as if he's imitating me:

A roof overhead, I don't ask a lot

A cat, geraniums in a pot, your hand in mine

And maybe you have delusions of grandeur too

In the middle of the night—I'm not sure which one—I wake up and go to the bathroom. This is the first time I've done that since the last night I spent with Sam. Now, as a considerably younger man, I don't usually feel the need to get up. Maybe I drank too much water before I went to bed. I come back from peeing, get in bed, and lie on my side, facing out, toward the front of the house.

I start to drift off again.

Then I remember: when I came back from the bathroom, I crossed around the bed to get into my side. I crossed around *her* side.

My eyes snap open.

I'm facing away from her.

Who is she? Who am I in bed with? Someone is sleeping on the other side of me. I can hear her breathing.

I remember my father's basement during a year we lived in New Jersey because of his work. I woke up once, realizing I was cold and that I was sleeping on something hard and unyielding. It was the Ping-Pong table we had in the recreation room. I had walked down from the second floor, gone through the kitchen, opened the basement door, walked barefooted down the slatted wood stairway, passed the furnace, gone into the recreation room with the linoleum floor and dropped acoustical ceiling, and laid down on the Ping-Pong table.

It was terrifying, waking up on a hard, cold surface in a pitch-black space I didn't recognize. What was worse, I knew I'd been told to go there. I had no choice. It was like a dark part of me, a part I had no wakeful access to, was willing me to do something and I had no say in the matter.

This feels like that. I'm sharing this bed with my wife, but I don't know which wife. I'm pretty sure it's not Sam. How could it be? But it couldn't be Fleury. She's in Michigan.

Who is this? I can still hear her breathing.

There's no light in the room, but I summon all my courage and slowly turn over.

It's a woman; it's a woman's breathing. She's turned away from me; I think she's covered to her neck with a sheet and blanket, but in this blackness, I still can't make out who it is.

It can't be Sam, but I'm terrified it's not.

I don't reach out to her. If it were Sam with me in this strange place, she'd know I'm looking at her. I can't tell whether she's young or old.

After a minute, I say, "Sam?"

Drowsily, she turns over. It's still too dark to see her.

I hear half-words, whispered low, then: "Danny?"

It's Sam. I don't say anything; I don't want her to disappear.

As if I were in my own bed in Valley Glen, I gradually relax.

When I wake up, it's morning. Remembering, I'm afraid to open my eyes.

When I do, I'm alone.

10

PATRICIA

I'm with Patricia, my therapist in the seventies. I thought she was excellent. I know that's not much of an endorsement. She's a bit younger than she was when I used to see her twice a week at her office in a small, two-story building on Weatherly Street, about a mile east of the Beverly Hills commercial district, Rodeo Drive and all that.

She agreed to see me this time when I told her I was referred by the Southern California Psychology Association, which was the guild or organization I mentioned earlier, that provided the auspices that cleared me to see her the first time.

Patricia used to be an actress. Then, when she was still in her twenties, she decided that life was not for her. She earned her Ph.D. and started a private practice. Many of her clients are actors. She has a special understanding of the problems of an actor's life, as well as being one of the smartest people I've ever known.

We stare at each other. This Patricia has never seen me before.

She's attractive. I didn't use to think much about that. She's a small, not delicate woman, but with fine features and smiling, deep brown eyes. I always liked that. I always liked her look. She's probably in her early-to-mid thirties and has hints of premature gray in her otherwise jet-black hair.

"Okay," she says, "let's begin with why you're here." I laugh. She narrows her eyes slightly. "It is a serious question. I need to decide if I can help you."

"I'm not sure I can explain."

She smiles patiently. "Try."

I dive in. It's the only way therapy works. "Okay, I'm lost in time." She waits for me to amplify. "I drove over the hill to this side the other day. I live in The Valley ... used to. And ... now, I live on this side. ..." It isn't until this second that I truly recognize how stupid this is, what an insane thing to say to anyone. "And, you see, now I'm living where I used to live many years ago, which—I know sounds ... uh, crazy. It seems as if some ... I don't know, *force* has placed me in the circumstances of a life I lived forty-seven years ago."

She lowers her gaze for two beats, then looks at me again. "How old are you?"

"According to my driver's license, I'm twenty-seven."

"Then how could you have been ... *anywhere* forty-seven years ago?"

"Yes, well, that's the problem, you see. The thing is, I went on aging. And in at least part of my mind—the more substantial part, the part I think with, I guess—I'm in my mid-seventies."

She stares at me for a long time, unblinking. "Are you married?"

"Yes. Well ... I feel married. I mean the old man in me is married. But I think the person you're looking at is divorced. I haven't found Samantha yet—the wife I grow old with. Or will grow old with ... I hope." I realize tears are forming in my eyes. "I don't know where she is. And I have no notion how to find her."

My glassy gaze meets hers and I remember why I stayed with her the first time. She has compassion. She has to think I'm off my rocker, but I remember now that she has the ability to go along with whatever mad thing that comes out of my mouth if she's convinced I mean it. She never judged the words I was saying, just tried to make sense out of them in her own mind toward the goal of helping me. And I can tell by the look in her eyes that she knows I mean—or at least *think* I mean—what I'm saying, insane as it is.

"Are you on any drugs?"

"Well, not now," I say. "I was. I mean the old me, the other me, was. I had a bad back, which I took pain medication for. Well, and also a statin."

"What's a statin?"

I remember statins haven't been introduced into commercial use yet. "Uh, it's something that … I think it reduces cholesterol levels and helps prevent heart attacks."

"I see."

She doesn't see. "They're proactive, statin drugs. Jeez, that may not be a commonly used word yet either."

"I know what proactive means."

"Of course. Sorry." She is looking at a man, sitting across from her, who's obviously delusional. And I don't know how to convince her otherwise. I blurt out: "You're an artist. You were raised in Brooklyn, went to NYU, did graduate work at Columbia, but didn't like the academic side of the art world and dropped out and became an actress for a while. Your husband is a … well, maybe he's not yet, but he's going to be an internist. It takes a while, to get set up as a family doctor, doesn't it, especially if you don't start until after you've done a tour in the Peace Corps? I know you have a scar the size of a dime under your hair, behind your left ear. Sometimes, when you're concentrating, you stroke it lightly with your left forefinger. You didn't tell me how you got the scar, but for some reason you mentioned it was about the size of a dime."

Her eyes are wide. "*How do you know any of this?*"

"I'm telling you I used to be one of your … patients. But it was sometime into the future. Will you see me? Will you treat me? Now? I mean, in this time."

"I would like to know how you know these things about me."

"They leaked out," I say. "Over a period of five years of therapy, I found out these things about your life. I know you have a dog, a Weimaraner, or you will have. You told me."

She frowns. "I had a Weimaraner, but she died."

"Then you're going to get another one." I feel in some part of myself that's she's beginning to believe there's … *got* to be *something* in what I'm saying. "Do you believe I might not be as crazy as I sound?"

She treats my plea as a rhetorical question. "I didn't ask you—how did you find my name? Did someone refer you?"

"Yes, in a way …"

"In a way?"

"Yeah. I mean, a friend who saw another therapist was told I should call the Southern California Psychology Association, and they gave me your number." I shrug, and show her something I imagine is a plaintive look—hopeful that she'll justify to herself going along with me for now. Then later, I'm imagining, she'll join me in trying to figure out how I lost my way in life. And then maybe she'll somehow explain why it has split off into these … two strands—or more, for all I know.

"Give me your phone number," she says. "I'll … give you my answer after I've had some time to think it over."

I rattle off the number on the rotary phone at 1809 Benedict, then ask, "What if I'm not home?"

"I'll leave a message. Do you have an answering service?"

"Uh … yes, I do." She looks at me oddly again as I remind myself that people don't use answering machines or voicemail yet. There's no texting or e-mails. I get up. "You will call me?"

"Yes," says Patricia, also standing. "I'll call you and give you my answer."

"I hope it's yes."

"We'll see. I have to think about it."

"I'm not crazy." I remember Nixon telling the world he was not a crook.

Then I remember Nixon is still president. I'm pretty sure he'll resign later this year, August I think.

When I get home, it crosses my mind to call a couple of old friends, but I don't do it. When marriages break up, old friendships can get unsettled for a while. Also, the idea of holding myself together as only the version of me those people know, and not giving away that in essence I'm two people now, seems too daunting at the moment. Also, even though they're my friends, the interests we shared are unlikely to be *alive* anymore—a little like going back to a place you once worked. Those colleagues, co-workers, friends may still be there, but pages have been turned in the book of what you shared with them, and not only would it not be the same, it would be awkward and unnatural to pretend it was. That must be close to why Thomas Wolfe said, "You can't go home again."

In my latest Samantha dream, it's morning, right after we've done our reading together. I walk out into our backyard that wasn't this beautiful when we bought the house. Standing on the grass, I look to the north. In the lower, right quadrant of my field of vision is our Meyer lemon tree, eight feet tall and seven feet in diameter. It yields beautiful fruit and the blossoms are my favorite outdoor fragrance in the world. On the left side of this angle on the world is the giant Chinese elm that dominates our backyard. It reminds me of a weeping willow. It's early in spring; it's already greened out (it *is* southern California) and will stay so for many months to come.

Lifting my gaze above the houses beyond our back wall, I see the rounded top of a seventy-five-foot fan palm, its fronds swaying in a soft spring breeze. To the east, willow leaf clouds streaked with ribbons of red, violet, blue, and an array of pastels are leisurely floating toward the south, as if they're on their way to Mexico, but they've got all the time in the world to get there.

I think the essence of the spiritual reading Samantha and I did was this: by changing old patterns, we can change the world we live in. I've been working at this since before I met Samantha—at first with no success at all. I've learned that if I'm loving I'm going to live in a loving world; if I'm fearful I'm going to live in a fearful world: same world.

Now, in this dream, in one of the back corners of our garden, I sit down in a lawn chair covered with chipped white paint. I'm in a patch of sunlight on a homely brick patio I laid ... I couldn't even guess when. There's a patch of bamboo stumps pushing up between the bricks, resolute in their desire to flourish again. It feels like a combination of disturbing and brave.

I lean my head back, letting the sun bathe my face, and thank God for the comforting warmth, for the birdsong, for the fresh spring smells, for the breeze on my arms and face, for my life. Still leaning back, I pray for another miracle.

For Samantha.

And then I wake up to a life where there *is* a Samantha, but she may as well be wearing a flashing neon sign: NO ACCESS, DANNY MAYTREE

I don't know why I should be surprised that I dream about her almost every night. Is she trying to communicate with me? Maybe she's suggesting that I get off my ass and figure out how to get back to her. I haven't accomplished anything so far. I've written bits and pieces of a screenplay, hoping in the most upside-down way imaginable (I realize how crazy this is) that producing a cheapie movie about my recent *life* will in some way get me back to Valley Glen in 2021. I know that sounds like begging for a miracle, which I don't think works, but I'm not sure I'm not already receiving a set of directions, one at a time, that I have yet to decipher, but when I do, I will have no choice but to follow.

For now, making this movie is the one action I know how to take and I've got to take it. I remember that if there are miracles, they're endless. Like for example: here I am—here everybody is—set down on this spiraling blue marble, each of us encased in a bewilderingly high-tech body, floating along with everyone and everything else through zillions of stars and infinite space.

If a miracle is available to me, I have to do something about it myself. If fate or whatever has scattered me into some coextending world, I have to get past this feeling of emptiness. I need a sign. And I need to recognize guidance when I get it.

I must also never forget that in the end, no matter how many wise people I listen to, *my* truth exists within *me.*

The rest is words, something somebody else said.

11

(1974) VALORY VALENTINE

Drinking late morning coffee in my home on Benedict Canyon Drive, I realize I haven't checked the mail—not that I'm expecting anything. I walk outside to the arched door in the wall that surrounds the front yard and open it. There are three pieces of junk mail. I take it out, go back in, and close the heavy wooden door behind me.

As I approach the front steps of my house, someone leans on a car horn. They do it again, and I guess it shouldn't, but it enrages me. I run out through the side gate and am standing by the Audi when a red Mercedes convertible, just north of my house, revs up, peels out with tires squealing, and takes off, headed south, in the direction of Beverly Hills. It has to be going at least sixty miles per hour by now. I am livid. I don't have children who could be killed by this kind of mindlessness; maybe it's existential disorientation, but I'm not spending even a moment trying to be philosophical about this, as I probably would a few years later. No other cars have passed since the Mercedes. I pull car keys out of my pocket, throw myself into the Audi, and take off in pursuit of the malefactor.

And now I'm a malefactor. Briefly, I'm clocking seventy and I have him in my sights. Just before we reach Sunset, I wait for a car to go by in the other direction and swerve around the Mercedes, which has now slowed down, doubtless in bewilderment at what the crazy guy behind him is doing.

As I pass Mercedes Guy, I start to press directly into him. Not wanting to be sideswiped, he slams on the brakes and pulls over. I screech to a stop in front of him and jump out, as if I'm a pissed off cop.

Approaching the driver on foot, I can see he's a young white man with a deep tan, wearing rimless glasses. He looks frightened. I see there's a pretty, dark-haired woman in the passenger seat.

"I've got a child!" I bellow at the guy. I guess I feel I need a little more moral authority than just being a deranged vigilante. "You could have fucking killed my little girl!"

He looks like he's about to cry. "Didn't you ever have a really lousy day?" he says. He glances over at the woman next to him. She turns away, as if she's embarrassed, or perhaps simply disgusted by her companion's behavior. Or mine.

Meanwhile, I'm now feeling terrible for this guy. Yes, he risked the lives of himself, his companion, and innocent bystanders, but something in me says, does anyone deserve to feel as bad as this guy obviously does now? I know it's incongruous, probably misplaced, but I can't help feeling sorry for him.

"And what was the honking about?"

He shakes his head helplessly.

"Well, just … don't do it again," I tell him. He nods convulsively, tears now running down his cheeks. "Are you okay, ma'am?" I ask Pretty Dark Hair.

She nods and murmurs, "Yeah, yes, I'm fine." She's staring at me. I find it impossible not to stare back.

She gets out of the Mercedes, crosses around to me, eyes on me the whole way, and says, "Would you take me home?"

I glance at the guy in the Mercedes. He's dabbing at his red face with what looks like an old T-shirt.

I look back at the woman. "Sure, I'll give you a ride. Where do you live?"

Seemingly unruffled, she says, "In The Valley." I can't stop looking at her. She has sharp features, like one of Pedro Almodóvar's women, but they're still feminine enough that she can be called pretty. She has hypnotic green eyes that look deep into mine. One of those eyes, her right one, seems a little more northerly on her face than the other. It's a distinct peculiarity, but integral to her strangely sexy face.

I tear my gaze away and look back at the crying driver. "Are you okay?"

He sniffles, nods, and says in a reedy, breaking voice, "Yeah, I'm all right." He takes in a deep, spasmodic breath. "Didn't you ever have a really shitty day?"

"Yeah," I say, realizing the dark-haired woman is getting into the passenger seat of my car. "I'm sorry about yours. It looks like it's about to get worse." I can't think of anything else to say except, "Don't drive so fast." I walk back to my car and get in next to the one-high-eyed woman.

Maybe that man's day is actually getting better, and it's mine that's about to get worse.

She seems to understand that I don't want to drive away until the guy in the Mercedes has.

Two or three minutes later, he wipes his face with the T-shirt, starts his car again and heads south, his left turn signal on as he approaches Sunset.

I look over at my new companion, who's staring straight ahead. I can't imagine what she's thinking. I start up the Audi, wait for traffic to clear, do a three-point turn, and head back north on Benedict.

After a couple hundred yards, she says, "What's your name?"

"Daniel Maytree."

"The actor?"

"Jesus, how did you know that? No one knows my name. *Almost* no one."

"I do."

"Jesus."

"I didn't recognize you right away," she says in a low, velvety voice, "but now I can see it's you. It's nice to meet you."

"Have you seen something I was in?" *God, actors never change.*

"I saw *Holiday in the Park* and something else ..." She searches her memory. "*Little Girl, Lost.* Right? Weren't you in that?" I nod modestly.

"Is that why you chased us? Because fans, or I guess crazy people, come around and honk their horns?" She remembers something. "Didn't I see an interview with you in the *Hollywood Reporter* and you talked about people honking in front of actors' houses?"

"Yeah, I think I did say something about that. I can't imagine what actual movie stars go through with that kind of junk. You read the *Hollywood Reporter*?"

She shrugs. "Yeah, Sometimes."

"Why did that guy honk his horn like that?"

"I said something that … uh, I guess irritated him. And he couldn't come up with the right words. So he blasted his horn at me."

"What did you say to him?"

"I don't know. Nothing much. It doesn't take much with him." She changes the subject without drawing breath. "You got another movie lined up? I mean, what are you doing now?"

"Not much. Research." *It's the kind of thing we always say.*

"For what?"

I look at her. She's probably not quite thirty, in great shape, firm without looking like she goes to the gym every day. Her green eyes are captivating, although as I say a bit out of balance, and so a little disconcerting at the same time. Nevertheless, they're the kind of eyes some women are blessed with that, when used in a targeted way, can stop a man in his tracks.

"My name is Valory Valentine," she says, not seeming to mind that I haven't asked.

"I'm sorry. That was rude of me." I look over at her. "Is that a stage name?"

"No, it isn't. My mother was a little … she liked to be different. And the Valory is spelled with an *o.*"

"Pardon?"

"V-a-l-o-r-y."

"Oh. Interesting." I look back at the road and see that I'm about to veer off onto Farley, which slides off Benedict just north of Cielo, infamous as the street Sharon Tate lived on, and where she and the other victims were killed by the Manson Family in 1969. That was somewhere near five years ago.

"So, what are you researching?" she says.

"I'm thinking of writing something for myself and see if I can get it produced, something low-budget. This is still the time when ... I mean, it's possible *these* days, that if you can write something for yourself and you've got some ... a little ... traction in the business, you can find financing on your own. Or, you know, with a little help."

"You're funny."

"Am I? I don't know. I'm uh, I guess, a little ... I haven't been in a kind of a ... situation like this. ... Jeez." I sound like I'm playing the bumbling suitor who gets the girl's sympathy, but never the girl.

She smiles. "Sounds great. What'll it be about—your movie?"

"I'm not exactly sure. I am sort of interested in time travel, or something like it—I don't know why—and I've been thinking of writing something about ... I'm not sure exactly. Probably a love story, something that hooks up with time." I shrug and pretend to concentrate on my driving. "I'd like it to be a sort of romance that jumps back and forth in time." She's frowning. "I mean it's about a guy who's in love with a woman, and then he loses her by getting thrown back in time. And then he's lost." Her eyes are on the road in front of us, but she is clearly listening, so I rattle on, saying far more than I mean to. "And then finally the movie is about his finding his way back to his wife ... he's deeply in love with his wife."

"So is that what you're researching, a way for him to do that, to get back, or forward, to where he came from?"

"Yes, that's it."

She thinks about that. "Will there be anything else, any action?"

"Well, yeah, sure. You've got to have some action. Or maybe a woman to be a temptation along the way, before he can get back ... or rather ahead."

"Who's the woman?"

"Pardon? ... Oh, I see. I don't know, maybe someone like you. Maybe today—as it turns out—I'm researching you."

A trace of a smile. "Well, I think it's a wonderful idea, making your movie. I'll bet you could turn out something fascinating."

"You think so?"

"I absolutely do." She nods her head, confirming her approval of the idea. "Why don't we stop at your house and catch our breath." This is at a moment when I'm straightening the car after a curve. I notice her gaze is fixed on my house, out of all the other pretty homes on Benedict Canyon Drive, as it comes into view.

"Do you know where I *live*?"

"Evidently," she says, as I slow down.

"What do you mean 'evidently'?"

"Is this where you live, up here?" She points at my house.

"Yes, it *is*. *How did you know?*"

She looks over at me, unfazed by the question. "Not a clue."

"I'm lost," I say, laughing *casually*, after we've had a couple of glasses of wine. (I offered her coffee or a soft drink, but she asked me if I had any white wine.)

She makes the universal listening sound, "Hmmm." I wait for her to go on, but she doesn't. "This is not the sort of thing you tell someone you just met, is it?"

"Hmmm."

"Uh-huh. The reason I say that is because recently I actually ... lost my *good* friend and ... you know, confidante."

"Your wife?"

"I beg your pardon?"

"Your wife."

"Well, yes." *How did she know I was talking about my wife?* "Well anyway, I know it sounds odd, but I'd rather not talk about her."

"I understand."

She can't understand, but I nod. "Have you ever lost someone you were … involved with and you never saw it coming?"

She thinks about it. "No, I don't think so. I always saw it coming. I knew Tad—he's the man you chased after—was on his way out. I knew he wasn't going to last long before I got into your car."

"Just wasn't the right one, huh?" I add to fill a void.

"The crying didn't help."

"You don't like to see a man cry?"

"No, it's okay for a man to cry. And I'd never seen him cry before. It's just that there's something … whiney about Tad. Childish, I guess. Tad is childish. That wears you down."

"I'm sorry," I say.

"Oh, that's okay. It wasn't your fault. The writing was on the wall."

"Ta-ta, Tad, huh?"

She smiles. "Yeah. Ta-ta, Tad. And he kept calling me 'Val'. I hated that."

"Don't like nicknames?"

"Not that one, not for people who don't *know* me."

"Listen … *really*, how did you know I live here?"

She frowns. "I didn't. It was like … I don't know; I guessed. And said it out loud. Does that sound strange?"

"It's actually more than strange. I mean, doesn't it seem strange to you?"

"I suppose it is, huh? But it … this just looked like your house." She gazes around. "It's a nice house."

"Thanks."

She knew it was my house, as we were driving, as it came into view—who knows, maybe *before* it came into view. Or at least she *sensed* it. I'm sure of that. And now, again, she seems so nonchalant about it. I wonder if she's psychic.

"I hope it all works out for you," she says.

"Thanks."

She frowns. "Do you have a couch? Well, of course you do." She stands up. "Would you mind if I have a ten-minute lie-down? I'm suddenly very tired."

"No, I don't mind. Would you like to lie down in a bed?"

"Point me to a sofa, if that's okay?"

This seems odd, but I say, "Sure, that's fine."

After she's settled in, on a sofa in the library, I put an afghan over her and close the blinds.

As she murmurs "thank you" in a low, velvety voice, the phone rings. I say, "Let yourself sleep a while."

"I just want to rest for a few minutes," she says. "You'd better answer your phone."

John Yort doesn't waste time with hellos. "Stanley Kubrick wants to meet you." No words come to me. "Danny? Are you there?"

"Why would *Stanley Kubrick* want to see *me*?"

"I can't say for sure, but you know he's seen film on you, right?"

"Is this a joke, John? I thought he said no to me a long time ago."

"He wants to fly you to Ireland. The rumor is he's going to replace Ryan O'Neal in *Barry Lyndon*."

"What? Why? I'd heard it through the grapevine Kubrick thought O'Neal was too pretty, but—"

"That's not it. *I* heard Kubrick was less than pleased with the kid's acting. Too wooden. Kubrick supposedly said a two-by-four has more charisma. I also heard Kubrick asked O'Neal to cut his leg off, so the scenes where the Lyndon character—whose leg gets amputated—would look more realistic."

"Kubrick was joking, of course," I suggest.

"I guess, but we're talking about Stanley Kubrick, so who knows? Anyway, O'Neal apparently didn't think it was funny."

"What about Robert Redford?" I say. "He was Kubrick's first choice."

"Still not available."

I feel as if my jaw has come detached from my head. This didn't happen the last time through. I think back to whatever I might have heard about the filming of *Barry Lyndon* so far. "Where'd you hear all these rumors? I'm almost positive they've been shooting *Barry Lyndon* since last year. That was a year ago he saw film on me, right?"

"About."

"The studio's not going to let him throw away months of work."

"Well, I guess they are."

"Pardon me, John, but who called you on this?"

"Stanley Kubrick."

"Aw, come on. Stanley Kubrick's not going to call you and then fly me to Ireland." Brief pause. "Is he?"

"I just got off the phone with him."

"How do you know it was him?"

John makes a harsh exhaling sound, like the sound of a tea-kettle just before it starts screaming at you. "Who's going to call me and pretend to be Stanley Kubrick? He sounded English."

"Lots of people think Stanley Kubrick is English, but he's American. He was raised in the Bronx."

"Well, maybe that was a Bronx thing I was hearing."

"John, the Bronx sounds like a lot of things, none of them British."

"I've seen Stanley Kubrick interviewed," he says. "This *sounded* like Stanley Kubrick."

I don't know what to say. Years ago this would have been my dream come true. "Did he say the studio would call you with the flight details and an offer?"

"He said we'd be hearing from them."

"I know I read it in *Variety*, John—*Barry Lyndon* had been shooting since the middle of '73. They can't reshoot the whole film."

"Are you going to argue with me about possibly the best job you will ever get?"

"No, but it doesn't make any sense."

"I've got a call coming in. Don't go away. I'll get back to you."

He hangs up.

Nothing like this happened the last time. What have I done to change anything? Why would a big thing like this that didn't happen the first time happen now?

Then it dawns on me: somebody has to be playing a dumb Hollywood joke on John. If it happened the last time, he found out about it and didn't make that silly phone call to me. Nothing has changed from my original timeline, unless you count the aliens in the bathtub, and that was mescaline.

I go back into the library and find Valory rolled over on her side, facing the back of the couch. I pull the afghan up over her shoulders. She's wearing a musky perfume. I never much liked the musky part of the sixties and seventies, but it's sexy on Valory. I try not to think about that.

I go upstairs to my office to do some writing. I'm not sure what, but I've got to do *something*. I sit down at my old ... *Look at that. I didn't think about it before: a Smith Corona typewriter.* I don't know if that company has gone out of business in the time I come from or not, but wouldn't working for them be a little like having a job with the Bubonic typewriter company? I think of the millions of people who will be affected by COVID-19. I consider saying something about the future pandemic, but I can't imagine what exactly I'd say.

I remember the notebook in my pants pocket. And my favorite pen, my voice-activated SpyGuy, the perfect pocket tool for a writer in 2021. I'm still wearing the same loose-fit blue jeans that feel way too roomy now, on my slimmer frame, and the light tan sweater I was wearing the day I drove into my past life.

Jesus.

I stare at the notebook and my SpyGuy for a while, then put them back in my pocket. I hadn't thought about it before, but why would something in my pocket go back in time with me?

Why would my *clothes* go back with me? For the same reason my skin did.

There are no rules for something like this any more than there are rules for ... anything you don't know the rules for. The spiritual reading Sam and I have been doing for years tells me that, as with gravity and electricity, there are spiritual rules. These are unseen laws of cause and effect, never-changing principles, like the one that tells us that under the right circumstances an acorn becomes an oak tree. There are many—probably an infinite number—of inexorable laws I don't understand: charges, principles, rules. Someone asked Edison to explain electricity.

He reportedly said: *"Electricity simply is. Use it."* He also said to a new staff member in his laboratory, after that assistant had asked him about laboratory rules: *"Hell! There ain't no rules around here! We are tryin' to accomplish somep'n!"*

So in my pocket, I have my twenty-first century SpyGuy. It doesn't make any sense, but who am I to say so? At this moment—*especially* at this moment—I may be the last person on earth qualified to talk about such a thing.

One of the nicest aspects of our spiritual reading is that, little by little, I've come to believe that Samantha and I are as much of spiritual reality now as we will ever be. But along with that I've developed a small recognition of the scantness of my knowledge of such things, and an unsettling awareness of how infinite are the number of penetrating volumes on this subject that I've not only never read, but most of which I've never heard of. True, I read *The Bhagavad Gita: A Walkthrough for Westerners*. But I don't think I understood most of it and mainly it made me realize more than ever how little I know.

In the meantime, since this lifetime is all we're aware of, I don't want to lose a second more of my time with Sam than I have to. I insert a piece of paper I've taken out of a woven straw basket, roll it into position in my Smith Corona, begin, and watch as my fingers start to move. They don't seem connected to me. I guess I'm letting whatever string of words sitting beneath the surface rise up into consciousness. For instance, sometimes it's a scene with characters that feel as if they're absolute strangers—people I had no idea were in me. It's a little like trying to go to sleep at night and you can't, and after a while you see a tumble of images beneath your eyelids in the darkness. These images are vivid, and you have never in your life seen them before, but there they are.

I walk in front of a nightspot (I've typed). There's a cordial mood to this cabaret, a satisfying texture and warmth, even if its specialty is the blues. The song the current singer, a woman, is singing is slow, passionate, and haunting.

It's late in the evening.
The sun is all gone.

"Go on in. Give a listen. This girl's got a magic to stir men's blood."

This has been addressed to me by an aging ticket taker with a seedy elegance that lies somewhere between old-world *savoir faire* and Damon Runyon, and maybe once, lifetimes ago, he was in a John Cassavetes film. Now that I think about it, he looks like Cassavetes (Mia Farrow's nefarious husband in *Rosemary's Baby*).

"She dispenses the magic of the blues in there," he tells me.

Me and my baby
Keep hangin' on—

"Tell me something," I say, not knowing why I'm asking *him*. "I was making a turn off Sunset Boulevard in LA, but I'm not sure I ever came out of that turn. Do you know why?"

"How could I answer a question like that?"

"I think you know things. You know, the way some people seem to have the answers?"

He doesn't even look puzzled.

Never leave, never leave

On his silence, I say, "Do you know where Samantha is?"

"Which one? The old lady?"

"She's not an old lady."

Never leave,

"I guess it depends on who you ask." The ticket taker points at a young boy, who, in the 1980s or '90s, might have been called a slacker kid, slouching against a building. "If you showed that kid the Samantha in question, he'd tell you she was an old lady."

Never leave

"She is my *Velveteen Rabbit*," I tell him. "If this slacker kid chooses to see her that way, as something past its prime, what do I care? ... Maybe this whole hallucination I appear to be caught in was designed to suggest a dimension of love to me that I wasn't able to understand until now."

"Whatever you say. Back to the old lady: maybe she's where you left her."

"She is not."

Never leave my soul.

"When did you look last?"

"Yesterday ... last week ... I'm not sure ..."

"Hey, Scooby-Doo," says the slacker kid, squinching his eyes. "I know you from somewhere, don't I? Not sure where. ... but *somewhere.*"

The ticket taker says to me, "Look again where you looked last time."

"This *is* a blues club, right?" I say.

"Right," he answers, "but you're not yet even close to coming out the other side."

"I don't know you. What right do you have to tell me how to find my wife?"

"Whatever right you give me."

"I seen you somewhere, Scooby-Doo," says the slacker kid. "It'll come to me. You wait. It'll come to me. You wait."

It feels as if maybe I'm taking a shot at some lunatic metaphorical version of the story I'm living. I don't know what I'm thinking. Nevertheless, I put in another piece of paper and start to write it in screenplay form.

After I've been working for what seems like an hour, maybe more, my concentration breaks and I remember I have a guest. I get up, feeling the surprising pleasure of no stiffness in my back or any of my joints from sitting at the desk, typing long enough to have come up with five pages. I hurry downstairs and into the library.

Valory is gone.

I look out the mullioned living room window at my two cars, my Firebird and the Audi. They're where I left them. This doesn't make any sense. 1809 Benedict is not what you would call reasonable walking distance from anything—not Beverly Hills and certainly not the San Fernando Valley, which is where she said she wanted me to take her.

I'm not sure why, but I choose the Audi again. Then I drive over the Santa Monica Mountains into The Valley, going slowly, keeping my eyes peeled for any sign of Valory.

She must have hitched a ride. I turn around and drive back south, past 1809 Benedict, and down to Sunset.

Still no Valory.

Back home, I think of phoning someone for help, but I can't think who. I'm sure she's okay; she's in no way the clichéd helpless female, but I want to find her. I know it's illogical, but it seemed as if she might somehow, in some obscure manner, be able to help me, as if maybe she knows something she's not aware she knows. It feels crucial that I find her. If she knows *anything,* I've got to figure out whatever it might be.

But why would she know anything? She's someone I … happened to pick up at the foot of Benedict Canyon Drive.

Who knew, without me telling her, where I live.

I walk around the house, trying to think what to do. There's a piano in the dining room. I must have seen it before, but this is the first time I've noticed it. I used to think of it mostly as decoration. Once in a while, I sat down and picked out a melody with my right hand.

Today, I pull out the piano bench, sit, lift the keyboard cover, and play *Moonlight Sonata* not too badly. That has to count as proof that I am carrying the second half of my life around with me as I live through my younger years again. In my first 1974 I couldn't play much more than "Chopsticks." Now, I can play everything I learned between my late thirties and age seventy-five.

That should mean I'm smarter this time through. You'd think I'd behave that way, that I wouldn't involve myself in a dangerous high-speed car chase. Being able to play *Moonlight Sonata* and developing street smarts apparently do not come in the same package.

I find Valory's note.

Fleury put several little seventies magnets, colorful plastic flowers that look like they might have been designed by Peter Max, on our refrigerator. They're still there. Valory has written me a note in large block letters and left it on the refrigerator door.

It says: *Call me tomorrow. I think we should talk.*

It's signed "Valory," and she's written her phone number.

12

OLD FRIENDS

Most of my friends are actors, still living back in New York, and wouldn't know much about putting a movie together on a shoestring budget.

But I do have one old pal, named Lou Gefsky, who knows a few things. Lou started out to be an actor, then realized it wasn't in his blood. He loves show business though, has a passion for it. He wants as desperately to be a producer as I wanted be an actor. He longs to be the guy who calls the shots on major movies, but he knows he's going to have to start with something small. He moved to Hollywood three years ago and studied at the American Film Institute. He's worked with some first-rate people, but so far hasn't been able to put anything together on his own.

I know what I'm doing is irrational, but I can't let that bother me. There are no other roads open. I plan to return to Sam by immersing myself in my own story. Gandhi said (and I have to find some way to jackhammer this into my unconscious):

*"A man is but the product of his thoughts.
What he thinks, he becomes."*

I am looking at this as another way of saying: *"If you build it, they will come."* In the same spirit, if I set out on an odyssey and know—as I have known almost from the beginning—that my restless desire, my singular resolution is to return, then I will return. I *have* to believe what I *need* to believe. I am Odysseus in my own story. Odysseus returns to Penelope. Only then is his Odyssey complete.

I reach Lou on the phone and after talking for fifteen minutes, he agrees to work with me. He doesn't care how crazy my idea is. Lucky for me, story is not Lou's forte. I don't say a word to him about my motives. He assumes I'm in it for the same reasons of ambition he is. Lou thinks I want to be an auteur/ movie star, a Warren Beatty, or (still many years before his fall from favor) a Woody Allen. Maybe I could have entertained such a dream my first time through, but it doesn't interest me now.

Praying this is not rose-colored irrationality, I say to myself, "If I produce it, *she* will come."

If I produce it. I know nothing about producing. I'll have to improvise.

I'm not positive I have that skill anymore.

As an actor, it took me a long time to learn improvisation. For whatever Freudian reasons, plus being raised to think too much between the lines, I didn't have free, unfettered access to that gift—only occasionally and by accident did I stumble over it. (I hadn't yet learned: " ... *there ain't no rules ...! We're tryin' to accomplish somep'n!*") When I did find my connection with that slippery little prodigy in all of us, it was only when I took a hammer and chisel to my brain and splintered out the few shavings of ingenuity I could find there. And even that seemed to be only by persistence and dumb luck.

Is that something I can pray for, Samantha? Persistence and dumb luck?

I think of Zeke Bromley for the first time since my journey back. Zeke was my understudy in *Holiday in the Park* on Broadway, before I did the movie. He wasn't my understudy because I was better than he was; I simply got to the role first.

We soon became friends. Before I met Fleury, I used to hang out a lot with Zeke and his terrific wife, Liz Callahan. For a while Zeke and Liz were a Hollywood golden couple. Liz was a luminescent actress. She played nice supporting roles in a couple of small films, and then was cast as the ingénue lead in a costume epic that was nominated for several awards. She was one of a handful of the hottest young actresses in Hollywood when she quit. She told Zeke, "I can't stand the bullshit." By that time Zeke was no longer acting, but had started to make a pretty good living as a screenwriter.

I don't know if it was coincidental or not, but it was about that time that Zeke and Liz split up. I never understood why. Liz was in the midst of making a lot of changes that I don't think Zeke was ready to make. Liz moved to Kentucky, and as far as I know, still lives there.

Zeke and I were writing partners for a while. Zeke had a degree in journalism. We wrote plays together, fancying ourselves a contemporary generation George Kauffman and Moss Hart (*The Man Who Came to Dinner, You Can't Take It with You,* etc.). We had a few of our plays produced, mostly off-Broadway and in regional theaters. Zeke has been my best friend most of my adult life. He retired to New Hampshire a few years ago—said that he was tired of Southern California living.

Two years before the morning I went to Beverly Hills and got lost in this time/space continuum I'm bouncing around in, my friend Zeke had two heart attacks and a stroke. For most of the time since, he has been in an "assisted living facility." It's as if he's been sentenced to a kind of hospital/prison and will probably, although I pray not, be there for the rest of his life. I've talked to him almost every day since. He would do the same for me. Sam told me she thought I was wonderful to do that, but I think she knows the truth is I do it as much for myself as for Zeke. When you've been friends as long as we have, you talk easily about anything that occurs to you, and that's a relationship to treasure.

I guess it isn't so surprising that I think about him now. Since I've been back to the twentieth century, even though it doesn't make any sense, I've tried to reach Sam by phone a dozen times, both on her cell and our home number; it's simple desperation. My efforts were rewarded with: "The number you have dialed has either been changed or is out of service." Immediately after that message, the phone goes to sounds of static. Maybe that's because I'm not calling from the same phone system that will exist in 2021. I've dialed Sam's numbers for … however many days now, always with the same result.

Now, from restlessness, or force of habit, or maybe it's no more than nomadic distraction, I ring Zeke's number. How much time has gone by for him since the last time we spoke, I have no idea. He has, or will have, a cell phone next to his bed. I know he's no more likely to answer my call than Sam was, but I dial him anyway.

It's not the automated voice I expect. It's a croaky, coughing male voice.

I feel my throat tighten. *Zeke.*

It is distinctly his 2021 voice.

The first thing he hears me say is: *"Oh … my … God!"*

"Danny, is that you?" I can barely make him out. He has had trouble talking since his stroke. He didn't stop smoking when he should have, long ago, so his post-stroke life is complicated by emphysema.

I have trouble getting my words out, too. *"Zeke, can … you … hear me?"*

He clears his throat. "Sure, I can hear you. My ears still work fine."

My next utterance is: "I can't … believe I … reached you."

"Well, I'm glad you did. I was getting pissed off at you."

"Zeke, something crazy has happened to me."

"Okay, but what's new?"

"No no no, I mean you don't understand. I got lost." Silence on his end, then more coughing. "Zeke, I got lost. *Can you call Sam for me?*" He loves Sam as much as it's permissible to love your best friend's wife.

"Why don't you put her on the line?" he says.

"I can't. She's not with me."

"Shopping?"

"I don't know what she's doing. I've lost her."

"What do you mean, you've lost her?"

"Promise you won't tell me I'm crazy?"

"I won't promise any such thing."

"I've gone back in time ... to ... 1974 ... to when we were young. ... Zeke?"

There is a long pause before he says, "I wish you'd figure out some way for me to join you."

"Oh, Zeke, I miss you. And I can't tell you how much I miss Sam."

"Danny, what the fuck are you talking about?"

I try to figure out how to answer him, but by the time I do, he's in the middle of another coughing fit. He says, "Let's talk later, Danny. I just had my physical therapy. I've got to take a nap. Talk to you later, pal—"

"Zeke! Listen to me! Do me a favor, will you?"

I can tell I have his attention. "If I can, sure, Dan. How can I help you? You understand I am not in a ... position to do much."

"I know that. I'd like you to call Sam for me."

There's a brief pause. "Were you serious? You really ... can't find her?"

"Zeke, I am not kidding."

"What'll I tell her?" He clears away the beginnings of a cough. "That you've gone off your trolley and won't call her yourself?"

"No," I say as firmly as I can without sounding as lunatic as I feel. "Tell her what I told you—"

"You want me to tell her you're stuck in ... what, 1974, you said?"

I should have thought this out better, but who knew I'd reach Zeke? "Tell her I'm okay and that it may take me a while, but I will find my way. Tell her I'm out here and I will work my way back to her somehow. *I'm out here. I'm okay. I'm alive.* Have you got that, Zeke?"

"Aw, Danny," he says through another coughing fit, "you've gone around the bend."

"Just tell her I'm okay. Will you do that?"

After a beat, "All right, Dan."

"I'll call you tomorrow. Same time."

"Not tomorrow. They're taking me to the doctor."

"Okay, day after. Don't forget, Zeke. It's important."

"Gotcha. Anything else?"

"No, but don't forget to call Sam!"

He hangs up; I do too and stand where I am, breathing hard.

I pinch myself. Did you ever pinch yourself to see if you're there? It hurts—but not much. The reason is that if you hurt yourself on purpose, you don't hurt yourself enough to *really* hurt yourself, and the reason for that is that you don't *want* to hurt yourself. So you don't.

I want to believe I just talked to my best friend Zeke and that the Zeke I talked to is living in the twenty-first century and that he'll call Sam for me.

But that's crazy.

Of course, if my senses are to be believed, and knowing Zeke's voice, and with my ears telling me they did indeed hear what they *heard*, it is also true.

It is also true, if my senses are to be believed, that I am well into living through the year unto God I am living through for the second time.

I am not in a position to *not* believe *anything*.

Australian Aborigines talk about *dreamtime reality*. Is that what this is? It doesn't matter. My ignorance is fathomless. I have always been out of touch, a fish swimming in ink.

When you're out of touch with everything, including what you've always thought you knew, you have no choice but to improvise. The self-monitoring parts of the brain deactivate when you're lost in that tricky process. There's an increase in overall brain activity. It's an altered state, much like being under hypnosis, or on hallucinogenic drugs, or in that moment between waking and sleeping when you're not sure which reality is the true one—when *everything* is out of your control.

If I combine my deepest need with the one thing I know a tiny bit about, the flickering bubble-world of acting and movies, then the movie of my life—if it's an honest version and I'm not delirious—must reflect the gift of love I have received.

The universe contains thousands of kinds of invisible cause—acorns the human eye will never see, but that will nevertheless grow into oak trees.

All I want is one acorn.

These thoughts began to surface at the exact moment Valory Valentine knew where I lived when it was *impossible* for her to know where I lived. I had an overpowering intuition that my quest did not end when I took off from 2021 and landed in 1974. I have to have faith in that.

"If I have all faith, so as to remove mountains, but have not love, I am nothing." The flip side for me of that Bible verse? I had love. I have faith that it's still there.

Now all I have to do is move a mountain and begin a search for whatever the level of reality might be—and I hope I haven't already unthinkingly passed it—that Einstein was inferring when he said: *"You cannot solve a problem on the same level of reality that created it."*

I will begin by improvising and *believing* that this is a round trip I'm on, that there are no one-way odysseys.

13

LITTLE GIRL, LOST

The next morning I call Valory Valentine. After three rings, she says, "Hello, this is Valory's new answering machine. Isn't it wonderful? Please leave me a message, and at my utter convenience, I will return your call."

It's one of the first answering machines, which along with thousands of others, and later many millions more, will be taking away the livelihoods of the people who work for answering services.

As I begin to leave a few awkward words on this machine, Valory picks up the phone. "It's you," she says. "I was wondering when we'd talk."

She asks me if I'd like to meet her for lunch and suggests the Red Lantern Inn.

My breath catches. "What made you choose that?"

"Oh, I like it there" she says. "And I knew it would have meaning to you."

"*Why do you say that?*" I can almost smell the evening air that first night, when I walked into the Red Lantern with Samantha.

She doesn't even seem to hear the question. "I gave you a ring because I thought—"

"You didn't give me a ring. I called you."

It sounds as if she's tapping lightly on the mouthpiece with a fingertip. "Did you? Oh, of course. I left my number on your refrigerator."

"Right. Where did you disappear to? Did you walk all the way to … where did you go?"

"Oh, I found a ride easy enough. I should tell you I've been praying for you."

The tapping continues as I gather myself. "Maybe I should tell you I'm not religious."

"Neither am I," she says. I can picture her north eyebrow arching up.

"But I thought you said you prayed for me."

"You don't have to be religious to pray." The tapping stops. "All you have to do is understand that while you are a part of the big picture, you are not all of it. You're a tiny wave on an infinite ocean."

"I see."

"Would day after tomorrow, say, three thirty, work for you?" she says. "It's not so crowded then."

"Yeah, I guess."

"How's Mr. Yort?"

"My agent?" I remember the moment the phone rang when she was on the sofa in the library. "Did you hear my conversation?"

"A little. Before I fell asleep. I believe I heard you ask him why Stanley Kubrick would want to see you."

"You have supersonic hearing."

"Average. Did you meet Stanley Kubrick? That sounds like it could be a wonderful thing for you."

"It could have been." I can feel her penetrating eyes. I don't know why, but I tell her: "My hopes had gotten built up about the possibility of playing a ... wonderful role in his next movie. Somewhere along the line, possibly twice, he changed his mind and stayed with his original ... or second choice." I frown at the phone. "I don't know why I'm telling you all this. I don't even know you." I feel lightheaded. "If you want the truth, I'm a little scared of you."

"Why would you be scared of me?" Sensing my reaction, she adds: "What's so funny?"

"I don't know. I feel like I need to see you again, but I'm not sure why. It feels to me ... as if you might know, or might be able to ... *intuit* something useful to me ... or maybe I'm wrong. How *did* you know that was my house we were approaching when we were driving up Benedict Canyon? I forget your exact words, but when we got near it you said something about stopping and resting. It was as if you knew where I lived. ... But how did you know? I really would like an answer to that. And another thing: you said you understood why the Red Lantern would have meaning to me. How could you know that? That's *Twilight Zone* spooky."

"I'd like to tell you, but I'm not sure I can."

"What does that mean? Does this kind of thing happen to you often? And what was that ten-minute lie-down about?"

"It's something I do," she says. "I feel a need for a little rest sometimes. Sometimes it helps me gather my thoughts."

This feels like some kind of hippie thing, which I guess is natural enough; it's 1974. But something else about her is unsettling me. I feel like hanging up, but I don't. "I still don't understand how you know things there's no way for you to know."

"I don't like to talk about it. It's come up a few times in my life. ... It's kind of embarrassing."

"Do you have a sixth sense or something?"

"Something."

"But you don't know much about it?"

"Practically nothing." She sighs. It feels as if she's not so sure she wants to talk about this, but she goes on: "I mean, I'll go along for periods of time—weeks, sometimes months—and nothing spooky, as you called it, happens. Then all at once, something comes up like it has with you. And then, I don't know ... I try not to impose limitations on myself."

"What does *that* mean?"

She says something in response, but I don't think I've heard her. I don't know why, but I'm envisioning myself walking through a roofless, infinite house. I can see the room I'm walking through, look back toward the one I just came from and ahead to the next doorway, and maybe a little bit into the room I'm coming to. And that's about it. But if I could see the inside of this house from above, I could see someone—even if it's an imaginary someone, say, an imaginary me—going from room to room. From above, I'd have the advantage of a wider perspective, a teleological view, and I could see, if not the whole house, at least a wide screen version of it, an IMAX overview.

But I'd have to be God. Or a bird.

Valory says, "I'll give you that I've known some things I shouldn't, but ... I can't explain it. I can't figure it out myself. I've been to doctors ... I guess."

"You *guess*?"

"I mean specialists. No one seems to know what's going on inside my head—least of all me."

"What kind of doctors? What kind of specialists?"

"They're not exactly *real* doctors."

It feels as if we're both getting uncomfortable with this line of conversation, but that doesn't stop us. "Does it get in the way of your life?" I ask. "I mean, what do you do for a living?"

She taps on the mouthpiece again. "I've been doing personal assistant jobs for various people in the film industry for quite a while—actresses mainly."

"Has your psychic … *thing* gotten in the way of your doing that?"

"No. Most of the people I work with are actors. I'm sorry to say it, but most actors are so self-involved they don't take in that much about their immediate surroundings. Anyway, they don't notice me to speak of, and as long as I do what they want me to, everything seems to be okay." Again, the tapping stops. "Have you ever had a personal assistant?"

"No, I wouldn't know what assistance to ask for—other than to influence me to make smarter decisions. How did you come to be doing that kind of work?" I stop myself. "No no no. Let's wait and go on with this over a drink or something. We're jabbering like a couple of teenagers."

She laughs. "You're right. Let's finish this at the Red Lantern."

The Red Lantern.

Samantha.

When she was in her early twenties, working in her father's jewelry store, a thin old woman came into the store one day. The woman produced a delicate gold bracelet and asked how much she could get for it.

Still very young, Sam hadn't yet learned how difficult it can be for people to have to sell something personal.

She knew how to measure for old gold value. She weighed the bracelet. Gold was not very expensive at that time. She told the woman what its value was. It had only weighed out to be worth five dollars.

Sam told her so, not thinking she would sell it. The old woman said, "Okay."

Sam took the bracelet and gave her five dollars.

When the woman had gone, Sam went into the back office, showed her father the bracelet, described the woman, and told him what had happened, that she had paid the woman five dollars for it.

Sam's father, Raymond, said to her, "Did you kick her in the ass on the way out?"

Samantha knew instantly what he meant.

Although I've heard that story from Samantha three or four times, the most recent time she told it to me, I asked her what her father would have done in her place.

Without thinking about it, she said, "He would have weighed the bracelet and said to the lady, 'It's worth $100.' And then he would have given her the money."

She never got over it. Whenever she tells me about that incident, it brings tears to her eyes. It's something she's never forgotten.

That's Samantha's nature. I've never stopped being grateful to be living within the shelter of that kind of heart.

Coming over the hill on Escondido Drive, above the park, I see the signs of the location shoot I've driven to with cunning afore-thought (some research, culminating with a phone call to an old location manager friend). My heart skitters down to my stomach and back up to my throat. In the parking lot are photographic and dolly trucks, a crane truck, a dressing room trailer, a trailer shared by makeup and wardrobe, a honey wagon (mobile toilets), a flatbed truck, and a large rig for electrical. I get out of my Firebird, which I've driven today because it's sportier, more masculine. (Mercy. Am I doing that again?) I head toward the rocks, anxieties overcome by the excitement of the game, and walk up a long slope of hard-packed sand and crushed and broken brush, toward Vasquez Rocks Natural Area Park. Known for its geologic wonders, Vasquez Rocks has long been popular for theatrical and television location shoots, especially Westerns and sci-fi adventures requiring a barren or otherworldly landscape.

The set for the morning is a lean-to amidst a circle of yucca bushes. Behind a screen of junipers that look suspiciously transplanted is an oversized trailer that must have been hard to haul in through the rocks—the kind of challenge movie producers take on only to accommodate big stars or actors whose best-natured cooperation they need to curry.

The nameplate on the door informs me this is, as I was pretty sure it was—extrapolated from what my location manager pal said—the temporary home away from home of "HANNAH CASTLE."

A uniformed security man is leaning back in a canvas chair a few feet away from the trailer, smoking a cigarette and reading a newspaper. I stride to the door, take a step up the stairway, knock once, then step back down and move toward the guard, who is by now moving toward me, his face contorted in outrage, roaring, "Who the hell are you?"

"Listen," I say. "I'm an old friend of Hannah's. If she knew I was here, she'd want to see me."

Cords are bulging out of the chunky guard's neck. "We don't disturb Ms. Castle for nothin'. If you're a friend of hers, you know that."

"I'm on the film."

The guard frowns. "You an actor?"

"That's right."

"What's your name?" He looks at a notebook he's pulled from his pocket.

"Daniel Maytree."

The trailer door opens and a familiar voice says, "What is it, Ned?"

"I'm sorry, Ms. Castle. Guy here says he's an actor, but I don't think he's on the list."

"Hi, Hannah. It's me, Danny Maytree." I try to move around Ned, but he grabs my arm in a vice-like grip.

We both look at the woman standing in the open Winnebago door.

This is Hannah Castle. The second movie I did was called *Little Girl, Lost*. Because of the success of *Holiday in the Park*, I had enough "heat" to have some say in the casting of my next movie, a studio effort that was not exactly bad, but near enough. It got seen by a lot of people in the industry, but not because it was a good movie. It drew the attention it did because of Hannah Castle. She was magnetic and lovable in her role, more charming than anyone could have anticipated. She is charming enough in person, but, as happens with some actors, film brings her to luminous life. The dubious doorway to stardom has swung open to her.

It may or may not remain open.

Hannah Castle is not what many people would call a "nice person." If word of that gets widely revealed before she's had the chance to gather momentum, the door may slam shut in her face. For now though, in the backrooms of Hollywood, she's looking like a thoroughbred.

Because I've worked with her, I know her ambition is as innocent as Eve Harrington's in *All About Eve*—which is to say she's as sweet and pure as Caligula, perfectly willing to stab you in the back with that enchanting smile radiating across her innocent face. Working with her the first time, I felt, beneath the surface, hostility, deep-seated anger. She said cutting things behind people's backs. She wanted what she wanted. Any serenity she might seem to have had was for show.

But she was gifted at that act.

And now I'm here to ask a favor of Hannah Castle. If I can get her to be in my movie, I can probably raise the money to get it done. I'm also here because, in Hollywood parlance, "She owes me." She knows what that means. It has to be honored or word gets out, which can be death in Venice, Beverly Hills, and all the other Tinseltown branch communities. Breaking such unwritten laws is the most direct route to becoming *persona non grata* in the film world. If now isn't the time to use what little there is of a Hollywood ethical code to my advantage, I can't imagine when.

"It's okay, Ned. I'll see him," says Hannah.

In her trailer: "It's *so* good to see you, Danny."

God, she's sincere. She hands me an apple juice and sits down on an upholstered bench seat opposite the one she's guided me to. Between us is a laminate table with a woodgrain top.

"It's been a long time," I say, trying not to stare at her. "You look really good."

"I ought to. I've had a tiny bit of work done."

It crosses my mind to say, "Already?" She can't be thirty yet. It's too early to be tampering with her looks. On the other hand … what do I know? Maybe it's the perfect Hollywood stratagem for her. Even though on the surface and on film she is charming, disarming, and sweet, right beneath that veneer is the killer instinct of ... quite a few Hollywood megastars.

She presses lightly against her chin with the back of one hand. "Nothing much. I'm very lucky. Some of my ... *our* contemporaries aren't doing so well." She smiles, lips pressed together, and shakes her head. "What's your secret?"

"Oh... lucky, too, I guess."

"Do you live near here?"

"No, actually I came out to see you."

Her smile doesn't falter. "God, I'm amazed you got through all the, uh ..." She shrugs. "Well, you know how super-anal they can be with ... security." She shakes her head again. "You *really* do look fabulous. How do you do it?" She doesn't wait for a response. "Listen, I don't know what you're doing right now. I'm so out of ... I can't believe we've lost touch."

"I just turned down a thing." I say, showing her what I hope is my snuggly, down-home smile. "It was genuinely not good. They could take the film straight out of the camera and make guitar picks out of it. Save time and money."

"Oh God," she says with old pal collegiality. "I know what you mean. I've been getting a lot of those. Ray Stark called me with something. He said he had George Segal and that big new kid ... uh, Nick Nolte. Well, I *know* Nick. I called him." Her eyebrows furrow into the mock outrage she's so good at. "He never heard of the project. Better than that, he never met Ray Stark. I mean, I never knew what 'dirtbag' meant until after we did *Little Girl, Lost* and people started sniffing around after me. At first I was shocked, then ..."

She looks out the window in the direction of the set and back at me again, just above my eyes. "You didn't come out here to chitchat with me. Is there something I can do for you? How's Fleury?"

"We split up," I say.

"Aw, honey." God, she's good. She reaches out in what feels like heartfelt sympathy and holds my hand. "What happened? I *know* you. You didn't ... wander ..." She frowns. "Did you?"

"Not exactly. In a way, we both did. And ... yes, it was my fault."

She looks out the window again, thinking her own possibly parallel thoughts. "Well, to be honest, I never thought you were ... uh, you never seemed to me the soul mate types. ... Does that sound terrible?"

"No, not at all. ... *Really*, I think you're right. We ... You know how you can drift apart from somebody? You go along, you know, convincing yourself that you're making adult decisions and ..."

I'm aware I'm no more than mouthing strung-together words, Hollywood talk. When I was a young actor, I used to try to convince myself that I'd discovered a sure approach to surviving "showbiz" encounters. I told myself: if you need something too much—like approval, it takes away from them. If you leap directly to what you want and give away the fact that you're lost, they will feel lost too, and they hate that. Act as if you know who you are and they will want to attach themselves to it, because the great majority of them are lost just like you.

At this moment in her life, I think Hannah believes she's not part of that muddle. Does she understand where she is on the pyramid of Hollywood power? It appears as if she's on top to stay, but that's probably not true. It rarely is. I wonder if she knows that.

Why am I trying to guess her destiny? I'm not qualified. I don't know her circumstances or who she's become since I last saw her. I remind myself why I'm here: she's the best chance I have to get my project off the ground.

"I'm doing a movie," I say. "I'm putting it together myself."

I see the quick furtive look that comes across the faces of cornered movie stars. She wouldn't have looked this way before *Little Girl, Lost* made her as big in the business as she is now. It's fascinating how fast what's on the inside, down deep, leaks through to the surface once people have something to protect.

"I'm not looking for money," I say. "And I'm not trying to get you to make a 'star commitment' to my little … you know … *cheapie* flick." I can see the relief in her eyes, along with a lingering guardedness. "It's three lovely, sweet, perfect scenes for you," I say, despite the fact that I haven't written them yet. "If you like it, you're top billed and I'd only need you for three days, four at the most."

Her smile is gradual, deft, but almost indifferent. "I'd be helping you raise the rest of your money, wouldn't I?" Hollywood people are like politicians at asking questions that aren't questions.

I nod. As she draws a deep breath, I tell her, "You've got my word this is a savvy, sympathetic girl. You could toss it off in your sleep. I promise the audience will adore you—the way they always do." I smile ingratiatingly.

After a pause long enough to be uncomfortable, she says, "We'll let your agent know."

She stands up and smiles. The smile feels compassionate, even affectionate, but it's also my cue to leave.

"Thanks, Hannah," I say. "You are the absolute best!"

As I slither away from her, I hum the Gloria Gaynor hit *I Will Survive.*

I pull over at a Shell station, fill up my gas tank, and call my service from a public phone. I have one message. It's from my father's girlfriend, Brenda. Girlfriend is not right. They've lived together for at least twenty years, in the desert, east-southeast of LA, in Hemet.

I call Brenda, a frizzy-haired desert creature, a beauty in her day, also sweet and loving. My dad is luckier than he'll ever know to have found her. I'll never understand why she has stuck by him, as faithful as Lassie is to Timmy. We exchange hellos.

"Would you like a tortilla with your coffee?" she asks. "And please don't breathe into the phone. I hate it when you do that." Brenda is what she herself would call a character.

"But I'm on the phone, why are you offering me a tortilla?"

"Because you'll visit us again someday—unless you've erased your own father from your life. And when you do, I'd like to know what you want with your coffee. You'll find out soon enough what it's like to be old. I've tried to reach you on the phone, but you know I hate leaving messages on that service. Why aren't you ever home?"

"It's a long story," I say. "Plus I don't always answer my phone. If you don't leave a message, I may miss your call." I head her off. "I'll try to get better at answering in case it *is* you."

"This is a poor signal. Where are you?"

"Up in Canyon Country."

"What are you doing there?"

"I've been visiting a friend on location. At Vasquez Rocks."

"What's that?"

"It's a park with some big slanting rocks where they've shot a lot of movies. *Apache*, *The Sea of Grass*, and something called *Blazing Saddles* last year."

"I never heard of them."

"You'll hear about *Blazing Saddles* this year," I say.

"Your dad's doin' poorly."

"Oh shit."

"Don't curse."

"Sorry. How poorly?"

"It's the asthma."

I don't remind Brenda that it's not his asthma, it's emphysema. She doesn't like to think about that.

"And it's pretty bad this time. You'd better get down here. He doesn't say much about you, but I know he misses you."

"You've got amazing patience, Brenda. That's a nice gift to have."

"It wasn't a gift, honey. I had to earn it."

"You're something else."

"Thanks." I picture her warm smile. "I guess your dad's out of the woods for the moment. But he'd love to see you. Come as soon as you can manage it."

"Okay. I'll call you."

"Promise?"

How did my dad got so lucky? "Promise."

Driving back down the 5 Freeway, I think of a short story ("The Green Door") by O. Henry: "*... she opened her eyes. And the young man saw that hers, indeed, was the one missing face from his heart's gallery of intimate portraits.*"

I can see her next to me in the passenger seat, a hallucination, but better than no Sam at all. I can't talk to her, ask her advice for dealing with the plight we're in. I don't think hallucinations, especially from other eras, are much good for advice.

How about present time apparitions? Valory Valentine, for example? Maybe I should ask her when I see her.

I have to see her.

14

STANLEY KUBRICK

By the time I get to the phone, it's rung eight times. That means someone the answering service knows has asked to let them ring through. John Yort. "Where were you?" he says.

"I don't just hang around waiting for you to call me, John."

"Is your passport valid?"

"I think so. Why?"

"You're flying to Dublin tonight. Kubrick wants you there now."

"Aw, John, you expect me to go out to LAX on the off chance that Stanley Kubrick has left me a plane ticket to come replace Ryan O'Neal in a movie that's already more than half shot?"

"Sure, why not?"

"I'll tell you why not: because it's crazy. Who told you this? Come on, you're kidding me."

"I just got off the phone with him. It was him. I know his voice."

This is not some kind of April fool joke. John's not kidding. "Are you seriously telling me Stanley Kubrick wants me to fly to Dublin?"

"Yes, I am. And he wants you there now. Sooner than now. There's a ticket waiting for you at Pan Am."

"Did you talk to anybody at all from Warners?"

"No, Danny, I talked to Stanley Kubrick, like I said. I got off the phone with him five minutes ago. Aren't you listening to me?"

"You're serious, aren't you?"

"As a heart attack. You're flight's at eleven o'clock tonight. You have to be there by nine. Go pack."

I take a cab to LAX.

I have one small bag. I stand in line in front of the Pan Am desk and wait my turn.

An angular young woman, in her early thirties with a Romanesque nose and full, sexy lips, smiles at me. "Yes, sir?"

"I believe you have a ticket for me for the Dublin flight."

"Name?"

"Daniel Maytree."

She thumbs through to a list and scans it. "How do you spell that?"

"Like a sapling in springtime."

She glances at me, smiling, looks down again, then up once more, frowning. "I'm sorry, sir. I don't have a ticket for that flight under the name of Maytree."

"I was told there would be one waiting for me."

She looks down again and shakes her head. "I'm very sorry, sir."

I take a deep breath. This is what I expected. Why am I so gullible? Why is my hotshot agent so gullible? I thank the woman, turn, and walk away.

I haven't gone more than fifteen feet when I hear: "Sir?"

I stop and turn back to her.

"There is a message for you though. Or rather, an envelope with your name on it." She seems embarrassed at not having seen it immediately.

I go to the nearest bank of windows, stand at one of those long metal shelf-like things, and open the envelope. It reads:

"Sorry, my friend, I've changed my mind once again. I've got too damn much good footage with Ryan in it. If I could go back and physically dub you over him, I'd do it. I think it's the most beautiful film I've ever made. But since I have so much of it in the can, I have no choice but to stick with O'Neal. You will find, when you go to your bank, that I have deposited $50,000 in your account toward the project you're working on. Good luck with it. I know it will be memorable." It's signed "S.K."

Fifty thousand is almost exactly what I need to take the next serious step toward making my movie.

But how does Kubrick know about my movie? How does he know anything about me? And why did he decide to ...

How does it even occur to me to ask these questions? Haven't I learned by now not to be shocked by any of my new life's Alice-in-Wonderland moments?

I'm having a recurring nightmare. Having been thrown out of time as I know it and into eternity, I've started to wake up almost every night because I'm having a nightmare that I feel a wrenching need to escape.

This dream begins in deceptive beauty. I'm in a chair I sit in when I'm writing, looking through the sliding glass doors between our bedroom and the yard. Close to the window is a patch of limestone gravel, and beyond that, a large grass-covered mound of sandy soil, on top of which is a Japanese maple tree, low-lying juniper, a patch of decorative nandina, spider plants, a big lava rock that stands on end, and a large agave cactus. A cascade of bougainvillea, star jasmine and honeysuckle overflows a pergola above a 6 x 8-foot fishpond, stocked with fifteen huge goldfish and two koi. We used to have several big koi, but one nighttime raccoon attack put an end to them. Now we have an electrified fence, triggered by sunset. It would be hard to describe the effect the koi slaughter had on Sam. To the right, looking out the window, is a weathering redwood fence, and a whitewashed cement bench, which, if you squint your eyes and assume the right frame of mind, looks like marble. All of this feels like Queen Elizabeth II's line: "For me, heaven is likely to be a bit of a comedown."

Then, in the dream, Sam comes home.

She says she isn't feeling well. She usually cooks dinner, but this night I do that because she's barely able to move.

The next morning, she seems all right at first, but after being on her feet for about five minutes, she is struck by the same feelings she had yesterday, and once again she finds herself almost paralyzed by fatigue. I help her out to the car and drive her to the Providence Hospital emergency room. The doctor in charge is unable to make any diagnosis, so Sam is checked in and I call our family doctor. He comes over to the hospital during his lunch hour, gives Sam a cursory examination, and can't come to any conclusion. He gives instructions to run a series of tests. They don't turn up anything. They can't figure out why Sam is feeling this way, so they keep her in the hospital, "under observation."

On the morning of the third or fourth day, Sam whispers to me that she wants our friend Calvin to pay her a visit. Calvin is our lawyer. He shows up and Sam tells him and me what she wants to happen after she dies.

I wake up at this point. I've had this dream three or four nights now, and every one is the same: I wake up right after Sam has said she wants her sister Morgan and Grace to have any belongings of hers that I don't want.

What I don't want is for Sam to die. I cannot conceive of life without her. And yet, when I wake up from my nightmare, I remember I am living life without her.

I'm in the bed where Fleury and I used to sleep. It's about ten a.m. The phone rings. There's no caller ID, so I pick up the receiver. Maybe it's someone with a few answers. I'd settle for a couple of smart questions. I had my nightmare around three a.m. and ended up getting so little sleep that I feel older than the old man I was before I arrived here.

"Is this Daniel Maytree?" says the voice. It's Patricia, my therapist. I don't know why it surprises me. She was always honest and straightforward. It's like her to return my call, as she promised she would. "Yes, it is," I say. "Does this mean you'll see me?"

"Would you say the same things today you said when you came to see me? About living two lives?"

"Yes. I'd say what I told you before." There's a long pause. "Doctor?"

"We'll give it a try."

"Can't resist someone as wacko as me?"

"Yes, that's pretty close … but I don't think you're dangerous. Am I right in assuming that?"

That's a fair question. "Yes, yes. I've never hurt anyone in my life. … Well, if you don't count Melvin Kahn."

"Pardon?"

"He was a kid I played with in my dad's basement once. He was being rough with an electric train I'd been given and it … um … pissed me off. So I hit him. I mean, I don't think I hit him hard … but he stopped messing with my stuff like he was *trying* to break it after that."

"I don't think we have to worry about Melvin Kahn. From what you said the other day, you have bigger fish to fry."

I laugh. "Yes, I do. You're right. God, are you right. I'd like to find out, uh, which one of me is real."

"*Okay.* How about Thursday at four in the afternoon? Does that work for you?"

"Yes, I have no plans for … well, for anytime in the foreseeable future." I can't prevent myself from adding: "If there is a future."

There's a brief pause. "All right, I'll see you at four, this coming Thursday."

I call Zeke again forty-eight hours after our first talk. Again he answers with the voice I've come to recognize in my twenty-first century incarnation.

I ask him about Sam.

"I can't reach her," says Zeke.

"What do you *mean* you can't reach her?"

"What the fuck is going on, Danny? Your phone's not listed."

"What do you mean?"

"They tell me there is no such phone line in Valley Glen. Promise."

"Aw, come on. Of course there's a phone line. She can't have just disappeared."

"According to you, *you* did."

"Yeah, but … try Sam again tomorrow. Will you? Please?"

"Of course." He coughs for about ten seconds, apologizes, then says, "Have you ever considered the possibility that you sort of *cling* to Sam? Isn't that a no-no in your spiritual view of the world?"

This notion has a jarring effect on me. I give Zeke the answer I keep on hand for myself: "I know what you're saying, but I don't believe it's clinging for either Sam or me." I feel a chill between my shoulder blades. "Well, maybe more for me than Sam, but we both know the danger of that. We joke about it, call each other Cody, as in codependent. But I don't think either one of us is doing that." I clear my throat. "I change. She changes. But neither of us leans on the other one. We're in love. That does happen, you know."

Zeke tries with difficulty to clear his throat. "I guess that makes sense if you say so. Listen, Danny, they've come to give me a damn bath. Can you call me back again tomorrow?"

"Sure," I say. I add quickly: "… Zeke? Try Sam again. Please. She's got to be there."

"I will." The line goes dead.

In recent days I've caught up with John Yort via phone about the progress on my screenplay, my meeting with Hannah Castle, and Stanley Kubrick's out-of-the-blue largesse. Now, for the first time since I boomeranged back in time, we're meeting face to face at an outdoor café on Sunset Boulevard in Beverly Hills. He looks as I remember him, like a beautifully cared for shark, but dressed in expensive, casual clothes—a sage green Ralph Lauren polo shirt, flax-colored chinos, and a pair of white sneakers that probably cost more than his secretary earns in two weeks. I assume I look exactly as he remembers me. Fleury used to tell me she thought he had a crush on me. I never really noticed that, although I remember he once made a comment about my legs; he said he liked them, that I looked good in shorts. But he said it in passing, an offhand comment. I'm probably naïve ... or was. John is a good-looking man. I was at a meeting with a producer one time and he talked more about John than me. From the tenor of his remarks, it was pretty clear he found John carnally attractive. I mentioned earlier that I wasn't pretty like Ryan O'Neal. John was. I know being pretty and preferring men don't necessarily correlate. Anyway, I knew John was gay. He never made any advances to me. Maybe he guessed I'd demur and he didn't want to muddy the waters of our professional relationship.

The café reminds me of the funky vegan restaurant Woody Allen will use in *Annie Hall* a couple of years from now. John has an iced tea, which he's using to wash down the cheeseburger he wolfed down as if he were taking part in a cheeseburger-eating contest, the only rules of which are not getting any food stains on your simple but elegant wardrobe. It's part of the Hollywood agent syndrome; agents never seem to have enough time to get through their day's work. I'm having my second Heineken.

"John, will you talk to me now? *Can* you talk to me? You inhaled that thing." He's wiping his mouth with his napkin.

"Okay, there's good news and bad news about—what is it you're calling it?—oh yeah, *Hello, Rest of My Life*," he says, pronouncing the title with distaste. "The good news is, Hannah has agreed to do it. Four days. And she'll do it for minimum. Oh, and there's an optional fifth day if we need it, but that day will cost you more than your entire budget, so you'd better not need it."

"The bad news?"

He looks east toward the 9000 building where his agency is housed. He hisses out a breath between his teeth. It sounds like one of those small, deadly jungle snakes that give you almost no warning before they kill you. John is not the killer in this case. At this moment, he is concerned the two of us may end up victims.

"John, you're scaring me."

"They want the contract predated."

"What does that mean?"

He gives me the weary, savvy look he keeps handy for the uninformed and sighs. "It means they have something hinky up their sleeve."

"Like what?"

"Like I don't know what. But I don't trust them."

"You don't trust anybody. Do you think it's Hannah, or the people at William Morris?"

"Both. My best guess is that they're trying to duck out of something else. I've put out feelers, but I'm not getting any answers, at least so far. Bottom line: you don't have much room to maneuver."

"What are we going to do?"

"You're dead set on doing this thing?"

"I've told you, John, I don't have any choice. I can't explain the reasons to you. You'd tell me I was crazy. But look at it this way, if Stanley Kubrick has put up $50,000, it's worth your believing in it enough to help me out with this."

He gives me his medium gauge dry look. "What do you think I'm doing here?" He squints at me. "Maytree?"

"Yort?"

"You do understand what fire you're playing with, doing a project like this?"

"Sure."

"I don't believe you do. I've got the feeling you don't think Hollywood success is wholesome, or some fucking thing—not *New York Times* enough for your taste."

"That's not true."

"Isn't it?" He reaches into one of those oversized men's bags that were popular in the seventies among a certain set and pulls out a copy of *On Set,* an entertainment trade magazine of the time. He has it opened to an article about the actor Peter Finch. He's underlined a quotation from Mr. Finch. I read it.

"Success is a very tough mistress. For years, while you're struggling, she wants nothing to do with you. Then, one day you find yourself in the room with her and even though the key is on the inside, you can't leave. 'You've made your choice,' she says, 'I don't care how exhausted you are—you're going to stay here for the rest of your life making love to me.'"

I look up at John.

"The point is, he's right," he says. "If you grab that scarlet lady while it's a possibility, while you're *this* close to being in the room with her"—he holds a thumb and forefinger up about two inches apart—"that floozy ain't never gonna let you go."

"I understand," I tell him.

"You're not acting as if you do."

I assure him I know what he's saying. And I do. What I don't tell him is that I have no intention of acting on that knowledge. So I'm lying to him. And I feel bad for him. I'm wasting his time, using him.

Driving home (or maybe it was actually much later, like a character in a Kurt Vonnegut novel), I realize I was being less honest, more Hollywood than John was. It wasn't until that moment I knew that I didn't do as well as I could have the first time I lived through this because I was overflowing with fear. I didn't think I was worthy of unbridled success and I made stupid, self-defeating choices. I could list them, but that would be as self-defeating as having made them in the first place.

This time, I know there exists another kind of "making love." In the other kind, you give and receive. You're not selfish. Your lover isn't selfish. She's as much or more concerned with your happiness than she is with her own. There is no predatory ego with this kind of love. It enriches every corner of every life it touches.

The Dog in me says: *if you fully understood right this second what you have just said, you probably wouldn't be in the fix you're in.*

I am aware, having been in 1974 the second time for a while now, of an additional surprise sensation, a layer of peculiarity painted over a base coat of peculiarity. Even though it's similar to terrain I distinctly remember, it's also different in an alarming, ominous way.

I think of the warmth I feel with Sam. One night, she was reading to me and I thought of people I've known, people I've *been*—naked, anxious egos, with or without makeup. As Sam was reading to me that night, I had my head on the pillow next to hers; my arm lay across her stomach. I knew exactly who she was, but in a different way than anyone I'd ever known before. I said to her (she's used to me tossing non-sequiturs at her): "Do you know what I like about you?" She shot me a quizzical look as I stroked her hair. I said, "You never try to fabricate another *self*." Without thinking, she replied, "I can hardly keep track of the one."

I look out of the mullioned window at the southeast corner of my living room. Across Benedict Canyon Drive, the mountains rise steeply toward the east. Behind me they climb to the west. I lose the sun in this house about three or four in the afternoon, depending on the season. It's a beautiful house to live in. I love being inside of it, but I realize I don't love where it is. I have a limited perspective of the earth and sky around and above me. It feels as if my life here is more claustrophobic than I remember, completely hemmed in, and I recall why I got out the first time. I felt as if I were standing in a hole, but also raised like a car in a mechanic's inspection pit, and I was being examined up close, from every angle. I never did well under the kind of stress that comes with being tested, judged by strangers with faces I couldn't read, knowing that not only did my livelihood depend on their verdict, my *life* depended on it. I knew such feelings were not reasonable, but I didn't know how to banish them.

Once, when I was eight years old, I got up in the middle of the night, walked to the foot of my bed and peed on it. I guess I was asleep or maybe I was half asleep because, as I remember it now, it feels as if I was standing in a hole I couldn't climb out of, sort of asleep, but terrified, peeing on something I shouldn't be peeing on.

Then my father, who it turned out was awake and plastered, appeared at my doorway. At first, groggy and in between worlds, I couldn't read his face. As I became conscious, I could see he was yelling at me in what felt like anguish. I don't remember what he said, the words are muddled in my mind or forgotten, but whatever they were, they were uttered in fury and grief. There was never a moment of anything like, "That's okay, son, you didn't mean to. You were asleep." He *never* said, "We'll work through it, you'll get over it." There was a frenzy of rage and then he hit me, not with his fists, but with open hands, held rigid. They felt like fists. I've always wondered if, in some part of himself, he was trying not to hurt me.

He never said a word about it afterward.

I'm pretty sure I have a *samskara* from that night.

15

HOLLYWOOD AND HOPEFUL THINKING

get on the Hollywood freeway at Highland, headed toward The Valley. As I do, a man in a pickup truck swerves in behind me. He's tailgating me. I look in my rearview mirror and see that he's gesturing, for my benefit, with what appears to be a hammer. He's jabbing at the air with it in the cab of his pickup as if he's trying with the wrong part of the hammer to drive a nail through the roof. He's not much over one car length behind me.

The entrance to the freeway is back to being what it was before the state modernized it. I didn't realize this as I merged onto the freeway and I've edged this guy out. His response is that he's telling me if he gets a chance, he'll hammer my brains out and even that might not satisfy him.

Okay, so road rage was a thing even in 1974, but the rage hadn't evolved yet—as it will—from hammers to handguns. How do cops deal with this kind of thing? If I reported this incident to the California Highway Patrol, it wouldn't do any good. Never mind that he is justifiably irked at me for crowding into his lane. What happens when somebody like the guy in the pickup later commits a deadly crime of some kind? Who do the cops look for? Who commits a crime like this? A maniac does. The problem is, with so much insanity running through the whole culture, how does a busy police force go about finding the right maniac? If you were to line up the country's motorized maniacs toward the east from Los Angeles, they'd stretch … I don't know how far—maybe once around the Empire State Building and all the way back to California.

I make it alive to Lou Gefsky's office.

Lou is happy to be working with me. He's three, perhaps four years older than I am, a sharp guy who loves movies. I don't know how much feel he has for the artistries and various supplementary crafts of moviemaking, but film production is his dream. Plus, I think he's a natural businessman. He sees my project as a first stage steppingstone to the career he desperately wants to have. He has the makings of a good producer—not a killer one; he's too good-natured and kind. But he's smart, studied hard at the American Film Institute, and as I say, loves movies and is ambitious. Sometimes that's enough. Another plus, along with being a pleasant guy, he's got one of those faces people like on sight.

He's taken a lease on a dinky little office in North Hollywood. He doesn't have a secretary, but he's set up a limited liability company and he's been looking for a project.

I find him behind a neophyte executive's Al's Furniture office desk. It has a thin veneer meant to resemble oak, three utility drawers on one side, a shallow side-mount ball bearing drawer in the middle, and a large, brand-new blotter, a nice one, framed in a narrow red leatherette trimming. The blotter covers most of the desk's surface and looks more expensive than the forlorn piece of furniture it sits atop. The only item on the blotter is a large amber glass ashtray.

Lou has a sunshiny smile on his face. He's ready to produce *Hello, Rest of My Life.*

He's become a cigar smoker, I think because he feels it's appropriate to the job. I don't think the habit will last. I get the impression he's trying to conceal the fact that he's not enjoying the one he's smoking now.

He sucks in a mouthful, ruminates the smoke around for a while, and blows it out in a way that suggests he can't get rid of it fast enough. He says, "I read the material you sent me. I like it." He frowns, then smiles again. "I don't understand it, but I like it. You've got a problem though. You've got too damn many locations. We're putting this together for a song. I think I have a commitment for forty thousand."

I haven't mentioned the Stanley Kubrick money yet and won't until I know for sure it's in my bank account. (I know this is adding up to more than the thirty thousand I told John Yort I would need. Reality is a mischievous monkey.)

Lou goes on: "I think by the time we're finished, and on the basis of you getting Hannah to headline"—he tosses me the bone you have to feed to the hungry actor who's trying to push the buttons on his own career—"along with yourself, of course. With the two of you in place, we can double that. But Danny, you can't do thirty-four locations, and the way I figure it, well over a couple hundred setups for a hundred twenty grand. We can probably get ourselves about ten between us on personal credit. I hope yours is decent. And I hate to ask it, but what's the outstanding mortgage on your house?"

"I'll look into that," I tell him. "I'm pretty sure I'll be able to help, but I've got to check on a couple of things... Can we talk about this later? I'm afraid I'm about to say something politically incorrect."

"Politically incorrect? What's that mean?"

I can't possibly cover this ground. "Uh ... I think it means you don't want to say something that would hurt the feelings of an ethnic minority, or a ... a certain group of people—say, divorce lawyers."

He represses a frown. "Yeah, okay, but we're going to have to beg, borrow, or steal a lot of stuff. The borrowing's cheap, same with the begging. But the stealing makes me nervous. We're going to have to buy film stock, rent all the camera and electrical. ... We'll steal all the locations we can, but we're going to have to get at least a *few* permits. And in a way, I gotta tell you, Hannah is a double-edged sword."

I haven't mentioned to him the fact that I'm a little unsure at this moment about Hannah Castle.

"We'll have to pay SAG minimum to all the actors," he goes on. "We'll do favored nations of course, everyone but Hannah, but that still means pension, health, and welfare costs. It's going to add up. And we will get caught location stealing a couple of times; we're going to have to have something put aside for fines. I'll be able to do some wangling and get those minimized, but we've got to have a little cash for when I can't and have to do some payoffs."

"I don't want to make this a big deal production," I tell him.

"That goes without saying. But you want to do it right, don't you?"

I'm nodding my head and sighing. "Yes, of course."

"And there's *other* stuff. We also have to find out if Hannah's got a hard stop worked into her next contract. I read about her thing with Peter Bart at Paramount; her next picture, you know what I mean? They're going to want to be guaranteed Hannah's there for the first day of shooting." He's looking at the glum expression on my face. "Look, I've got a woman who can do costume and makeup both. That's a big savings. And she's wonderful. I can get Boswell to do payroll. They owe me a favor. We'll try to duck around the Teamsters. I know a guy with a warehouse in Reseda we can use for the things we can't grab on the street and shoot at my sister's house, et cetera, et cetera. I can get us a sweet deal on the camera package, but …"

He sighs, picks up his cigar out of the amber ashtray and rolls it meditatively between a thumb and forefinger. "Am I depressing you?"

"Yes, a little." I look at the pitiful expression on his face. Even if I weren't doing all this for my own reasons, I'd love to make it work, if only to do something nice for Lou. As millennials will say, he *thirsty*. He leans back precariously in his wobbly desk chair and I imagine him flipping backwards, head over heels, like Buster Keaton.

But he doesn't, and I feel a moment of optimism, not to mention gratitude that Lou has agreed to produce this … whatever it turns out to be.

"One more thing," says Lou. "Not sure why we haven't brought this up yet. Who're we going to get to direct this turkey?"

I smile at him and with both forefingers point at myself.

"Aw, Danny, you're not a director." He's been hoping I would change my mind on this.

"True enough, but neither are most directors. If we could afford one of the good ones, I'd be a happy guy. But we don't have time to sift through the chaff of the DGA—not for what we're willing to pay. And you know as well as I do how long it would take to seduce one of the first-rate guys."

What Lou doesn't know is that I have close to fifty years of experience watching directors direct. It's backbreaking work, but if you know the basics, doing a journeyman job of quarterbacking a film is not rocket science. Even so, never in my wildest dreams did I imagine myself a movie director. And now I *are* one.

Rue Lefanty sits down next to me on my front steps. It seems she's taken a liking to me.

"I asked you earlier if you live here," she says. "You said, 'I think so.' What does that mean?"

"Oh, I live here all right. My wife and I split up. I guess I was feeling uncertain about my future."

Rue furrows her brow as much as a young teenager can do that. It's complemented by a curl of the lip that must be ongoing with teenage girls since at least the signing of the Magna Carta.

"What school do you go to?" I ask. For some reason, this girl gives me an awkward feeling of being confronted.

"I'm an autodidact."

"You don't go to school?"

"Right."

"What do your parents do?"

"My dad travels."

"I see. Your mom?"

"She's not around much either."

"So, who homeschools you?"

"Nobody. I told you, I'm an autodidact. I learn on my own."

"What do you learn?"

"Oh, lotsa things. I talk to people. I learn from them. I'm talking to you, learning from you."

"I doubt if you're going to learn much from *me*." What a strange kid this is. She doesn't appear to be uncared for, but I wonder who does look after her. "How old are you?" I say.

"Fourteen, the last I checked."

"Well, you've learned how to be a smart-ass."

She grins. "Yeah, I think I'm coming along okay on that. I may go into comedy; you know, those smart-ass women who act all wiser than they could possibly be, but they try to make you think that's how they are all the time. As if they get up out of bed every day all hip and have something clever to say about their kitchen and their breakfast and their funny-looking husband. That's who I want to be."

"I think you're well on your way."

I see someone approaching us on foot, jogging up the east side of Benedict. Noticing my gaze, Rue peers back over her shoulder.

"That guy's more than just out for a jog," I say. "Look at him, he's *flying*." The man doesn't even glance in our direction as he comes even with us. "He's going to have a heart attack."

Rue shrugs. "He's a young man. Young people don't usually get heart attacks from running, do they? They get tired, but big deal."

The man continues north. "Look at him though; he *blew* by us."

She shrugs again. "Back to you," she says. "Right now the class is studying you. You say you're uncertain about your future. Isn't everybody?"

She is indeed studying me. I wonder what she's thinking.

"So, tell me something about yourself," she says. "And I don't mean some movie star crap."

"Okay. My life was going along pretty well and then I met this cheeky kid."

"But you like me, don't you?"

I grin at her. "Yes, I like you. ... Okay, well, I'm not sure, but maybe what I'm doing is ... living from day to day, hoping to ..."

"To what?"

"I don't know ... find the love of my life maybe ... eventually, of course. I just got divorced."

"You could marry me in a few years if you don't find this love of your life before then. You could wait until I grow up. I mean, maybe fate is at work and it turns out *I'm* the love of your life."

"I'm twice as old as you are."

"Who cares? There's fifteen, twenty years difference in lots of marriages."

"Hey, we're studying me, remember? I've got to figure myself out before I make actual marriage plans again—especially marriage plans to little girls thirteen years younger than I am."

"I could start wearing makeup," she says. "That way you could get an idea what kind of a lady I'll turn into." She flashes a playful smile. "But no funny business till I'm sixteen. Got it?"

"Got it."

"Then I could begin by driving you places, and if you drink too much like almost every other grownup I ever knew, I can pick you up and get you home safe. So, tell me something else about yourself—and no movie star junk."

"Listen," I say, "maybe I can be a better learning tool for you if you try to learn from me, not about me. Maybe you can find out something about *you* from me. You could tell me anything you'd like to about yourself and find out if I know anything useful to you. Pretend I'm your therapist—a trainee."

She frowns. "What could you tell me about myself?"

"Okay. Well, for example, you're fourteen. Have you ever been in love?"

Her frown deepens. She looks off at the hills rising on the east side of Benedict Canyon. She takes me in again. "I want to say no because I don't like him anymore, but I was … kinda. I don't ever want to be again. It was awful. In fact, I don't want to think about it. Why do you ask me that?"

"Was it wonderful? While it was happening?"

She glares at me and lifts her shoulders, indicating maybe it wasn't *too* bad. "But I hate him." Now she regards me with what feels like a flash of adult perception. It's an unexpected moment of something like mutual empathy.

"I'm sorry," I say.

She lifts her chin. "It's okay. Next time, I'm going to get myself an older man." She smiles at me. "This is my rueful smile."

"I'd call it more of a wry smirk. The right guy will be lucky enough to fall in love with you one day."

"I wonder what it's like …"

"What?"

"I don't know. I guess I was wondering what it would be like to be a married grown-up … woman … in a happy marriage—not like yours."

I'd like to give her an honest answer to that. "Of course, I don't know this firsthand," I say, "but I've seen a few good marriages." She's watching me with a fixed look, paying close attention. "I think when you're part of an older couple and you're both in love, it's hard for younger people to understand …" I'm aware of what I'm saying; it feels odd saying it to this girl, but that doesn't stop me. "There are things that go on in ... mature relationships that most young people don't recognize; it's hard to imagine when you're younger. It's painful for ... older people too—I would *imagine*—as painful as it is when you're young and in love. When you're older and in love, the thought of losing it is agonizing. You must know or at least be able to imagine what I mean."

She is studying me.

"And you can't picture the world without that other person; that's something indescribable. You've heard about an elderly husband or wife dying, and a lot of times, you find out that the other one goes soon afterward. It's not only because it isn't as much fun as it used to be; it's because—at least in some cases—their best possible world has vanished. Even though getting old is not a bed of roses." She's gazing straight into my eyes. "You're smart. You must understand what I mean; they have wrinkles, and aches and pains, and all the rest of it." This has started to feel ... uncalled for, saying this to this kid, but she's listening intently to me, and anyway she doesn't feel like a kid. "You don't have to worry about that—you're young. But with an old couple, their loved one is still young and beautiful to them, and you can't bear the thought of her going to heaven ... or wherever ... without you—or you going first might be even worse because you'd feel like you were leaving her alone and lonely. And I think especially if you don't believe in heaven, or don't feel that hopeful ... thing about it, non-existence can seem to be the ... best choice."

Still gazing straight into my eyes, Rue says, "I'm surprised you got divorced." Oddly, her facial expressions are reminding me of someone.

"It *can* take a long time to grow up." Caught in her stare, I wonder again what she's thinking and why I'm telling her all this. She's interested; I guess that's enough. "Young people see an older couple holding hands and they say, 'Isn't that sweet and cute.' But that's not what it is. It's tender and deep. It's grown into real love. And if you're lucky enough to find it, you are lucky indeed."

Rue flashes what I think of as an old soul smile. "Okay, maybe I'm convinced," she says. "So for you, what you need to do is get over yourself, right? All that blowing your actor horn stuff, and being a big star and everything. How do we get rid of that?"

"The thought of changing my path worries me," I tell her. "The thought of *not* changing my path worries me."

She frowns and mulls this over. "Do you have any kids?"

"Why do you ask that?"

"Felt like it."

"Mm–hmm. Well, maybe, maybe not."

She grins at me.

"And you can write in your autodidact book that smart-assery isn't the best learning tool in the world," I say.

"Neither is talking to people like a politician."

"God, you're precocious."

"I think at fourteen it's too late for precocious."

"How about cheeky? Is cheeky okay?"

"Can't we just call me smart?" she says. "Smart, but still young."

"That's a lucky thing to be."

She reaches her arms up and out, stretching. "All right, if I can't marry you, maybe I can junk my parents—they aren't around enough to matter anyway—and be your kid." On my look, she says, "You'd be a young father, but who cares? Come on, it'd be fun. You could give me advice and so on. You know, *Father Knows Best.*"

"How do you know about that?"

She looks at me like I just fell off the moon. "Reruns." She spreads her arms again, palms up, says, "See ya," and scampers up the hill.

The mockingbird announces he's back and shows me his Navajo underwings.

If God is in everything, this mockingbird is ... the Deity. If so, he is presently working on His mockingbird-doing-a-blue-jay impression. Or is that a frog? It sounds a little like a frog too. But He's God; He's already a frog if that's His pleasure. He doesn't have to impersonate one.

If I lived in Valley Glen in the twenty-first century, I'd go inside and Google whether mockingbirds do frog impersonations ... or talk to actors. I've never run into any frogs in LA—except maybe a television producer or two.

I feel scattered this afternoon. I've had atrial fibrillation (an erratic heartbeat, which will come to be known as A-fib in years to come) for a long time now. I'm not sure exactly when I developed it, but as I got to be sixty and over, I remember it depleted my energy sometimes, not completely and not that often; it was just an occasional bother. It's not uncommon. About one in ten people over the age of seventy have it. Lots of young people have it too. The odd thing is I seem to have brought it back with me, kind of like my clothing, my skin, and my SpyGuy. Sometimes I get more tired than a twenty-seven-year-old should get.

I imagine my mockingbird, as God, peering down at His divine Universe as I—a part of His Universe and Him too, I'm told—try to prevent any further interior slippage, or for that matter, the whole cosmos from skidding out of chaos into oblivion.

I sit at the kitchen table, pick up a pencil and legal pad, and try to come up with anything in my narrative that may have possible cinematic substance, but I'm not having much luck. It's hard to make cinematic sense out of a story that makes no sense in the first place.

I spent most of the first half of my life guided by my pitiful bleeding ego, which the spiritual people tell me, until I want to stab them in the forehead, is not an ideal way to live. I know the world, for the most part, thinks the spiritual people are nuts, but after a lifetime of watching, it looks to me as if the *world* is nuts. We keep on doing awful things, and awful things keep being thrust back at us—like what blew wide open in 2020, the year before this adventure began. All the sages in our planet's history continue to say, "As you sew, so shall you reap." Isn't that what keeps happening to us with numbing regularity?

The sages say we're interconnected and need to have faith that we are—that if we do that, and try hard enough, we can move mountains, and do it to constructive, worthwhile ends, nipping in the bud any more wars, plagues, and famines.

Just on the gambling chance that's true, who's crazy—the people who urge life, love, wisdom, intelligence, peace, creativity, kindness, forgiveness, beauty, and joy, or those who squinch their eyes, stamp their feet, and tell us that all men are *not* created equal?

If faith does work—*and for sure, nobody has proved that it doesn't*—what could it hurt to give it a shot, to try to think more along positive lines? For example, we could tell ourselves we are not bound by yesterday's mistakes, that if we want something within the laws of nature, which we now know are far more expansive than we ever imagined, we can have it.

I hear Sam's voice from the other room: "Come to bed, darling." I picture a faint smile playing at the corners of her mouth. "You're giving a lecture, and nobody but me can hear you."

"I'm grateful for that," I say. "I thank God every day that you're in the other room, waiting for me."

"Does God ever say you're welcome?"

But now I'm angry at her for not actually being there. Worse, she's gone all smarty-pants. The Samantha I've constructed to deliver myself from solitude is not the real one. She's like the me I'm trying to escape. I've said that Sam's presence, even a sketchy facsimile is good enough. That's a lie. I need to feel her heart beat. My version is not the real Samantha. It's like symbolic logic. The symbols are there to assist you in getting to the point. It's the method, the mechanism, not the real thing.

"But I'm only here because I love you, Danny."

And that's all it takes. A fuzzy impersonation of his beloved turns out to be good enough to forgive the impersonator his wishful dreaming.

16

~

MAKING BEAUTY

P atricia sits in her swivel desk chair, facing me. We're in her office in Beverly Hills. There is a small waiting room outside. I'm sitting at one end of a plain but fairly comfortable couch. It looks like it was bought at a wholesale office furniture store. Same with Patricia's desk. This psychologist's office has been put together to say as little as possible about anything, especially the therapist.

We're having a moment of silence. I've had a lot of those with Patricia. Finally she says, "You say your career crashed. Why do you think that happened?"

"I wasn't happy."

"Why?"

"I'm not sure. It felt like … It felt like my career was more important than … being happy. It got to be that the things I was doing within the … cage of my career didn't make me feel good. What the career was about was okay. And I loved the creative part. I didn't even mind the showbiz cage the career was in. It's not show business itself, it's the tricks and somersaults they make you do—the way *they* want you to do them. That's got to be true with almost anyone who works as hired help. That kind of stuff can begin to give you the creeps. I guess if I'd been one of the ones on top of the pyramid, that might have been okay. But there's an albatross in that too. I knew a handful of those people. Nearly all of them live in a glass cage. That's creepy."

"So, what did you do?"

"Most people, if they're wage earners, they've got to do their jobs. I did that. But after a while, I couldn't stop thinking about the sort of relentless competitiveness in the Hollywood air. I hated that more than the somersaults. One day I began to wonder what it would be like if I concentrated more on trying to be happy and maybe not worry so much about money, career status, and all that. Then I met Sam. … I'm not sure which came first."

"And you couldn't manage to be happy and competitive at the same time?"

She expects me to think about this before I answer, but after a lifetime of watching myself in and out of show business, I don't need to. "There's a kind of meanness that goes with the never-ending competition. And it's almost all competing—most of it is a relentless dog-eat-dog aggressiveness. Maybe that's okay when you're a young dog and you love fighting and snarling and tumbling around, nipping at all the other puppies. But there comes a time when you just want to take the sun, lick your wounds— maybe even other people's wounds— because you know what it feels like to be wounded, and you don't want to wound even one more dog."

I look at her for a while, unable to think of any more to say on this subject. I remember this is not like normal conversation. Most of the time, she doesn't respond after I've unburdened myself. She's watching me. It doesn't make me feel uncomfortable the way it used to, so I open my mouth again, curious myself, to see what will come out next.

"There's a line that's said in theater and acting and movies before you start to work: 'Let's go make beauty.' It's half ironic. It comes from a good place, and it's a sweet ideal, to make beauty—but that prompting, that charge to 'go make beauty' contains the inference that we live in a world that's not already beautiful. And even with all the slings and arrows that go along with being alive—loss, sickness, death, a thousand forms of arrogance and cruelty, all the bad stuff—I began to want to spend every bit of the rest of my time enjoying my ... existence. I wanted to breathe. And along the way, I discovered Sam and began to see generosity in her and possibilities I'd never dreamed of. And I'm not putting down movies, theater, or music or all the best of it. At its best, it's wonderful, it's delirious sunshine-over-a-green-meadow sublime. But it's also ten thousand miles away from show business. And show 'business' is still that jumble of snarling dogs. And once I'd lived in this 'new' world I'd never understood I was already in, the last thing I wanted to do was go back to 'showbiz.' I mean, some people handle it fine; many of them have a sense of proportion. They know how to assign real values to real things, how to separate joy and enthusiasm from foolishness."

"But isn't everything show business in a way?" she says. "Business, politics, the majority of the things people have to do to make a living?"

"Are you giving a speech or asking a question?"

"I figured you were giving a speech; you wouldn't mind if I gave a little one."

I can't tell her she's wrong. "Yeah, well ... the speech I was giving was at least one part bullshit anyway. It feels like there's no ass I wouldn't kiss to play a role I really wanted to play."

She smiles.

"Okay," I say. "I've got something that'll interest you. The day after I arrived here … You know what I'm talking about, right?"

Her eyebrows lift, giving me a grudging go-ahead.

"I was in Beverly Hills, parked on the street. I saw that the Beverly Theatre was showing a revival of *Adam's Rib*, an old Tracy/Hepburn film. Something about it seemed wrong."

"What was that?"

"I don't mean the movie. I mean the marquee I saw from probably a little less than hundred yards away as I was sitting in my car. The title of the movie was in large block letters. The stars were billed above that. There wasn't room to place the names of the two of them on one line, so, Spencer Tracy, who was always billed first, was listed SPENCER, then beneath that, TRACY. SPENCER took up two more spaces than TRACY, right underneath it.

"On the right side, also above the title, I saw HEPBURN directly beneath her first name. But her first name, KATHARINE, should have been, like Tracy's, two spaces longer than her last name under it, but it wasn't, it was shorter. I figured maybe they'd run out of the necessary letters and billed her as Kate or something. I didn't think much about it at the time."

"What are you saying?"

"Several nights after that, I figured out what I'd *really* seen. The Beverly Theatre was advertising their current feature, a revival of *Adam's Rib*, starring Tracy and Hepburn, but they were advertising it with the wrong Hepburn. The marquee clearly said: Spencer Tracy and *Audrey* Hepburn in *Adam's Rib*.

"Why would they … How can you be sure?"

"Her last name was longer than her first. On the day it happened, I saw what I expected to see. Later, I realized what I'd actually seen. I saw the name *Audrey* where I should have seen *Katharine*. It's the truth. I *saw* the name Audrey."

"But you said you were almost a hundred yards away."

I stand up and look out her window. "I can read the license plate on the Volvo next to that driveway. "It's MRY4372." I sit down again. "It's a big marquee. I *saw* the name Audrey. I know I did."

"But you're remembering it. You know memory is unreliable." She shakes her head. "It was a mistake of some kind."

"I don't think so. Those women are two of the biggest stars in the history of Hollywood. Somebody would have caught that mistake the same day. Anyway, that theater is about a mile from here. I passed it on the way to see you today. I stopped and asked the woman in the ticket booth when *Adam's Rib* had closed. She was young, about my age. She didn't know what I was talking about, said she'd never heard of *Adam's Rib*. I asked her how long she'd been working there. She said a year and a half. I told her I'd seen *Adam's Rib* on the marquee … very recently. She told me I must be thinking of some other theater, that they'd been playing *The Godfather Part II* for the past ten weeks. Can you imagine any way to account for this, for *any* of this?"

"Yes, I can," she says. "The woman in the ticket booth is mistaken. Or you were mistaken about what you thought you remembered. There is some reasonable explanation."

I don't respond to her. I know what I saw. I also know I sound crazy again. Maybe I didn't see what I thought I saw.

"Okay, how about this?" I say. "When I was your patient the first time, I had, a few years before that, made my … debut movie performance. It was called *I'll Live Till I Die*. Over forty-seven years later, before the experience I related to you of finding myself *tossed* back in time, I saw a revival of that movie. There was an aerial shot in the original version. It was of Benedict Canyon and the house I later bought and lived in until shortly before I started to see you—the first time." She's watching me, unblinking. "When I see that aerial shot years later, in 2021, my house on Benedict Canyon will not be in the film. The aerial shot will still be there, but where my house had been previously, *and where it is NOW*, there will be nothing but trees and weeds. I am not exaggerating or stretching the truth. I am not making any of this up. I sat through that damned movie almost three times. The house I lived in had disappeared. Do you have any … can you imagine any possible explanation? I ask because I'm living in that same house right now."

Patricia is looking at her hands.

"I've read just a little bit about what the quantum … people have postulated." … German physicist Max Born talked about probability waves in 1926. According to him and lots of physicists, that means a single particle can exist in multiple locations at the same time. A lot of those people have said … or *will* say that whether we know it or not, mankind has been thrust onto a new playing field and that a whole lot of things are going to end up—not until this knowledge has been put to use—being way less predictable than we've always thought. … So let me ask you again, do you have any explanation for the disappearance, and apparent reappearance, of my house?"

She blinks for a few seconds, thinking. Finally she says, with a tiny shrug, "Parallel universes?"

I laugh. "That's got to be it. So, what's the next step? You ship me off to Camarillo?" (That's a mental health institution between Los Angeles and Oxnard.)

"Afraid not. You've got to be way nuttier than living in a parallel universe to get into Camarillo."

"And I don't suppose we should talk about *Adam's Rib* anymore."

"Let's not." She looks at the small clock she always keeps facing her on her desk. "I'm afraid our time is up."

"Will you keep seeing me?"

"Yes, I will. Shall we do the same time next week?"

"No. Sooner," I say. "I need help now."

She studies me, then looks at her appointment book. "I can make an opening tomorrow at eleven."

"I'll be here."

My next call to Zeke was twenty-four hours after our second conversation. He didn't answer the phone. Instead, I was greeted after three rings by the flat, Upper Midwest intonations of an operator who asked me, "What number did you call, please?" I told her and she informed me there was no such line in service; in fact, the area code I'd called didn't exist.

I tried again. Different operator—out of Atlanta I'd guess, judging by the musicality and soft Rs of her speech—same result.

For a while, I was depressed. But single states of mind are not hanging around long lately, and I don't know what the rules are for intertemporal telephone calls. I'll try him later.

Back to my screenplay. I think the events it portrays will have to be as they happened. I will play myself in the film—if it gets made. As with any film project, no one could predict what its chances are for success.

I get up, walk from my office into my darkened bedroom, and lie down.

You have to presume with a story like this that it's a long shot at best, but you don't know that for sure. It'll never be a blockbuster, but that's not my concern; my concern is what I hope to see out of this project.

"A miracle," says Sam again in the other room in the back of my mind.

That a film ever gets made is a miracle. That a film propels an actor to great success is uncommon. That a film propels an actor forty-seven years into the future is probably—although I can't say anything for sure—unprecedented.

I should make it clear that *I do not truly expect to do this* any-more than in an allegorical or some kind of subconscious way—the same kind of way that when I wake up (I pray) from all this, I may understand that my original trip here, the one after the night I did all those drugs, was on another level of consciousness, somehow metaphorical and not an actual journey through time. Still, as Sam says, I am looking for a miracle—to the best of my extremely limited knowledge, unprecedented.

I ask her, "Can a miracle be metaphorical and still be a miracle?"

No response.

Anyway, unprecedented things happen all the time. They are happening, right now, to me and around me. I reach over, find the cord for my lamp on the bedside table and switch it on. The moment I see the room I'm lying in, I feel cold. I hold my arm in front of me, crooked at the elbow. There is no fall-ing flesh on my forearm next to my bicep. I'd gotten used to some of the signs of age. It's not that I wasn't aware of them, but that I'd come to a time in my life when I rarely thought about such things. I didn't care. I think it's possible that when you feel loved, aside from periodic anxieties about losing that love, there is little to worry about. When you're loved, you live forever. Or am I crazy?

"Very," says Sam. I picture her at the dining room table, working at her computer. It's late at night. I'm ready for her to come to bed and read to me but so far, except for shouting "A miracle" and "Very" at me, she's ignoring me. Eventually though, she'll turn off her computer, come into the bedroom, get her pajamas, go into the bathroom, change into them, brush her teeth and the rest, come back into our room to her side of the bed, get in, and ask me for the book.

I'll hand it to her. I think we're still somewhere near the end of *The Secret Garden.* We'll talk a while, then she'll start to read from where we left off last time.

And that is—although of course it isn't fleshed out yet—the essence and soul of the story for my movie. The only thing I need to finesse is how to make sure I'm in the right bedroom at the right time.

"You chose the right one the last time," says Sam. "Do it again."

"How?"

"I can't answer that. The ball's in your court." I know she's smiling at me. "Go ahead, take a swing at it."

"Okay. Einstein said, '*Time is not at all what it seems to be. It is not flowing in one direction, and the future exists simultaneously with the past.*' "

"Yes? And so?"

"I don't know. It felt like it might be useful. Gotta keep trying."

"Try again. Try better."

"Circumstances that seem wrong can be altered," I say tentatively. "Old thought patterns, like politicians who've been elected too many times and hate to be disagreed with, or perhaps weren't qualified for the work in the first place, can be … voted out of office. I don't know how it's going to happen, but I don't know how anything is going to happen. Who can say how the unseen becomes the seen, or how the disincarnate—you, for example—can take form … pull into the driveway, come into the house, and ask me to go outside and help you carry the groceries in?"

"But who do you get to help *you, now*?" she says. "How about our spiritual readings? Can you think of anything there you can use?"

"Maybe. But it also seems likely, in my second 1974, that anything that offers a simple explanation is going turn out to be a booby trap."

She's gone again. I can feel it. I remove the yellow pad from my chest and toss it and my pencil onto the floor next to me.

I remember a story about a trapper in Alaska. Out in the deep wilderness, he finds himself lost and alone, without food or drink or any hope of survival. He's an atheist, but thinks "what the hell" and gives prayer a try.

Later, in a tavern, he tells the bartender that he does not believe in a God who answers prayers. He tells the bartender his story. He says, "I prayed and prayed and God did not lift a finger to help me."

The bartender says, "But you're here, aren't you?"

The trapper replies, "Yeah, but I wouldn't be if that fucking Eskimo hadn't happened by."

I don't know where or when, but I believe my Eskimo is on his way.

I'm in the next morning's eleven o'clock session with Patricia. Again, I'm feeling scattered.

Patricia's eyes are closed. Her head is bent forward and both hands are steepled together, the tips of her middle fingers touching the tip of her nose. She says, "Describe Samantha for me."

"You mean what she looks like?"

"No, I don't need to know that, unless you want to tell me. I assume you like the way she looks." I nod. "I mean, tell me a little about who she is. I'd like to know."

"I married her on a Saturday afternoon a couple of years after we'd met. It was a little chapel in Santa Monica, the Ivy Cottage. I saw her ... glow when I looked over at ... my ..." The memory of it stops me. "... *fiancée* across the aisle from me, facing the nice middle-aged woman who was about to marry us.

"It was an ordinary event—a high point in a person's life, but still an everyday happening. But now this beautiful girl/woman I was marrying was bathed in light, as if there were a string of skylights in the ceiling of the Ivy Cottage, or thousands of stars all focused on her. She was lit from without and within for all of that day and night. And that was the second time I knew for sure that whatever happened in our future, I had come home."

"What was the first time?"

"It was a while after we met. She came up a flight of stairs, and I remember it was as if she was glowing, but at the same time I could see beneath the surface of her, and I realized the more deeply I looked into her the lovelier she was. It's hard to know where to begin to tell you what I'd like to tell you about her. With Samantha I could say something foolish or ... any stupid thing that came out of my mouth and she never made me feel humiliated. She never makes me feel small." I look into Patricia's eyes for several seconds. Neither of us blink. "The first time in therapy with you, I told you something—I don't remember what—but it was something embarrassing, *humiliating*, and I saw in your eyes ... *a compassion* that's still frozen in my memory, a lifetime later. Sam has that too. She wouldn't begin to know *how* to humiliate anybody; she feels contempt for nothing."

I stroke my chin several times and wonder if I look like Pontius Pilate. "With her, I stopped being as temperamental as I used to be. It was a *little* tricky at the beginning, but after a while I understood, and have ever since, that she ... doesn't *judge* me. And after a while, it got so that I wasn't judging her either. Or other people, or even *myself*—well, as much as I used to anyway. So I guess I've gotten to be ... nicer than I was before Sam.

"We say 'I love you' or 'Love you' almost every time we say goodbye on the phone. It's gotten to be a habit; we say it a lot—with cell phones and everything. ..." (I explain to Patricia about cell phones, which causes her to blink several times.) "I guess we say 'Love you' a few times a day—so much so, that it's almost my default way to say goodbye. Once in a while, I've said 'I love you' to people I wouldn't ordinarily say I love you to. And I think sometimes they're a little lost for words. Most people manage to take it in stride ... I think, but it must seem a tiny bit odd—for example, when I tell the plumber I love him.

"Sometimes I've complained about the way she's done something or not done it and she says, 'You'll be sorry when I'm dead and in the bury hole.' That's not funny, now that we're older. The thought of all of a sudden not having the one who makes your life most livable is as far from funny as you can get."

I'm aware of Patricia staring at me.

"And even though I've been with her all these years—and this is ... *odd* to me—I still feel like I'm drifting up. Samantha became a definition for me of something that ... lifted me above whatever low point I'd allowed myself to sink to. I'd watch her sleep or cook or read or do anything, anything at all. And it didn't matter what angle or lighting I was seeing her from or in.

Every snapshot of her was instantly a ..." I stop myself. "I understand this might be a little cloying to you ..."

Her expression doesn't change.

"And it's not *always* milk and honey, martinis and Chardonnay with Samantha," I say. "We have both, on more than one occasion, stalked out to the car, gotten in, and driven off. I've had it with her, or she's had it with me. We can't take any more. Each of us has had one version or another of driving down to the end of the block, or perhaps even as far as the next community away—within the San Fernando Valley—to Studio City or Encino.

"Then ... we've both had the experience of pulling over to the side of the road and thinking, 'Yeah, but where am I going to go now? I'm not happy anywhere other than at home with that lousy bitch/bastard.'

"At that point, what we're already feeling sets in. It's an unnamable sadness at being without the other one. We start feeling a little sniffly. But then I think, yeah, but how do I go back without feeling like a jerk? Ah! I know. I'll go to Walgreens, buy her a bouquet of flowers and maybe her favorite candy bar.

"And then I do, and I take it home to her. Usually, I apologize for being such an overbearing prick. Then she says, 'How do you put up with me?' And I tell her it's easy. On the occasions when one or both of us has simply been snarky, but not to the point of causing the other to drive away, we soon find the right moment to reach over and pet the other one, until the other one feels forgiving—sometimes we stick our tongues out at each other. And then it's all over. None of these tiffs ever last more than a few minutes; the longest can go an hour and a half or two.

"And then we make up—which, now that I think about it, is so much fun that the other part doesn't seem so bad.".

Neither Patricia nor I say a word for another long moment.

"And then sometimes I'll look at her when she's asleep and find myself lost in the sheer perfection of her—the shape of her nose, the way her ears stick out very slightly at the tops, like an elf's ears. There is nothing about her that is not exactly as it should be. I *know* that's crazy, but no one could convince me that I'm wrong. She's more than my dream come true; she is what God had in mind when he said, 'And now I think I'll make a woman.'"

"Jesus."

"Yeah, I don't blame you. Maybe some people—maybe a lot of people, I don't know—understand this, but I never did before. I didn't know that love is a kind of religion. If you truly love one person, it *can* spread out and you can find yourself loving life, learning to love the entire world. … Well anyway, most of it."

Patricia is looking at me with a countenance I remember well. I don't even have to see that to feel what's underneath it after all the time I've spent with her. She's using her professional demeanor to disguise … something like warmth. You go into therapy and you're like any two human beings who are honing in on the same wavelength. There's often—or there should be—an intimate understanding that develops between you that supersedes the hierarchy between doctor and patient, expert and neophyte. We are two people. She doesn't know everything that's going on inside me, and I know only a limited bit of what's going on with her. She has intuition about me; that's her profession. But also, I have intuition about her—not because I have anything like her understanding, but because I'm a sometimes-insightful human, same as her. In this case, I'm not the same one who came to her a lifetime ago. I benefited from the first time with her, and also from the time I spent growing old with Sam, letting resentments—most of them extremely petty—dissolve behind me, along with most of my fear, and a great deal of my anger. Corny as it sounds, I've found the place where I'm happy. It's allowed me to drift up toward what was always within me: the better part of myself.

I say, "Sam is straightforward in kind of the way you are. She doesn't make leading-me-on noises." I love that about Patricia too. "That's one of the things about her," I say. "She lets me fill in the gaps, or sometimes we just let the gaps happen. I'd come to expect that in therapy, from you. But people in conversation so often—without even knowing they're doing it—try to lead you to where they want you to go, or they try to coerce you to go there. And sometimes you go there just to please them. Then the relationship gets off-kilter, turns into a fraudulent, volatile manacle of interdependence because one person is trying to steer the other, and then that begins to work both ways and the whole thing gets unhealthy. Sam never tries to steer me. She lets me go where I want. Or if I don't know where I want to go, she gives me the space and time to let me figure it out—even if I don't do that until mid-sentence on my way to where I think I want to get to. So the whole thing has the space to get honest and then more so. There's a lack of pressure to make up stuff to fill uncomfortable pauses."

Patricia remains entirely still, listening.

"And so I began to see her letting me learn by finding out where I wanted to go, or what I was trying to learn from the better part of myself, not from words I mouthed to keep the relationship afloat."

Patricia says nothing, and my hunch is she has no wisdom to pass on to me, at least for now; she's not trying to lead me any-where. She continues watching me.

Finally, she looks at her clock and says she'll see me at eleven the morning after tomorrow.

Driving home, I think of something I'd thought of saying to Patricia when I was talking about my marriage to Sam having the occasional sticky patch. I didn't want to talk about the coronavirus and the upside-down culture, because to whatever extent she's managing to suspend her disbelief and go along with my insanity, I didn't want to cast any kind of shadow over the future. If I'd been at all able to describe the atmosphere enshrouding that time, I think it might have made her unhappy. The sixties and seventies had unquestionable downsides, but they were also a time of hope and positive change. I didn't have the heart to tell her about 2020, in many ways one of the saddest years since the World War II era.

Sam and I got along beautifully during the COVID-19 quarantine, but not during every moment of it. One day, early on, we had a disagreement over something trivial (always the case). I got in the car and drove around for a while, then came back to our neighborhood. I parked a few blocks away from our house, next to the Valley College athletic stadium. Not many people were out; it was late afternoon on a quarantine Saturday. With mask in hand in case I got close to somebody, I walked through the gate and stood as near as I could to the football field. The yard lines were marked, the goalposts in place at both ends of the field.

I wasn't thinking about Sam; I'd slipped into my old habit of feeling sorry for myself. I couldn't have told you what I was sorry for myself about. I hadn't worked that out. What I did know was that I was feeling the blues and hadn't yet even begun to consider how I might come out the other side of them. I was reveling in my blues. Like the old days, I'd once again made my own bed, badly—and some pigheaded part of me was enjoying lying there on that nasty, lumpy mattress. I was having fun being miserable.

A little time passed, and the truly miserable part of being miserable began to set in. I had not yet figured out, after the 97,000[th] time of going through this, that when I make my bed badly, I have two choices: lie in the stupid lumpy thing the way it is or get up and remake the motherfucker.

Looking out at the football field, I remembered what it felt like to be a boy, running out onto that field, leaping as high as I could and catching—or simply trying to catch—a football. I could smell the grass. (Although it was a sense memory—the Valley College football field has artificial turf.) I felt good and young. Deep inside me, I had a flash of that exhilarating, youthful immortal feeling.

It was a late afternoon. My telephone sounded an emergency alert. It was telling me that a curfew had been called by the mayor of Los Angeles. A Minneapolis policeman had murdered a black man named George Floyd, and people were rioting, looting, and protesting all around the country, especially in big cities.

I drove home. Sam knew what was happening. Neither of us could remember what our argument had been about.

17

THE RED LANTERN INN

I meet Valory Valentine at the Red Lantern at three thirty in the afternoon. Maybe it was only coincidence that she chose the same restaurant where Sam and I had our first date.

Still, why did she say she knew it would have meaning to me?

The Red Lantern is one of the most popular restaurants in this part of the San Fernando Valley. Founded by Joe Capra, Frank's nephew, in 1956, it has an old Hollywood feel to it. Right now, in the middle of the afternoon, midway between lunch and dinner, it's doing brisk enough business to keep the staff well occupied.

I tell the slim, pretty girl at the reception podium that I'm meeting a friend. The girl smiles at me in a flirtatious way I haven't experienced for a long time, hands me a menu, and leads me into the wood-paneled restaurant. It's darker at this time of day than I would have expected. The booths are as I remember them, covered with shiny red leather. The receptionist leads me to one that could accommodate five people. It's opposite a wide aisle across from the bar.

Valory is seated facing the bar but looking at me as I approach. She smiles warmly, apparently happy to see me.

I sit on the booth's semi-circular bench. I'm gripped by déjà vu. The booth's red leather has a soft, buttery feel to it. I slide around toward her, but not too close.

"What made you choose this place?"

"I like it here," she says. "And I thought you would."

"I know, you told me over the phone. What did you mean by that?"

She takes a sip from the Dubonnet with a twist, half finished, in front of her. It feels as if she has no immediate intention to answer my question. She smiles, a distracted Mona Lisa, and nods, looking over my shoulder.

"Would you like a drink?" she says.

"Sorry, I didn't see you," I say to a tall, silver-haired waiter with bushy white eyebrows and the dark feel of a gypsy, made darker by an aura of an indentured servant with no hope of living long enough to be granted freedom. He's scowling at me.

"I don't usually drink during the day," I say with a social unease I don't remember feeling for half a lifetime. "I guess I'll have a Guinness, if you've got that."

"Draft or bottle." It's not a question, kind of a foreshadowing.

"Draft," I say. He's already heading back to the bar.

I look at Valory. It floods my mind again how weird this is; I'm in Sam's and my place with *another woman, a woman I'm squeamishly attracted to.* I can't turn around and walk out. I can't *not* find out whatever she knows—if she knows anything.

"What did you mean when you said you've been praying for me?"

"Anything interesting happen since we spoke?" she says.

I frown. "Yes. Stanley Kubrick gave me some money."

"Oh?"

"I'm not positive why, but maybe he's just a kind man. My hopes had gotten built up. ... And, uh, he found out that I was trying to make my own movie, the low-budget thing I told you about. And he deposited ... uh ... He deposited $50,000 in my bank account. It looks like I am going to be able to make my film because of Stanley Kubrick's generosity."

"Guilt money?"

"Why do you say ... No! He didn't have to do that. He was in a position to be kind, and he was. Why am I telling you all this? I don't even know you."

"I'll tell you one thing about me," she says. "I'm the biggest supporter you have of your movie project."

"Really? Well ... thank you." My beer hasn't even been brought to me, but I'm feeling lightheaded. "To be honest, I don't know ... exactly what I'm doing here."

"I know that," she says, and changes the subject. "There's some political violence going on in Ireland. I think Kubrick is going to finish up the film in England, and I don't believe there is any way he's going to fire Ryan O'Neal."

"That's what *I* said."

She shrugs. "Then I guess you were right. It's a lucky thing you got your guilt money. Or maybe it wasn't only luck." She smiles, almost twinkles, then looks up at a painting of a sporting dog above the bar. "Do you have any pets?"

"What?"

"Pets. Do you have any?"

"No ... not at the moment."

"Good. I hate the pet industry. There are people starving in this world and the pet food and pet toy industry and all of that ... takes food out of starving people's mouths."

I can't think of a response to that. I had coffee with Lou Gefsky at Du-pars diner on Ventura Boulevard near Laurel before I came here. When I told him our angel was Stanley Kubrick, his mouth dropped open. "You're shitting me."

That caused me to think of my father; when something surprised or shocked me and I'd gone slack-jawed, he would often say, "Shut your mouth."

Lou and I both ignored our coffee and started to make plans to put our modest production on its feet.

Lou said, "Why the fuck would Stanley Kubrick give you $50,000?"

"Good question. I wish I had an answer. I suppose if I told you he wanted me to replace Ryan O'Neal in *Barry Lyndon* but changed his mind and decided to give me $50,000 instead, you'd find that hard to believe."

Lou stared at me.

"I dunno. Maybe he was trying to buy me off, so I wouldn't start a rumor that Stanley Kubrick gave serious thought to shooting his latest project through the kneecap."

Lou continued to look at me, disoriented, then put his palms to his temples and raked his fingers back through his hair as if he were doing an impression of a giddy celebutante. "It matters not to me who you had to do whatever to, to get the dough. I'm just glad you've got it."

I'm staring at Valory. "What did you mean you'd been praying for me?"

"Just that. And who knows? Maybe I influenced the money from Kubrick." She smiles and winks.

I try to renew my focus. "I don't understand how you know things there's no way for you to know," I say. "How? Would you please tell me?"

She seems to be thinking that over and I realize this strange woman, riddled with *Twilight Zone* vibes, is about to become the second person I've told my story to. I don't understand why this is so, but I think it is. "Is there anything you know that I should know too, that you haven't mentioned?"

She smiles as if she's privy to some inside joke about me. Or maybe she's hit my paranoia button. "Again with the questions, like our phone conversation. Why are you so interested in me and what I know? You're not like most actors."

"Maybe I outgrew … whatever it is most actors are."

"You're too young to have outgrown it."

"Not exactly." Every instinct I have tells me I should be mistrustful of this woman. With Patricia, it's natural to tell her what's on my mind. With Valory, it feels as if I'm with Angela Lansbury in the first version of *The Manchurian Candidate*, and she's just asked me to take out a deck of cards and play solitaire until I draw the queen of diamonds. And when I inevitably do, I'll tell her everything, or do anything she wants me to.

"I've told my old therapist about a few things she was not prepared to hear," I say. "I was wondering if you might be … willing to hear them." Am I trying to seize her when-Mommy-tells-Raymond-to-play-solitaire moment?

"What do you mean your old therapist? Is the therapist old?"

"No, I mean my *used-to-be* therapist. I was … Never mind; maybe I'll explain it to you later. And also there's this girl …"

"Girl?"

I have no idea why I bring up Rue. "Yeah … yes. Well, there is another girl I'm sharing a few personal things with—I do not mean the same things I feel the urge to tell you. We've befriended each other, this girl and I, because she's … *there*, I guess. And she is a *girl*. She's fourteen years old. She lives up the street behind my Benedict Canyon house."

"I don't understand."

"I can't imagine why you would."

"No, no, I mean there is no one behind you except that music composer who lives in the house behind yours on Wilkie."

"What do you mean?"

"I mean look at your *Thomas Guide*. There is no other house but the one behind you on Wilkie Street. Wilkie is a one-house street. The only one who lives in that house is an eighty-year-old composer named Richard Eberly, who used to be under contract to MGM. And he doesn't have a daughter or a grand-daughter or a girl of any description living with him."

"No, no, Wilkie Street goes up into the hills behind my house."

She shakes her head. "Have you ever taken the trouble to walk up that street?" I shrug. "There is a house just behind you, then the little road we're talking about, Wilkie Street, curves around to the back of that house where there's a cul-de-sac. And that's it. No more Wilkie Street."

"But all of those streets that branch off Benedict wind up into the hills."

"Not Wilkie," she says. "Wilkie is a one-house street."

"Then how did the girl manage to be going that fast?"

"I beg your pardon?"

"Why would you know what's on Wilkie Street?"

"*Thomas Guide*," she says.

"Why would you find the one page in a *Thomas Guide* that has my address on it and look to see what surrounds my house? Why would you do that?"

She puts her index finger to her upper lip again and looks at me as if she's conducting a séance and trying to read my mind at the same time. "I was in your house. I was curious to see where you lived. I looked you up in my *Thomas Guide*. Nothing unusual in that."

"But ... how did you know an eighty-year-old composer lived in the house behind me?"

"Tad must have told me."

"Tad was doing some pretty fancy driving to be giving a guided tour of Benedict Canyon. Or is that why he stopped just north of my house?"

"I don't think so. I think he pulled over—it happened to be near your house—to get a Maalox out of the glove compartment. Tad has an acid stomach. He must have already known before that day that Mr. Eberly lived behind you. I'm sure he wasn't thinking about that anyway. When Tad's in his car, that's all that's on his mind, his car. Wouldn't matter what was coming out of his mouth."

There doesn't seem to be any point in trying to explain to this woman that I saw a teenage girl going faster on a skateboard than she could possibly have been traveling if she'd only begun from a cul-de-sac behind the composer's house. I smile lamely as our waiter approaches with my beer and sets it in front of me.

After I've watched him walk away, I find Valory gazing at me. "You were going to tell me something," she says.

I take a sizable gulp of beer, still trying to understand this urge I have to spill my guts to her. She seems to know things other people don't. "What I was saying is that you're about to become the second woman I tell my story to—if you care to listen."

"Of course I'll listen."

Again, I feel as helpless as the unwitting communist pawn "Raymond" (Laurence Harvey) in *The Manchurian Candidate*. "This is the second time I've lived through the year 1974," I say. "I've been here before. Nixon is still president, right? Don't ask me why I say that. ... I'm ... double-checking. I haven't been watching the news because ... I'm out of the habit." (I don't add that in the time I came from, it had gotten depressing to watch the ebbing away of "civilized news," that jackals—despite a couple of seeming recent upticks in the exercise of human decency—are both making and reporting it, and that, to some people, certain words like "unscrupulous" and "shameless" are practically compliments.)

She blinks. "It looks like he's in a lot of trouble, but so far, Nixon is still president."

"I'm sorry, what is the date today? I ... lose track lately."

"It's April 17, 1974. What do you mean, you've been here before?"

And I tell her: "I have lived until the year 2021, forty-seven years from now. I got married for a second time. I met a woman named Samantha on a blind date. We lived together for two years, then we got married. I've been married to her ever since." I cover my mouth and Edvard Munch's *The Scream* flutters through my mind, an oscillating mocking version, looking, I swear, something like the queen of diamonds. I stare up into the darkness above our candlelit table. "But then somehow I ... ended up back in time." I gaze at her with what might be the pleading look of a sick little boy, wanting mommy to fix him.

"So that makes you crazy. Is that what you're thinking?"

I laugh, sounding, I fear, very much like a crazy person. "By any standard I ever heard of. But you see, you can't call me disconnected or ... anything, because you're living on another planet yourself."

She smiles and regards me with her séance look. "How little you know." She looks up and to the left, in the direction of the long row of bottles over the bar. "But I suppose in a way that's true. Still, there is a huge difference between having a sixth sense and being thrown back in time."

"But you are listening to me. I wasn't expecting anyone would do that. I expected to be ... isolated, lost. But I've now found two women who have become my ... kind of confidantes, even though I haven't told the other one everything I'm telling you. And then there's the teenage girl I mentioned. It feels like I've got my own set of the three Furies. These two women and this funny little girl seem ... I dunno, interested in me, unglued as I probably am."

Valory has a way sometimes, like right now, of appearing to look at the center of my forehead, as if searching for my third eye.

"Maybe you can see," I say, "that, to me, that's very interesting. It makes me feel almost as if it's possible for me to find some ... *help*, some ... guidance back to my wife, and that I've got a chance for a happy ending."

"Yes, but wouldn't your happy ending include becoming an old man again? How old were you when you got ... *thrown* back in time?"

"Seventy-five."

"So you're saying you would rather be seventy-five again, forty-seven years into the future, than be a young man with his whole life ahead of him?"

"It sounds crazy, I know, but you're young."

"So are you," she says.

"No, I only look young. I'm a version of Dorian Gray."

"Maybe I am too."

I'm thinking several thoughts at the same time, but I go on talking: "Did you come from another time too?" I laugh, as if I've attempted a bad joke. The joke didn't work, but that doesn't stop me. "Do you know how *much* life is not what most of us are used to thinking it is?"

She smiles, studies me for a long moment, then says in low velvety tones: "So do we get to have fun with these bodies in the meantime?"

I'm *married. Hasn't she been listening?* And why hasn't she reacted with more surprise to my story? I don't see how there's any chance Valory Valentine is a coincidence. She looked me up in the *Thomas Guide*. She shouldn't be having this strange effect on me. I'm in a restaurant in 1974 with this enigmatical woman, who looks like she stepped out of a Pedro Almodóvar movie, even though Señor Almodóvar is still a young man. I've been married to the love of my life for nearly forty years, and this strange woman is giving me an erection.

She reaches out and strokes my hand. "Listen," she says, "if you want to find your Samantha, you will find her. I know it."

But the look in her eyes hasn't changed and my erection hasn't deflated.

After early dinner, she asks me if I'd like to come up to her place.

I don't know how to respond. It doesn't feel like a smart thing to do. But since I don't have much in the way of a private life these days, and Sam isn't waiting for me at home ...

I am lying to myself. I am compelled to follow this woman. I assure myself everything is all right and ask her where she lives.

"On Senalda, off of Outpost Drive."

I follow her yellow Datsun minivan down to Ventura, then east, then south. Just past Barham she takes a right and I follow her up through a cobweb of winding streets into an upscale hillside neighborhood.

When I called Zeke again about noon, I got the same result as the last time. I was standing in our kitchen, trying to let myself be open to any spirits of improvisation that happened to be hanging around. I found a large container of frozen orange juice in the freezer. I have no idea how long it had been in there. Not forty-seven years—I don't think refrigerators last that long. As I thawed out the cylinder of what used to be twenty or so oranges, I remembered talking to Zeke maybe two or three days earlier. But I could no longer do that. The lines of communication to him were now closed, at least to me. I was staring out the window and I heard a faceless director call "Cut!" I stepped away from the set, and there she was, off camera: Sam. I stared at her. Everywhere I looked, there she was.

If you become immersed in one thing, one human being— as I have with Sam—and for whatever reason you remain fixed on what has come to be a single point of concentration, you grow conscious of the fact that this object or person is traveling more and more slowly as she drifts through your awareness. You're locked in on her like a shooter with a target in his crosshairs. And when it's working the way it's supposed to, that's all you see.

The problematical news is that it doesn't always work the way it's supposed to. During those *other* moments, all laws go backwards. I've been told and have read, more often than I'm comfortable with, that objective reality doesn't exist. But then of course that law will end up having to go backwards too, and it may turn out that all those people pulling the handles on slot machines in Las Vegas are the ones who really know their stuff. They'll patiently explain to me that they have risen to a higher level of perception, and that what I have thought is reality is not even close to being that, which then means I am not following this bizarre, Picassoesque woman, who gives me repeated hard-ons, to her home in the Hollywood Hills in 1974, which year, in all my gullibility, I would have thought I'd already been given my one and only crack at.

18

THE LIGHT THAT BREAKS
HEARTS IN LOS ANGELES

Valory Valentine pulls her Datsun into the driveway of
a well-cared-for California bungalow, and I park my
Audi out front. It's a pleasing, quiet neighborhood, as
much as I can judge in the evening light. Forty-seven years from
now hillside property like this, no matter the house, will sell
for extortionate prices. Valory's bungalow, not much more than
a skillfully expanded chalet, is a harmonious fit with this hillside neighborhood, nested, from what I can see, among Brazilian
pepper, elm, and liquidambar trees. She waits for me to come
up the front walk, and unlocks an arched front doorway on the
relatively broad veranda, under an overhanging eave. She reaches
in, snaps on a front hall light, and beckons me to follow her in.

She crosses around to the other side of a linoleum-topped
counter between the pine-paneled living room and kitchen.

"Would you like something to drink?"

"Do you have a beer?"

"Sure." She goes to the refrigerator. "Guinness?"

"Nobody keeps Guinness in their fridge."

She smiles. "I ain't nobody."

"No, you're not that. Yeah, sure, Guinness would be great."

Outside Valory's living room picture window is another angle on LA, one of those backdrops that always catch you off guard. You wouldn't see anything like this in any other city— Boston, Chicago, Atlanta. And certainly New York and San Francisco, even Miami and Seattle, know how to behave like cities, but unless you're high in a skyscraper, you never look out and see this kind of great sprawling display of color.

It's sunset. "The light that breaks hearts in Los Angeles" is sweeping in iridescent arcs and golden flares across the LA basin. Streams of phosphorescent lime green, the final pulsating shafts of evening sunlight, slice over the Hollywood Bowl, defying the dark that moves catlike out of San Bernardino to the east, like the army at Dunsinane, but still with enough wingding of its own to display a splashy dot matrix rainbow, a raffish Jackson Pollock spattering of speckled crimsons, magentas, aquamarine, cobalt and cornflower blues, intertwining into a tangle of deep purples creeping up and over their garden walls, a blowout farewell performance, before melding up into the dusty diamond sky and the haze of LA that never ceases stalking, day or night.

I turn around and find Valory watching me.

"When you wake up from a bad dream," she says, "what do you think happens?" She hands me a beer in a large cut-glass mug. "Do you think the part of your brain that creates dreams just shuts down, as if the coming of wakefulness switches off the dreamer in you?"

"May I ask you an impertinent question?" I say.

She smiles and takes a sip of Chardonnay. "Of course."

"Are you by any chance a witch? I ask because you occasionally say some version of what's already going on in the back of my mind. You know what I mean? How do you do that?"

Her laugh contains satisfaction, almost glee. "I haven't a clue, but yes, for all I know that is true—that there is a little of the … occult in my blood. I've wondered the same thing. I don't know why I say … a whole lot of what I say. Then sometimes I get … call them … premonitions. I don't know how it happens or why. It's a kind of clairvoyance or precognition. I can't explain it. Deep down, everybody knows telepathic communications, premonitions, do happen. Occasionally—not always—I get vibrations about what … some people will do under certain circumstances. Second sight is a real thing. I think I just have it a little more than most."

"And that's something else about you; you seem to have this sort of soft-sell insight about yourself, which leads me to ask you again, do you *truly* not know how you picked up on where my house is? I know you said you don't like to talk about it, but it feels almost as if—maybe because it was my house—as if your clairvoyance, your foresight, in this case concerns me too."

"I guess I felt we were approaching a … home that might be yours."

Which tells me nothing.

Outside her window, the cinematographer has signaled his gaffers and they've flicked on a legion of klieg lights that burst into a final surge of illumination of the LA basin all the way to the horizon.

"You told me you knew I could find Sam," I say. "How? I mean, I know where she is right now. But I don't want to take the chance that I'd screw it all up by trying to make contact with her too soon. I think, if I were to find her when we're both still relatively young, I'd need to find her at the right moment, six years from now, when we first met. What would I do in the meantime? Can you help me with that?"

"That does sound like the tricky part." She rakes a hand through her silky chestnut hair. "I could help you pass the time."

I show her a sickly smile. "Well, that's another tricky part. ... I can't do that, but I don't want you lose to interest in me, if you know what I mean." I don't want to give her the wrong impression, but I also don't trust my own intentions. "What I'm saying is, I don't think it would be that easy to find companionship—anyone—who'd be willing to listen to the kind of craziness I'm telling you. But that means, if I spend time with you, I have to keep myself—no offense—alert."

"I understand." She forms a smile that seems to come from a hidden chest of humor. "My luck." She looks at me with a gaze I couldn't possibly turn away from. "You won't mind if I keep trying, will you?"

"But isn't that awkward for both of us?"

"Maybe." She reaches out and touches my face, my cheek. Then, as I flash again on *Manchurian Candidate*, this time the mother-and-son incestuous kiss, she turns and drifts over to a two-seater Chesterfield, and sits down at one end of it.

"Listen," I say, "I'm ... uh, flattered you feel that way. And it's not like me. I used to—a long, long time ago—jump at ... implied opportunity." God, how do I say this? "I just can't ... or rather I mustn't be ... unfaithful to Sam."

"Even if you never see her again ... as the Sam you knew? And say it ends up that you had to wait those several years? You don't seem to me to be the kind of man who can live a monk's life that long. Anyway, how do you know you'd have the same result with her you did the first time?"

Shit! I have an instinct to slap my forehead, but it's such a cliché. "Of course! You're right! ... But what if ... What if I *can*, in fact, as I've been fantasizing I might, find a way to get back to her *now*—I mean, directly back to where I came from? I can't hang around six years, hoping to duplicate something that I *know cannot* be duplicated. Life doesn't work that way. You cannot *forge*—make a counterfeit copy of—a moment in time. You can't pour the cream out of the cup of coffee back into the creamer from whence it came. But if I could find a way to get back to her the way she was the last time we were together, that would be the ... answer to my prayer."

She frowns. "But, as we said, even if you could, you'd be an old man."

"I wouldn't care if Sam was there."

She shakes her head; her hair fans out and she smooths it back with both hands. "Anyway, maybe I've changed my mind. As you suggest, it's possible I'm a witch. We blow with the wind."

I'm staring at her again, out of my depth. There is no chair within comfortable conversation distance from her. I cross toward her and sit down at the other end of her small sofa, placing my beer on the end table. She's watching me. I interlace the fingers of my hands and look at my thumbs. I actually twiddle them. I say, "Do you think this could be a continuation of my dream life? Can you ..." She's giving me the same hypnotic look she did in the restaurant. "Is it possible I've somehow made you up? What I'm living through cannot happen. I am not in 1974 for the second time, with an attractive woman, who has just said ..."

She grins at me. "So, if I'm not real, why worry about it?"

"I don't know how not to." I concentrate on keeping my mind from careening off where I don't want it to go. "What I want more than anything—again, no offense—is to be, yes, an old man, forty-seven years into the future. I have, delusional as it might seem, some sort of long-view knowledge of my beginning all the way through to ... *approaching* my ending, as most of us perceive endings. And even though I want to keep on living like anybody else ... and yes, I know it's mad ... but I want my life, the time before Sam, to fly by as quickly as possible."

Above us is a skylight I didn't notice until now. She clasps her hands behind her neck and looks up into the night. "The explanation for you thinking I'm witchlike hooks up with one of the reasons I'm more attracted to you than I would normally be. It's because I can tell you know as well as I do that we live on a speck of dust, the minutest possible speck by cosmic standards. And you understand what I'm talking about and I find that sexy."

I show her my most incorruptible smile. It's also my lamest.

She smiles back, eyes twinkling, looks off, lowers her hands and regards me again. "If the earth and all of the life on it was placed next to a dust mote, and we looked at both of these 'objects'—the dust mote relative to us, and the earth relative to the cosmos—through a high-powered microscope, we would be able to see the dust mote, but not earth. That's how important we are in the overall scheme of things. So because we now know Darwin's theory of the evolution of the species on this dust mote, and have chewed, for a nanosecond, on what he figured out a couple of hundred years ago, we now leap to the conclusion that we are in possession of some pretty serious knowledge. Enough so that we deduce—from our fathomless wisdom, acquired through an immeasurably minuscule span of time—that we understand even the tiniest ort of cosmic knowledge." She spreads her arms, palms up. "Are we crazy?"

"You've given this some thought."

"Not that much. You don't have to be a deep thinker to realize we know nothing. That's not an exaggeration. I don't mean we know next to nothing. I mean ... we do not know *anything*."

"I know one thing for certain," I say. "I'm not living in my own time. I'm not living in the time I came from."

"Your real home is in the twenty-first century?"

"Yes, recently crossed over into the third decade of it." I study the look on her face. "What do you think when I say that?"

"Well, it's obvious you expect me to be surprised."

"Right. Why aren't you?"

She looks up again into the nighttime over Los Angeles. "I'm not sure. What makes you think you came from 2021?"

I tell her step by step what happened on that first day, leaving out not one detail.

She doesn't even look puzzled.

"Doesn't any of what I'm saying affect you? It doesn't seem to. Are you quietly thinking I'm crazy?"

"Normally, I would be, I guess. But—and I don't know why—right now, I'm simply thinking this is ... your story, and I'm listening to it."

"Well, it seems crazy to me."

She stares at the center of my forehead, then deep into my eyes again.

"Let me ask you something," I say, standing up, stretching my arms casually, in a way that feels like bad acting. "How did you really know about me as an actor? No one does, not really. I always hoped I would have a big career, fans and all that. That was part of being successful—for good or bad—but I don't have that yet, and ... never will. You work in the industry, right?"

She nods, gazing at me.

"I still don't know much about what it's like to be a film actor. The me I am now … God, I'll *never* get used to this. … The me I am … *now* is from New York—at least most of the last few years."

"And before that?"

"I was raised …" I remember my conversation with Brenda. "Would you like to drive down to Hemet with me and visit my father?" I do not know why I've asked this woman to drive out to the desert with me. Well, maybe I do, but I don't want to think about it.

"Hemet?" she says.

"Yeah. He's an actor, my dad, many years retired. He lives near Hemet."

She smiles up at me with her combination dreamlike and penetrating look. "Okay." She didn't even seem to think about it.

"Uh … nice," I say, "I'll warn you right now, he's got this redneck thing he slips into from time to time. I was never sure why." I cross away from her. "I don't think it's who he is. Maybe he just misses being an actor." I examine a primitive bronze sculpture of … I don't know what it is.

"Sounds interesting."

"Yeah, well, not exactly." She did *not* answer my question about how she knew what it *feels* as if she knows about me as an actor.

Still gazing at me with the same look, she says, "Let me try something."

She sets her wine glass down, gets up, glides over to me, and puts her arms around my neck. She's almost as tall as I am. Again she's looking into my eyes, unblinking. I feel chills, the kind you get when you've got a flu coming on.

She leans in and kisses me.

I kiss her back. I don't mean to, but I do. I have this young body and feeling her breasts against my chest, I instantly overcome my vows about keeping myself only unto Sam.

She pulls away and says, "Did that feel like a dream?"

"No. But still, how do I know it's not?"

"I guess you don't. In any case, you're apparently on *some* kind of trip. You might as well enjoy it while you're here." She gathers her sweater and begins to pull it over her head.

19

BIRD'S EYE

don't know if she completes the action.

I'm winding west along Mulholland Drive toward Benedict Canyon.

I'm on the crest of the mountains that separate the San Fernando Valley from the LA basin.

There used to be a sameness to the years I lived through; it was interesting, unfolding life, but there was a sort of predictable evenness to it. Then, at some point, around when Fleury and I separated, time began to play games like a puppy that lies still or moves only languidly for a time; then, the following moment, it's flying toward the next object of its puppy passions. If I had to live through some of the life I remember living and knew it would play out as it did the first time, I'm not sure I could stand the strain. I don't know that I could make it through the next six years, even if I changed everything about it from what it was the first time I lived through it. With Sam—although time passed quickly—at least it had conscious, lively value. More than that, it brought with it an exhilaration, a satisfaction I never knew during my fulltime professional show-off years.

I feel the same chills I felt ten minutes ago.

Even if I changed my mind and went back, Valory would probably have changed her mind. And then I'd say, "I'm really glad because this time I don't know if I would have been able to stop myself."

If she did something like she did before, like taking her sweater off … maybe I wouldn't be able to walk away from that twice in a row. How can I know? It would be a mixture between sad and …

I see Sam, sitting in the passenger seat next to me. She's crying.

I cry at the sad parts of movies.

Now we're both crying.

It's magic hour on our back porch. With a pencil, Samantha has drawn two lines on a piece of paper. "Here's the block," she says. "We lived on this corner." She makes a tiny square for her house where the two lines meet.

"I'd go down the block to the grocery store, up in here somewhere." She taps her pencil midway along the first line. "And my mother would have given me the list. And I would go there and I'd give the man the list. And he would fill it."

I say, "Where was the Sharon Bigly incident in relation to that?"

"Oh. Okay. Sylvia Winters lived on one of the other corners across from us, and Dee Ann Knibloe next door to her. And across from them was the public school, kitty-corner from our house. But I didn't go to it; I went to the Catholic school. I had to go allll the way up this block." With a flourish, she draws a new line from the opposite end of the line where she's placed her own house. "What are you laughing at?"

"*Nothing.*"

"*Anyway ... and the Catholic school was up this hill right here.*" She waves her pencil over the line she's now established as going up a hill. "*And at the top was my school.*" She takes a sip of wine. "*It wasn't so bad in nice weather, but in the winter, in the cold, we were all bundled up in our snowsuits.*" As she thinks back, I see seven-year-old Sam, barely able to walk in her multi-layered snowsuit, roly-poly and lovable like Ralphie's little brother in A Christmas Story. "*But the Sharon Bigly incident was not up at the very top,*" she says.

"*Was this a fancy area?*"

She frowns at me. "*I didn't know what fancy was. Carbon Falls was ALL not fancy.*"

"*And they didn't have any falls either.*"

"*Right. I guess there might have been a wealthier area. ... I think there were some bigger homes up there.*" She looks off into middle distance. "*Anyway, here's our house on this corner. And across the street was a big vacant field. All the kids used to pick violets. There were rampant violets.*"

"*In the spring,*" I add.

"*Of course in the spring. And in the winter, there was a hill that went off from the intersection we lived next to. We were on the flat part, but up in this other direction*"—she draws a new line—"*the street started to rise, and the hill was steep enough that everybody came there to do their sledding. They'd block off car traffic and all the kids would go up the hill and they came down on their sleds into this intersection, the one in front of our house.*

"*And then other times ... My bedroom was right on the corner and ... and I used to see the headlights of the cars on my wall. I loved that. I'd hear the car coming, then I'd see the lights move across my wall.*"

She points with her pencil again. "*So, back to my school. Here is the little street that goes up to it, and right around here is where it happened.*"

"*You got her,*" *I say in a mock-villainous voice.*

"*There was wild mint that grew up there and that's where it happened. She and I were there picking mint one day, and I'd found out that she'd told on me.*"

"*What had you done?*"

"*Just something I wasn't supposed to do. And she told my mother about it. And I either got a spanking or a reprimand of some kind.*"

"*But what had you done?*"

"*I don't know. Some kind of transgression.*"

"*You must have done something bad.*"

"*I told a lie, I think. So anyway, Sharon and I were friends and we were in there picking mint. And I said, 'You told on me.'*"

Sam gazes at me, a hurt look on her face. "*It was something that was supposed to be a secret, and it was an awful betrayal, a terrible feeling of betrayal. And I didn't beat her up, I just pushed her a little bit. It was more of a …*"

"*A reprimand?*" *I say.*

"*Well … it was more of a … it wasn't really a physical hurting punishment, but mentally hurting her.*"

"*But you wanted to hurt her.*"

"*Yes.*" *She frowns, feeling bad.* "*If I ever see her again, I'll tell her I am really sorry about that.*" *She looks at me sadly.* "*I've tried to track her down, on the internet, but …*"

"*Oh, poor Sharon,*" *I emote broadly.* "*She probably wakes up mornings and thinks, 'Ooooh, Samantha. How could you?'*"

Sam nods. "*She was a cute little girl. She had dark hair and she always wore it in two braids. Sweet little girl … And her mother … they didn't have much money. Her mother was very thin.*"

"*Why?*"

"*I dunno. Her mother used to bake bread and go around the neighborhood selling it.*"

"Aww, man." I can see a frail-looking woman coming up the side-walk trailing an old Radio Flyer wagon behind her.

"It was good bread," says Sam. *"We used to buy her bread."*

I nearly miss a curve. I have to pay attention. I have to watch the life I'm living right now, whatever that life is; I don't want to give it away.

I had a friend named Howard McGee, an actor I used to drink with at Joe Allen's. One night, Howard was drinking there, then later ended up on Mulholland on his way home.

He missed a turn and plunged to his death. Simple as that: no more Howard. I wonder how the time passed for Howard as he and his car were flying off Mulholland into the canyon below. If everything is laid out consistent with my memories, Howard is still alive and working both in New York and out here. He drinks at the Joe Allen's in New York when he's there. If he's working in LA now, he's probably drinking at the Beverly Hills Joe Allen's—at this moment.

Could I go tell him that he should be careful when driving on Mulholland?

If he said that to me, I'd think he'd had a few too many.

As I'm approaching Benedict Canyon, still headed west, I hear them before I see them. Two fire trucks on the Valley side of the road, a third one approaching. Lights blinking, people collecting on the side of the road like droplets in a puddle. The traffic is stopped in both directions.

I pull over, park, walk around a bend to the front, and see the fire.

It's a conflagration—a rambling redwood house with a slate tile roof fully ablaze. The firefighters aim two large hoses at what's left of the house, dousing the fire.

At the moment, it seems to be having no effect.

Through the turmoil I see a man holding a woman against his chest, standing thirty feet from the blazing house. The woman is rocking her head back and forth, her whole body shaking.

Looking around, I see twenty or more people, neighbors, I assume. They're all staring somber-eyed at the charred house, locked together as witnesses to this inferno.

The woman tucked under the man's arms wails and tries to break away from him, screaming, "Please! Please!" Her next words are lost in sobs.

A young woman, another neighbor, I guess, her hands held up to her chin as if praying, stands nearby. She's about thirty, pretty—or she would be. Her face is red. She's been crying too. She glances at me with grief in her eyes.

Stupidly, I say to her, "They can't get everybody out?"

The woman shakes her head, eyes wet. "Their little girl is trapped in there."

The woman in the man's arms screams again: "Please! Please! Somebody save my little girl! She's only seven years old! Don't let her burn! She's my baby!" She buries her head in her husband's chest.

I look at one of the firefighters, standing helpless, as slate tiles fall from the crumbling roof, thunking to the ground.

I hear a man's voice, angry. "Can't you do something? You're just standing there."

I'm not sure whether it's a man or a woman, but now I hear someone else yell, "What's that?" I look toward the east end of the house. Through the fire's dull roar, I'm barely able to hear a low, intense growl. It sounds like a dog. It's not a combative growl, but one of concentrated effort.

We all see it now, fur black with soot, its teeth bared down as it pulls something out from under a fallen beam, squeezing through a small gap.

My breath catches … only to release when I see that he's pulling a child, a little girl, gripping a clump of her pajamas between his teeth, stopping periodically to get a new purchase on her pajama top, then tugging her out some more. At the moment he's gotten her out of the house, a slate tile falls, grazing the dog, but missing the little girl.

A firefighter runs in and scoops up the little girl in his arms.

As the flames eat the house, I watch the mother's silhouette dart across the empty perimeter toward the firefighter, who meets her midway carrying her daughter. As the mother's arms wrap around the child, I see joy and relief reflected in her posture. Etched in the smiles and applause of the bystanders is a beholding of what feels like a miracle, a rebirth.

It's gut-wrenching, watching the scene around me, aware of the feeling of renewal and resurrection at the same moment this family's home, all their possessions, memorabilia, all of it, is going up in smoke. They have lost everything—except life. They have their life together, and no doubt their love—deepening, I imagine. They may not have any of their *things* anymore, but they've got each other.

As I walk back to my car, I see the dog that saved the little girl. He's still covered in layers of ash and soot. He turns and limps by me, headed west, and I notice an irregular patch on his right side.

Chills pulse through me, but the rational part of me knows it's impossible that my dog from the future has just saved the life of a little girl in 1974.

There is a message on my service from Lou Gefsky. It's only 9:45 at night so I give him a ring.

"I hate to tell you this, Danny, but we've got trouble."

"What kind of trouble?"

"Hannah trouble."

"Oh boy."

"I'd like to tell you it's not as bad as it sounds, but I'd be lying. It's worse."

"How much worse?"

"She's backed out."

It feels like someone has clamped a pair of ice tongs on my intestines. "But she signed a contract."

"Yes, but she left herself an out. Remember she wanted the contract predated? We didn't know why and told ourselves it didn't matter. … We spoke too soon. It mattered a lot. It gave her an out on her other project. And here's the interesting part: turns out she's got *two* predated contracts, and we are, with the meager clout we have, low man on the predated contract pole. Even if we wanted to sue her, it would take years to get it to court, and by that time we'd be real lucky to have jobs in the William Morris mailroom. This is not to mention that these scuzzballs, under careful guidance, are extremely gifted at hiding from subpoenas."

"But how can she do that?"

"You're talking like you think she's got some sort of moral code, Danny—which you know better than. She's working her way up to the million dollar club. She's playing the old climbing-over-low-rollers-like-us game."

"Isn't there any kind of pressure we can put on her?"

Lou makes a moaning sound. I can see his head shaking as if it's set to a metronome. "No," he says, "neither can the other guys do anything to her. She's got some smart, ruthless people working for her. We are all up the creek with Hannah Castle and she currently owns the paddle."

"I'd like to borrow it."

Neither of us has words for a moment. "Hannah Castle couldn't care less if we bleed to death. You gotta learn to pick your friends better, Danny."

"I didn't pick her; she got *cast* into my life, and yours too I'm afraid."

"Right ... so, do we have a plan B? I've been racking my brain. The only thing I can come up with is your friend, Liz Callahan."

"She quit the business, Lou."

"Yeah, I know. Fuckin' shame." I hear him take a deep breath. "Let's try to get a good night's sleep ... *any* night's sleep. And talk tomorrow. Maybe we'll be hit by a stroke of ... *anything* useful."

That night, I look down and see that I'm flying, sailing high above Venice, Santa Monica, then out over the ocean. I can feel the breeze enveloping my body like cool silk. I turn back toward land and as I do, I see the underside of my own wing; it has a Navajo pattern. I'm my mockingbird, soaring back over land, then north toward the Santa Monica Mountains.

Now, I'm miles inland and high over Benedict Canyon Drive. It's the middle of the day. The stream of cars going north and south is sparse in both directions. I can see that I'm approaching my house.

A red Mercedes convertible is headed south. As it reaches a point about twenty, twenty-five yards north of 1809, it pulls over. Although I can't tell who the driver is, I know that he's turned off the engine.

I see someone come out of the front door of my house and experience a dread that feels like drug withdrawal, realizing it's me. I walk toward the arched wooden gate, open it, remove the mail from the mailbox, go back inside, and close the gate behind me.

As I head back toward the house, the Mercedes driver leans on his horn. After about three beats, I sprint through the gate and am standing next to my Audi as he guns the engine. Tires squealing, the Mercedes lurches forward, hurtling south.

I am enraged.

I wake up, or dream I do.

I dial Zeke several times again. No luck.

I hear a booming voice in the back of my head. It sounds like my father. With appaling glee, the voice says in rumbling, actor tones: "*Harebrained.*"

It's nine in the morning. I'm feeling the island fever I recently discovered is part of living in this beautiful house. I go out the back door and look up at the house behind me, owned, I've now learned, by a composer of music scores.

With some difficulty, I loosen the latch on the long wooden gate that fronts on Wilkie Street. I walk up towards the house behind me. Wilkie curves towards the left behind the composer's house. For the first time in my life (either of them), I walk up Wilkie, past the house behind mine.

It's exactly as Valory described it. Behind the composer's house is a cul-de-sac. If Rue were to begin skateboarding toward Benedict Canyon Drive from this rounded dead end of a short street, she could not get nearly as much momentum as she had the day I met her. When I first saw her on her skateboard, she was flying—as if she was nearly airborne. Despite the fact that the composer's house is slightly above mine and the hills behind it rise steeply, Wilkie Street itself is relatively flat, no more than a minor slope.

Where is Rue Lefanty?

Who is she?

20

A VENUS FLYTRAP
BY ANY OTHER NAME

I am in the middle of my eleven o'clock session with Patricia. I've told her that Valory has volunteered to drive down to Hemet with me.

"What does she want?" says Patricia.

I think of the rage I felt when the Mercedes squealed out from just north of my house on Benedict Canyon the day I met Valory. I felt an echo of that during the dream I had about it. It made me see how volatile I must have been when I was young the first time. John Yort mentioned my hot temper. I think I've been with Sam so many years I long ago stopped thinking about that part of myself.

But it did not ... vanish.

I think Valory somehow, by means I can't imagine, *knew* I was in front of my house that day and that I might react exactly as I did: jump into my car and follow them.

Was that one of her "premonitions"? And why me?

That's the reason for the anger I've felt since I had that dream. *She planned it. I know she did.* She had seen a little interview I did where I mentioned hating people who honked their car horns in front of actors' houses. What made her decide to ... What a devious way to go about it. And what did she want?

Patricia says, "Are you with me?"

"Yes!"

"I asked you what does your new friend Valory want?" She's staring at me, unblinking.

"She's not exactly my friend. I'm ... temporarily involved with her."

"Temporarily?"

"I don't know. I think she's ... interested in me. Do you believe in premonitions?"

She blinks. "Sure, doesn't everybody?"

"Do you believe someone can predict the future?"

"I don't know. Maybe. Rarely."

"Rarely," I repeat.

"Why?"

"I don't know. It just crossed my mind."

"I see. ... Can we get back to ... *Why* do you think this woman is interested in you?"

"I don't know. Maybe she's attracted to me." I don't say anything to her about what I think might be the calculated way Valory chose to meet me.

"But you've told her about Samantha," says Patricia. "And if you speak to her about your 'future wife' the same way you do to me, she no doubt understands, aside from the fact that you're crazy in some other ways too, that you have"—her eyes narrow very slightly—"an obsession with Samantha."

"Yes, but she still seems to be … interested in me."

"Why?"

"I don't know." There's an edge to my voice.

"Tell me anything else about her."

I look around the room, trying to think what I might say. "She hates the pet industry. Pet food. Pet toys."

Patricia waits for me to amplify, but I can't think of anything to add. "Are you attracted to her?"

"Yes. She's sexy."

"And you've said no to her?"

"Yes."

"Then I have to ask you again, what does she want?"

"She enjoys my company."

She shakes her head and makes a little humming sound. "No, I don't think so. Is it possible she knows you as an actor? You remember I deal with actors. And you know that sometimes actors are, in one way or another, stalked by fans—not the usual fan. And every once in a while, an actor is stalked by a fan who has severe problems. Do you think it's possible that Valory has severe problems, off the chart problems?"

"Maybe. But whatever they are, they're not exactly obvious."

She shoots me a doubtful expression, then looks out the window at the crape myrtle trees. "I'm pretty sure the notion that she simply enjoys your company is bullshit."

In the years I was with Patricia she never once said anything like that. "How?" I ask her. "How is it bullshit?"

She frowns. "You're an actor. You know you shape a character's words and actions by understanding what the character wants, *really* wants, not some 'she wants to be happy' nonsense, but something deep in her gut that she wants. The character you're describing isn't spending time with you only because she enjoys your company. So I ask you one more time, what does she want?"

I look out the window too, as if I'm trying to decide which one, among the row of crape myrtles, she's concentrating on. "I don't know. She's kind of a philosopher or just a … student of life; she has that in her."

"Why are you so angry?"

"I'm not angry!"

Patricia lets that hang in the air, then: "Nobody's just a student of life and that's it."

"But I *am* telling her I'm from the twenty-first century. She's fascinated. Anybody would be."

"Oh, you bet they would, but I don't think that's what's going on. I think anybody even a little bit normal would get out of there as fast as they could. Or if they're the kind of loose cannon 'philosopher' you describe, they'd have sex with you and *then* get out of there as fast as they could." She frowns. "Unless …"

"Unless what?"

"If you came back from 2021, and she's about your age, then maybe …"

"*What*? What are you talking about? You don't really believe my story, do you?"

"No, I do not," she says. "But I also can't dismiss the fact that you know a long list—a list that defies probability—of things about me that you have no right to know. What I'm saying is, I now feel as if you're not the only one. I feel like I've lost my bearings too. *Of course* I don't believe anything you've told me. I can't. I live in a world of facts like I've always assumed everybody who's sane does. And I am a … doctor." She massages both of her temples with her fingertips. "Forgive me. Listen, I know you're having a strange experience. But the fact is, you have passed it on to me. Other than this unhinged story of your being a time-traveler, you impress me as a reasonable, fairly well-adjusted man. It's not professional for me to say this, but you have drawn me in … about as much as I can allow you to."

She stands, walks to the window, and stares down at the street below. "I should ask you to leave right now, but I can't. Once you've exhausted every commonsense resource you can think of, traveled down every rational avenue …" She moves back to her chair, sits, places her elbows on her knees, clasping her hands in front of her. "I believe it's possible that something very much out of the ordinary has happened to you. Your story is too consistent—nutty, but consistent. I cannot dismiss it. I *want* to more than I can tell you, but I know myself. I have always been one of those people with her feet on the ground. That's why I got out of acting. Actors are not great actors because they have common sense.

"On the other hand …" She shrugs. "I distrust inflexible 'realists.' People are attracted to a narrative that makes sense of the world, solid science and all that, a world of pure logic; it gives them a feeling of control. But that *can also* be awfully arrogant. Allowing that some paranormal phenomena are genuine drives those people crazy, but the grinding evidence in support of *some* psychic activity being authentic is overwhelming—and I'm not talking about anything anecdotal. The point is that I have too much common sense not to understand that you are not consciously making up a single thing you've told me. My instincts are good in this area. I trust myself. Now let's try to figure out what's going on with you, because I must tell you, it's now going on with me too."

She leans back in her chair, lightly stroking the scar behind her left ear with her left forefinger. "Look, I do not believe you are a time-traveler. I do not *think* this Valory is anything more or less than a lunatic fan. But since you believe what you believe, we have to start somewhere. You are sure that you never met this woman, this Valory, before in either of—I can't believe I'm saying this—your ... *incarnations?* Maybe we're talking about something that happened previously *in your mind* or hers and they became interwoven in some bizarre way. Whatever the case may be, the specifics don't matter; we do have to begin somewhere."

I look down at the gray Berber carpeted floor for several seconds. "It's *possible*," I say. "It's possible I remember her from ... *something ... somewhere*, but I don't know what or where, and I don't think I ever saw this woman before. She doesn't have the kind of face you forget."

She presses her lips together and blinks. "Well, I think you'd better do some serious sorting through your memory. I don't care which century you pick to search through, but pick one, and try to remember how you know this woman. And if you can't find her there, look somewhere else. Scour through every connection you can think of that might hook up with Valory Valentine. That's not exactly a forgettable name—if she's always gone by that name." She stares at me. "If she's a young woman, the odds are fairly good that she would still be alive in 2021. Maybe you were aware of her during that ... 'period of your existence.'" She looks over my shoulder, shaking her head in self-disgust.

"How do I do any of this? I can't say to myself, 'Remember' and expect myself ... my *self* ... to do what it's told. My mind doesn't work that way."

"Everyone's mind works that way. Do this: take a few minutes before you go to bed at night and ask your unconscious—however you think of your unconscious—ask that part of you that quietly watches you live your life to deliver to your consciousness any buried memory you have of this woman. It may be a long way back that you encountered her, and I'm not saying this will work, but it's possible. It's a valid approach."

"I like that word: valid."

She narrows her eyes. "Do you?"

"It sounds crazy to me," I tell her. "Maybe it would work with some people, but I doubt if it will with me."

"You should know this from ..." She drops her gaze, and with two fingers taps lightly on her forehead. " ... from *before*. Your unconscious is aware of some things your conscious mind knows almost nothing about—things you can't see when you're awake, only when your mind is 'in the dark.' It's like trying to see stars during the day; they're still there, but you can't see them until the sun goes down." She holds her hands up, palms toward me in surrender mode. "Look, maybe it won't work for you, I don't know." She clasps her hands, stands, moves to the window and looks out in the direction of Beverly Hills, Westwood, Santa Monica, and the Pacific Ocean. "But maybe it will. Who the hell knows?"

On my way home from my session, as I wait for the light to change on Cañon at Sunset, about to cross over to Benedict Canyon, Rue Lefanty floats through my mind. Where does she *really* live? Will I ever see her again?

I think about a seventy-some-year-old Valory. Could she have traveled from 2021 to 1974 like I did? Why would that ... *coincidence* happen? And of course, the sixty-four bushels of gold question: *how?*

And how did *I* do it—if I am, in fact, in 1974? Were my conversations with Zeke no more than random upheavals in my liquefying brain? Whatever is going on inside my … *being*, it's clear I am gathering some firsthand experience of the inner composition of my mind, or my madness.

I think I'd already anticipated Patricia's advice; that's why I'm going to have company on my trip to Hemet. I don't think I have any choice but to follow Valory Valentine down whatever back street she may lead me.

Please, God, it's only until I learn whatever I need to learn from her.

As I lie down in my bed, I repeat the name Valory Valentine several times, trying to plant the idea of her in a prominent place in my unconscious.

I'm told my unconscious, my sub-conscious, is *subjective*; it's "under the direction of" my conscious. So then, my unconscious—that bottomless pit of mostly useless *stuff*—is supposed to follow the orders of my conscious. The problem is that my conscious(ness) has always been a backward child, a few giant steps behind the rest of the class. I guess it can utter a few directions, but what self-respecting unconscious would listen to it? It's been burned enough by useless information (mairzy doats and dozy doats and liddle lamzy divey, itsy bitsy teeny weeny yellow polkadot bikini, etc. I've got a boxcar full of yak shavings in the back of my brain). Patricia explained this by telling me my unconscious has no volition, no initiative; it does not reason, but simply takes direction. It also holds infinitely more than my conscious mind can contain at any one time. What I am going to be trying to do now is to locate, within my vast storehouse of unconscious data, any bits of "forgotten" information—especially as may connect with Valory Valentine.

Okay, I'll try. I'm willing to give anything a go. Maybe Patricia is right. I don't remember ever having a more active dream life than I'm having lately.

In the next one, which seems more real than ever, I drive to Samantha's apartment late one night. It's the one she was living in when we had our blind date. I park up the street from the entrance. She has to walk up two flights of outdoor cement steps to get to the cantilevered third floor apartment.

I've had a few drinks by the time I arrive. In fact, I've got a fifth of Gordon's gin with me—for company. After I've had a couple more slugs, doing nothing but staring off into the darkness, I get out of my car, walk a few steps to the bottom of the stairs leading up to her apartment, plunk myself down on a wrought iron bench with wooden slats, and wait for her. I'm obviously not thinking clearly in this dream. I don't know what I expect Samantha's reaction to be when she sees me, if she sees me. For some nonsensical reason I expect her to recognize me this time; I expect her to see the love of her life and run into my arms.

I get up and stumble the few feet to her street, Fairview, in Studio City. I see the lights of a car moving in my direction. There's not a lot of traffic at this time of night, so when I see those lights approaching, something—I don't know what; maybe I'm delirious at the possibility of seeing her—causes me to plod out into the middle of Fairview, eyes at half-mast.

I have not given the driver of the Volkswagen Golf time to stop. In slow motion, it feels to me, she hits me.

The next thing I know, I'm waking up, feeling no pain, probably because it's a dream. Samantha is leaning over me, her hair enveloping me in a silky cocoon. She is holding a cool washcloth to my forehead. Apparently, she was able to apply the brakes quickly enough not to seriously injure me. Whatever happened, it's the nicest accident I've ever been involved in.

Another dissolve, a time-lapse. Actually it feels like several time lapses. In these sequences, she's above me again. Again, it feels as if I'm in a safe, warm, sexy, silken cocoon. I look into Sam's eyes as if for the first time. Is there a word for their color? Caribbean? So many shades of blue, they're uncountable.

Music plays over this scene. I think it's Andy Williams, singing something about looking into your eyes. And it feels as if I am simultaneously in every one of the many mansions of what heaven must be for me, because I know there will be no more tears and never, ever another goodbye.

This dream is especially confusing because it feels like a lucid dream, the kind in which you know you're dreaming. Most flying dreams are lucid dreams. My dream of being the mockingbird was a lucid dream. In any case, this dream of being with Sam feels doubly real, containing at least two separate planes of unconsciousness, and I realize I'm praying this dream will never leave me, not in 1974, not in 2021, not ever. Whatever this place is, I want to stay in it the rest of my life.

As I go on with that life, the world will be with me, but I will always be able to look out of my eyes and into Samantha's, whether she's physically with me, or whether she's in what the world calls another generation.

Another attack of doubt: I'm not sure if it's the young Sam I'm with or the older one. I feel a chill through my entire body and am aware that time in both of my lives has dwindled; it's almost spent. I am being given a kind of death row moment, in this case one final wish.

I look into Sam's eyes and whisper to her, "All I want is one more hour with you."

21

ENCOURAGEMENT

I reach an old friend who used to be best friends with Zeke's wife, Liz. I'm guessing they're still in touch so I gave him a ring. He remembers me, knows I'm a friend of Liz's, and after a little half-truth explaining, gives me her telephone number in Newport, Kentucky.

I thank him, hang up, and dial the number for Liz.

Because I live in Los Angeles where most of the people I know (or knew) often don't answer the phone themselves, but have their services or machines pick up calls they haven't been expecting, I'm surprised to hear Liz answer after two rings.

There is a husky, warm timbre to her voice. I remember thinking she's as nice as she is beautiful and how lucky I thought Zeke was. Too bad they couldn't make their marriage work. I always thought they were crazy about each other.

"Liz, is that you?"

There is only a moment's pause. "Danny?"

She sounds surprised. But why shouldn't she be? We haven't spoken for ... a long time.

"Oh, Danny, Danny, oh good Lord. I've missed you."

"Hi, Liz, I can't tell you how wonderful it is to hear your voice."

"What are you doing? I mean, what have you been up to?"

"Kind of a long story."

"Zeke hasn't mentioned your name for a while, and I've been up to my eyeballs in my painting and sculpture. I'm doing both now. Usually, I'll get involved with a painting project for about a week, and the next week, I find myself working on a new wire sculpture. And in case you're about to ask me if I miss acting, the answer is a resounding no. … God, and I'm telling you all about myself, just like an actress. Tell me anything about yourself."

"Do you talk to Zeke at all?" I say.

There's a brief pause. "What do you mean?" I frown at her through over two thousand miles of AT&T lines. "I talk to him every day."

I'm silent. Finally: "You call him long distance, or he calls you, every day? You might as well not have bothered getting divorced."

There's another long pause. "Danny, what are you talking about? We didn't get divorced. We're … what's the term they're using? Codependent. I don't think either one of us would survive a day without the other."

"But I remember …"

"Oh, we had a couple of bad moments, but we worked those out."

"So you're saying he moved to Kentucky with you?"

"Yes. Well, it was kind of contingent on his quitting smoking. But he did that. I know it wasn't easy for him, poor lamb. But he did it. And he's able to do his writing as well here as he could in LA."

"I'm shocked."

I can almost see her frown. "I'm not sure why you should be," she says. "Haven't you been talking to him lately?"

"Uh ... no, I guess it's been a while."

"Yeah, well. ... Anyway, I hope someday you'll be able to put Fleury behind you and find the perfect one—she's out there, waiting for you."

"Liz?"

"Yeah?"

"Would you consider coming out of retirement for a week of work?" I quickly add: "You'd be saving my life."

"Oh, Danny." There's disappointment in her voice. "Oh, Danny, I gave that up. You know that. I can't stand that whole end-less stream of Hollywood ... horseshit. I live in a state famous for horses. We don't have 1 percent of the horseshit you have in Hol-lywood. You know how I feel about it. We've talked about this."

"But you were doing so well. You had more ... *heat* in Hol-lywood than almost anyone I know." She's quiet. I blurt out: "I am in a bind." Lost in talking to my old friend, I feel myself veering off the track. "I don't know what I am anymore, Liz. Or even, to be honest, *who* I am. I don't know where to begin to look for myself. Somewhere in here, maybe a few days ago, it felt as if I was begin-ning to lose time ... maybe a week? I dunno." Naturally, I don't mention that I also lost forty-seven years. "I missed an appoint-ment or two. My producer had to track me down. ... It's no more than showbiz nerves, my usual wonkiness, I guess, but—"

"Danny, what is it? You don't sound ..." She's lost for the word that describes however it is I should sound.

"I know I don't, Liz. But I do know that if I can get this movie I'm working on into production, I feel in my guts that somehow I'll be able to get back to myself. It'll save my life."

"Give me your number," says Liz, not happy. Before we hang up, she says, sounding wistful and as loving as I remember her, "Aw, Danny, you're still a baby."

I'm doing a few things around the house and packing a bag in preparation for driving down to the desert when Liz calls me back.

"You sounded desperate," she says.

CLOSE–UP: DESPERATE ACTOR, LOST IN TIME AND SPACE, LAUGHS WRYLY.

"Danny? Are you okay?"

"Yeah, I'm okay in the sense that I'm still breathing and thrilled to hear your voice again."

There's a long pause on the other end. Then Liz says, "How long do you need me for?"

My lungs fill with oxygen. "A week, at the outside."

There is a pause. I hear shallow, even breathing on her end. "I'll do it. When do you need me?"

"Oh, God, thank you, Liz. Can I give you an on–or–about?"

"Why not? It looks like I'm back in showbiz for a week."

I get her address, promise her the script as soon as I can finish it and get it to her, and we hang up. When I'm playing a role as well as I can play it, it's because I've found my performance in the other actor's eyes. That's an old line, but good actors keep saying it (I remember hearing Alan Alda say it in an acting workshop). Liz is a great actor. I'll have a better chance of finding the performance I need with someone that good.

I'm feeling a strong flicker of hope.

I would file the telephone call I get next under the heading of coincidence if I still believed there was such a thing.

"How ... did ... you get ... my number?" I say to Zeke.

There's a long beat. "I don't know," says Zeke. "The same way you reached me. I dialed the number I remember and—"

"But we're in different ..."

"I will always know your telephone number. He coughs a few times, clears his throat, then says, "Danny, I always know where you are. We've been friends for about fifty years. How could I *not* know how to reach you?"

Again, this makes no sense to me, but by now I'm not sure I care. "What made you decide to call me at this particular moment?"

Zeke says, "Because I have to tell you I got a letter from Sam."

I hear my own intake of breath. "When?"

"I don't know. They gave it to me today, but I'm not sure when it was delivered." He coughs. "Sometimes this place is a little sloppy with things like getting your mail right up to you."

"When was it written?"

"It says Wednesday the fifth at the top."

"The fifth of what?"

"I don't know. I guess this month. What month is this?"

"Aw, Zeke, I don't know what month it is where you are. Can you read the letter to me?"

"I don't know, Danny. She wrote it to *me*."

"Is it about me?"

"It's all about you."

"Zeke, I am lost. I still can't find Sam. Please, help me. If you got a letter from Sam, read it to me."

He coughs again, then says, "Maybe I should."

"Yes. You should. Read it to me."

"It's kinda long. I'm not sure I can make it all the way through."

I don't say anything.

"But I'll try."

"Yeah, Zeke, try. Read it to me."

He clears his throat. "Dear Zeke, sometimes I have a little trouble talking to you on the phone. I'm not sure why. It's not you. I can understand you all right. I am so sorry you're having to go through that experience. I think of you every day. I know Danny does too. But then, he talks to you almost every day, right? Rhetorical question.

"I'm writing because I am worried about Danny. If I tell you this on the phone, it's going to put too much pressure on you, and I don't want to do that. I know, I'm doing it anyway, but at least this way you can think about it a little, maybe jot down a couple of thoughts.

"My problem is I don't know what's going on with Danny, but something is. He doesn't seem to be here lately and I don't know how to find him. I mean, we are living in the same house together, but it's as if somehow my husband is slipping away from me. And I don't know what to do about it. The only other person who knows him as well as I do is you. But I'm thinking we don't know him in the same way and maybe you can understand some things that are going on with him now in a way that I can't.

"I know the slipping away from me part doesn't make any sense. He's crazy about me. I'm aware I don't have to tell you that; not to mention seventy-five-year-old men rarely leave their wives. So I'm not worried about anything like that. What I am worried about—and maybe this sounds crazy—is that he may have made me more important than I should be, to the exclusion of everything else in his life. If you asked him, I know he would tell you himself that's unhealthy. I know it's unhealthy. He needs something I can't give him, but he's not looking for whatever that might be anyplace else—which scares me. It's as if he feels that this phase of his life, these years with me now, are so good that somehow they're bound to end up driving him away from me in a way neither of us can understand. It's like 'too much of a good thing.' I think he feels that, in some manner, his lucky streak has got to end, almost as if an unhappy ending is what he deserves.

"I don't expect any of this to make sense to you; it doesn't make sense to me. I'm writing this to you now on the long shot chance that you might have some idea what I can do ... to turn this around, so that we can get back to the life we've always had together. That's all I want now. I want our life to be the way it used to be. I want Danny to be happy. And I don't need to add I want to be happy too. We have cocktails every night. He always seems to want to go back in time and talk about our first days together (I don't mean our *very* first days) and I don't want to do that so often, at least not the way he does. If life doesn't move forward, it's not life; it's trying to capture something that can't be captured. It's putting your existence under glass. I don't want to live that way. I am sure Danny doesn't want to either. But he can't seem to pull himself off this path he's heading down—this path toward living in times that are already gone, which makes it impossible to create new times."

Zeke takes several seconds to cough and clear his throat, then continues reading.

"Anyway, give this some thought, will you? I'm not trying to go behind Danny's back. I've never kept secrets from him, except during a few of those first weeks after our blind date. But our life together is better when he's working on something that isn't about me.

"The ironic thing is I don't think he knows how often, from my point of view, the essence of it is the other way around. I was on the other side of the Santa Monicas one day, coming out of a 7-Eleven. I was at least seven or eight miles away from our home, over the mountains in this sprawling city, walking to my car, and I looked up and saw Danny, leaning against his Firebird in a tiny parking lot, grinning at me. It doesn't make any sense, but that's one of my happiest memories—seeing Danny when I hadn't expected to. It was purely by accident that he was over there too and he'd seen my car in that parking lot, but it was like a Christmas surprise, the best present I could have hoped for. I know he loves me, but I'm not sure if he knows how much he constantly fills my heart with joy.

"But even so, it seems I don't obsess on it the way he does. I'm a little afraid that if he keeps on making his wife the pivot point of his life, he may lose his direction. Danny is my life, Zeke, but I know it's not a healthy one if I don't keep my own separate identity.

"Talk to him about it, will you, old friend?

"I love you. My heart is always with you.

"Sam."

There is a pause before Zeke says to me, "Well, I guess that's it, Danny. I think reading Sam's letter to you constitutes talking to you about it. I don't know what else I can add. You told me you're lost in time. But you're not. I've found you. The way I look at it, it's up to you to help Samantha find you too. Bye, pal."

He hangs up before I have a chance to tell him that his wife is coming to LA soon, to be in a movie I'm writing, the whole purpose of which is to help Samantha find me again.

I walk into the living room, look around me at the beautiful Benedict Canyon home I'm living in. Has everything that's happened since the morning I kissed Sam goodbye and set out to drive over the Santa Monica mountains, including this moment, been a lucid dream?

But you can't drive into a lucid dream. You cannot turn on the ignition, listen to the motor turn over and drive into any form of clarity, into a 3D, waking sense of yourself; you will remain as uninformed as when you started. Lucid dreams *can* mesh dreams and reality, I guess, but without conscious waking help, the engine of your focused dreaming will never have turned over in the first place. I told Patricia I cannot say, "Remember" and expect my "self" to do what it's told. My mind doesn't work that way." She said, "Everyone's mind works that way."

Okay, maybe, but what I seem to be missing, in order to gain access to the mysterious mechanism of my mind, is one of those horrible folded-up, tissue-thin instruction sheets, like the ones they give you with unassembled IKEA products.

I'm not going to pinch myself again. I've tried that a few more times since I first mentioned it.

I'm starting to bruise.

22

DAD

It's late afternoon on a Friday. Valory is with me. I've gotten off the San Bernardino Freeway and we're headed south toward Hemet to visit my dad, who has been failing physically for the last five years—or maybe for his entire life. When I told Brenda we were on our way down, she said we should hurry. She doesn't take everything my dad says too seriously, but he's told her he thinks he's dying … again. Well, you never know, and I have no accurate memory of when he died my first time through.

Acres of mesquites vanish to our rear. The passing desert transforms, as if we're speeding across an animated patchwork quilt from one panel onto another. This new square is dotted with low cactus and scattered limestone rocks, absorbing the late afternoon rays of sunlight.

Because my father has already died over and over in my mind, and because he's an inescapable influence in my life, I see him watching me as I approach. But he's not "with me"; he's never "with me." His mind is wandering. He can't stay in a moment, even the stillness of this dazzling pre-sunset that turns the cliffs on the eastern horizon into a sweeping console of gold that shimmers as if God just this second thought of it.

Valory says, "Why's he live out here?"

"I don't know the answer to that. Never did."

"My God, there's nothing here."

"There's a thriving fundamentalist movement where we're going. And I know it's pretty hot today, but in the winter it can get real nippy."

"How hot does it get?"

"Sometimes the highs hover in the 120s."

"Who lives out here?" says Valory.

"Oh … people—listless, sorta belligerent people. I'm sorry; that's not nice. They do have *The Ramona Pageant*. If you don't know about that, it's an outdoor historical drama, performed in a natural amphitheater, about the Native American people in this part of the country, focusing on the trials and tribulations of a pair of star-crossed lovers. It's a mostly volunteer effort and kind of a big deal with the locals. The play draws pretty big crowds every year; they've been putting it on since the 1920s. Anyway, when they heard my father was an actor they asked him to be in it. But he said no. He was a 'star' and wouldn't do it unless he could be the lead. You can imagine their reaction. They didn't want a grizzled old Hollywood Anglo has-been as the hero of *The Ramona Pageant*.

"We're coming up to Ramona Expressway now, which is normally a road you want to avoid. They don't maintain it well. That's why we're driving my Audi today. I don't like to expose my Firebird to roads like this. I figure we'll be okay. God knows where I'd get an Audi fixed out here."

"That wouldn't really count as a slur on the citizenry." Valory looks out at a bleak stretch of *Mad Max*-like passing scenery and adds, "It's not all as monotonous as this bit ... is it?

"No, but most of it is." I squint out the driver's side window at "this bit" of desert wasteland and its endless dispersal of cactus, like headstones in a haphazard cemetery. "It's also a place people come to when they're ready to die. So, there's something sort of sad about it. Not that it's not sad enough all on its own. It's got more than its share of extremists, racists, and hillbillies. The school district is so bad that for quite a while they were required to offer parents the opportunity to send their kids elsewhere. I once heard a joke about Hemet: 'I heard my neighbor beating up his wife. I called the cops, but they didn't come. They were too busy beating up their own wives.'"

"Was he a good father, your dad?" She glances at me. "What's that look?"

"He was never home that much as I was growing up. He worked in dinner theaters around the country when that was popular. In a way, most of what I know of him is from clips of celluloid on which he smiles, gets angry, persuasive, friendly, clever, outraged, tender ... surprised, but never alive. It doesn't matter that he's still breathing—if he is still breathing."

Valory lifts her eyebrows at this last comment and asks me more about him, but I can't think of much more I want to say to her about my father, except ... I tell her about St. Louis.

"He reached his high point of ... not exactly fame," I say, "when I was still a toddler."

"How so?"

"It was in St. Louis. I remember being out on something they used to call an airing deck. But I think it was a kind of balcony that was over an alley. My dad was doing a play. My mother and I were with him. We'd all come out from LA."

"What play?" Valory is wearing dark glasses, which is disappointing. I can't see her eyes. She's looking at me, but I can't read her expression. I feel a breaker of erotic urges, imagining those eyes, but she frowns at me.

"Hollywood actors didn't often do plays in those days," I tell her. "But Marlon Brando and the Actors Studio were in the news back then. I think somebody convinced my dad he should get a reputation as a stage actor in order to be taken more seriously. So the way I heard it, a few years later somebody wanted him to go to St. Louis and do Stanley Kowalski in *A Streetcar Named Desire* and he took the job. And my mother and I went with him."

"Do you remember it at all?"

"Not exactly. I heard later it turned out my dad wasn't a good fit for Stanley. In fact, the local papers in St. Louis made fun of him. And I guess they made such a fuss over my dad being … pretty lousy that it drew the attention of the national press. And so they went out to see just how bad my dad was as Stanley Kowalski. And I guess they all agreed with the St. Louis critics and it became kind of a theater world cause célèbre, how bad my dad's Stanley was. And then it was national news for a little while.

"Well, that would have been okay," I say, "and it would have blown over and maybe my dad would have let it fade from his memory. But evidently, he wasn't able to do that. And when he got back to Hollywood he couldn't get a job anymore. He didn't have a wonderful contract with his studio in the first place. But they dropped him just like that … and he never did anything half-worthwhile again … shit jobs and dinner theater for the rest of his working life."

"What's that got to do with the airing deck?"

"Nothing. Except I guess my dad could see the writing on the wall. And one day in St. Louis he got violent—like Stanley Kowalski in *Streetcar*—and even though I was eighteen months old and the doctors said there was no way I could remember anything about that time …"

"What?"

"I knew they were wrong. Because I remember one day my father came home. It must have been after a matinee because it was still light out on that airing deck. I was in some kind of play-pen. My mother came out and picked me up—I don't know if she was trying to protect me, or probably both of us. And my dad followed her out to where we were. And he grabbed me from her. I can still almost feel the pain in my shoulder, or maybe it's that I imagine I can, I'm not sure. And he grabbed me with one hand, and he hit my mother with the back of his other hand … and I heard her scream."

Valory takes off her sunglasses. "What happened?"

"We were on the fourth floor. Dad had knocked her over the railing. I remember her kind of balancing on top, like a tennis ball on top of the net, bouncing, equivocating, suspended in time before it decides which way to drop.

"Then my mother dropped—on the other side. There was an alley below us, cement. She died."

"My God! What happened? I mean … she *died*? He slapped her and she fell to her death?" Valory's forehead creases with what I think is horror, but then she brings her hand to her mouth and stifles a laugh.

"Lord," I say. "I don't think of that as a funny story."

She covers her amusement. "Yeah, but after time has passed …"

Valory only now heard that story.

She turns solemn. "But he didn't mean to. ... Was he prosecuted?"

"No, it was ruled an accident. And I think it probably was ... if you don't count the physical abuse that precipitated it."

She looks off at the passing desert. "I suppose your father was pretty naturally frustrated at the time."

Who is this woman? "You mean if you get really bad reviews, you're allowed to kill your wife?"

"That's not what I mean. I was just trying to understand. I mean, I'm sorry, but your mother was ... *gone* by that time. I was thinking about the survivors, you and your father."

"You're about to meet the other survivor."

That introduction had to wait. Dad had become a prodigious afternoon napper in recent years and was taking a siesta when we arrived. Brenda warned us not to disturb the hibernating "bear."

I'm standing in the kitchen of my father's house in Passion Falls, a "suburb" of Hemet, a hundred miles from Beverly Hills, looking out the window at Brenda and Valory, sitting in an inviting little oasis that Brenda has put together about thirty yards behind the house. It consists of an eclectic mix of outdoor furniture, lovingly assembled from garage sales and antique stores. There's a padded wrought iron bench, two mismatched but comfortable looking wrought iron chairs, and an Adirondack chair, painted white. The area is surrounded by three palm trees and protected from the sun by a goldenrod yellow, triangular sail canopy, attached to the trunks by a braided nautical rope.

At the moment, Brenda is petting a dog sitting docilely next to her. I didn't know Brenda and my father had a dog. I don't remember that from the first time through. Maybe I didn't notice. The late afternoon desert sun, slanting in from behind us, has set the San Jacinto Peak aglow and is bathing this side of the mountains in a rosy yellow-gold. I wonder what my father is going to think of Valory when he gets up from his afternoon nap.

I see Brenda rise and head toward the house. As she approaches the kitchen door, Valory stands up from her chair and holds her hand out to the dog, half-hidden behind the Adirondack chair, a little hard to make out in the glare of the sunlight.

Valory stoops, reaching out to pet it.

Now she pulls up and I see the dog in clearer lighting. His teeth are bared. He snaps at her, then does it again, moving steadily toward her. Valory retreats a step, holding her bitten hand. She whirls away from the dog and runs toward the house. Brenda meets her at the door. As I head out of the kitchen, Brenda is hurrying after the dog, scolding him, chasing him away.

As I reach Valory, I say, "Are you okay?"

"I am not okay! That dog bit me!" We both turn back to see Brenda still chasing the dog, who disappears over a rise.

I take Valory into the kitchen, trying to soothe her, assuring her she's going to be fine. It's not having much effect. The bite doesn't seem bad, and it strikes me that Valory has the makings of a drama queen. Brenda joins us and produces a first aid kit, from which she takes out antiseptic and bandages.

"Wasn't that your dog?" I ask Brenda.

"No. I've seen him wandering around the village once in a while. I'm shocked. He's always seemed harmless, friendly. But I can't say I know him."

"You were petting him."

"He just wandered by," says Brenda. "He's usually so sweet."

"Sweet to you," says Valory. "He didn't like *me*."

"I am so sorry, sweetheart," says Brenda. "The people in the village seem to be fond of him, but no one can figure out who he belongs to."

I'm looking out the window as Brenda continues to minister to Valory's wounds. Valory looks away, the way people do when having blood drawn.

I see the dog, standing in Brenda's oasis. He's returned. I can see him clearly now in the late afternoon sun.

"Where are you going?" says Valory as I open the kitchen door.

"I'll be right back."

The dog is still standing beneath the sail canopy as I approach. He doesn't move. His body faces toward my left, but his head is cocked in my direction. He's watching me.

As I've almost reached him, he turns in the other direction.

An irregular brown patch covers much of the right side of his light tan body. Again, he stops moving. Now he sits.

I sit next to him.

"What are you doing here? You don't bite."

He smiles at me.

"I wish you could *really* talk, not just when I'm smashed or stoned or whatever. And that's odd—I haven't even been drinking today, not yet. What are you doing here?" He's still smiling. "I know you're in there." He's just looking at me. He's a dead ringer for Tali in 2021. "Why don't we pretend this is another mescaline trip I'm on, and you're my dog. Or if you prefer, I'm one of your humans and we're sitting here talking about old times, except in reverse, because old times for us are future times—that haven't happened yet. It would be so reassuring." Again, I say, "I wish you could talk."

He unfolds himself, licks my face, sits back again, and stares at me in that way I'm so fond of. "Oh, I can talk. It's just that—like always—I need you to provide me with the words."

"Wow."

"So, what do we have in mind?" says Tali.

I blink a few times. "All right, to begin with … did you follow me back in time?"

He looks pensive.

"Did you drag a little girl out of a burning house a few nights ago?"

"I'm not sure."

"What does that mean?"

"It means I don't remember doing that, but I guess it's possible. I'm pretty certain that if I saw a little girl in a burning house, I'd do my best to be helpful, but I don't recall the specific incident. Why? Did you see me do that? If you saw me do that, maybe I did. I'd like to think I did. I'd feel good about that."

"Okay," I say, "I'll ask you again: did you follow me back in time?"

He looks at me with his amiable *what-is-your-PROBLEM?* eyes. "I don't follow you; I go where I'm needed. I never know where or when that's going to be, but I'm always prepared—you could think of me as a canine Boy Scout if you like. I've given you sort of temporal custody of me, but you don't own me, if that's what you're thinking. Nobody owns anything."

"Are you a reflection of me?"

"Not that I know of. I'm me."

"I can see that, but who are you?"

"Oh, you want to know who I *am!*"

"Why did you bite Valory?"

"Is that her name?"

"Yes."

"It wasn't personal. And I didn't actually hurt her. It's just that she was threatening me. You know how dogs hate to be threatened—even nice dogs like me." He sighs, as much as a dog can do that. "Look, despite what I said about nobody owning anything, you belong to Sam, and I'm very territorial when it comes to you and Sam. Simple as that."

"Is there anything else about Valory you think I should know?"

"Valory?"

"The woman you bit."

"I didn't bite her ... exactly. I sent her a little message."

"Is there something I should know about her that I don't?"

Tali gazes over my shoulder, apparently reflecting on the question. "Look Danny, you—all on your own—have a better set of psychological assessment tools than I do. It looks to me like she just wants to know where you've buried your bones. More than that, it's hard to read what's on her mind. I *can* tell you this: when you picked that lady up, you picked up a piece of work."

He smiles at me again, but it's as if his atoms and molecules are floating out like aerosol spray mist in all directions. I don't know if it's because of the drive across the desert, and maybe I'm a little tired and spacey from that, but anyway, Tali is no longer with me.

When I get back to the house, Valory asks me, "What happened out there? What were you doing?"

I look out the window at Brenda's oasis where, three minutes ago, I was sitting with my dog Tali.

Brenda grins at me, a penetrative kind of grin. "Oh, Danny's a strange one, he is. You never know when he's going to plunk down somewhere and go all inside himself. He's a strange one."

A while later, still in my father's house in Passion Falls, Dad gazes out at his backyard, the rusty barbecue grill, a scrawny mesquite, and Brenda's brave attempt at a lawn—sparse, the color of old and dry tobacco, gone almost entirely to crab grass, tinged with a hazy, LA basin-infused sunset. Brenda's little oasis setting is the only part of the house's surroundings she's been able to partway tame.

It turns out my father is not dying, not at the moment.

"Brenda, bring these people glasses of white wine," says Dad. "We're going to have to prune that tree."

"I know, Frank."

"It's blocking my whole view of your little picnic ground thing out there. It's starting to muck with my soul." Brenda made him stop cussing a few years ago, but he still gets close.

"White wine good for you?" I say to Valory. She nods and I say, "Could you please do me a gin and tonic, Brenda?"

"Better bring him the bottle," says my dad. Humor.

Brenda always lets my father be a fool, but never makes him feel like one. She smiles, nods, and goes off to get us our drinks.

"What's your name again?" says my dad.

"This is my friend, Valory," I tell him.

"Nice to meet you, Mr. Maytree," she says for the second time.

For at least the third time he gives her the once-over. "Yeah, same here." Then, looking after Brenda: "I talk and talk lately and she doesn't understand me. To be honest, I don't understand myself, not a single thing I'm saying. But I guess I can understand what a pleasure it is that my son has brought such a gorgeous guest with him."

"Thank you, Mr. Maytree. I like your home."

"Do you? I guess it's okay if you're a Zuni or a Hopi or one of those burnished Pueblo people. Sometimes I try to imagine those Asians who migrated here from Siberia. You'd think they wouldn't have come this far south, maybe stopped in Oregon or San Francisco. Of all the godforsaken places on earth, why would they pick this one?"

"Why did you pick it?" says Valory.

"I didn't pick it, it picked me." He looks around him at the adobe walls and the Native American art. "Brenda has done a great job with what she has to work with. I gotta hand it to her. And the price is right. I can't cavil about the rent."

"I think it's beautiful," says Valory. "It seems to suit you."

"That's real depressing," says my father. "But maybe you're right." Apropos of nothing, he adds, "The workings of my mind feel as trite as a sitcom, and as pointless." I'm not sure which one of us he's saying this to. "I got a solicitation in the mail today that said, 'Open immediately.' I spent fifteen minutes thinking of a response and finally settled on, 'Go flock yourself immediately.' I didn't actually write it and put it in the mail, but I'm afraid that's next."

With my best-humored smile, I say, "I'm not sure they'd be that offended by you telling them to flock themselves."

He glances distantly at me. He looks like an old doll with a painted-on smile, except the smile has faded from being left out in the desert too long. He has a fish-eyed look, a cheerless ventriloquist dummy that got thrown into the corner where it flopped onto its back and it's staring up into the air. He sighs and lowers his gaze to his Chardonnay. "I add string to the spool of my health during the daytime, eating all her ridiculous health foods, and then, in the evening, she uncorks the wine, because she knows she can't say no to me, and ..." He makes a *phssht* sound, like fishing line spinning out from a casting rod.

"You don't drink that much anymore," I say. "Do you? You know the doctor said it can ... be very bad for you."

"I know. It almost killed me last week, or yesterday, or whenever I was sick."

"That's why I'm here," I say. "Brenda was worried about you."

"Fooled her though, didn't I?" He regards me with the stubborn look of a sixteen-year-old looking you straight in the eye as he produces a pack of cigarettes and takes one out and lights it. "It's going to take a lot more than asthma to kill me."

"You're a tough old bird," I say with a carefully crafted pleasant smile.

He half-echoes the effort, blinks, and looks out at the mesquite tree. "My mother had her own demons."

I don't think I ever knew that, but I don't ask what he means because he'll either complete the thought or he won't. ... *Shit. That's coldhearted. Did I ever ask my father about his childhood? I can't remember. I don't think so. He never volunteered anything.* I look to see where Brenda is with our wine and gin. She's still out in the kitchen. I think of Samantha back ... *sideways* in time and wonder if my father would have been able to recognize her for who she is. Hard not to.

We have a dinner of flour tortillas filled with cheese, lettuce, and ground beef, and tortilla chips with a salsa hot enough to spike your pulse rate. Brenda has also made a Mexican salad, with olives, romaine lettuce, and a mixture of some other greens I'm not familiar with. We drink an Argentinian Beaujolais and top the meal off with flan and coffee.

After dinner, my father sits down at the piano and plays and sings a lot of the same stuff I remember him playing and singing when I was growing up.

At one point he croons, "Somebody stole my gal / Somebody stole my pal ..."

He stops, turns, and with a straight face says to me: "I suppose you think it's kind of ironical, my singing that particular song, right?"

I don't say, "Ironical doesn't cover it, Dad," I shrug and smile as genially as I can.

He grunts, turns back to the piano and plays a sprightly version of *12th St. Rag.*

He's still pretty good. Even though I got more attention in the world of show business than he did, he's much more of a natural entertainer than I am. I think … I hope, I'm a better actor than he was, but that's partly because I'm not quite his kind of hammy, although I'm afraid there are a few similarities between us, genetic mannerisms or something. I've always had trouble with that.

Later, sitting in front of the fire drinking brandy, which Dad insists on having despite his faltering health, Valory appears to be studying him. Brenda has gone to bed.

"So, tell me about your son," she says.

"What about him?"

"Has he been a good boy? Have you enjoyed calling him 'son'?"

Dad chuckles. I haven't heard him laugh in … longer than I can remember.

"Well, he thinks he's a better actor than I am."

"I don't think that," I say, smiling.

"Is he?" Valory asks him again.

"I'll tell you something, honey. I haven't the faintest idea. I never understood any of it. I never knew anybody who did. As for good actors, except for a few freaks—Spencer Tracy, Henry Fonda, Katharine Hepburn, and a handful of fancy-pants like that—it's not always so easy to tell the difference between good acting and bad. If you're reasonably smart and you can make yourself sound sincere, and you don't overact too much, like I guess I did sometimes, or underact when you should be making it broad, then all you've got to do is show up and say your words. If they like the cut of your jib, then for as long as they do, you're fartin' through silk." He glances at me. "Got yourself a delightful little *chiquita* this time." He looks at Valory again. "What do you do for a living, sweetie?"

"I'm a personal assistant in the movie business," she tells him.

"Who have you assisted?"

"Oh, quite a few people. Carrie Snodgress, Paula Prentiss, Hannah Castle, Candice Bergen ..." She throws me a furtive glance. "Whoever needs assistance in the movie business. I'm kind of a Jill of all trades in that line of work."

My father glances over at me and says, "Shut your mouth."

I feel like someone has jammed my fingers into a light socket. *It is brand-new information for me that she has worked for Hannah.* "Are you still working for her?" I say. "Hannah, I mean."

"Oh, I thought I told you. That gig came to an end a while ago."

There's no point in trying to straighten this out now. Judging by her crooked smile, Valory is about as smashed as I am. But she didn't drop that piece of information at this moment on purpose. Why would she do that?

Later, after Valory has gone to bed, my father and I are still in front of the fire. We're each drinking our third brandy. Maybe because of the brandy and the news about Hannah, or perhaps it's because feeling I've been lied to always puts me in a dark mood,

I say to him, "Did you ever love me, Dad? No, I take it back. Did you ever … like me?"

He yawns. *Yawns. I shouldn't have gone down this road, but I can't take it back now.*

"The reason I ask is, I have no memory of you giving me— as far as I could make out—any conscious thought at all. Did you ever do that?" He frowns at me. "I mean, maybe I've missed something, and in your own peculiar way you're crazy about me. And I've never understood it before. Is that possible?"

He narrows his eyes, searching, I assume, for a clever response.

"You may wonder why I've waited till now to ask a question like that. I'll tell you. I didn't have the guts the first time through, but I'm not nervous about whatever you might say … or do anymore." I don't bother to fill him in on any of the details of my current cosmic experience; he'd think it was the alcohol, or drugs. Anyway, I'm being reminded again of his gift for not listening.

His look splinters on mine, perhaps in fact recalling times when he didn't think I was much worth taking note of, other than as something to use for target practice when the urge struck him. And now I'm sitting a few feet away, talking to him for what may be the last time, asking him questions that may or may not embarrass him to death.

"Not easy for me either," he says, "to look back on what I was a part of." It's said with his contrarian air. Noticing that I'm gazing at a picture of a beautiful, dark-skinned Native American woman on the wall, he slips into a nonspecific redneck accent: "You ain't a man till you had a dark meat." That's been said like an actor with only contempt for this character, demonstrating that he could play this role if he wanted to, but also that he is a decent, sensitive performer who would never stoop to that sort of unkindness, professionally or otherwise.

"Why do you do that, Dad? It's just ... *mean*. What makes you think it serves any purpose to say something like that out loud?"

He blinks his eyes at me rapidly. I must look like a strobing light show to him. Now, he resumes his usual mid-American oratory, touched slightly by the flat Michigan vowels of his upbringing that make, for example, "pass" rhyme with "chaos." He scrapes the back of one hand over the stubble on his chin. "You don't have a feel for irony, do you, kiddo? I've been on the right side of good and worthwhile causes all my life. But you've got to have a little levity from time to time. We've all got to be allowed to be a little irreverent once in a while. That's something you just never understood."

I understand he would not in any sense know what "politically incorrect" means. "I am revolted, Dad, by what I didn't say 'Oh, shut up' to. But I was ... petrified, or maybe—giving myself a huge benefit of the doubt—I didn't know any better."

He frowns at his brandy. "You won't be here when I do die. I don't think it's going to take long for me to go once it starts for real. I've lived too hard. I'll explode or something—like most alcoholics."

"I admire your self-recognition."

"Do you?" He studies me, and for a fraction of a second I imagine he almost cares. "But you don't admire much else about me, right?"

"Not much."

"What are you looking for?"

"I beg your pardon?"

"Why do you stay in LA?"

"I don't know. It's my home."

He snorts a monosyllabic chortle that turns into a coughing spasm.

When he's partially recovered, I say, "You seem to care about every worthwhile cause in the world, but sometimes I think you don't like other people, especially me." *I could let it go at that, but I don't.* "Well, maybe that's not true. Maybe it's just all of us and you can't love anyone."

He stares at me through eyes watery from the coughing, still trying to clear his throat. Finally, he manages, "You need a shit-load of help, Danny boy."

I wonder how much of this conversation has been an inevitable, equal and opposite reaction to my earlier limp attempts to play the role of caring son. "Maybe we could seek out a little family therapy, Dad, you and I. Even after all these years maybe we could finally develop a little father-son kind of … regard for each other."

He's terminally ill, I don't expect to see him again, and a couple of generations later, as if it's a skill I've been practicing every day of my life, I'm as handy as I always was at taking dead aim at his open wounds.

23

JOHN CASSAVETES

After Dad retires to his bedroom, I go into his den and discover he has an early videocassette home recording system hooked up to his television. I'm familiar with the system; it was pricey (as expensive as some cars) and high-tech back in the day—that is, *this* day—but went the way of the dodo when VHS came along. Few homes had one in 1974; I'm surprised Dad does. He has a sizable collection of videotapes. I pick one arbitrarily, stick it in the clunky, big-as-a-Buick console's slot, and turn it on.

I don't know what I'm watching—I'm a lot befuddled by brandy—but the camera is following an actor who looks like my father, or maybe even a little like me. Yes, it's definitely me, *not* my father. Jesus. All I had was some gin and tonic, a few glasses of wine, and a … little brandy. That's not too much … I'm a young man; that shouldn't be enough to …

Who is this man I'm watching?

In a tracking shot, the young man (I'll go ahead and call him me for now) is wandering along Broadway in Manhattan late at night.

I stop in front of a nightclub and say to the ticket taker, *"I'm looking for my Velma. I can't find her."* No, that's another movie. That's *Farewell, My Lovely*, based or *Murder, My Sweet*, an earlier version.

"Maybe she's where you left her," says the familiar-looking ticket taker in the booth in front of the nightclub.

"She's not." I hear a voice singing from inside the nightclub. *Goodbye, Old Girl ...*

"What's the deal?" I say to this ticket taker, who is beyond question the one I thought I'd left on a piece of paper, a page I typed on my Smith Corona that never made it into the script I'm writing. I never got around to giving the character a name, but I realize that who I had in mind, and who I'm now seeing on this videotape as the ticket taker, is the actual actor/director John Cassavetes.

I say, "What is this?"

"Only a guess," he says. "Maybe it's the blues you've got to go through before you come out the other side."

"Do you know where Samantha is?"

"The old lady?"

"She's not an old lady."

"That's what you said the last time." He points at the same slacker kid as before, slouching against a building. "If you showed that kid the Samantha in question, he'd still tell you she's an old lady."

"He doesn't know."

"Then, maybe she's where you left her."

"She's not."

The slacker kid is looking at me with frowning curiosity. I point to him and say to Cassavetes, "I recognize this kid from before."

The kid sits up straight. His sleepy eyes grow wide. "Hey, Scooby-Doo," he says. "Sup?" He says it again, except more drawn out: "Su-uup?" He scrambles to his knees into a kind of shambly prayer position. His eyes have gone as round as half-dollars. "Oh dude, I *know* you. *Sunset Island*, isn't that right? That's right, isn't it? Zat right? Oh dude! Oh man, that's classic."

"What does he mean?" I ask Cassavetes.

"Looks like he knows you."

"It's like the road not taken, but you took it," says the kid. "You were in *Sunset Island*."

"I was not!" It feels as if I've yelled this at him.

He's undaunted. "Oh man. Oh dude. Dude, that's classic. *Sunset Island*! Shit the bed. And here you are, right here. And I met you. I'm still *meeting* you! Right now, right here in the Big Apple. It's you."

"It's not me," I say. "I didn't do *Sunset Island*."

But I don't want him to feel humiliated. If he believes, based on what I would think is the slimmest possible chance in this constantly expanding universe, that on some forgotten plane of reality I was actually in *Sunset Island*, what purpose would it serve to make him feel bad about it now?

I shrug and say, "Well … thanks."

"No, man. Shit the bed. They'll never believe me. First I run into Mickey Mantle, and now you."

He sits back down and goes silent, still gripped in his reverence for me and this moment of his existence.

I whisper to Cassavetes, "I really wasn't in *Sunset Island*. I turned it down."

He shrugs as if it couldn't matter less to him, and now, looking around, I'm not sure if I'm in front of a nightclub or a movie theater ... or it might be a rapid transit token booth, down in the subway.

"Listen good," says Cassavetes. "Think back to the call you got the night before you left home. Are you with me?"

"Yes, sir," I say. This guy seems to be in possession of some important information. "I remember that call," I say. "It was from my agent."

"No. Guess again."

"Sure it was. He told me I had an acting interview the next day." I feel like crying. I don't know the answer to this, and for the who-knows-how-many-zillionth time I'm trapped in ... *time*, repeatedly shattering and reemerging in the unending moment of the turn I made from Sunset onto Benedict. The act of hanging that right, begun in innocence, has become an apparent transgression, and I don't seem to have the power to forgive myself.

"Before you wander down that identical road again," he says, "let me straighten you out on something. That was not your agent who called you. That was a woman."

He's right. *How did I forget that?*

"It was a woman's voice you never heard before. What made you think that call came from your agent?"

"Where *did* it come from?"

"Can you remember the voice?"

"Not exactly. It sounded familiar, I think. But I don't remember in what way."

"Think again. Who have you known in your life with a mysterious, velvety voice? What's her name?"

I stare at him. For a millisecond he reminds me of my old camp counselor, Jim Ball. "Velma ... no, *Valory. Valory Valentine!*"

"And the next morning, you drove over the Santa Monica Mountains into Beverly Hills for a meeting."

"But I don't remember that meeting. What am I supposed to take from all this? If you're saying Valory Valentine was in 2021 with me, I will tell you that's not true. The voice I heard—and this was before I took those extra pills that night—was not the voice of an old lady. It was a distinctively young, sexy voice."

"Very good. Everyone learns what you're beginning to learn in their own peculiar way."

"What am I learning?"

"That everything, time included—especially time—unfolds in inconsistent, not necessarily harmonious chunks. Your job is to make as much sense as you can out of the bits and pieces you've been given." He starts to turn away; then, with a canny performer's *savior faire*, swings back. "Oh, and one little piece of advice: you've had the good fortune along the way to have been taught the distinction between substantial and silly. Most people know the difference deep within them, but they ignore it all their lives when they're confronted with the baubles, bangles, and bric-a-brac the world, like a carnival barker, holds in front of them."

"I don't understand."

He lowers his head, this fabulous Cassavetes character, and says with measured patience, "What I'm recommending, pally, is that you not be a schmuck any more than you have to, and that you do not forget to"—he smiles, eyes a-twinkle—"put the gels in the instruments, then you feel better. *But …*"

"But what?"

"*There is always a new show. Then that one closes and another one opens. We know that all certainties turn out to be the beginning of a new creative series. You've got to be bright enough to remember that each show requires a new and appropriate set of gels. But—and, most importantly, you have to remember this—the source of the light shining through the gels remains the same. Always."*

He nods at the man in the token booth, who's looking at me with dull impatience.

Without buying a token, I shuffle off to the side of the booth. Cassavetes drifts after me. "Let me ask you just a couple more things," I say, turning back.

"The floor is yours."

"What about that Tracy-Hepburn marquee I saw with the wrong Hepburn displayed?"

"What about it? I thought the girl in the box office explained that movie didn't show at the Beverly Theatre in 1974, that they were showing *Godfather Part II* when you saw the marquee."

"Then why did I see what I saw?"

"I can't say," he says, "but you *have* asked the pertinent question. And you already know the answer—although you don't seem to know you know it. You have been selective in what you wish to experience, at least when you believe you have a choice in the matter."

"I don't understand."

"I know you don't. So here it is: life is not a cabaret, it's a metaphor—everything, all of it. It never stops. Sometimes it's vague and amorphous, sometimes it's quite literal. The important part of it is this: everything we see—when we are not convinced that it's imposed on us from the outside—is what we *want* to see. Before you met the old lady, who was your favorite actress? Who did you have a schoolboy crush on?"

"I don't know, I guess Audrey Hepburn."

He nods. "But then you grew up and met Samantha. You fell in love with Samantha. You married her. She became your mate."

"Oh shit, are you telling me *Adam's Rib* is a metaphor and I didn't really see what I thought I saw, that I saw instead a … kind of analogy, or another form of what I'm seeking, what I'm longing for?"

"*I'm* not telling you that."

I sulk, as I always do when somebody knows something I don't know, but it feels as if I *should* know.

Despite my lifelong pleasure in pouting, I am not sure how much time I have with this guy, so I forge ahead. "What do you know about time traveling dogs?"

He grins Cassavetes' cool, lopsided grin. "Oh, you already know the answer to that. You don't expect one figment to explain another one, do you?"

"I can hope."

"I know. I like that about you. I'll bet that's one of the things Samantha likes too." He glances at the subway token booth. "You got thirty cents?" he says. "You got thirty cents, you can go a long way in this town. You can be on Broadway, or you can toddle off all the way to Canarsie. It all depends on whether it's you giving the directions, or the nameless desperado in the outback of your brain."

And now it's not a subway booth, it's an old-time movie theater.

I'm sitting in the front row, looking up at a two-character scene. The actors are Samantha and Danny. It's easy to see the Danny character feels he's being judged and that he's been pronounced guilty even before the jury goes out.

We're having cocktails. I don't know whether it's 2021 or 2011, or it could be anytime. I think about the pyramid meetings we got involved with shortly after we met. (It was one of those things where you go to a *gathering and each person pays a buy-in fee—in this particular scheme, $500. Eventually you had a chance to make many times that. Of course, in the end more people lost their money than won any. They were popular, those pyramid meetings, for a short while in Hollywood, until everybody caught on and it was time to move on to the next flimflam.)*

"And the time when we were involved in that pyramid scheme," I say to Sam. "Then it split apart and you went off your way and I went mine. And then one night you came back with $5,000, which seemed like a lot of money at the time. It is a lot of money. And you said here's your half. … It wasn't because you were honest and did that, because—I know—we had agreed on that. I would have done it for you as well."

"Of course you would have," says Sam. "We'd made a deal. Our pyramid meetings split off, growing exponentially as it all expanded into more and more groups. And we said we don't know if either one of us is going to win, and if one of us does, which one it will be."

"Of course," I say too quickly.

A questioning look caroms off her countenance. I've told her many times that I grew up saying what was convenient, what would keep me out of trouble. She's always told me she believes every word I say. But sometimes that seems like a big task, to be as trustworthy as Sam believes I am—or wants to believe I am. Growing up in my household, which mostly meant my dad, you were honest when it was useful. It takes some adjusting for a naïf like I was to learn to live in a world of truth.

"Whatever somebody wins, we'll divvy it up," says Sam. "That's what we decided."

"Right. And then when I had that surgery, you stayed with me every day, and every night, well past when you were supposed to leave. You stayed until the last moment. And I saw that you were this great … stand-up pal, as well as everything else. And I'd never encountered that in my life—not the way you did it. Did you just think that was the right thing to do?"

"No," says Sam. "You needed me. I mean, there were nurses and everything, but ..."

"You didn't want to go, I remember that."

"I would have stayed all night. But they made me leave," she says.

How can it be that sometimes Sam's generosity is so unnerving?

She frowns. "But ... back to something we said before ... the splitting of the money. I was surprised that YOU were surprised that I split it without question."

"Yeah, but you hadn't spent six years living with Fleury, and you weren't raised by my dad."

"That's true," she says, "but we had a deal and we kept to it. I couldn't have even entertained the idea of not doing what we said we would."

"It was the sweetness of it when you said, 'Here's yours.' It was deep in the center of me that I could read such a ... a built-in generosity in you."

She laughs. "It was only money. ... If it had been key lime pie you'd have had a little trouble."

I'm not missing, in this conversation, the unsmiling larceny that still lives in me, like deeply embedded rust in the walls of my consciousness. I know a layer or two of rehabilitative paint is not going to refurbish me. It hasn't yet.

Could the replaying of this memory and the knowledge that I've changed, and am changing, light my way back to my wife?

But without Sam's support to help me, this thought instantly evaporates.

"That part of me may never get cured," I say, waking myself up in the middle of the night in my father's house in Passion Falls.

"How do I live with that, Patricia?"

24

RAINY AFTERNOON IN TINSELTOWN

I wake up in a strange bed in a strange bedroom feeling a terrible case of jealousy. It's a sensation I don't recall having since maybe my teen years, or when Sam first told me about the time I went off to Portland a month after our Red Lantern "blind date," and she had gone to Palm Springs with Mike, her previous boyfriend. She told me she was sad, so she went off to see her mother and Grace and to hang out with … *her previous boyfriend*. I can't think about it.

Is Samantha sad now? This minute? Is she lonely? God knows it would be natural. Mike got married; it wouldn't be him, but wouldn't it be reasonable for her to find *some* company, someone to spend time with? I don't know how long I've been gone by her measure of time, but I would think it would be long enough for her to wonder if I'm ever going to find my way back to her.

I won't think about it.

On our way back to LA, driving across the late morning desert, I tell Valory I'm sorry about my father. I've drunk three cups of coffee. I'm still a little foggy, not to mention the hangover and the acid in my esophagus from the coffee.

"No need to apologize," she says. "He's a character, but I like characters. They make the world interesting."

I glance at her and see that she's frowning.

"I'll tell you what I don't like though. I don't like stray dogs that bite."

"Brenda says he's usually harmless."

Valory holds up her bandaged left hand. "This is not from harmless."

"You'll be fine. I know."

"*How* do you know?"

"Brenda says he's been seen around the village for quite a while, which means he doesn't have rabies. Call your doctor, if you like, and check to see if your tetanus shots are up to date. Otherwise, don't worry about it."

She shrugs.

"Why didn't you tell me you'd worked for Hannah Castle?"

She's brilliantly casual. "I don't know, it never came up."

"Was it until recently that you were with her?"

"A little while ago."

"Was it before or after you and I met that you … parted ways with her?"

"I think it was before. Why do you want to know about her?"

"But you knew she was going to be in my movie."

"I didn't want to prejudice you."

"And back to the day we met, you *pretended* to have trouble remembering *Little Girl, Lost,* the movie that made her a star."

"That was probably just me, trying to put her out of my mind."

"You didn't like her?"

Her eyes flash. "No. If you must know, I wasn't crazy about her." I seem to have worked my way around to the windward side of Valory's temper—me and the pet food industry. She says, "Being around Hannah Castle is like picking your way across an unexploded bomb field."

She saw me in the movie with Hannah, whom she'd worked for. Then she met me BY ACCIDENT.

On the street where I live.

I force myself to say, "*Was* it an *accident* that we met the way we did?"

She shoots me a death glare. "Of course!" After a split second her gaze drifts up and off toward a caravan of puffy white clouds scudding by in the northwest sky. It doesn't seem profitable (or safe) to corner her any further. My spine is made of jellybeans; I'm *afraid* of Valory Valentine.

After a mile or so, she says, "You're the one who initiated this journey you think you're on. You do know that."

"Why would I do that? Or *how* could I initiate a trip back in time, which as far as I know has never been done by anyone."

"We don't know why we do most of what we do. I don't know why you chose to set off on this journey you think you're on. I'm pretty sure you did it by choice, unconsciously maybe, but by choice. As to *how* you did it—*if* you actually did it—I have no more of a clue than you do."

"But why would I leave what it took me a lifetime to find?"

"We don't necessarily do what we do because we want it," she says. "Sometimes it's because we think that's our 'lot,' our 'fate,' our hand playing itself out. Maybe you've always known you don't deserve Sam. Maybe that's why you're here."

"How can you *possibly know* ... I mean what makes you say that?"

I feel her staring at me. "Or maybe you're here because you've always been here, straight through since you were born. Maybe there is no Samantha."

I wish she'd shut up. I remember Sam's trick when I yak at her about some impassioned preoccupation I can no longer keep to myself, but she's trying to concentrate on something of her own. She simply tunes me out. It's a self-protective device.

Valory's mouth continues to move.

"I had to kiss a couple of frogs before I met you," says Sam. We're having a bottle of wine on the back porch, magic hour. "He had to be smart, but sensitive." She smiles. "Dangerous, but goofy. And he had to be kind and he had to like poetry. And he had to be good. He had to be good and nice. And also not too predictable."

We are halfway through a bottle of wine, both slightly buzzed.

I say, "Tell me again what it was like before we met, when you were at loose ends."

"You mean just before we met?"

"Right."

In the weeks after we got together, as I looked at the books in her house, I found various notes to herself that tied in with what she was reading. They were sad, most of them. They reminded me of Doc in Steinbeck's Sweet Thursday. *In the first part of that book, he has voices inside of him. I forget what the first two of his three voices said, but the third one, the low voice from the deepest place inside himself, every once in a while cried out: "Lonesome." That's the voice I heard coming from Sam's notes to herself. I don't know if she was aware at the time that I'd seen them. Later, she knew I'd read them. She didn't seem to mind, but we were together by then, and told each other everything anyway.*

Sam says, "I was tired of being with people I wasn't that interested in. I chose to be by myself most of the time." She gazes off, maybe back into the months before we met. "My cats. Before I had the cats, I was a little crazy, going out at night and driving all over the city and up the coast ... to get out. I'd see people riding in their cars or walking down the street ... or I'd see houses with the windows lit up and I'd say to myself there's people in there, having fun and being together. I knew I should have been going down to Palm Springs, to my mom's place, to spend time with Gracie. But I didn't hold myself in very high regard at the time and I wasn't going to do anyone any good. Anyway, I felt isolated. I remember I even thought about taking out one of those billboards like some crazy Hollywood wannabe. But mine would've tried to describe who I was looking for."

"Who were you looking for?"

"You. I wanted to reach out and touch that smile you're wearing right now."

After she's reached over and tapped my lips with her fingertips, I say, "You mentioned that couple you saw one time."

"Yeah. One night I went for a walk up the hill. You remember that hill?"

"Sure."

"Well, I went out. It wasn't long before sunset, and I went for a walk up the hill. I didn't have a dog or anything. I walked up to the top. And way up at the top of the hill was a nice house. It was on a corner. The yard was wrapped around it."

"Nice area."

"Yeah, very nice area. And it had one of those split-rail fences. And there was an old lady—seemed like an old lady at the time—and she had a straw hat on and she was working in the yard, planting flowers or pulling weeds." She looks out at our backyard now, which is vibrant emerald green with the lush winter rye grass we put in every year. The

little Meyer lemon tree beneath the Chinese elm loves the combination of light and shade it lives in, and the lemons are a rich cadmium yellow, almost orange. "And right around the corner of the house," she says, "was a man, her husband; I presumed it was her husband. They looked like an old couple. They weren't side by side, working …"

She flashes an unguarded smile, and I feel a warmth for her I rarely felt during the first half of my life.

She says, "And the fading sunlight was so nice and the air … It looked like … I don't know, they could have been at each other's throats after the sun went down. But at that moment they looked like they were a happily married older couple that had been together for a long, long time and I thought: that's what I want." *She gazes off, lost in the moment.* "If I was who I am now, I might have gone up there and talked to her. I'd tell that old lady what I'd been thinking. 'And I wonder if I could talk to you about it?' I'd say. And the old lady would say, 'Of course.' And that would make her feel good, which would make me feel good."

"And then," *I say to Sam,* "the old man would come around the corner and, not seeing you, he'd say, 'Hello, rest of my life.'"

Sam smiles at me in the way that predictably turns me to butter.

"You'll want to be careful how you handle Hannah."

I think of one of those huge, swiveling satellite dishes. I set my machinery in motion and now, for reasons unknown but *with no qualms, I engage with Valory.*

"We lost Hannah," I tell her. "She's not going to be in the movie. Didn't you already know that?"

She's gazing at her hands in her lap. "No, I didn't. You didn't tell me." A half mile later, she says, "So, what are you going to do?"

"Liz Callahan is going to play the role."

After another long silence, she says, "I thought she quit the business."

"She did, but she's an old friend of mine."

"That's nice. She's wonderful."

"Yes, she is. We're lucky."

Valory is quiet for another mile or so. Then: "Do you think Liz might need a personal assistant?"

"I think she's got somebody she worked with before."

I feel her staring at me.

I remember the time during the first part of the COVID-19 quarantine, a few days after George Floyd was killed by the Minneapolis policeman. It was the day Sam and I had the fight—I forget about what—and I drove away and ended up looking out at the Valley College football field. I remember the anger I felt before I got in the car.

During that time between us there was a particular moment when I was … enraged. I couldn't gloss it over and Sam saw it. A little later, she said, "I hate the look on your face when you get that angry." I knew exactly what she was talking about and felt the shame that goes along with that. That anger is something in me I rarely think about anymore and obviously sometimes deny. As an old man, it's *almost* gone. I would have thought I'd purged my ghosts, especially that one. Apparently not.

I don't mind that I'm human, that I still get angry sometimes. I expect that. But in whatever life remains to me, I don't want to hurt anyone with it ever again, especially Samantha. Ever.

Anyone.

When I get Valory home, it's begun to rain, hard. It's a deluge for Southern California, dramatically so for May in Southern California; large raindrops carried on the wind burst against the windows.

She asks me if I'd like to come in and dry off. I'm not wet, but I accept her invitation.

She makes coffee. We sip it and gaze out the living room picture window at rain-soaked Los Angeles. It looks like a picture painted with overdiluted watercolors that someone hung too soon, its pigments trickling down the painting, blurring whatever the artist had in mind.

"Did you follow me back in time?" I say.

She frowns, then grins. "You're asking if *I'm* a *time-traveler*? Are you seriously ... No, I am not. As far as I know—in my 'travels'—there is no such thing, despite the fact that you evidently think you're one."

"I don't know what I am. I am just here with you. At this moment, right now, that's *all* there is."

She nods. "Maybe we've come together for a reason. Maybe we ..." She extends her arms like a college lecturer who's just had a fabulous mid-sentence insight. "Listen, I don't know what goes on in your brain any more than you know what's happening in mine, but this is life. Crazy things happen in life. Not everything you think you 'dream' *is* a dream. Some things that seem to be real are not what they appear to be. But the opposite is true too, kind of a reverse déjà vu. How about this? You saw this vision of a woman you call Samantha in a dream and now you've made her real. You're telling me in effect that I'm the dream, but from the evidence of our being here, standing next to each other, looking out at rainy LA, it seems entirely possible that you have it backwards. All we have to go on is what's here at this very moment."

"Isn't that close to what I just said?"

She half-smiles, then gazes into my eyes. She reaches a hand out and caresses one side of my face with her fingertips. "Right here, right now, this very second, I am touching you. Would you like to slip into my bed and talk about reality?"

I shake my head. She finally drops her hand. I'm looking at the window in front of me. I see a blurry face in the patterns of dripping water.

"I am *not* going to get into your bed. *You* encouraged my movie idea to get back to Sam. You suggested that you may have helped manifest the Kubrick money."

"Oh, that's only me. I talk big. Come on. You're crazy, I'm crazy. Why not? You keep telling me, between the lines and—not always so subtly—that you want to. You've been doing that since we met."

"Yes, I know, but I finally do *have some lines*. It took me lifetimes, but I drew them myself, with a *lot* of help, and whatever's within my lines is there for a reason. I don't want what I've drawn lines around, what I've fenced off based on well-considered judgement for a change, to get out and go wandering off again."

She smiles. "You're protesting way too much. Come on. We're the only ones at any kind of risk by doing whatever we want."

"No." I reach into my pocket. I'd been thinking of doing this before. I produce SpyGuy. "Let me play you something."

"What's that?" She's staring at the futuristic pen.

"It's a recording device, invented in the twenty-first century. This is a conversation I had a few weeks ago, in 2021."

I explain to her that I've inserted all the necessary descriptive stuff—what was happening and who was talking.

Heading east on Oxnard toward the 170 Freeway, on our way to visit friends, Sam is driving and whistling "In the Wee Small Hours of the Morning."

I tell her, *"We just passed the glass store with the sign that says 'Last Chance for Glass Before Freeway.'"*

"It's not on this street," Sam says.

"Yes, it is."

"No, it's not," she corrects me. *"It's on Oxnard."*

"This IS Oxnard."

"Oh, yeah … but the glass store is in back. There's something else on the street where the glass store used to be. Am I in the right lane to get on the freeway?" She provides her own answer. *"Okay, I stay to the right, then when we get on the freeway, I'll be on the right again to get onto the 134."*

"Uh-huh. This is the Bruce T. Hinman Memorial Interchange [aka the Hollywood Split]," I tell her later as we approach it.

About two minutes after that, we're now headed east on the 134, she says, *"Who is Bruce T. Hinman?"*

"A California Highway Patrol officer who was killed by a drunk driver somewhere around here."

She likes that. *"Oh, that's really nice,"* she says. *"Good people should be memorialized."* She thinks about that for a while before she whistles *"In the Wee Small Hours of the Morning"* again. Now she says, *"Did you know Justin Timberlake has a melon named after him?"*

"No."

She takes a sip from a bottle of something she has in the cup holder between us. *"It's yellow,"* she says.

"Pardon?"

"His melon."

I can't think of what to say to that. *"What are you drinking?"* I ask.

"Coconut pineapple drink. You can have a sip. Two sips." I see she's smiling at me. *"Are you recording what we're saying?"* She nods at SpyGuy.

"Yeah, but don't be self-conscious about it." I say.

"Oh, I won't. I'll forget." She looks ahead and slightly to the right. "They've been building this thing coming up on the right for years now." She looks off at Griffith Park. "And it's so beautiful here. Then they do this." She points ahead at the huge structure she was talking about.

"Do you know what it is?" I ask her.

"Something connected to the studio."

"Which one?"

Disney or Warner, she suggests, obviously not pleased by what's being built next to Griffith Park, whether it's Disney or Warner who's building it.

"It's a nice smog-free day though," I say.

"Smog-free?" I'm not sure if she's disagreeing with me, but I'll never know because now she says about the traffic: "Where are all of these people going?"

"I don't know. It's the weekend."

She sighs and looks off at Griffith Park again, smiling. "This is where I used to ride my horse."

When Sam was still a teenager, her younger (by two years) sister Morgan never stopped hinting to her parents that the only thing she wanted in the whole world was a horse. Finally, her parents, who couldn't afford it, bought her one. Sam, who has always loved animals, wanted a horse too. Her parents couldn't get one for Morgan and not for Sam. So, Sam and her sister each had a horse. They kept them in a stable on the north side of Griffith Park.

Sam loved her horse. She loved taking care of it; she loved riding it on the horse paths through Griffith Park.

One day many years ago, almost back to hippie times, Sam was riding along one of the paths. She saw a man on a picnic table, off to the side. As she approached him, she could see that he was wearing a big smile but no pants.

The man waved his arms, apparently quite proud, and said, "Can you dig it? Can you dig it?"

Sam smiled at him, said, "Colossal; I'm speechless," and trotted on.

"You're right about the traffic," I tell her.

"Is this lane okay?" she asks, but once again answers her own question. I know this because she says, "This guy is slow."

"How do you know it's a guy?"

"I don't. We'll find out."

She pulls even with the car, now to our right, and we can see it's a woman talking on a cell phone.

Neither of us says anything for several moments until Sam asks me, "Do you know how to say ambulance in Spanish?"

"Ambulansay."

She laughs.

"How DO you say it?" I ask her. Sam speaks pretty decent Spanish.

"I don't know. I thought maybe you did." After another moment, she says, "I know how to say lawyer."

"Okay."

"Abogado."

"Has that come in handy for you in the past?"

"No. But I see it a lot. Hey, look." She points to a sign on the back of a truck. It reads "Haunted Hayrides." Beneath that it shows the telephone number you call if you'd like to go on a haunted hayride.

Sam says, "You don't have a toothpick on you, do you?"

We both laugh as I say, "No, but I've recorded that for my novel."

"Booga booga," she says. "See if that shows up in your novel."

"I like it."

She smiles at me and sighs as traffic slows up, then starts whistling "In the Wee Small Hours of the Morning" again until she glances around us and says, "I just love this part of old Hollywood. It's as magical as ever." She looks over at me. "What are you staring at?"

"You."

"Why?"

"I was thinking I can't believe I found you on a blind date."

She smiles. *"I can't either. I had trouble enough when I could see them ahead of time."*

"You did see me ahead of time."

She smiles. *"That was entirely different."*

She pulls into the parking lot of the apartment building our friends live in, finds a space, and says to me, *"Do you have enough room to get out?"*

"Yes, I do."

She's already out of the car. *"Oh, would you hand me the keys?"* she says. *"I left them in there."*

"You also left the engine running."

"Oh, sorry. I was thinking of Bruce T. Hinman. I wish there was a way, a meaningful way, we could memorialize all those people from ... you know, last year ... and ... so forth, as we go along."

I nod, turn the engine off, and we go in to visit our friends.

Valory stares at me, then at my SpyGuy. Finally she says, "Who's Justin Timberlake?"

"Do you really not know?"

She gazes out into the rain. There is a barely visible hairline crack across one of two long, vertical panes of glass on either side of the picture window.

"He's an actor and singer."

Water seems to be puddling above the crack, as if the rain, which had been dripping down the pane in this spot, is now being held in place by tiny unseen hands, parallel with the floor. It's a horizontal rain puddle the size of an elongated quarter.

It bursts loose into three rivulets. Each finds its meandering path toward the bottom of the pane until I can no longer distinguish it from the glass.

Valory glances at me, then looks out the window again, watching this distorted, rain-drenched image of LA. She says, "I suppose you've guessed I've followed ... a few actors over the years, people who live and work and try to have lives worth living in this 'town'. I'm sure you know what my experience has been." She doesn't expect a response; I'm pretty sure she doesn't want one. "It's a world of me, me, me, but ... still, there's something about it." She squints at me with what might be—for her—an embarrassed smile.

She still scares me. I don't ask her any more questions.

"It rubs me the wrong way to say this," she says, "but congratulations."

"For what?"

"For *her*. For finding a ..." She looks for the right venomous word and settles on "*grownup* relationship." After a long pause, she says, "I wonder where this 'Sam' of yours really is."

I shake my head.

After a half-minute or so pause, still looking off into the rain, she says, "Maybe time travelers are simply those of us who feel we are." She half smiles, then shakes her head absently and frowns at me as if she'd forgotten I was there.

"Thanks for the interesting trip," she says. "Now, get the hell out of here."

25

THE CURSE

Time, in its mischievous way, continues to make as much sense as usual. Time is the leader, me the follower in the dance of all my days and nights. It whirls me around as if I were a city boy, raised in the country, say in a cranberry bog. I have no experience of walking, let alone dancing in my bog. Maybe I could manage some primitive sort of waltz clog in it, but on dance floors with a follow spot on me, I'm hopeless. And I'm scared. And I miss my bog. And someone has turned out the lights. And I'm slogging around here in the dark.

I wish a few of time's events would unfold in some semi-organized manner for a change, not so suddenly throwing me into illumination after what feels like a lifetime in the shadows. I'd like it if some of the people in my life would behave a tiny bit predictably. I wish some of time's little unanticipated shuffle steps were preceded by a warning bell, and when it went clang, clang, I could brace myself, grab on to something sturdy, and hang on to it until the newest quakes settle back again into the relatively reliable tremors of day-to-day living.

I've driven over the hill to Radford. Lou Gefsky's office is now the production headquarters for *Hello, Rest of My Life*. We have an unending number of details to work out as we prepare for shooting. We still haven't bought our film stock. We've worked out deals for camera and electrical, but we've barely spent a penny for permits so far, and we won't be able to sidestep that much longer.

Lou and our production assistant, Bo Spence, have been scouting locations, most of which we've got a pretty good chance of "stealing." For example, we're going to be using the park in Sherman Oaks between Riverside and Magnolia—the one I ran across in the ecstasy of realizing I had become a young man again. We will be using that location at the beginning of the final sequences. My conceit is that if I can exactly duplicate the full feeling of exuberance of being a rejuvenated twenty-seven-year-old, it will then take me the other way, in the direction from which I came, and back to Samantha.

We should be able to set up, shoot, and get out of that park by the time someone decides to report us. Los Angeles being Los Angeles, stealing locations happens all the time. It's like gardeners with their leaf blowers, the local mow-blow-and-go guys. The leaf blowers are illegal, but there aren't enough police to enforce that law. There are almost as many low-budget filmmakers stealing locations in LA as there are leaf-blowing desperados. After we've stolen the shots we need, we can do pick-ups and close-ups somewhere else.

The first thing Lou says to me today is: "Did you hear about Hannah?"

"What?"

"They've canceled the production she stepped over so many bodies to make happen."

"Why?"

"You didn't hear?" I shake my head. "She's come down with some sort of rare … disease."

"What disease?"

"Something called Moebius syndrome." Seeing my puzzled look, he says, "God knows. I'm told it's a rare, isolated disease that causes complete facial paralysis."

"I thought that was Bell's palsy."

"No, I looked it up. Bell's palsy usually affects only part of the face and most often it goes away eventually, sometimes within a few days. This thing Hannah's got never goes away."

"Never?" Lou shakes his head. "You mean she can't act anymore? That seems like pretty severe karma."

"No one is ever likely to see her in public again," he says. "She can't even close her eyes or look from side to side."

"My God."

"The crazy thing is that she can still potentially live a long, productive life. They say that after a while, the people close to victims of this disease forget they even have it."

"Yeah, but it's not going to be easy for Hannah to forget. Her whole life is about being an actress. What a horrible fate. I'm not crazy about the little … but Jesus."

"Sorry to sound mercenary," says Lou, "but thank God we've got Liz."

"I can't help thinking God kind of overdid His eye-for-an-eye thing with Hannah though. I guess it couldn't hurt to say a prayer for her."

Lou frowns. "That's the second time I've heard you say something like that. When did you get religion?"

"I guess … a little while ago. It's not exactly religion. I just think we should do the best we can for other people. We're all in the same boat."

"Yes, and Hannah pretty much drove a spike through ours."

"I know, but … it looks like she's already paying a price." We both think about Hannah's fate for a few seconds, then I repeat what I heard: "She can't look from side to side?"

I place my hands on the sides of my face like horse blinders, so that I can't see anything peripherally. Even imagining the sensation of not being able to see what might be approaching from the sides is distressing. "It would be torture to go through life like this."

"I guess so." Lou's gaze flashes to the ceiling, possibly saying he'd be pleased if I'd shelve all tenderhearted ruminating on the unfortunate Ms. Castle for the moment. "Okay," he goes on, "what do you say we talk story and a few other basics?" He picks up a sheaf of papers I drove over to him yesterday and hefts it in one hand, demonstrating how little I've delivered to him so far. He riffles through the pages, then drops the sheaf on his desk.

"I get it up to as far as you've gone. I even sort of understand that it's a good tale, a little surreal, but good. But when we get to the part where you've been here for a while, and you get your best friend—and okay, I'm even buying that he's forty-seven years forward in time, up in 2021 you say, and yet you can talk to him on the telephone, God knows how—and that this friend has led you to think of his wife, who was a kind of star and then quit, which by the way shows a lot of common sense, if you ask me. But anyway, she's going to be your new costar after we've lost the brassy little tart who turns out to be the essence of the step-on-your-face-to-get-where-she's-going movie starlet. I'm sorry, was that … what did you say before, politically incorrect? I'll sure as shit never begin to understand that concept. But you say where you came from—and I'm going to have to have about a dozen years of therapy to deal with the whole experience of your idea of the future ...

"Anyway," Lou goes on, "it's at this point in the story that I'm in way over my head. So you go to that park in Sherman Oaks, and you're going to run across it, and then you'll head back, but you'll never make it because you've zipped forty-seven years forward in time and you're reunited with your wife, Samantha, you call her in the script—and thank God we've got Liz to play her. But you haven't shown me one fucking page that really explains the underpinnings—some solid back-story—on the *old*, the *aged* you."

"I will put that into the screenplay," I promise.

"By the way," he says, "we haven't hired a makeup person yet, and it's going to be a pretty serious challenge to age you forty-seven years. No comment on your talent, Danny, but it's going to be a hell of a stretch to make you look seventy-five, and if we can't do that we're going to end up looking like the school play."

"Lou, I told you you're going to have to take a few things on faith."

"Well, that's all swell, but faith is one thing; planning on production contingencies is another. Throw me a fucking bone here. I'm producing this piece of shit. I need you to be open with me. We can't shoot these final scenes without some infor-mation—especially information that has to do with preparations I'm going to have to make in order to even begin to shoot the final scenes of this turkey. Give me a break here. You're not doing this all on your own, Mr. Auteur."

He grins. "I'm sorry, Danny, that's a terrible thing to call anybody."

"Hey, Lou?"

"Yes, Dan?"

"If I happened not to be around after our final shooting day, the one in the park in Sherman Oaks, would you be okay on your own?"

"What are you talking about?"

"I don't know. But imagine if, during the run, something happened to me. Anything's possible. You'd be able to edit the film and find distributors, right?"

"You are an absolute fruitcake, man. I'm not even going to respond to that."

As I said before, I do not anticipate going on an actual journey through time, but rather, for lack of the right word, a metaphorical one, harmonious with some level of perception I may or may not—probably never will—understand. Some of my dreams are idle, wishful thinking, but I have to believe a dream *can* be the first stage of a miracle. *"Dreams come true. Without that possibility nature would not incite us to have them,"* said (or will say) John Updike. I've seen it demonstrated; I got what I specifically wished for—even though I didn't know I was wishing for it, even though it turns out I didn't want it.

My present way of thinking is telling me that some of Valory Valentine has rubbed off on me, wicked witch or not. I'm counting on getting all the way to the end of my intricate, impossible equation with no justification, only a matching miracle in the form of my return trip to 2021. This is as possible as me pulling my keys out of my pocket and unlocking the door to my twenty-seven-year-old self. Of course, I don't know how it will happen; life is miraculous, but it never promises it's going to reveal its innermost secrets.

I know if I had to sell this movie idea to backers, I'd give them a big fat laugh. Well, maybe not; they're money people, not that famous for their rich senses of humor.

Back to life revealing its innermost secrets. As an old man living in Valley Glen, one thing was beginning to leak through to my consciousness. I try to communicate that to myself right now. I relax my shoulders and all the muscles around my heart and let go of all doubt, all skepticism, all disbelief. "I am the captain of my soul."

"Try lieutenant. No, make that corporal. I'd demote you to private, but you're probably on the right track and I don't want you to lose heart; it's just that something about you makes me love messing with your mind."

I ignore Tali and remind myself of what I was beginning to learn about that thing that happens to people when they get older, that thing that only occurs rarely during their youthful delusion of immortality.

"Tell me, oh omniscient master of mine, what might that be?"

"Something earlier generations were not able to see as clearly. We now had something the previous generations of 'seniors' didn't have. We had, despite all of the terrifying downsides, things like social media. Don't laugh."

He is watching me, not smiling or laughing, but patiently waiting for an answer, so I try.

"I was able to see between the lines that other people my age had grown spiritual interests that were not so quietly wishing to be expressed. I could feel what was no less than an epidemic of divine discontent. These older people wanted to know what's coming next. They didn't, in their hearts, believe that they had been set down on this planet, as babies, with the sole purpose of growing up, working until they fell over, or it became too painful to move anymore, and then dying and becoming extinct. They felt deep in their hearts, where the truth lives, that it had to mean more than that."

"Let me guess. Life is a fountain?"

"That's actually not too bad, but I can do better. During our most recent years together, Samantha and I have every morning been dipping into an assortment of spiritual readings. You may not have been aware; you were on the floor sleeping through most of it."

"Oh, I heard."

"Right. So you know we sampled from every belief system we could find. Skip to ... this moment. It seems to me that everything we absorbed through all those years distills down to these words attributed to Jesus Christ."

"Yes?"

"'It is done unto you as you believe.'"

"I hate religion."

"It's not only religion, or anyway, it's philosophy too. They overlap."

"If you say so."

"All right, how about this? A Japanese scientist named Masaru Emoto wrote a book several years ago—not religious, not even spiritual—called *The Hidden Messages in Water*. In it, he says that because a cloud is made up of water and *we're* mostly water, if we focus on a cloud long enough with relaxed concentration and tell it we would like it to dissipate, that before long it will. Then, he says, we're supposed to say thank you. I was skeptical about that until I tried it for myself."

"Yes?"

"I've been dissolving clouds for years. Just for the fun of it. A few *whatevers* ago, I saw five clouds. They looked like the five fingerprints of a huge hand in the sky. They weren't large clouds, but they weren't insignificant either. First, I dissolved the pinky finger cloud, then the index finger cloud, then the middle finger, then the thumb cloud, and finally the ring finger.

"As far as I was concerned, Dr. Emoto's hypothesis was proven. I know lots of people who've had the same experience. There are many, I am aware, who don't and won't believe it. You can demonstrate it to them and they'll say, 'It was going to disappear anyway.' But if I can choose the order in which I want several clouds to disappear, and then I follow Dr. Emoto's procedure, and if they disappear in the order I asked them to, and I can do it repeatedly, how can I not take that seriously? ... Tali?"

"When I first looked at you from inside the cage, God help me, I had no idea that my assignment would turn out to be trying to guide back to safe harbor an oracular, celestial-navigating, cloud-dissolving ego addict, whose drug of choice was introspection."

A good thing about losing Hannah and gaining Liz, aside from the fact that she's a joy to be around: Liz has agreed to work non-union, which means we can circumvent a whole lot of other union stuff and worry about it later. If we don't get caught.

I spoke to Liz, told her about Valory Valentine, then hired her to be Liz's assistant. I had a gut feeling they'd get along, that Liz could handle her fine and get the best out of her. Liz will need all the help we can give her, and I'm positive, off the wall as she is, that Valory is superb at what she does. Whatever that second sight thing she has turns out to be—if anyone ever knows what it turns out to be—I want it on my side. I hope I'm not fooling myself.

I remember something called Zeno's Paradoxes. I have no idea why I think of that now. It's got to have something to do with ... *something*.

Liz will stay with me in the house on Benedict Canyon. Zeke couldn't come because he had a made-for-TV script to finish, and as usual with Zeke, he let the deadline sneak up on him, and he couldn't come to Los Angeles to be here while Liz did her four days' work on the film.

Liz is as lovely and radiant as ever. I know this because I remember her from the first time through at almost this moment in time. She's not exactly a beauty queen, but her delicate face is framed in a cloud of soft toffee-colored hair, and most people, myself included, only have to look at her once to find themselves unconditionally charmed. She is also the least showbizzy person I have ever met in my showbiz life. Maybe that accounts for her having walked away from it even though she was doing extraordinarily well, and despite the fact that she had been, as they used to say in the Hollywood of mid-century and before, "groomed for stardom."

But Liz decided that she and stardom were going to be a lousy match. She thinks the culture of celebrity is too stupid for civilized conversation.

Fortunately for my purposes, not enough time has passed since she left Tinseltown forever (she thought) that she isn't still dazzling enough to Hollywood money people to draw vulturous interest.

In the script I'm writing, Liz will play the Samantha character. Most of her four days on the film will consist of a montage, occasionally stopping for a quick dialogue scene. She and Daniel, the character I'm playing, will meet, court, and fall in love. This will be followed by three brief scenes that show how devoted Daniel and Samantha are to each other. To add to the drama, on the afternoon of the last day of the shoot I will do the run across Sherman Oaks Park, just as I did in real life in 2021, the day I was swept back to 1974. However, I have cheated and have Liz with me when I take off to run across the park.

But I never come back. Liz crisscrosses the park looking for me. Finally, she calls the police, but of course I've disappeared into the world of 1974. We don't see her again until the final sequence, when she is sick in the hospital. Because she is very sick, something in me wants so badly to be with her that I'm able to bridge the gap and come back to the point in time (2021) when this whole delirium began.

She is in her hospital room, close to dying. When she sees me …

Well, I've got to keep a little surprise alive in this story.

My phone rings. I pick up the receiver.

"Danny?"

"Hi, Hannah. I'm surprised to hear from you."

She seems startled. "It sounds like you expected me to call."

"No, but I've been thinking about you."

Without further preamble: "Did you hire Valory Valentine?"

"How would you know that?"

"The Hollywood grapevine."

"Somebody ought to patent that."

"That was a big mistake," says Hannah.

I remember what Lou told me about Hannah no more than two hours ago. "Listen, I was so sorry to hear what happened to you."

Hannah is silent for a long moment. "It didn't just happen. It happened to me on purpose. This goddamn disease was … *inflicted* on me. I know this sounds strange in this fucking modern world, but Valory Valentine has some kind of … I don't know, ancient powers. I didn't like the way things were going with her, so I fired her. The reason this thing happened to me is that she put … I know this will sound crazy to you, but she told me herself, she put a curse on me."

I make an involuntary laughing sound. "I beg your pardon?"

"I can't think of any other way to say it," says Hannah.

"Curses, black magic, that kind of thing, only work if you believe in them. You don't believe in that kind of crap."

"I do now, Danny. She told me something bad was going to happen to me. And it did. Part of the reason I fired her was that she gave me the heebie-jeebies with all her mystical shit."

"But it's been proven that voodoo, for example, only works on people who believe in voodoo. There was a study, I think at Yale, in the nineties. Oops."

"Oops what?" She waits for me to answer, but I can't think how to do that. "Never mind, Danny. I am telling you that if I were you, I'd be *extremely* careful around Valory Valentine."

"I am sorry this thing happened to you. You let us down, but you didn't deserve this. Is there anything I can do for you?"

"Boy, does this not sound like you. Well, maybe it does. You're in show business. You know how to make nice."

"Is that the way you remember me?"

She seems to think about that. "I don't know. I do remember you had a pretty good temper when we did *Little Girl*."

"Did I?"

"I didn't want to cross you. It seems as if you've changed. I don't know, mellowed or something."

"Maybe," I say. I don't tell her that getting humbled (flattened) by show business and aging forty-seven years would mellow Rasputin. It flashes through my mind how frail human beings are, how dear we can be with our preening and strutting. I think again of what Hannah is going through and say, "I am sorry for what you're having to deal with, sweetie. But life will get better for you ... eventually."

"Promise?" There is an edge of ridicule to the way she says it, and I don't think she realizes how plaintive and broken-hearted it sounds.

"Promise," I say.

She takes in an extended breath, sibilant; it sounds as if whatever she's feeling, she's feeling it deeply.

It makes me remember what a good actor she was.

26

THE RESSURECTION OF RUE

'm sitting across from John Yort, who is at his desk at IAA (International Artists Agency) in the 9000 building a little west of San Vicente on Sunset Boulevard. He's talking on the phone with notoriously temperamental Elizabeth Eisley, apparently not having an easy time of it. It turns out she has not been given the dressing room she was promised and is upset about it. John puts her on speakerphone so I can hear the conversation. She's not just a little upset about her undersized dressing room; this feels more like a death in the family.

I wave to John to please turn Elizabeth off. She's harshing my mellow. But John's a tiny bit of a sadist and doesn't turn her off or down, so I stand up, go to the window, and look down at Sunset Boulevard, four stories below us. It's what you would expect: modishly dressed men and women in their twenties and thirties moving a touch more slowly than they would be if they were in any other city. It's as if there is a pedestrian speed limit in West Hollywood and Beverly Hills. Success is mandatory on whatever level you're looking for it, but it's a corollary that you must not look desperate as you pursue it. If you do, and people catch you at it, they will look at you askance. And if you're the kind of person who's looked at askance in these neighborhoods, you're doing something very wrong; you're not playing the game in the appropriate unnameable spirit of the game. You are either worried, studiedly unworried, palpably anxious, too friendly, visibly needy, or any combination of the above.

Needy is the worst. If you need your success too much, you're missing the whole point. I'm not sure what the point is, but that's not the point. In any event, if you want to know what cool really is (or isn't), walk down the west end of the Sunset Strip anytime and you'll get a firsthand look at the anxiety, desperation, and neediness of people slogging through Hell day after day, as casually as corpses, trying to catch a glimpse of Heaven. I came up with a rule (later than it was useful to me to have a rule, but anyway): If you *want* to be the best, go for it. If you *need* to be the best, it'll be a cold day in no-way, no-how.

I see something that electrifies me. A girl has rolled by on a bicycle headed east on the south side of the street, below me.

It was Rue Lefanty. I'm certain it was Rue, dressed in her usual T-shirt and jeans.

I don't have any choice. I say "Later" to John and rush out of his office, leaving him alone with Elizabeth Eisley and her undersized dressing room.

The elevators are all either above me or below me, so I run down the stairway to the first floor. In front of the building, I can still see Rue. At least I think that's her. She's about three blocks to the east of me on the other side of San Vicente. I'm parked on the street about a block away. I run to the Audi, get into it, and start weaving my way east as quickly as I can. The late afternoon traffic is thick, hostile. None of the other motorists like it that

I am trying to get where I'm going faster than they can get to their destination; I'm veering from lane to lane. I'd feel the same in their place. I want to tell Neil Diamond that LA is not in any way "lay-back" on the Sunset Strip at four in the afternoon on a weekday—well, except on the sidewalk, where they're all wearing their obsessive glory-or-die-trying masks.

I am not gaining any ground on the bicyclist. She's still about three blocks ahead of me. I can see now that she's angling to the right off Sunset onto Holloway. When I reach Holloway, I follow her east, past Alta Loma, where Fleury and I lived at the Sunset Marquis Hotel when we first came out from New York City. I couldn't possibly list all the luminaries who have lived in that place—maybe as much as a half of the actor membership of the Academy of Motion Picture Arts and Sciences.

The girl on the bicycle turns left on La Cienega. As I reach that corner, I take a left too, and by that time I can see her two or three blocks ahead of me turning right onto Fountain Boulevard. I follow her, I think gaining a little ground, but when I reach Fountain, she's still more than two blocks ahead of me, headed east again. I track her on Fountain, past Hacienda and Olive. Still about a block and a half ahead of me, she turns left on De Longpre.

It's a little slower going for her, peddling uphill on De Longpre. I'm within a block of her as the street curves to the right. I'm nearly positive it's Rue. I stick my head out the window of my Audi and shout, "Rue! Rue, please stop!" She either doesn't hear me, or doesn't want to let me know she does. She looks over her shoulder, mindful of the traffic; I don't know if it's my imagination or not, but for a split-second, she seems to flash me her impish grin.

She passes Actors Studio West, pedals another block, gets off her bike, leans it against a building on the north side of De Longpre and, not bothering to lock it, runs inside.

With little trouble at this hour, I find a nearby parking place and enter the building where she did.

It's an apartment complex. Next to the entrance is a brass plate that reads: *Casa Del Sol.* There are two stories, with a pair of staircases, one to the left, one to the right, rising up to a mezzanine walkway that surrounds and overlooks a Mexican-tiled common area on the ground floor below, and from which residents of the second floor have access to their apartments. High above the common area is a skylight. Late in the afternoon, it casts a hazy pink blush over the interior of this charming 1920s complex of about fourteen units. I have entered it through a doorless archway.

I don't see anyone. I have no idea which apartment Rue may have entered. But she definitely came into this building. I can't think what to do, but I have to make a move; I need to talk to her.

I start at the first apartment to my right on the ground floor and knock on the door. From inside, a youngish-sounding male voice says, "Who's is it?"

I can't think how I should best respond. "I'm looking for a teenage girl who just came into the building," I say.

After no more than five seconds, the door swings open. A young man in his late twenties, medium height, in a tan sweatshirt, stands in the entryway gazing at me as if I was an even more offensive presence than he'd expected. He has a large head squatting on narrow shoulders; he looks like a large extended thumb.

"I know that's a … uh, strange thing to knock at your door and ask you," I say. "But I'm trying to locate a missing girl."

"You fuzz?"

I smile and shake my head; I haven't heard that expression for a while. "No, I'm not with the police. I'm a family friend. And uh … did you by any chance happen to see a fourteen-year-old girl, pretty, light brown hair, come into the building a minute or two ago?"

"I'm a writer, man. I'm in the middle of writing." He points behind him at a desk with a typewriter on it. "I don't notice anything while I'm writing." He's glaring at me; it looks as if he's about to slam the door in my face.

"Oh. Okay, sorry to bother you." I move toward the next apartment as the writer firmly shuts his apartment door.

As I proceed with the rest of the apartments on the first floor (Rue has to be in this building), I realize that my A-fib has sapped my energy. I'm young. I don't know why this should be. Back in my twenty-first century life with Sam, I once complained to my cardiologist that I napped a lot. He said, "What's wrong with that?"

But now I'm twenty-seven. I shouldn't be this tired. Oh well, my strength will flow back. It always does. I guess I have reason to be tired now. I've been chasing this girl, adrenalin exploding through my body, for what seems like half an hour.

There's no response from within three of the units, even though I knock for at least thirty seconds at each one. The other three on the ground floor are occupied, but no one has seen a fourteen-year-old girl come into this apartment building.

I climb to the second floor and start again, beginning on my left, intending, as with the first floor, to go apartment by apartment.

I skip the third one, because I see the doorway to the fourth apartment is ajar.

I tap lightly on that door with a knuckle of my forefinger. No sound from within. I tap again. Still nothing.

I push the door open a little more and take a tentative step into a darkened apartment living room. Heavy shades are pulled. A little darker, the room could be used for developing photographs. "Is anybody home?"

I hear what sounds like a faint rustling from another room.

I lift my voice. "Excuse me? … *Excuse me?*"

After three or four seconds, a girl's voice responds curtly. "Who is it?"

"I'm sorry to bother you," I say, "but could I ask you a couple of questions?" That sounded like Rue. If it is, I have more than a couple of questions—like, who is she? Where does she live? How did she come to be flying down Wilkie Street that day when Wilkie is not steep enough or long enough for her to have been traveling as fast as she was? And why did she say she lived on that street when there are no other houses on it? Where does she really live? And how do I end up talking to her in an old apartment building in West Hollywood near the Actors Studio? But mostly I want to know: Are you Rue Lefanty? And if so, what is going on with you that someway connects to me?

"What kind of questions?" says the girl from the other room.

"I'm looking for a girl," I say. *Brilliant.*

"What girl?"

"Well, kind of a … missing person. Could you please come out so I can talk to you … face to face?"

It feels as if she might be thinking about that. "Anything you have to ask me I can answer from in here. I've always enjoyed a certain amount of anonymity."

Enjoyed a certain amount of anonymity? "I'm sorry to be so insistent, but part of the question I have to ask you depends on what you look like."

She doesn't wait to answer. "Well, that sounds pretty impertinent."

It's Rue. That was her voice. "If I could see you for one second," I say, "it might solve a lot of things for me. … I'm not sure what." Silence. "And then of course I'd leave you alone right away."

"You sound kind of weird," says this girl who *has* to be Rue.

I'm beginning to feel a little out of control, desperate. "Come on, please let me take a look at you. I have to know if you are who I think you are."

"Who do you think I am?"

"I think you're my new friend, Rue."

"What kind of a dumb name is that? I think you'd better leave."

I feel wired, ten-cups-of-coffee wired. Nothing wrong with my energy now. Without a word I cross to the doorway through which her voice is emanating.

It's not a bathroom. It's a bedroom, I think. The high arched ceiling seems to glow as if faintly illuminated in dappled lavender and gold, although I can't see the bed or, for that matter, the room itself much better than the living room I'm still half-standing in. I'm between the two rooms, under the header of the doorframe.

"Can you shed some light?" I say. "I mean, turn on the light?"

I hear her breathing. Fifteen seconds pass before overhead room lights snap on. Although I can't make her out distinctly, it is Rue. It is unquestionably Rue.

"Who are you?" I ask.

"I'll give that some thought," she says. "Do you happen to know what Zeno's Paradox of the Tortoise and Achilles is?"

I *know* this. It's came up yesterday or … recently. Didn't it? But right now, it seems as if it must be in some vault in my brain I've lost the key to.

Rue keeps talking. She's still in the shadows, but it's her; I know it is. "Paraphrased," she says, "this particular Paradox, one of nine, says that if you have to travel one mile, you begin by covering the first half-mile. Next, you cover half the remaining distance. Then you travel half of the *next* remaining distance. There is always a remaining distance. But imagine how close you can finally get—within breathing distance, within reaching-out-and-touching distance. Doesn't that feel as if it might be close enough?"

"I don't know what you mean."

"I think it's time to move on. Let's take a moment and talk about guilt, movie star. Unless I'm mistaken, and I rarely am, you've been thinking that your trip backward in time may turn out to have been no more than some combination of guilt and the cocktail of drugs you ingested that night. But if that were the case, how do you explain me? If you're trying to eradicate your underlying feelings of failure and the residual shame you've always felt, especially in regard to Samantha, why do I pop up again and again to assure you—through my demeanor and the fact of my landing in your particular life—that those are the last things in the world Samantha would want you to feel?"

"But who are you, really?"

"Oh, who am I *really*?" She shakes her head and shows me a not unpleasant smirk. "You'll find out soon enough. Now, may I please return to edifying your sorry ass?"

"Okay."

"Okay. I won't ask you why you feel guilty," she says. "We both know why. You have not forgiven yourself as any other creator would forgive his creation. You're the one who made the mistakes you made; you're the first one who has to forgive them. Everyone—I mean everyone—makes mistakes. Mother Teresa was a pill. The Dalai Lama was a bad, bad boy more often than you'd guess. Gandhi, St. Augustine, Thomas Aquinas, fuhged-daboudit." She grins. "I'll admit that you yourself have made some dillies along the way. But that is neither here nor there, because everyone has made her or his own set of mistakes. It's a rule of human existence. I'm amazed you haven't digested that one by now."

I start to ask her some of the many questions I need to, but she holds up her hand, as if she's stopping traffic. "You need to let me finish, Mr. Wonderful. A body does not get that many chances to hear the voice of his creator in a form as adorable as I am. Now listen to me: it does not even matter that you may not believe a force of energy that reflects you also created you. If you don't think that's the case, then more than ever you need to know that you are responsible for this ever-guarded, so-called Danny Maytree, wandering around time and space."

"But—"

"Don't but me, or I'll disappear into thin air again, then you'll be sorry."

As my father so often advised me, I button my lip.

"If we don't forgive ourselves," she goes on, "then we can't forgive other people, and if we can't forgive other people, we are dead in the water. Now"—she rubs her small, slender hands together and smiles sweetly—"here it is: work your way back in your mind to the beginning of time—even if you no longer believe in time. As you travel counterclockwise, you will discover that it all becomes simpler and simpler. Complex forms, such as ourselves, evolved from less complex forms, finally narrowing down, ever so long ago, into cells and miniscule viruses, then further down to atoms, protons, neutrons, and electrons, which are no more or less than crystallizations of pure energy."

I think she closes her eyes for a moment, for all I know imagining the tiniest increment of pure energy. "That's what you are," she says. "That's what I am. That's what Sam is. A leaf, a tree, a dog, a flea on a dog, a mountain, a mole—that's what *everything* is. You can't leave anything out. We are all energy and nothing but energy. Now, back to your precious guilt: there is no evil energy. There is no benevolent energy. There is only energy that we as humans, at the top of the food chain, if you will, are allowed to use for good or ill. Most of us try to use it for good. If we make a mistake, the next time around we correct it, constantly trying to move toward the light. Then, when we make another mistake, we learn how to correct that one too, again always moving toward the light. That's what *you* do. That's what you're doing right this moment. That's what you, as you, have no choice but to do."

She shakes her head almost imperceptibly and smiles. "God, you would think after all those mornings, reading all that metaphysical crap with Sam, you would know this by now."

She sighs, as if happy to have gotten that off her chest.

She makes a funny face, crosses her eyes, and says, "Now get thee gone, movie star."

Late in the afternoon I go to Ralph's Market, then home again. I put the things that need refrigeration away and then get to an overdue cleanup of the kitchen before I put the rest of the groceries away. Before it's entirely dark, I go out the back gate and walk up Wilkie to the other side of the house that overlooks mine, the composer's house. It's a shallow slope from the cul-de-sac on the other side of that house down to Benedict. There is no way that Rue could've been traveling as fast as she was the first time I saw her. And yet I *did* see her; I didn't imagine that—unless my whole existence for the last however long has been my imagination. Maybe Rue found a way to push off on her skateboard so hard that it gave her more momentum than I can envision. But I'm almost sure that's not possible; when I saw her that day, she was flying.

It seems equally impossible that I was sitting in John Yort's office at IAA this afternoon and saw the same girl, who I guess may now qualify as a figment of my imagination, riding a bicycle.

No. I saw her. I saw Rue Lefanty rolling east, on Sunset Boulevard.

I go back into the house, ravenous, and heat two chicken pot-pies. I cut a head of iceberg lettuce in half, pour bottled French dressing all over both halves, eat this meal that Sam would make a funny face over, and try to reconstruct the day.

Is it *possible* I fabricated Rue Lefanty this afternoon? Could today's sighting and *Casa Del Sol* be a vision of some kind?

I called John when I got home.

"Where'd you go?" he said.

"I had kind of an emergency." I told him that's why I called, to apologize for that. He didn't seem to question it; it probably sounded like just another one of those innocuous fibs Hollywood people are so practiced at.

Maybe I ran out of his office for no other reason than a sudden need to be anywhere other than an office at ITA with John and the displeased voice of Elizabeth Eisley. I do remember feeling kind of dizzy when I saw—or thought I saw—Rue Lefanty ride by on the bicycle.

But the next thing I could swear to was waking up from a nap on the couch in the library at 1809 Benedict, remembering having been involved in a car-and-bicycle chase down the Sunset Strip, ending up on De Longpre in an apartment building near the Actors Studio, where I imagined I found Rue Lefanty, although I certainly couldn't swear that I ever really found her, or if we spoke to each other. More disquieting than that, I couldn't swear that Rue exists.

The next thing I remember is waking up from that dream, that ... flight of imagination, and driving down to Beverly Hills to shop for groceries.

I wish I'd checked my odometer before I started this day.

27

SPYGUY

I have my nightmare about Sam getting sick again. As usual, I take her to the hospital on the morning of the second day. But in this dream, when I arrive at the hospital a few days later, the nurse at the reception desk calls me over to her. She looks down, shakes her head slightly, and tells me that Sam died ten minutes ago.

In this time, here in 1974, I wake up crying and can't seem to stop myself. I cry harder than I can ever remember crying in my life. If only I could get back to her, maybe I could do something—give her mouth-to-mouth resuscitation. I know it doesn't make any sense. I know she hasn't died; I know that she's working at her father's jewelry store. Yet the depth of sorrow I feel is bottomless.

Preparations move along even faster than the usual frenetic pace that sets in when you get close to the first day of filming. There's still far too much to do before we actually start.

The best thing that's happened to me in my re-acquaintance with the movie business is Lou Gefsky. If there is any justice in showbiz, which there famously isn't, Lou is going to have a wonderful career as a movie producer. He's efficient, smart, knows how to cut corners when corners need to be cut, has the necessary killer instinct without being an actual killer, along with the potential to be that rarest of all types among Hollywood producers: a good human whom people respect, and for whom they gladly do their best work.

That's the good news. The bad is that Lou is only one human being, and slippery indeed is the perilous incline to the summit of which he's been given to push his burden. Ambitious and gifted as he is, he's not ruthless enough to turn everybody around him into Type A zealots like himself, who will happily throw themselves in front of a threshing machine to get the movie shot and in the can. Add to that he's got only a shoestring budget with which to accomplish his Sisyphean task.

Most of this work I have to leave to Lou. Meanwhile, I've got a world of things to do myself. There is no question about the need to do them and I am going to, as soon as I can narrow down a little more precisely—or at all—what those things are, so we can get this enterprise rolling.

I feel the need for a joke here, some kind of treacle cutter, but I don't have it. I look around, hoping Tali will show up and to give me one, but whenever I need him in my life, he's masterfully absent. Let me see, if I were a wiseass, time-traveling dog, what would I say to my charge at this moment? Maybe I'd be kind enough to tell him to keep his eyes on the road, that he is starting to make some solid progress, beginning with the fact that he's finally got his guilt, that remorseless, everlasting monkey, off his back.

But the circus is still in town.

I telephone Valory Valentine.

"Did you tell Hannah Castle that you'd put a curse on her?"

Silence from Valory. Now she breathes heavily, and in her lowest register, dense velvet, she says, with what may even be the tiniest note of remorse: "Yes."

"You know she's not very bright. She believed you. Would you please call her and tell her you've lifted that curse?" She doesn't respond. "You're ruining that woman's life. Shame on you."

"Jesus, a girl can't have any fun anymore." She taps on the phone, then says in a testy tone of voice, "I was going to call her. I don't like being fired. She fired me. After all I'd done for her, she fired me. I was only kidding with the curse."

"You can't kid; you're too good at it." I change the subject. "Valory, how long have you been … following my career?"

She's quiet again, then, sounding subdued: "I'm just a hobby-ist. Every once in a while I see an actor or an actress who especially interests me. When I saw you in *Little Girl* with Hannah … I'm *not* a stalker." She trails off again. "I just … *like* certain actors … actresses … it's all the same to me."

"You got your friend Tad to honk his horn, burn rubber and then squeal out from just north of my house that day, didn't you?" She makes a surprised little squeak. "And if I hadn't taken that bait, you'd have gotten to me some other way, wouldn't you?"

There's a long silence before she says, almost under her breath, "Probably."

"Please take the curse off Hannah. And don't forget to tell her you did."

"I don't put curses on anyone. Nobody does."

"I know that, but she doesn't. Call her and tell her you've removed it."

After a long silence: "Okay. But I'm only doing it because you asked me to."

"Have you been talking to Liz?" I say.

"Yeah." She sounds enthusiastic now. "She seems nice. I like her."

"Well, don't like her too much. She's happily married, and she wouldn't like it if her assistant ... liked her too much."

"I'll like her exactly the right amount, asshole."

"And have Tad give my agent a ring. Tell him to say I recommended him. Tad's a good actor, very persuasive. He *is* an actor, right?"

"Of course. I'll tell him that."

"How's his acid stomach, by the way?"

"What?"

"Never mind."

"Oh. Oh, yeah. It's much better." I can picture the fey smile she gets when she's cornered. "He doesn't have to take Maalox anymore. ... Now, I've got something for you," she says. "Someone you need to see. She's a gypsy."

"You're kidding."

"I am not."

"What does she do?"

"You never know with her," she says. "Maybe she'll do a reading for you. If she likes you, she may make some suggestions. She lives out past Calabasas."

"Calabasas? I don't have time to trek out to Calabasas to meet a gypsy."

"Whatever your problem with Calabasas is, you'd better get over it. You're going to need Cassandra's help."

"Cassandra? You're kidding. Isn't she the one who told the Trojans not to bring the horse inside the city walls and nobody paid any attention to her?"

"Never mind the Trojans," she says. "You're going to want to hear what Cassandra has to tell you."

"This is not going to involve anything crazy, is it?"

"Crazy to you, not to her." The mid-afternoon sunlight filling the room dims, then brightens.

"It's okay either way."

"Tomorrow about two all right?"

"Better make it three thirty or later if possible. Hey, haven't they been having some brush fires in Calabasas?"

"I don't know, but if she tells us to come, don't worry about it. Brush fires don't mess with Cassandra; she's a force of nature all on her own. I'll check about the time and get back to you. I'll pick you up. You may not want to drive afterward."

"What's she going to do to me?"

"She's not going to hurt you or anything."

"That's nice."

"It's just that you may have a little trouble focusing for a while."

"How was your drive in?" I ask Liz. She rented a car and came directly to 1809 Benedict.

"Nothing I didn't expect," she says. "It's LA."

"It's not so bad."

She gives me her tender, bemused smile. "No, it is. It's … *so bad*. All you poor unfortunates, plunked down together on this big parcel of desert—not big enough, when you think about it—sagebrush in your sushi, coyotes eating your cats, too many freeways, too few freeways, the most bizarre sense of reality per capita in the world. And now you've got the annual wildfires and brush fires blazing up and down the state again, a little early this year. ..." She stops herself, seeing the look on my face, probably mistaking it for hurt feelings on behalf of LA. She reaches out and puts her hand on my cheek.

I put my hand over hers. "I am so happy you're going to be doing this with me."

"Only you, Danny. Only for you. When do I meet Valory? She sounds nice."

I'm sitting in Patricia's office. We've listened to the conversation I had with Sam that I earlier played for Valory. She asked me if she could see SpyGuy. Now, she's holding him, turning him over, examining him curiously.

"I told you I hired Valory, right?"

"Yes, but haven't we established that Valory has something awfully close to a character disorder?"

"But that doesn't mean she's not good at her work."

She shrugs, watching me, idly caressing SpyGuy.

"Maybe everything I'm living through is no more than a perfect punishment I've designed for myself. Maybe I've deprived myself of what I love most."

I read in her expression what I always do when I say something like that: nothing.

"May I ask you a question?"

"Sure.

"Can lucid dreams be more than dreams?"

"How do you mean?"

"I had a dream about Samantha. It was a lucid dream, but it feels as if I've had it more than once."

"And your question is?"

"Is it possible to have something like, I dunno, transient amnesia or something. ... And later to dream about what you can't remember in waking life, in a very realistic kind of way—maybe more than once?"

Patricia glances out the window and back. "I've never come across such a thing in my practice, but I've read about cases not dissimilar to what you're describing. So I guess the answer to your question is a qualified yes. Why do you ask?"

"Because I had a dream where I ran into Samantha ..." I chuckle. "... or she ran into me ... with her car, about six years before ... oh ... shit. About six years before I ... *will* meet her. But that's not possible, is it—that such a thing actually happened?"

"Do you remember this incident happening?"

"No. I don't think so. Not while I was awake."

She studies me. "You're not subject to blackouts, are you?"

"Not unless my whole current existence is a blackout."

She strokes the area behind her left ear. "Then it probably didn't happen. But you know by now that I am not an authority on what goes on inside your brain. I can only go by what you tell me."

"The thing is," I say, "I've had that dream twice now, maybe more."

She shrugs. "Well, repetitive dreams are not unusual."

"Lucid dreams seem so real, don't they?" I say. "But I know mine *are not* real. For example, I also dreamed I was a bird, flying over the Pacific and then Benedict Canyon, and that can't be—"

"Did you fly over your house in that dream?"

"Uh ... yes. Why?"

"I don't know. You said you found your house missing in a movie about that area. I just wondered if the house was there when you flew over it."

"Yes, it was there, but ..." I forgot how she can piss me off sometimes. "So anyway, my dream about ... Samantha running into me is no more than a dream, right?"

"I don't know. I'm 99-percent-to-infinity positive that you can't turn yourself into a bird, but I can't guarantee you didn't have a real-life experience on the ground that you later dreamed about."

"So it's possible for me to have been hit by a car, right?"

"Do you have any bruises?"

"No."

She spreads her hands, palms up, and smiles. "Then I would guess no one hit you with a car either."

There doesn't seem to be any point in pursuing this. After a half-minute or so, I say, "Were you a good actress?"

That surprises her. "Why do you ask me that?" She frowns at SpyGuy and hands him back to me.

"I'll bet you were, but the thing you didn't like was how out of control you have to be when you're acting."

Silence.

"Lee Strasburg said: *'Acting isn't something you do. Instead of doing it, it occurs. If you're going to start with logic, you might as well give up. You have conscious preparation, but you have unconscious results.'* Do you know the story about Laurence Olivier doing the August Strindberg play?"

"I don't think so," she says.

"I'm sure there's more than one version of this, but the story I heard is that Olivier was doing a Strindberg play, *The Father*, I think. Toward the end of his career, he'd been stricken by a horrible case of stage fright. On the night in question, he'd almost had to be pushed onstage.

"But the performance went well. Extremely well. When he came offstage after the final curtain, he rushed to his dressing room, distraught. The stage manager followed him and found him sitting at his makeup table, head down, helplessly weeping.

The worried stage manager said, 'What's the matter, Larry? You just gave one of the finest performances of your career.' Olivier said, 'I know, dear boy. I just don't know how I did it.'"

Patricia is frowning at me. "What's your point?"

I realize I'm giggling.

After about ten seconds, she says, "Are you all right?"

I'm still giggling; tears are rolling down my face. I say, "Do any of us know how we do what we do?"

Patricia keeps a box of Kleenex on her desk. She hands me a few.

My giggling fit comes to an end and I ask her, "Do you know how you do what you do?"

She looks at me without expression, then, along with a spreading girlish smile, her dark brown eyes turn warm and she shakes her head no.

I pat at my cheeks with the Kleenex, and finally understand—or at least I think I do, in the most general way—how I will make my transition:

No matter how terrified I feel, I will allow myself to be pushed onstage.

Early that evening, I call my father's house.

Brenda answers and I ask her how he's doing.

"Oh, about the same," she says. "He's fine though. There's nothing for you to worry about. At least not now."

I wish Brenda had been around for my formative years. "He's lucky to have you."

"That's sweet of you, darlin'. But I always think I'm the lucky one."

"That's what I mean. May I talk to him?"

She's surprised. "Sure, I'll take the phone into him. Just a second, honey."

I hear her moving into the next room, then a rustling, then my dad's gravelly voice. "What is it, Dan? You need money?"

"No, Dad, I don't need any money. I called to tell you something."

"What?"

"I wanted to tell you … that I forgive you."

He clears his throat. "For what, Dan?"

"For everything."

"Yeah, but for what especially?"

I try to think of a subtle way to say it, then settle on: "For what happened to my mother."

There is a long pause. "I didn't do it on purpose."

"Yeah, I know that. I also know it's been weighing on you."

Sharp, sardonic, little more than a whisper, he laughs. "All my life."

"I know."

"Do you?"

"Yeah, I do, Dad."

He clears his throat again, which takes a while, then says, "Thanks for calling, Dan."

"You're welcome. Goodbye."

I can still hear him breathing on the other end of the line.

28

CALABASAS

Valory picks me up in her yellow Datsun minivan and we drive out the 101 Freeway toward Oxnard and Ventura. Exiting at Las Virgenes Road, we head south, passing Liberty Canyon and Mulholland Highway. It feels as if we're moving more quickly than possible away from Lotusland. Valory seems perfectly comfortable driving out here. I'm not quite so easy about it.

"Is that haze over there smoke?" I say.

She looks ahead and to the side and shrugs. "Maybe a little."

"You told me the fires weren't this far to the east."

"I guess the wind has turned a bit." She makes a face similar to the one teachers use for little boys who ask too many questions. "We're nowhere near the fires. The news said they were way west of here. Isn't that what you heard? You've got a television."

"I don't watch the news," I tell her. "That's definitely smoke out there and we're heading directly for it, to talk to a fortune-teller with the same name as a prophetess of doom nobody believed."

Valory shakes her head in studied patience. "We're not going to be with her long. We'll head back home as soon as we've talked to her a little while."

She sees I'm still looking at the haze to the west, grins at me and says, "Now, don't be yella, Danny."

I smile lamely because I'm feeling quite yella indeed. My A-fib is rattling my heart all over the place. This seems like the dumbest time possible to drive this far out into the wilderness. What if there's more smoke in the air than we can see?

We turn west on Waycross Drive, a dirt road that takes us over Malibu Creek, which is the conduit conveying the runoff from Conejo Valley and the Simi Hills to Santa Monica Bay in Malibu.

A quarter mile past the creek, we turn south on Century Mountain Way. It feels like we're in some of that desolate landscape near Las Vegas, but it's Los Angeles. The countryside we're driving through is covered with a botanist's inventory of desert fringe weeds and grasses and occasional scraggly junipers or mesquite trees, bravely trying to hang onto life by means of the flimsiest channels of nourishment this side of Death Valley. I'm imagining how quickly an out-of-control brush fire would gallop across this terrain, and good luck to any life-forms, like humans for example, that happen to get in the way of it.

Valory has told me to keep my eye out for Tarver Road. It's only by luck that I see it. The street sign is hanging by a nail, in an up-and-down attitude. We go left on it, back toward Malibu Creek, which is the only way you can go.

We bump along Tarver Road, which isn't a road; it's more of an arbitrary runnel of stones and dirt, laid across this barren landscape with no apparent purpose other than for people like us who want to pretend it's a road.

Coming around a hillock of stones, dirt, and sand, covered with more weeds and grasses, and topped by a twisted palo brea tree, we see a haphazard conglomeration of a house, made up of severely faded aqua blue siding—composed of some material I don't recognize—and what looks like a wrecking yard's collection of formerly red bricks with faded stenciled advertising on them, assembled with no regard for whatever the advertisements used to advertise. These elements have been thrown together into what looks like a three or four room house, topped by maybe five layers of tarpaper roofing. A shiny white door that looks like it was painted no less recently than last week beckons from the center (more or less) of the front porch, which is nothing but a few scattered sandstones.

Over the door, in loving calligraphy, is a robin's egg blue metal sign that says: CASSANDRA'S PLACE. Below that, in smaller block letters, is a warning that reads: KNOW YOUR FUTURE IF YOU DARE.

As Valory and I get out of the Datsun, the shiny front door opens, a woman emerges and smiles at us. She's almost pretty, not the frowzy desert character I expected. It looks like she's got all her teeth. Her long black hair is striated by streaks of aqua blue, apparently her favorite color.

By way of greeting, she says, "We may be in for a teensy bit of trouble. The winds have shifted and instead of blowing past us towards Santa Monica Bay, they seem to be pushing that danged brush fire right at us. We can begin in the house if you like," she adds, "but I think before long we're going to want to get our butts down to the creek. Haven't got any rags in the back of that thing, do you?" She points at the Datsun.

Valory admits she has no rags with her.

"It doesn't matter," says Cassandra. "I've got a bunch of old clothes we can use. I'm a little embarrassed though. Haven't done any laundry in a month or two. Not to worry—we'll soak them in the creek anyway."

I whisper to Valory, "Why do we need wet rags?"

"I think you're supposed to breathe through them if the smoke gets too thick."

Cassandra has overheard us. "They say it can stop your lungs from getting scorched." She shrugs. "I don't know that for sure. Never tried it myself."

She grins, then fixes her gaze on me. I fancy I must look to her like one of the terrified woodland creatures in the forest fire scene in *Bambi*. "Why, you poor thing. We'll just get our behinds down to the creek directly." Now, as if searching her own mind, she says, "Do you, aside from the cliché gobbledygook of it, have any understanding of quantum mechanics?" She studies my eyes and smiles. "Oh, never mind. What do you know about plain old physics, high school level, say?"

I don't want to appear entirely ignorant. I tell her, "I know that Einstein proved, mathematically I guess, that the only absolute reality in the universe is light ... the speed of it. When he did that, time became, well ..."

She gives me a few seconds to produce an answer. I don't seem to be able to, so she says, "The essence of ambiguity?"

"Yes," I tell her. "That sounds right. I mean, most of it doesn't go any deeper than that with me, but I do keep trying to under-stand ..."

"Roger that." She glances at Valory, then back at me. "I think I got my work cut out with you."

"What do you mean?" I'm not sure whether she's referring to my ignorance of physics or my Bambi impression.

"Come here and give me a hand, Val." She looks back at me. "This poor boy's whatchamacallit is way too erratic for him to help us. I wouldn't even ask him to carry my undies, poor honey."

Two minutes later, both the women are headed down toward Malibu Creek, their arms full of Cassandra's laundry. Trailing along behind them, I can clearly make out that the smoke is now upon us.

"What are we going to do?" I ask them in squeaky adolescent tones.

"Take to the creek," says Cassandra, shrugging again.

Valory smiles at me like someone had just suggested we carry our picnic basket down to the stream, then maybe Renoir will wander along with his easel, canvas, and paints, render us immortal, then ship us off to the Louvre.

By the time we make it to the creek, you can cut the air with a machete. After they've rinsed out Cassandra's laundry, we lie down in the creek bed, next to the water, and breathe the cool, moist air through Cassandra's various items of clothing. I wonder if I look as funny as they do. I guess I must.

As we wait for the smoke to pass, the two women talk in whispers. I don't understand what they're saying; the T-shirts on their faces aren't helping. After a little while, it becomes pretty obvious we are not going to be burned alive, which, along with her gentle demeanor, almost makes me believe in Cassandra. And now we no longer have to breathe through her waterlogged clothes.

I feel hot breath. I'm lying on my back and it's coming from behind me. I look up and see that a dog with chocolate brown eyes is standing there, looking down at me.

I reach up and scritch him behind the ears. Even upside down I can see that he's smiling at me.

"Hi, baby." I don't usually have affectionate names for him, but I'm feeling terrific affection for him right now. He turns around and crouches down next to me.

"Where did you find him?" I say in the direction of the two women, still whispering. Remembering Valory's feelings about the "pet industry," I wonder what her reaction will be, but she doesn't seem surprised or concerned.

"He belonged to a friend of mine," says Cassandra, glancing at us. "You remember Dorothy, don't you, Val?"

"Sure."

"She moved on to the next place," says Cassandra to me. "She lived in Beverly Hills. I never thought that was a good place for this dog anyway, and at the end of her time here, Dorothy agreed with me."

She chuckles. "Although to tell you the truth, it doesn't matter what address this furry little boy has. He's a citizen of the world. I love that about him." "What's his name?" I ask. She smiles at me as I look at his tag. "Never mind," I say. I'm squinting at the silver medallion attached to his collar. It says: "Talisman." There's a phone number beneath it: CR-62754.

"How long have you had him?"

"Oh, he's not mine," says Cassandra. "He belongs wherever he's needed, wherever he's valued."

She leans in and takes one of my hands in hers. "So, what brings you out my way today, young man?" She doesn't give me a chance to answer. "You're an actor, I'll bet. Valory just loves actors. Some more than others." She winks at Valory. "It's a safe bet you're one of the ones she's taken a special shine to."

By now, all four of us are wet and muddy.

"You seem to know things," I say to Cassandra. "May I ask you a question?"

"Sure."

"Is everything in life random? I ask because I think if I could find an all-inclusive principle, one that I could actually *use*— from my just-another-lost-in-time-person's point of view—in the same sort of way, I guess, that Einstein was looking for a field theory that would combine general relativity and quantum mechanics to create a theory of everything. That's right, yes?"

Her eyes are sparkling. "Yes, it is."

"If I could get someone," I go on, "like you for example, someone about whom people could say, 'Yeah, well, she might be someone worth listening to. ...' If I could do that, get someone like you to give me a comprehensive answer to my larger question, then I might begin to learn more or less where I am. I might begin to know which number to put my money on, if you know what I mean."

"Not exactly," says Cassandra. "But okay, here: think of all those botanists and zoologists out there, all those students of life. They all learned early on that living things are made up of atoms, the building blocks of the universe. They also learned that those atoms do not work in a self-sufficient manner. They depend on each other. So the answer to your question is that *something* makes them cooperate. You can call that *something* whatever you like. Most of you give it the name *God* ... or ... whatever. Another theory is 'natural selection.' And who am I to argue? But I will tell you this. If it's Darwin's theory we're talking about, and if that turns out to be the overriding truth behind *everything*, behind *all of it*, then that 'natural selection' is *one smart cookie*.

"That's all I've got that means anything at all," she says, smiling. "Something is making this whole thing work." She spreads her arms. "I hope one of those scientists out there will wrestle this conundrum to the ground and make it explain itself." She looks up at the vast canopy of sky above us. "Although I would hate to lose the *magic* of this whole glorious … experience, wouldn't you?"

She doesn't wait for me to answer. I realize by now that I'm not minding lying here in the mud, especially when I consider the alternative, choking to death from smoke inhalation.

Cassandra squeezes my hands hard for about twenty seconds. Then, slowly, as if a mystical light is dawning in her, she says, "Uh-oh … I see what's going on with you."

I don't have the strength to question her.

"I don't think I'm going to have any trouble convincing you to go sleepy-bye for a while," she says. "I've got some work to do on you. Fortunately, it doesn't demand that you be there; I have a feeling your conscious presence is a little more surgically precise than is useful right at this moment. Let yourself go and understand that when you see a mirage as what it is, it is no longer a mirage. Treat yourself to a deep look into Tali's eyes. Memorize what you see there. Then if one day you should happen to lose hope for even an instant, you can call on what you saw in his loving eyes and remember that you're timeless."

As I start to drift off, Cassandra speaks a few words to Valory that I don't understand. Finally, she laughs and says, "Thanks, Velma. Love you."

Did she say Velma?

The rest of this strikes only the outermost reaches of my awareness because I am already lost in the depths of Tali's eyes, looking faraway into something like a nighttime Fourth of July celebration. I'm in my mother's arms, although it couldn't be my mother; she died when I was too young to remember what it felt like to be held by her. It doesn't matter. I was promised that the probability model I live in has more dimensions than I ever knew, that I was not the only outlier. And that promise was honored. I'm sheltered in encircling arms, looking up into the midnight blue skies and a rainbow of fireworks, stars, planets, and meteors streaming in a million directions in this singular moment around and above me.

I'm not afraid. I'm safe and held and watched over. And even the darkness is friendly and cares about me as it gently eases me down.

29

PRODUCTION (YOU CANNOT FORGE A MOMENT IN TIME)

I have a screenplay. It's a mess, but it's nearly complete; it is, for good or ill, a reflection of my story. Thank God, Lou and the skeleton staff he's assembled, most of whom will also be part of the skeleton crew, have accomplished most of the "development hell" phases that precede the production of any film. This was actually accomplished some time ago. The staff/crew have been paid enough to keep body and soul together (well, body—I can't truly speak for my own soul, let alone anyone else's). They have been promised back-end payments (ha ha). I pray there will *be* back-end payments. It only happens if the film turns a profit, and with low-budget films that's a rare occurrence—which is a shame because I know of few people who work harder than the crews of such films. I've never known exactly why. I tell myself it's love, but it's got to be a form of masochism too. I know if it's at all possible, Lou will break his back to see that everyone is paid.

But as I've tried to make clear before, if it all works out the way I want it to, I will never see that happen.

One of my favorite definitions of theater is: "Life with the dull parts left out." I'm going to leave out most of the dull parts that lead up to the shooting of *Hello, Rest of My Life*. In fact, I'm going to leave out most of the shooting. If you've ever watched a movie being filmed, you're familiar with dull parts. Lou and I both know the folks at Paramount, Universal, and Columbia (which still exists in 1974, barely) would get a good belly laugh if they could see what we've done in the way of pre-production and production so far, and how we've approached each phase of it.

I have to address what I expect to happen when I am no longer around to help Lou complete the film, and with any luck, find distributors. Without a lot of advance hoopla, Liz and I, even though we've done pretty well in our careers up to now, are not going to—as the Hollywood money people like to say—draw flies.

Hello, Rest of My Life will only make back its investment if it's lucky and influential film critics of the time, like Roger Ebert, Gene Siskel, and Pauline Kael, are enthusiastic about it. Lou is philosophical. He knows, as far as his own career is concerned, the important thing is that people in the filmmaking community recognize his efforts as skillful, savvy, and (one of the favorite words applied to new filmmaking artists) *breakthrough*. In his less confident moments recently, Lou has been saying, "What the hell, it's Stanley Kubrick's money." Although the truth is it's not all Stanley Kubrick's money. A lot of it has come from the surprisingly red tape-free remortgaging of my home on Benedict Canyon, which has more than doubled in value since I bought it—and most of it is mine, even considering the settlement I made with Fleury. I did end up with the house, and now that lucky investment is partly responsible for the financing of a very iffy film.

Almost all of the movie is now shot. The cast and crew are running on fumes. We filmed the scenes with "Valory," "my dad," and "Brenda." I won't burden you with the fictional names I've given them, or the names of the actors who are playing them at a place that belongs to an uncle of our first assistant director—who, coincidentally, is also our second assistant director and set designer. We chose the uncle's simple but beautiful Southwestern-style home in Twentynine Palms because it's in a scenically beautiful location, with Joshua Tree National Park in the background.

We shot the "Daniel"-at-home scenes, that I felt needed to be in the story, in and around my place on Benedict Canyon. We got a few complaints from neighbors, but nothing to slow us down. People are pretty blasé about film crews shooting in and around LA.

Liz and I have shot the montage I mentioned. I think it went nicely. Liz is happy, and aside from the gratitude I feel for being able to lose myself in her eyes, I have confidence in her instincts. Lou seems okay with it too, although I can't say I trust his. He's a nuts-and-bolts guy, not a student of "cinema," the art form. In fact, despite his passion for the business, I think he believes a lot of it is pretty silly. I guess maybe he's right to some degree. I love it anyway.

Since I'm the nominal director of "this turkey" (as Lou can't stop calling it), you'd think I'd be seeing all the dailies. I haven't seen any. Lou says they look pretty good, but again I'm not sure he's much of a judge.

I can't think of filmmaking results anymore. I have to concentrate on shooting the movie and getting us to the point in it when the Daniel character runs across the park. When it's finally time for us to film that tracking shot, it seems as important as any moment in my life (both of them) that my concentration be focused on exactly what it should be focused on.

As for my own acting instincts up to now, they can be summed up in a scene we shot in which "Daniel" (the character), wondering whether his film will accomplish its purpose or not, looks at himself in a mirror, holds a forefinger up to his mouth, and watches himself flap the finger up and down between his lips as he hums and produces the cliché idiot sound. He could be a character in a Samuel Beckett play.

As I look at what I'm writing, just for the fun of it, I do that piece of business now. It's quite enjoyable. I should have tried this instead of smoking, back in the time when I used to go through a pack a day. I can hear Lauren Bacall saying, "Anybody got a match?" Bogie tosses her a pack because that's what the script bids him to do, but then instead of smoking a cigarette himself, he puts a finger to his lips and goes, *Bubbada-bubbada-bubbada-bubbada*, which causes him to grin Humphrey Bogart's wonderful, goofy grin, and that would have been a hell of a lot better than the esophageal cancer that did him in at the age of fifty-seven.

In my last conversation with Zeke, he again expressed feelings of doubt about my whole journey back into our youth (well, my youth).

I say, "Are you going to tell me it's not possible I'm experiencing what I'm experiencing?"

"No, I don't have a broad enough frame of reference to say that. What I do believe is that it's impossible that I am talking to you in 1974 from my ... fucking nursing home in 2021. That I don't believe."

"But we are talking, right? And I give you my word I am sitting at the table you and I used to play chess at next to the window that faces south in my old house on Benedict Canyon."

There is a brief pause before Zeke says, "Well you're not at your usual phone number in Valley Glen; I know that. I can't reach Sam. So you're somewhere other than where I normally find you." He clears his throat. "So, who am I to say where you are or aren't? You tell me I called you earlier at the number you're calling me from now. I have no reason not to believe you; as you know, my sense of conscious reality is also a little fickle these days. And you've never lied to me."

"Right. And I spent an evening with my dad ..."

"Who died well over thirty years ago, right?"

"Right. So let me make you a provisional promise: we are going to see each other soon."

"Where? In heaven?"

"I can't tell you where, Zeke. If I could, I don't think it would happen. That's the provisional part. But ... it's going to happen."

"If it wasn't you talking, I'd say you're being cruel."

"I'm telling you what I think."

There's a pause as I hear Zeke take a labored breath. "Okay, Danny. If you say so, I believe it. I hope you're not screwing this up, that you're not bringing down the wrath of the gods by breaking some cosmic rule and saying out loud what's going to happen. I know that notoriously pisses them off. My memory is that between the time you tell me you're living in and the time you met Sam, you were—to be generous—a galloping luna-tic." He has another coughing fit and takes a long breath. "But otherwise, other than lightning bolts being hurled at us, I am—God help us—with you on anything you say."

Following the afternoon with Cassandra and the brush fires, I found myself at my bar, drinking White Horse whiskey, remembering what feels more like a dream than real life.

Valory called to ask me how I felt.

"I'm okay. Did I see you today?"

She laughed. "We drove out to see Cassandra. You don't remember?"

"Kind of, I do. I think it's starting to float back to me. But I'm not real sure. What did we do there?"

"Feel your pulse."

I did. It was as steady as a rock. "What happened?" I must have sounded like I was in shock. "What did she do? I am feeling an unusual rush of energy."

"She helped you understand the means you need to use in order to go where you need to go—back to Samantha."

"I don't understand. My heartbeat is normal—for the first time in … I don't know how long. I'm grateful." I took a couple of deep breaths, still with two fingers on my pulse, the phone receiver held between my shoulder and my ear.

"Cassandra didn't do it all by herself. She needed your faith. She reminded you of the heart you didn't know you still had."

"But how will that get me back?"

"'There are more things in heaven and earth …' Remember?" When I didn't respond, she said, "Haven't we learned anything? Going by what Cassandra says—and more and more it seems I don't have any choice but to believe her: 'Moving a bit of time this way and that is not nearly as big an accomplishment as mending a heart.'"

"What's your story?" I said. "How did you fall victim to ... this fan thing?"

Out of an obstinate silence, she said, "I told you. I'm a hobbyist."

"And you want *nothing* from what you collect?"

"A stamp collector doesn't own her stamps," she said. "Any more than anybody really *owns* anything. Most of us know that. It very often moves into addiction territory. Addicts don't mean to hurt people, but sometimes it happens in order to get whatever fix the addict needs. Oh, honey, as you understand by now, I don't know what I'm doing any more than you do. I don't want to hurt people, but I do ... sometimes."

"Can't help yourself?"

She sighed. "I'm afraid I've still got a long way to go. Maybe I am a little jealous of you."

"Why?"

"You have something I don't. Maybe that's why I wanted you. By this time, you don't find fault with anyone—if you don't count yourself—and I've begun to see how nicely that works for you. I think you're even beginning to forgive yourself, and I'm jealous. Also—and I know this is not enlightened of me—it drove me up the wall that I was less appealing to you than an old lady. ... But since we saw Cassandra ... I no longer doubt anything you say."

"I probably would have felt the same," I said, "in your place, in another time." She started to ride over me, but I kept talking: "You've told me that if I get my wish it will include being an old man. I guess so, but I'm beginning to develop a renewed gift of enthusiasm. They tell us that's a blessing of youth, but they're wrong. What 'they' don't seem to know is that enthusiasm is a much better measuring stick of life than biology; it doesn't have the limitations of 'aging.' I was bit by bit beginning to realize, as I got older, that my mind—and I don't care how it sounds—is an eternal springtime. I want to recapture that. Our age is of trivial concern. Sam and I both want to go on sharing springtime."

"I understand all that shit," said Valory. "But you'd be *old*. Your time would be limited. The moment would come, sooner than you'd guess, when you'd have to acknowledge that death is the landlord; that you and Samantha are only tenants and that time, or whatever you decide to call it, would soon run out."

"I know that," I said. "But being away from her has shed light where there wasn't nearly enough before. I know now that Sam realizes, along with me, that death can be liberating. Understanding that can set you free to seize the gift you've been given. Shouldn't all of us live with the certain knowledge that our next breath may be our last? If we did that, wouldn't we be turning every moment, every split second of our lives into a diamond of infinite facets? That's what *I* want: that moment, that over-and-over endless moment with—"

"Yes, I know who with," said Valory. "You don't have to say her name again." After a long pause, she said, "I'm still jealous. And I'm going to hate to lose you."

"Me too." There was a good long pause before I finally said, "Hey, Velma, how did you know I'd follow you that day you were with Tad?"

She began tapping on the phone. "I … learned quite a bit about you from Hannah, and from looking in on you once in a while. And I told you I read that interview you did in the *Hollywood Reporter*. It was a calculated guess. I knew about what time you go out to get your mail every day, when you're home. And I knew you had a … temper. And if that hadn't gone according to plan I'd have gotten to you some other way." The phone tapping stopped. "But I enjoyed the way it worked out. It amused me."

"How did Tad feel about it?"

"Oh, well … Tad was extremely confused. He's a little like Hannah, a Hollywood phenomenon. Yes. Tad was confused. He wasn't *pretending* to cry when you yelled at him. … *What did you just call me?*"

"You mean, Velma?"

"Where did you hear that?"

"I've heard it at least a couple of times. Is that your real name?"

She tapped on the phone again. Finally: "Velma was a Raymond Chandler character in *Farewell, My Lovely*."

"I know."

She was now tapping steadily on the phone. "That character is married to a judge. She kills people who find out she used to be a prostitute. Nobody else is named Velma, at least not in 'my time.' I hated being … that name. So I changed it when I was still a girl. I wanted something elegant. I chose Valory with an *o*."

"Cassandra called you Velma."

"She's allowed."

"But I heard your voice in 2021. You told me your name was Velma and that I had an audition in Beverly Hills. Your voice is distinctive. Even over the phone. I'm good at identifying voices. They're like snowflakes; no two are exactly alike—years from now they'll be using voices as a form of identifying people. I heard *your voice* tell me I had an acting audition the next day."

"How is that possible?"

"You don't believe you might have called me back to this time? You think it's impossible that you were there, where I was, and that you did that, said that?"

The tapping stopped again and there was a long silence on her end. I wished she was in the room with me. I'd like to have reached out and given her a pet. I'd like to have made her feel better.

Velma and Valory need a lot of petting.

Maybe it has something to do with my new heart that I find myself slipping through this timeless, space-less universe, through a transparent layer cake of magical magentas, indigos, Tokyo blues, spring yellows, millennium golds, chrysalis pinks, deep lavenders, rose blushers, velvet greens, special rose pinks, electric lilacs, virgin blues, and—because life has to have comedy or it's not life—the three bastard ambers.

As I emerge, I see Rue, smiling sweetly.

"A couple more words for you, grandpa."

"What did you call me?"

"Just a term of endearment. Try to pay attention before I go back to being—"

"What?"

"Never mind. Give me a couple more minutes."

"All right."

"All right." She shows me the same grin she wore when she rose up out of the ivy on Wilkie Street the day I met her. "Okay: most people are panicky at the idea of jumping onto a better track of being. They persistently remain in the cowboy stage of their evolution, far less kind and forgiving than they ought to be—not only for other people's good, but for their own; being generous and good-hearted is, in its own way, selfish." She raises her hands, palms toward me, in case I might decide to interrupt her. "Being human is never a piece of cake," she says. "It never will be until you see the universe for what it is: harmonious, light years more glorious than you'd ever guess going by all the bad little boys and girls branding each other with pitiless, scarring heartaches, turning this beautiful playground you've been given into coliseums, battlegrounds, pits of hell.

"But—and this is the wonderful part—it can only be that when you allow it to be. You have a choice. God slipped a miracle card into your deck. You make the world what it is. You are free. You lock yourselves up once in a while, but you are still 100 percent free, always. Most of you have known for generations, in your hearts when they're healthy, that you're the creations of something unspeakably beautiful. Since God, the nickname most of you use for the vast Celestial Intelligence, has to make you out of Himself, you are immortal. Of course, your bodies are not; most of you figured that one out by the time you were five or so. But you are—even those of you who don't know you are—extraordinarily beautiful spiritual essences that go on long past the end of time.

"To return to you: Is Danny Maytree really here? Or are you back where you came from with Samantha? Don't bother; those were rhetorical questions. You are living an eternal life right now, this second. The world keeps telling us what we're supposed to be, but the world is wrong. Once more: you are free; you have the choice to be where you want to be. Where do you want to be?"

"You know the answer to that."

"Yes, I do, but the point is, this is it, right here, right now, talking to me or to Sam—who is waiting for you. The essential element of all of it is *you*. We love you, not that wonderful body you're walking around in, and not the aging one lying in a hospital bed right now."

"What are you talking about, lying in a hospital bed?"

"That's not you either. There go all those doctors, scurrying around, exercising their miniscule medical school learning. What gullible sawbones believes in his or her heart that chipping away with their little saws and chisels, trying to recreate perfection, is going to do the job solely from their medical school 'expertise' and their extremely limited experience at manipulating their little stone axes? What they really are, are Michelangelos. Michelangelo doesn't sculpt *David* all by himself. He has help—the help of the same genius who created a rose, a sunset, the depths of the Adriatic Sea, the incredible spray of bougainvillea bursting up over your garage behind your house, or this tiny ant that just made its way up onto my pinky finger. Do you think poor, deaf, little Ludwig van Beethoven wrote all those incredible symphonies only out of the insignificant physical organism given the name Ludwig van Beethoven by *seine mama und papa*?

"We don't do any of the good stuff without lots and lots of help. All the little inventions—the wheel, the printing press, the personal computer, digital technology, SpyGuy—added up cannot even begin to touch the beauty, the perfection of that Chinese elm growing in your yard in Valley Glen. And wherever you go there will be more perfection. How it got there, and continues to get there, is apparently not for you to know—at least not yet.

"You look out your window now and see a mockingbird. Is this your old mockingbird friend? It doesn't matter—certainly not to him. Nothing matters but mercy and compassion and what you ask for. You've learned mercy and compassion, and you have asked for Sam. Will you, in your heart, be surprised when you find her? Your heart has been mended. Can't you let it go at that? Are you listening?"

"I'm trying."

"Do that. Somewhere deep inside of you, you are aware of everything except who you are. You see the thoughts, events, and emotions that pass in front of you. You see your mockingbird, but you don't see you. You need help if you want to see what the world calls Danny Maytree."

"I don't understand."

"I know you don't. That's been the problem. You haven't understood that although you have never known who you are, you were lucky enough to find someone in your world who did."

"Sam?"

"Yes, Sam," she says. "And Sam more than just knows who you are; she loves who you are and that will take you a long way into this spiral galaxy."

"Are you saying all I need is Sam?"

"*No*, I am *not* saying that! Do you think all Samantha needs is you? Don't be silly. We all need each other. I'm telling you that getting back to Sam would be a perfect place to begin the next leg of your journey, and maybe the next—who knows?"

She shakes her head. "Listen, leading man, humanity does not operate on the star system. Try to get that through you head. Life is an ensemble production. You managed to get yourself into a nice two-hander. Maybe it will have a long run. Maybe it will have a long, long run. That would be wonderful. But the world keeps turning.

She sighs and once again shows me her sweet, pixie smile. "Okay, I've done all I can do with you. I guess all that's left for me to say is: break a leg."

30

THE MARTINI SHOT

We are in the park, setting up to shoot the final sequence.

I am still locked up in my own little time capsule conundrum. I'm not sure if what I'm seeing now is fantasy or memory, or if I'm actually standing here and what I think I'm seeing is what I'm seeing.

Except this is Sherman Oaks Park. The electrifying sensations I'm having, the lights and colors swirling through my mind, may be inappropriate to the moment. I should be concentrating on the run I'm about to make from east to west across the park to Van Nuys and back again.

I'm standing at the east end, just inside the parking lot on Hazeltine Avenue, looking west toward where the sun is beginning to set, no less beautiful than it is over the Pacific Coast, spreading its kaleidoscopic glow the length of the Los Angeles basin, from the coast to San Bernardino, a hundred miles to the east, and equally sharing its enchantment with the San Fernando Valley.

The park is surrounded by and filled with islands of trees more robust and beautiful than they have a right to be in this smog-steeped valley. There must be at least two dozen different kinds of trees, but the only ones I know are the Mexican fan palms, several varieties of pines and cedars, and a single Italian cypress; all of them congregated in a random pattern, the cypress towering above the rest, like that boy in the sixth grade who looks like he should be in the eighth. All of these trees are reaching for the sky, happy to be what they are, where they are, lavishly blooming as if all the world is as it should be.

But something is not quite right with this picture. Or possibly it was the last time I was here that it was off. It's beautiful; there's nothing … exactly wrong with it, but something chafes at the back of my mind. Maybe it's only a moment of déjà vu. I remember running across this park the day it all began; or at least I remember part of it. I was on the north side, a little below Magnolia Boulevard, as I am now. I remember noticing a crew was shooting a film on the south side of the park. It didn't occur to me to go over and see what was being filmed that day. I felt jealous, I remember, that other people were working and I wasn't. Now I am, but I couldn't care less if it's the last time I ever playact.

(Given the opportunity, I … *might* want to rethink this last sentence.)

Our camera rig is set up and ready to go. I look over at the south edge of the park. On that side, I see someone who could almost be me. It looks like my friend Zeke when he was younger and healthier, as long ago as when he was my understudy—a job he had partly because we looked quite a bit like each other. If I were he at this moment, especially in my current frame of mind, looking at me across this distance, I'd wonder which of us was which.

We are using a primitive early version of the Steadicam, first introduced as the Brown Stabilizer in 1975, and now being tried out in a couple of early incarnations in order to iron out some of the kinks. Lou Gefsky and Gene Blanchard, a brilliant young cinematographer, came up with the rig we're using. It includes an experimental silent cart created under the same principles as the Steadicam and capable of keeping reliable pace with me as I run across the park.

We need to get this in one take. Even at age twenty-seven I am not going to be able to do this more than once without a several minute layover, and we don't have time for that. I notice a slice of pinkish, golden light over the tree line and wonder if anyone looking out a window of one of the residences, or the squat commercial buildings that line the west side of Van Nuys Boulevard, is watching us. Maybe no one is. After all, it's just another humdrum day in La-La Land.

When I get back to Hazeltine, the one-mile run completed, I may be back to Danny Maytree's original life—if, going by my fluky history, this is no more than the acid trip it may turn out to be.

I may not.

Either way, if I've learned anything at all, I will be more aware than I was before that life is exactly as rich as I will let it be.

The last shot of the movie is called the martini shot.

God, I'd like to have one right now. No rocks, no olives. No vermouth.

"Two things," said Valory on the phone.

"All right."

"I have to ask you something before you make your final decision to go back, or to try to go back."

"All right."

"You said you wouldn't mind being an old man. What about this worldwide plague?"

My blood froze.

"As you know, it hasn't ceased to exist in your other time. You've gotten vaccinations, but nothing is 100 percent yet."

"How do you know anything about this?"

"I have sources," she said.

"Cassandra?"

She took a deep breath, but ignored me, going on from where she'd left off. "There are no guarantees that it won't keep mutating. You're not going to be a young man if you get there, Danny. I don't know how good your lungs are at seventy-five. You used to be a smoker. You have ... or had atrial fibrillation. You might not survive this ... thing, or the next one, if you got it. You told me you wouldn't mind being old if you were with Sam. But old and dead are two different things."

"Nothing in life is 100 percent. How do you know anything about this?"

"I've told you before, my beamish boy, I don't know how I know a lot of what I know." She tapped the phone a few times. "Yes, it was Cassandra, but also ..."

"Also what?"

She paused. "Also, never mind. I'll just leave it that I have the odd paranormal moment, but Cassandra is the real thing. She said the pandemic we're discussing isn't only a virus, like a flu that hits and then goes away and never comes back. This one, and all that comes along with it, is part of a greater message. The world you go back to—if your mad plan works—would be unlike the world you lived in most of your life. You would have Sam, but the world would be moving into a new chapter; it would feel like a foreign land to you. I know you're shaking your head. Why are you doing that?"

"If the world changes, it changes. Sam is my home."

"And if Sam ceases to exist?"

"Well, it's more likely to be the other way around. And if that should happen, then I'll invoke the "Danny Boy" rule, as Sam would for me."

"And what is the 'Danny Boy' rule?"

"And you will bend and tell me that you love me.

And I shall sleep in peace until you come to me."

"Sam is still my home. Do you understand? … Are you there?"

"I'm here," she said.

"And the second thing? You mentioned a second thing."

She took a deep breath. "Actually, there is a third thing. They both have to do with Cassandra. The last time I talked to her she told me I would *'somehow know you again, in another time.'* She said we would know each other, but we wouldn't understand that we did because somewhere along the way you changed course."

"What does that mean?"

"She didn't tell me. We're both going to have to guess at that one until we know. Cassandra was always hard to read."

"What do you mean *was*?"

"The brush fires swept through Calabasas again. I got a telephone message. You need to hear this."

"Okay."

"We won't be talking for a … for a while," said Valory. "Be with God, Danny."

She played Cassandra's message:

"It looks like my wet underwear is not going to save me this time and I'll soon be off to the next place. Obviously, I have no idea where that might be. I'll try to at least give you a hint—that is, if I find out myself. Please don't try to save me; don't do anything heroic. It wouldn't work the way you'd hope it would.

"Tell that boy, Danny, to remember that he has been occupying at least two super positions. He's in more than one location and more than one time. He's lost track of which is which. Although it is physics, and he told me he understood that, I don't think he does. Come to think of it, I don't think I do either. The quantum mechanics people call it decoherence. I've read about that, struggled with it till my eyes bleed. It hasn't helped much—not that it matters.

"Wait! Just tell him this. Tell him what Buddha said:

"'We are what we think. All that we are arises with our thoughts. With our thoughts, we make our world.'

"Danny's world is now his world—not partly, because Samantha is in it, but completely because forgiveness always turns the world right side up.

"Tell him to go run across his park. Run as fast as he can. If he does that with all of his brand-new heart, he cannot fail."

31

ROUND-TRIP ODYSSEY

Where am I? It feels like I'm in a car, like I'm being driven somewhere; I don't know where. The road is bumpy. I don't think I'm sitting up. I can't be. I can't see. I don't have my bearings. In the leaky lifeboat of my brain, I don't remember when I ever did. It takes a long time for my past to learn to tell itself apart from every other delusion. It never stops whispering ominous asides in all the rooms I can no longer afford to remain inside.

"Okay, now it's behind me. I'm listening. I am no longer contrite and fearful."

The old man takes his own sweet time before he responds, "What happened?"

"You're going to have to be more specific, Dad."

"We were doing okay, weren't we?" He sounds oddly conciliatory. "You were grown up by then, at least in years."

"I was pretending."

"For the first time I could recall, we weren't fighting."

"We weren't fighting," I say, "because you were drinking every waking hour and never listening."

"I was listening."

"Only when you talked."

My father groans at the injustice. "So let me go then. You forgave me, remember?"

"Yes, I know, but this is still real life and the scoundrel doesn't nod his head and stroll docilely away like a sweet old Hindu cow. He remains in the unquiet ideas that drag and plead, one lonely argument at a time, to give them just one more listen. And the crazy thing is, my habitual first response is to re-engage in the same old way. But, dear old man, you're not only forgiven, you're dead, and therefore left behind; and more and more you are only a speck on my horizon. I love you, but if it's all the same to you, I'd just as soon not talk to you anymore."

And every time I say that he vaporizes—for a little longer each time.

I don't know what time it is, but why would I expect to? I've never known.

But boy, do I not know what time it is now.

Have I died? Is this one of *those* things?

No, wait. I left my home and went someplace far away ... someplace that felt both familiar and strange. It was not my home. I left what had become my source. ... But I'm young again. I remember that now. Aren't I?

But hang on. I didn't want to be just young. That in itself is meaningless.

I hear something I immediately forget from a voice I don't recognize. It's the voice of a young woman, maybe even a girl, but to be honest, I'm not sure what the source of the voice is.

It's the wrong source in the wrong style. I met the source, or what I took to be the sustaining component of my happiness. But I left her. I didn't mean to. It just happened, one of those things that happens … crazy. A bell rings now and then. No, not a bell, a buzzing. Or it could be a motor of some kind. Except this buzzing feels as if it's in my head. I don't understand that.

Why would I expect to? I haven't understood anything for longer than I can remember, which is a funny expression because everything is for longer than I remember. It's not exactly a buzzing I'm hearing. It's a cue of some kind, a cue to say my first line. It's kind of comforting, hearing my cue. It means I'm still in the show. But maybe that's not so comforting. I don't know my line. Still, it's better than the buzzing. And even if I don't know what to say, I can ad lib for a while, can't I? I can *improvise*. Except—shit—I wasn't so good at that, was I? And even if I knew my line, I'm not sure I could say it; I'm afraid this new play is in a foreign language, one I don't speak. Ambulansay? *Nein. Ich spreche kein Deutsch.*

No question I'm on my back. I'm being driven somewhere. Except that doesn't make sense. Try again: I left my home. Then on Sunset, I took the second turn north. If I'd gone south instead, I would have turned onto Cañon Drive. … Oh, I see. I'm on a loop of film, going around and around, endlessly repeating what there is no longer any incentive to repeat. Maybe it doesn't matter. All I have is this moment, now. "The only moment the infinite ever knows."

I must be imagining it, but I hear the *ca-chunkata-chunkata-chunkata* of a subway or a railroad, as the conveyance that's transporting me carries me through the day or the night; I can't tell. No, but this can't be a train, at least not at this moment. This is not a railway car. I recognize the feel of steel wheels on

steel rails; this is not that. The vehicle I'm in is on … tires? Air?
It's smooth now, no more *ca-chunkata*, but there is also a no-
nonsense but dreamy sensation of speed. The light that passes is
moving rearward, which means I'm hurtling ahead into some
form of futurity. Whatever force is carrying me is in a hurry
to get me where it wants me to be. Good. I don't know what's
happening, but speed is important, I'm sure of it. I can't wait
to find out where I'm going, even as, I confess, I'm enjoying
going there.

One of the sweet things about your mind being in all times
and places in that only moment the infinite ever knows, is that,
out of nowhere, even as you're surging ahead—you can be
brushing your teeth, or replacing a broken shoelace, or watching
your wife in bed, lying in the middle of our California king, her
head half on her pillow, half on my shoulder, flickering slightly
as if she's lit by candlelight. You can be fully aware of the whistle
of the train it turns out you must be on after all, even as it's
somewhere off in the distance, its mournful cry as intoxicating as the rest of it. You can, in the same endless moment, taste
and smell the prairies, woodlands, freshwater lakes, the corn and
wheat fields, the shining steel rails across the backcountry this
train everlastingly passes through—in this case, the backcountry
of your mind. You can maintain your merciful embrace of everything your life will ever be, and even if you've never been here,
you've *been* here. You recognize the feeling on your skin of the
sweeping winds howling in from … no one knows where. And
isn't that comforting too?

But I think I'm crying. My wife is in a hospital. I remember her
getting sick; it scared me, I thought I'd never see her again. There
was … something else. And someone mentioned doctors and a

hospital and ... something ... a *toll booth*? A ticket booth? No, it was *inside* the theater!

A *movie*. I was in a movie. I produced a movie. I directed it too. Imagine that. It wasn't as easy as I thought. I remember my friends Liz and Zeke, but I can't place them somehow. I thought he'd grown old, but I'm not so sure now. I don't know where he is. And Liz wasn't Liz either. Liz was ...

A good actor. And if *she* found *her* performance in *my* eyes, as I did mine in hers, that made her ... that made her *Samantha*! I found Sam!

And I know *when* I found her.

I found her before I found her, near her apartment. Something happened to me. It didn't hurt. Gordon's gin. And then ... I don't remember. I can't even begin to count how many years I was without her.

"Samantha, Samantha, Sam, I've been looking for you all my life."

Someone shushes me gently.

Someone is holding a cool washcloth to my face, patting me, petting me. I'm speaking; I'm sure of it. I say, "Help me. Help me. ... Why won't you talk to me?" I hear voices. I hear ... it could be a nurse. It must be, or some kind of caregiver, but I can't see her. I am unconscious, an unconscious question mark. I do remember I'm on an odyssey. Someone told me odysseys are never one-way; they have to be round-trip. When Odysseus gets home, Penelope will be waiting.

Another hallucination, a vision: a giant cup of coffee, but the cream is flowing out of it, up into a white ceramic creamer, and the coffee is back to being black again.

And now that's gone and I'm in the gallery overlooking a surgical theater. But I'm also the patient. From this unique catbird seat I can see—no, *feel* everything, with a sightless person's enhanced perception.

Back to the nurse. I study her. Her concentration is specific to the immediate task. She is focused on the part of the body she is working on, washing and caressing it with mild soap and warm water. The tenderness of caring for the particular part of the patient this nurse is working on is thorough and undivided—until she moves onto the next area; and now this new convergence of her attention is total in its absorption.

There is an agile perception behind this nurse's eyes, an inborn grasp of the relationship between the parts and the whole, an insight that transforms into soothing care of the whole patient by concentrating on each component, on each part of the whole, in the most sensible order, until the patient is loved—and there is no righter word—back into well-being, into perfect harmony with himself.

I still can't see, but I can hear everything around me.

And now, I *feel* her hand. It's on my face. I've reached up and touched her hand on my face. This nurse. This nurse is caring—what a wonderful word, a valid word. This nurse has time to care for me. Has she been on duty all day? All night? That's not possible. It feels as if my head ... she's stroking my head. There's the cool washcloth again. How long has this been?

I'm not writing or recording or doing anything secondhand anymore. I'm at home, or if not at home, I'm in a hospital bed and it might as well be home. This wonderful nurse is caring for me. A nurse. I feel safe and held and watched over.

No. This is not a nurse. ... I can smell her. She smells of lilacs and lavender and lemon blossoms, "L" things.

"Sam, it's me. Can you hear me?"

"Yes, Danny. I hear you."

32

PENELOPE

"Danny? Danny, are you okay?"

"Yes. Where did you go?"

"Nowhere. I'm right here. You just drifted off for a few seconds."

"I've been remembering when we first met on that blind date, at the Red Lantern."

"No, that wasn't how we met—not how we *first* met. We met the night you were outside my apartment, six years earlier. You remember. You shuffled out in front of my car, as I was about to pull into my garage. I hit you. I knocked you down. Don't you remember that? … Danny?"

"I'm not sure."

"It's okay, honey. That memory has always been a little unreliable for you. You stayed with me for a week. Don't look that way. Don't worry, sweetie. It's okay. Your doctors told us some memory loss is nothing to worry about with people who've gone through a physical and psychological trauma."

"Tell me about that night."

"You mean our first night together? You want to hear this now?"

"Yes."

"All right. I tried to take you to a hospital. You said, 'Please *don't*. It'll ruin everything.' You told me you were fine. I could tell you were a little drunk, but—"

"But why didn't you call an ambulansay? I mean an ambulance."

"You were shaken up ... but you actually did seem okay. You're probably right though. I don't understand why I didn't. But you were so dear. And finally I believed you when you said you weren't hurt. You were able to walk all right. You hadn't hit your head on the pavement. I helped you upstairs into my apartment. I was going to let you lie down for a while ... And then you stayed with me. For a week."

"A week? ... What is it, Sam? Are you okay? You're crying."

"I'm just so grateful to have you ... What do you mean, *am I okay*? You're the one who's had the heart attack."

"A heart attack?"

"Yes, we *told* you. ... But you're going to be all right. You're fine. There's no permanent damage. You were told."

"Okay. ... God Sam, it's been so long since you held my hand. What else did I say to you the first night?"

"You really want to ... All right. It was late. I'd just gotten back from one of my ... I've told you about my late-night drives."

"I thought that was later."

"Later *and* sooner. I was lonely. ... It was a funny... not so funny time in my life. ... And then I found you—actually, I *hit* you with my car. ... And then a week later you went away. You said it wasn't time yet. You said, 'It's six years until our night at the Red Lantern.' I had no idea what you were talking about. And then you almost pleaded; you said, 'Please wait. We've got to be sure it happens the way it did the first time, that we don't drift away from the original sequence.' After you left, I was angry. Then later, there was all my driving between LA and Palm Springs. By then I had lots of reasons to be angry. I thought, no matter what, I'll be damned if I'll wait six years for any man. *Six years* didn't make any sense. You left me a note. I've never shown it to you. I kept it. I'm not sure why. For a long while I thought I hated you. But as time passed …"

"But you did wait. We had the blind date I *knew* we would have."

"How, Danny? How did you know we'd have that? And how did you *know* I would wait? … What are you laughing at?"

"You said you'd be there. You never break your word."

"But it wasn't long after the blind date that you went off to do … that job in Portland. You broke up with me …"

"Samantha?"

"You'd asked me to wait for you for six years. And without really wanting to, I did. … I can see you don't remember this. … And then—*it blew me away*—six years later, you materialized at my apartment door for the blind date. And we've always laughed at what I said. I said, 'Not bad.' But I also—and you did not know this at the time—nearly fainted. I thought I'd been given the wrong name for the guy who was to show up for the blind date, or I misunderstood. I couldn't believe it was you. I didn't tell you anything about the first time because … well, you know why."

"I don't think I do …"

"Right. … And then a month or so later, you went off to do that job. You broke up with me. I wanted to kill you. And when you came back a month after *that*, you called me, and I came to that apartment you were living in. You buzzed me in. And as I came up the stairs, you said—although it wasn't out loud at the time, but somehow I heard your words anyway—you said, 'Hello, rest of my life.' And I guess I thought ... Jesus, I can't believe it, but I guess I'll forgive this man *anything*."

"In the end, we were meant to be. It was okay that you came to me."

"But, Danny, did I have no pride at all?"

"Could it have been as simple as ... you loved me?"

"Yes, in the end it *was* that simple. And you know, during the six years before our blind date I think I saw your image on TV once, maybe twice, but you know me, I don't watch television. I thought I was having, I dunno, a hallucination. It scared me. I turned it off. And I don't think during that whole week you ever told me what you did. When we talked, which I don't think was very much ... When we did ... it was about ... I don't know what it was about."

"Sam! It was not *just okay* that you drove to my apartment. I'd never been very happy about living in this ... skin. But when you came to me after I'd been away for that month, just the sweetness of that ... I began, too-too slowly at first, to see myself through your eyes. Then I was finally able to open my own a little. ... I remember that within thirty minutes of my half-witted breakup with you, you phoned me and said, 'You don't know what you're missing.' Well, when I got back from Portland, I began to understand what I would have missed, what I almost lost."

"You didn't understand, not entirely. That took you a while."

"In my dream, *you* were the one who was sick. You asked to see our lawyer. I was scared to death something would happen to you before I could tell you I love you. ... I mean really, *properly* tell you, *I LOVE YOU!*"

"I'm not sick, Danny, I'm fine, and you've told me you love me … many times. Now rest for a while. The doctor says you can have visitors, so we're having some a little later. Okay with you?"

"Who?"

"Liz and Zeke. They've been playing tennis at the college and they're going to drop by for a few minutes afterward. Is that okay? What are you grinning at?"

"Nothing. Nothing at all. Yes, that is okay."

"Good. And just so you know, I won't mind if you tell me you love me thousands of times more."

"Sam? Do you remember anything I said in the note I left you, in 1974?"

"I remember every word. You said: *'We aren't supposed to meet for six years. Wait for me, Samantha. It turns out I do have a chance to be a decent man after all, but it's going to take about six years longer, if you don't count the lifetime I've already spent with you.'* And of course there you lost me completely. And then you went on: *'I know it's a lot to ask,'* you said, *'but please wait for me. I'm going to do it. Wait for me, my love.'* And then you added: *'If we got together now, I'd just fuck it up. Sorry, but I know I would.'* And I said to myself, 'Well, maybe I *can* do it. I think I can—for *him.*' I realized, deep within me, that I'd already given you my heart and soul."

"Sam? What are you smiling at?"

"I know it's not funny, but I'm smiling at the fact that you haven't remembered that I've always had my *own* guilt. … You're falling asleep. Let yourself go …"

"Sam …?"

"Go to sleep."

EPILOGUE

~

GRACE

"Okay. I'm finally going to ask you what possessed you to try to run across Sherman Oaks Park at the age of seventy-five."

"I felt full of joy and youth. I thought I was twenty-seven."

"Well, don't ever do it again. We need you around here, all of us."

"Sam? A while ago, I don't remember when, you said something about guilt. What did you mean?"

"Oh, Danny. You've known this ever since ... I felt guilty around the time of our blind date for *storing* Grace down in Palm Springs during weekdays when I was working. I told myself she was better off with my mother. Danny ...?"

"So during our blind date at the Red Lantern, aside from a spooky feeling that I'd known you in another lifetime, *our* five-year-old daughter was living down in Palm Springs with her grandmother?"

"That's right. And I just heard her drive up."

"Oh my God."

"Don't be surprised when you see our little girl is a middle-aged woman. Why do you say 'oh my God'?"

"I don't know. It took me by surprise."

"I think that's an echo of our early days together. You had this schism between remembering and not. Sometimes I had to point to Gracie, who we've always agreed looks a lot like you, and you'd say, 'Oh, right.' Then we'd laugh."

"I remember that. … If Gracie's middle-aged, what's that make us?"

"It makes you too old to run across parks."

"No more running. I promise. I have no time to waste and whatever time I do have, I want to waste with you."

"Right. I hear footsteps."

"Sam, we need to get out once in a while, anywhere; just get out, together. Especially after last year and … *this* year. You know what I mean?"

"Yes."

"Hi, Grandma. Hi, Grandpa. I'll be right back. I told Mom I'd go help her bring in the groceries."

"Who was that?"

"That was Gracie's daughter. Your granddaughter. Get down, Tali. You can't jump on Daddy till he's feeling better."

"*Granddaughter?* What's her name?"

"Rue."

THE END

ACKNOWLEDGEMENTS

n the early 1960s, my favorite teacher in theater school (Claribel Baird) told me she thought I might make a living either acting or writing. I loved both, but I was unnaturally thirsty for approval and acting was more immediately rewarding in that regard, so I spent the first forty-five years of my professional life doing that.

Although I also had some writing success along the way, mostly plays, it didn't take long—three or four decades was all—to realize I wanted to write novels. When you write novels, I told myself, you don't have to listen to other people's advice.

I was misinformed.

I needed lots of advice. Richard Russo (*Empire Falls,* etc.) said I had to write at least a thousand shitty pages of prose before I could expect to "get good." So, I wrote at least a thousand such pages. Every page (I know in retrospect) qualified as shitty. I still write pages like that. The difference now is that I usually know which ones they are and throw them away.

I count on great editors to help me weed out the rest. The following people have been unbelievably generous in doing that:

My longtime play writing partner, Michael Norell, has done line-by-line edits of almost everything I've written. Kevin Cook has been the primary editor of all my books and he's done it with immeasurable savvy, diligence, and good humor. Pamela Cangioli contributed mightily, along with overseeing the whole editorial process.

George Foster has designed the covers for all of my books and he does it so beautifully, so expertly, that there is never one thing I can imagine improving.

Keri-Rae Barnum's guidance has been invaluable, her patience and kindness endless.

And to Amit Dey for his beautiful formatting.

Additional thanks to Michele Winkler, who has been a constant inspiration, Spyguy of Dallas TX, Chris Chesser, Beverly Vines Haines, Amy Collins, G. L. Blanchard, the superb author Scott Campbell, Sun Cooper, my sister Deb, and my eternally beautiful children, Abigail, Charlie, and Scott. Thanks to Abigail and Swamp Boogie Queen for permission to use the lyrics of *Never Leave*. Special thanks to my friend and former leading lady, Kendall Hailey, for her wisdom and kind support.

My wife Linda is the most common-sense content editor I've ever had. She's also patient; when I tell her she's wrong about some comment she's made, she smiles and says, "Okay." A little while later I usually come back and grudgingly tell her that maybe *most* of what she said makes ... "*some sense*." She's never been obnoxious when she's right—which, I've got to be honest, can really piss me off.

I should mention wonderful writers, in addition to the ones I've already cited, whose advice on writing has been invaluable: Anne Lamott (*Bird by Bird*) and Stephen King (*On Writing: A Memoir of the Craft*). Richard Russo's book on the subject is *The Destiny Thief.*

Lastly, thank you to all the great authors I have the opportunity and honor to read. This includes Elizabeth Forsythe Hailey, Ernest Holmes, Elizabeth Gilbert, Haruki Murakami, Anne Tyler, Margaret Atwood, Bret Easton Ellis ... the three Johns: Updike, Cheever, and Steinbeck ... Wallace Stegner, Bruce Wagner, Bruce Jay Friedman, Kurt Vonnegut, Thomas Pynchon ... the list goes on.

ABOUT THE AUTHOR

When Rick Lenz retired as a stage and film actor (playing opposite Ingrid Bergman, John Wayne, Lauren Bacall, Walter Matthau, Peter Sellers, etc.), his passion for drama refused to retire with him. Although he was an actor most of his life, he was also a seasoned writer. His plays have been produced Off-Broadway, on PBS television, and in regional theatres across the country. Rick's memoir *North of Hollywood* was called "masterful" by *Writer's Digest*. His first novel, *The Alexandrite* was named "one of the best books of the year" by Kirkus Reviews. Bret Easton Ellis called it "almost impossible to put down." Rick's books have won several awards, including, Readers Views (first place), the Chanticleer Somerset Grand Prize for Literary, Contemporary and Mainstream Fiction, an IPPY Award, and a Foreword Book of the Year.

He lives in Los Angeles with his wife Linda and an ever-shifting array of animals.

NOTE FROM THE AUTHOR

Dear Reader,

If you enjoyed *Hello, Rest of My Life*, please consider leaving a review on Goodreads, BookBub or one of your favorite online book selling sites.

Reviews are so important to an author. It doesn't have to be a long review, a sentence or two is fine, unless of course you'd like to say more.

I'd also love to connect with you online.

Website: www.ricklenz.com
Instagram: @RickLenz
Facebook: @RickLenzAuthor
YouTube: @RickLenz

With appreciation,

Rick Lenz

CPSIA information can be obtained
at www.ICGtesting.com
Printed in the USA
FSHW010144290921
85090FS